Finnegan Found

Surviving the POW Camps on the Yalu

D0877830

John N. Powers

ISBN: 978-0-578-68639-4

Other books by the author:
Bean Camp to Briar Patch – Life in the POW Camps of Korea
and Vietnam

How quickly we forget
The heroes we beget
When we send our boys
To war

A story untold, left in the dark for seventy years. This historical fiction novel tells that story, shines a light on that darkness. Now is the time for those men to be remembered, to finally be given the full measure of respect they earned so long ago.

JNP

Acknowledgments

A project like this takes a village. I am very grateful for the editorial work and advice from: Joan Brahmer, Linda Denissen, Larry Denissen, Stasia Frank, M.D., Dan Moericke, Richard Powers, M.D., Shirley Schmidt, and Kevin Wick.
And to Ned Bolenbaugh, for his questions in the beginning.

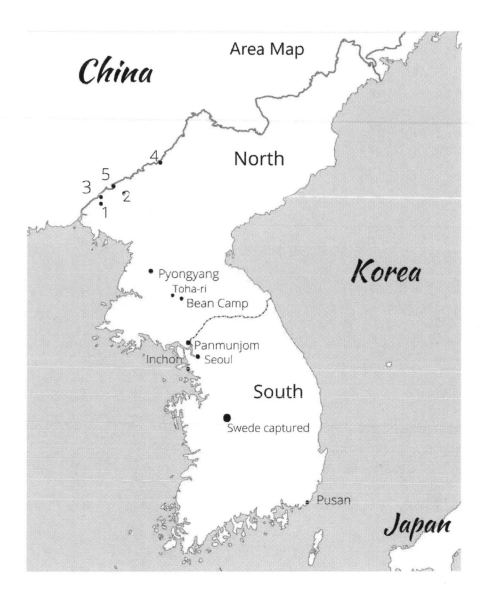

Be sure to read the historical background of this novel and the explanation of the cover art in the addendums.

Japan and Korea

July 1950

It was a perfect morning. Sun shining, birds singing, a slight morning breeze scented with fresh-cut hay in the field. And a breakfast made for a king. A breakfast only his mother could make, perfectly cooked pancakes with sausage and hot maple syrup. After a breakfast like this, a man could do anything. The only imperfection was the song a bird was singing outside the window. There was something wrong with that bird.

"Swede! Swede! Get up, man. We gotta pack up, we're on the move again."

Paul Larson jumped the time warp from his mother's kitchen to the sweaty darkness of his pup tent. Hadn't he just collapsed on top of his sleeping bag after coming off guard duty? His red-headed tent-mate, Ray Parker, was kicking his feet a little harder than Paul thought he ought to.

"Hey, take it easy. I'm awake."

"No man, really. Get outta the sack. The whole company is packin' up. We're outta here."

"Here" was a dry paddy - full of tents - in Japan. Just nine months before, Paul Larson had enlisted in the Army. The oldest of four children on a small farm in western Minnesota, he had graduated high school just a year ago. With no money available, Paul had seen the Army as the means to broaden his limited horizons and start saving for college. World War II was long over, the world a peaceful place, so his parents were not completely against the idea. His father just asked he wait until the fall harvest was in before he left.

"Swede" was born on an early November morning on a parade

ground at Fort Riley, Kansas. It was part of an age-old tradition when the drill sergeant put his scowling face inches away from the recruit's nose and growled, "Where you from boy?" The look and tone gave the distinct impression that whatever the answer, it would be distasteful.

"Minneota, Minnesota, Drill Sergeant!"

"Never heard of it. Name somebody important from Minnie-owe-tuh Minnie-sew-tuh," sneered the drill sergeant.

Without hesitation, Paul gave the name of his hometown war hero. "Val Bjornson, Drill Sergeant!"

"Jeezus! Bee-yorn-son from Minnie-owe-tuh, Minnie-sew-tuh! We got us a Swede boy here," the sergeant yelled in an exaggerated drawl. The newly named Swede did not react as the sergeant insulted anything and everything Swedish. He kind of reminded Swede of his high school basketball coach, but with a lot more profanity. Besides, somebody bad-mouthing the Swedes didn't bother Paul Larson - all his ancestors were Norwegian.

He was young but not stupid, so "Swede" didn't bother to correct the drill sergeant. He tried to maintain eye contact, knowing looking away would be a sign of weakness and then the harassment would increase. He had learned that lesson at an early age working with his uncles on the family farm and had it reinforced as the country kid on the high school basketball team. Paul had grown up working side by side with his father and uncles. His work ethic and demeanor around adults had earned him respect in the community. He was given responsibilities beyond the norm for a teenager, and that had given him an early insight as to how the world worked. His new name didn't change Paul a bit on the inside. Melvin R. Sweet, two ranks back, had a different outcome.

"Melvin are Sweet are he? Get down and give me twenty, Melvin Are. Best you learn right now there's nuthin' sweet around here."

Master Sergeant George W. Tucker had been around a while. He had served in China when he was younger than Swede and waded ashore on quite a few islands in the Pacific during the war. He had served with good leaders and bad, officers and NCOs. More than once he had been forced into taking charge because there was no one left above his pay grade. Those experiences had not always had a positive result, and he had the scars, both physical and emotional, as proof. Since then, he had made it a personal crusade to help develop leadership skills in troops under his command, whenever he could, in whatever way he could. This was his Army, and it needed good people.

The veteran drill sergeant saw more than a fit-looking, blue-eyed farm boy in front of him. The newly named Swede stood just under six feet, broad through the shoulders but otherwise slim. Tucker grabbed the kid's hands to inspect his fingernails for cleanliness. The hands were callused from hard work. His eyes, never flinching, gave a distinct sense of intelligence. So, the kid was added to his list for admittance into the Tucker School of Keep Your Head Out of Your Ass. Swede and two others in that batch of recruits were given extra duties and responsibilities. He tried to make them understand almost any problem they might encounter in his Army had a solution in the Manual. They didn't have to re-invent the wheel. The manual was based on years of experience. But sometimes problems had solutions only found *outside* the manual. Sometimes you found yourself in situations where no manual existed. He found Swede to be his best student and spent extra time with the Minnesota boy, usually in the form of profane rants on his lack of ability to perform to his full potential. They were followed by quieter, detailed suggestions on how to improve. The profanity was for the benefit of the rest of the company. The detailed discussions were for his students.

Swede responded well to the entire experience. He was enjoying the Army. As the oldest of his siblings, farm work had made him fit. Since age twelve he had been allowed to hunt on his own with the family .22 rifle and soon after with the .30-30 his grandfather had given him. He was used to hard work and life in the outdoors. Swede and the Army seemed to be a good fit, even if their breakfasts didn't match up to his mother's pancakes and sausages.

By early spring of 1950 Swede was in Japan, assigned to the 24th Infantry Division. The long boat trip across the Pacific had given him a quick look at Hawaii and the Philippines. Not bad for a kid who had never been more than fifty miles from home. Swede tried to soak up the foreign atmosphere of it all. He was in Japan, a place he had only seen in National Geographic! Life was a grand adventure.

Parker was right. They were "outta here." Trucks pulled up next to the bivouac area, sending diesel fumes and dust swirling through the hot air. A few hours later, the trucks rumbled up to a dock and the men hustled aboard a ship. Rumors bounced around about a problem in Korea, but most of the guys figured the whole thing was just part of the maneuvers. They spent the night at sea and their small flotilla pulled into a harbor the morning of 13 July. It could have been the Japanese coast for all they knew, but their captain confirmed it was Korea. That was all he confirmed. No one told them where they were or where they were going. Still, Swede was feeling good about being smart enough to enlist in the Army. Here he was in his third foreign country and just 19 years old.

But soon things got serious. They were told to grab ammunition and grenades and hop into the waiting trucks. As they started filling their ammo pouches, trucks pulled in loaded with wounded. Up to this point, many in the company were like Swede, too young and too ignorant to be afraid. Most of the guys in the unit had never fired a shot off the rifle range and had never been shot at. But a look at those wounded started them thinking maybe this was not Kansas anymore. They climbed aboard their trucks which took them to a railroad yard where they boarded a train. The scene was straight out of an old western, steam huffing out from the engine, the cowcatcher on the front, the old wooden bench seats. The company rode on the train for most of the day, constantly stopping and waiting, the cars screeching to a halt and then jerking forward again. Much of the conversation was about how soon this would all be over, and they could go back to the good life in Japan. Most of them were young and convinced they would win this little war, just like the Army had won the last war. Their age made them forget how long it had taken to win that last war. Most did not understand how poorly trained they were and how old their equipment was. So, they talked smart, partly from ignorance, partly from fear, but mostly because that's what young soldiers do. They talked smart and played cards, doing neither very well, but it passed the time.

Swede spent most of the time watching this new country. There was no war in sight, so his mind could still appreciate the beauty that rolled by. Brilliant green rice shoots stood in rows, the sun reflecting off the flooded paddies. Village after village of brown thatch-roofed huts contrasted with the green hills beyond. When the train stopped for the last time, they boarded trucks again and headed out of the town. The few Koreans they saw were walking along the same road - headed in the opposite direction. Most adults had a woven basket or an A-shaped frame on their back, the contents bending them forward as they trotted along. A few cows pulled two-wheeled carts. No one waved at the soldiers.

A few miles after crossing a river the trucks stopped in a little valley. By then some of the company had not slept in over twenty-four hours and all of them had only been fed once. Just when they needed some food and a rest, they were hustled off the trucks, marched up the valley, and then up the steep hillsides to what they were told were the front lines. The guys already on the hill looked more tired and hungry than the new guys. They also had a look about them Swede hadn't seen before. He learned soon enough what that look was - fear.

On Swede's hill there were two platoons. They had only their rifles - no automatic weapons, no mortars, no bazookas. The NCOs put the troops to work preparing better firing positions and making the hill more defensible. Nobody got much sleep that night. They were tired, hot, and hungry. Dirt and sweat added to their discomfort. They could see and hear artillery fire way out in front of them and it seemed somebody was constantly spotting movement coming up their hill and firing off rounds. Before daylight the next morning, the men were rousted out of their foxholes to the sound of gunfire and the light of flares overhead. Their gunfire and their flares. Swede couldn't see a thing other than glowing fog. He didn't see any of his buddies getting hit and he couldn't see anything to shoot at. His grandfather had taught him at a young age not to shoot unless he could see exactly what he was shooting at. Given the language he heard from the platoon sergeant, it seemed he agreed with Swede's grandfather. So he sat back against the side of his foxhole and tried to enjoy the cool of the morning, hoping breakfast was on the schedule. It wasn't.

A couple of hours later the fog lifted and the shooting started up again. This time they could see movement about a half-mile away. Their fox holes looked out over a low area of fields or paddies, with another ridge beyond that. Some points on that ridge were higher than they were. Paths of brown created a random pattern through the green rice paddies. On the far side a road traced the bottom slope of the distant ridge. Terraces stepped their way up that slope.

As Swede looked out over his M1, trying to find a target, there was an explosion far to his left. *Caruumph!* Without thinking, he stood up to see what was happening. They had never trained with mortar fire, so he had no idea he was in danger. Suddenly there was another explosion just thirty yards away. Before he could react, there was a third. A wall of noise and pressure slammed into him. As Ray pulled him down, there was a sharp blow to his arm. Then they were curled up in the bottom of their foxhole, crushing their helmets down on their heads. The ground bounced, again, and again. Dirt and rocks rained down, convincing them the next round would drop directly on their heads. Their senses were almost overwhelmed by the noise and the smells but when the sergeants started yelling at them to get up and point their rifles down the hill, Privates Larson and Parker did as they were ordered. There was nothing there.

After the first mortar barrage, they didn't take much rifle fire. There were a few North Korean tanks and troops in the valley to their front and more troops on the ridge beyond. They seemed to be ignoring the Americans on the hill. The platoons fired sporadically at the men in the valley, but distance and dust made it hard to see how effective they were. Probably not very, given the Koreans paid them little attention except for the occasional mortar round and machine-gun bursts from the far ridge. In between the incoming rounds, a medic patched up the wound on Swede's arm while reminding him to keep his head down. At mid-afternoon they were ordered off the hill by squads. By then most of Swede's ammo was gone and his canteen was long empty. Fear has a thirst.

The squad, or at least those still moving as a squad, didn't see anybody, American or North Korean, as they worked their way back to where the next line of defense was supposed to be. Later in the day they met up with what turned out to be a counterattack headed right back to the hill they had just left. They followed their mortar and artillery fire back up the hill just as full dark hit. Swede and Parker ended up in their old foxhole. Swede immediately set to work making it deeper and piling more dirt in front. He only did as Master Sergeant Tucker had so recently taught him, but many other foxholes on that hill would not have met with Tucker's approval. That fact was clear to the platoon sergeant as he went down the line. He realized Swede was doing exactly what needed to be done without waiting to be told. Swede was promoted to Private First Class on the spot and put in charge of the squad in the foxholes to either side.

The fact he had been promoted made Swede even more aware of their predicament. With only a few instructions he had the six foxholes in the center of that hill brought up to par. He then sent Parker and one man from each of the other foxholes to get more ammunition. They each came back with two bandoliers of loaded clips and more hand grenades. Then they sat back and waited.

An hour later the platoon sergeant came around handing out more ammunition and grenades. He whispered to them to toss one grenade each if they had movement in front of them but to be sure their imagination didn't run wild. Swede looked at him without saying anything and reached out to grab even more grenades and ammo from the box. He scooted over to the other foxholes and divvied up what he had. He designated one man in each foxhole to toss grenades and one to fire his rifle. "Place your bandolier where you can easily grab a new clip but not where it will get dumped in the bottom of the foxhole. When they hit us, start tossing those grenades. When the last one is gone, grab your rifle and join in. If you can, try to time it so we all don't have to change clips at the same time. But whatever you do, make your shots count."

Most of the company had only been out of basic training for a few months. At first the whole experience wasn't much different than basic. But that day had given them a fresh sense of reality. And now they were sitting in the dark waiting for the Koreans to come charging at them. They could see and hear an attack on the ridge to their right, noise like they had never heard before. There was a lot of noise in the valley in front of them, tracers drawing lines through the dark, and finally, the bugles. It sounded like the whole North Korean Army was blowing bugles.

A command was shouted down the line. "Fix bayonets!"

At that point there were no thoughts about home or any kind of pie. They were too busy trying not to be afraid, trying not to let the other guys see they were afraid, and trying to do what they were trained to do, wishing the attack would come before the fear broke them. One last bugle call and they got their wish. A flare went up and with no hesitation Parker tossed out his first grenade. There was a wall of men charging up the hill right at them, yelling and firing. Swede yelled at Parker to keep tossing while he opened fire with his rifle. All their training had been for this exact moment.

Parker was tossing them out as fast as he could while Swede kept up a rapid fire - point and squeeze, point and squeeze, *spriiing,* new clip. Picking his targets was simple, there was nothing but targets in front of them. Flares swinging from parachutes created a black and white field of dancing men and shadows. It was a county fair nightmare. One target fell down and another popped into view. But these targets were shooting back. Each man operated on training and reality, doing what had to be done while pushing back at the fear that said differently. Their only thinking was limited to the right here and now. No yesterday, no tomorrow, just now. The noise and heat and screams and fear of now. When the grenades were gone, Ray swung up his rifle and began firing.

A wall of men was charging at him, making so much noise Swede was transported to another place. A place where his hearing was almost gone, but his vision was crystal clear. He was aware of everything around him, but it was all in slow motion. There were flashes and smoke from this wall of men, silent explosions among them. At some point he emptied a clip and realized he had no time to reload. The wall was right in front of him. He pushed aside slow-motion bayonets with his rifle, stabbing back and swinging the butt at strange faces. The eyes in the faces didn't look at his, but beyond, as if he wasn't there. Objects thudded near his feet. He kicked them away without looking. More objects thudded near his feet, only these were bodies that he had dropped there. He realized he was almost out of ammunition. Finally, swinging his rifle back and forth, looking for his next target, Swede realized he could hear again. He and Parker were yelling, but there was nothing more to yell at, nothing more to shoot at, no more angry faces with blank eyes. Swede wasn't sure if it had all lasted two minutes or two hours.

The Koreans had pushed through their thin line and kept on going. Swede's squad had kept up such a heavy barrage of grenades and rifle fire the Koreans had, for the most part, gone around them like a rock in a stream. Some thought the Koreans had seemed more focused on getting over the hill than on killing the men in front of them. Others in the platoon hadn't been so lucky. As their hearing came back Swede and Parker could hear shouts from the wounded and dying.

While doing what they could for the wounded, the surviving NCOs came around and started organizing a withdrawal. Some soldiers were out of ammo and most were down to their last few clips. Nobody had any water and nobody had any food.

The platoon sergeant pointed them in the direction they needed to go and sent them off the hill by squads. It wasn't long before there were just four of them - Swede, Parker, and the two guys who had been in the foxhole to their left. Four young kids who were aging quickly. After stumbling off the hill just following the man in front of him, Swede wasn't sure what direction they were headed. Nobody had a compass. He held up the other three while he tried to get a fix on the North Star but couldn't find any stars. They kept turning away from gunfire until they could have been heading north for all he knew. By dawn they were lost and running on empty. They hadn't eaten in three days. They were exhausted, thirsty, hungry - and terrified. It was obvious there were North Koreans all around. The four crawled into some thick bushes to stay hidden during daylight. The plan was for one to stay awake for a few hours and then wake the next guy to keep watch. That was the plan.

The next thing he knew, somebody was kicking his foot. Swede figured it was his turn to keep a look-out. He opened his eyes to look up the barrel of a cannon held by a grinning midget. Later he realized the man wasn't that small and the rifle not that large. It was 15 July 1950. He had been in the Army just eight months. He had been in Korea just two days.

Somewhere in Korea

Jul-Sep 1950

There were four Americans sleeping on the ground, six Koreans standing there with rifles pointing at them. There was no question of what to do next. Their hands went up.

The young soldiers were probably lucky they had all fallen asleep. If they had been awake, they might have gotten into a shooting match as the Koreans approached. They were down to a few rounds each and there were North Korean troops everywhere. They were surrounded long before they left the hill the night before. The Koreans had just gone over and around the hill in the dark and kept on going. The Korean who seemed to be in charge of this group had them drop their equipment and went through their pockets. Any rings or watches disappeared into his pockets with a nod and a grin. Soon they stood in boots and fatigues, nothing more. They were lined up and marched back again toward the hills they had left the night before. Four dirty, hungry, scared kids-who were now prisoners-of-war.

The feelings Swede had at that point were hard to describe. It felt like he was in a different world altogether, as if he had stepped through time. Just a few hours before he had been part of this powerful military machine. All he had to do was his small part, knowing that everything else would be taken care of. He had rights and he had responsibilities. If there was a problem, he went to his corporal, his corporal went to his sergeant, and so on up the line. Then, in a flash, that reality was no more. He was tired, hot, dirty, hungry - and afraid.

Swede felt as if he was all alone in a very strange land. He was supposed to be responsible for these men but had no idea what to do. No idea what would happen next, not tomorrow, not next week, not in the next few minutes. He did not speak the language of his captors or have any understanding of what they were thinking. Swede assumed the chances were good they would all be shot and their bodies dumped in a ditch in this completely foreign place. He would never see home again, and his family would have no idea what happened to him.

Somehow Swede realized he was at a turning point. Fear was taking control of his every move. If he didn't do something to fight that fear, he would be lost. He started to look around instead of just following the man in front of him. Then he remembered a lecture given in a cold classroom during his training. The sergeant, a POW in Germany in World War II, had explained, "Your worst enemy is fear. Let it take control and you are finished. You won't be able to think clearly. So focus on something. What are their weapons like? What direction are you going? Can you hear anything that tells you where the good guys are? The sooner you start to assess what is happening and try to figure out how to make a really bad situation a little better, the sooner you start to take control of your life again. Take control of that fear. What exactly are you afraid of? Are you afraid they are going to kill you? Then look for the chance to run. Afraid you will starve to death? Find some food. Maybe they *will* kill you, maybe you *will* starve to death. But don't let fear defeat you. Look for a way to push that fear aside."

Swede decided he would walk slower so anybody coming to the rescue didn't have so far to go. Until he got a bayonet in the butt. Then he settled for paying attention to the terrain so he could figure out where they were. All he could come up with was they were headed north with tree-covered hills all around, but at least he was no longer feeling sorry for himself.

They were marched back to their hill from the night before and then into the valley beyond and then more hills and valleys. Along the way, they were joined by other groups of prisoners until there were probably fifty or more of them, with maybe fifteen guards. They marched for a couple of hours and then herded into a little wooded valley. What they guessed was a North Korean officer told them they would be "not shotted and go rest camp. Now sleeping." Any other directions given by the guards came through the means of pointing and grunting or the butt of a rifle in their back and yelling. The prisoners got the idea the guards were afraid planes might spot them, so they were to remain under the trees in the woods. Since Swede was a country boy who had not eaten for quite a while, he decided to see if there were any apple trees or berry bushes in their little forest. If he moved slowly and sat back down frequently none of the guards paid much attention. But not an apple to be found.

A voice called softly to him. "Hey kid. Over here." It was the platoon sergeant from the hill. He looked different. The confident authority was gone. "You did good up there, kid. Larson, right? Ya did good." Then he said nothing more, just sat and stared out over the group. Swede moved away. He finally sat back down next to Parker who said, "You thinkin' what I'm thinkin'?"

"I'm thinkin' I'm hungry, I don't know about you."

"I thought you were lookin' for a way to hit the road, go on the lam. I was hopin' you wouldn't just duck out without takin' me along." Ray had arrived in Japan at the same time as Swede. He was a city boy from Milwaukee, the same age as Swede. They were the two newest guys in the company, so it was only natural they became buddies.

Swede took a good look around. Most of those scattered under the trees seemed to be from his company, but none of the few NCOs or officers had made any attempt to organize them in any way. They hadn't been shot yet and it was beginning to look like that might not happen. He knew about the Geneva Convention. Executing prisoners was supposed to be a big no-no. Maybe these guys were going to follow the rules. But the rules probably said prisoners were supposed to be fed every now and then. The rules probably said something about taking care of the wounded. Neither of those seemed to be happening, and as far as he could see, none of his superiors had been complaining to their guards. Almost every face Swede looked at reflected shock or disbelief. Maybe it was time to take the advice of that instructor and start helping themselves.

He looked at Parker and nodded in agreement, "Maybe that's not such a bad idea." They talked in whispers about their situation. The farther north they were marched, the harder it would be for any of their guys to reach them. It looked like they would probably be moved out after dark, so they decided to slip further into the woods and hide out when the guards got them moving again. Just the two of them, any more and they would draw attention. So far no one had asked for names or serial numbers and they hadn't noticed the guards doing a headcount. That meant they might not be missed. They could either hide until the next counterattack or head south and try to make contact.

And it worked. The two slept on and off the rest of the day. At dusk they watched the guards rotate down to the road for their evening chow. Nothing was given to the prisoners, nothing to eat, nothing to drink. The same had been done for the wounded - nothing. Parker and Swede had moved as far away from the road as they could before they stretched out to sleep. They had decided to crawl into some bushes at the mid-point between two guards and try to hide. If spotted they would pretend to be sleeping. As luck would have it, the guards they were watching headed down to get some food before their replacements got back up from the road. That gave them the chance to move farther back into the woods than they originally planned before crawling under some bushes. When the new guards got to their posts and turned around to watch the prisoners, Swede and Parker were outside the perimeter.

Minutes later the guards herded everybody back out on the road and lined them up to head out. The two escapees waited to hear some kind of ruckus when the guards noticed two of their flock were missing. At the first sign of a problem, they were going to start running. But the column marched off and left them looking at each other in disbelief. For a few seconds Swede felt like he was playing hooky from school – a sense of complete freedom combined with the fear of being caught. Then he almost died from fright as a head popped out of the bushes next to them.

"I'm goin' with you guys." The head belonged to Danny Morgan. He had been in the foxhole next to them up on the hill and was with them when they were captured. Morgan was about a year older than either Swede or Ray, but they had been on a few work parties with him and sometimes hung out together in their free time back in Japan. There was something about him Swede didn't like, but since they didn't spend much time together, he didn't give it much thought.

"Jesus, Morgan!" yelled Ray. "Where did you come from?"

"Well, I was out for a walk in the park and then I saw you guys, so I thought I would come over and say hi," whispered Morgan. "Where the hell do you think I came from? Keep it down, you dumb shit."

Swede put his hand on Parker's shoulder to calm him down as he chuckled at Morgan's response. "We weren't exactly expecting any company, man." He looked downhill at the road where their fellow prisoners had just been to see if any guards came back to check on the noise. "We figured the guards might not notice they were missing one or two. You kind of took us by surprise."

"If you think three's a crowd you can try and catch up with the column, but I'm headed south," Morgan growled at Swede. "If you don't want me around, I'll head out by myself. I kinda figured you guys were up to something. When I saw you watchin' the guards while you tried to make like a bush I caught on."

"No, Morg. That's not it. When you poked your head out of the bushes, we thought we were done for. Three might be better than two anyway. Let's get outta here in case somebody comes lookin' for us." Swede waited a second for any reaction from the other two and then headed up the hill. He knew Danny Morgan to be mostly mouth, but this was not the time to argue about invitations.

The terrain they faced consisted of tree-covered ridges about four or five hundred feet high. Lesser rolling hills and fields separated the ridges. They stayed on the wooded ridges and hills as much as possible. Going across the open fields was tricky, but they used any cover they could, even crawling in some of the more open areas. Crossing footpaths and roads really got the adrenalin flowing as they could easily be spotted from the surrounding hills. By dawn they figured they should be getting close to the river they had crossed in the trucks a few days back. A small hill just ahead looked like a good spot to check their location and maybe hide out for the day. Moving up the hill, they found a few bodies - North Korean. On top, there were a few more bodies - American. They hadn't thought of checking the North Koreans for weapons and food but did try their luck with their own dead. They found one full canteen and one can of peaches. And Americans with their hands wired behind their backs and bullet holes in their heads. Somebody hadn't read the Geneva Convention after all. They moved away from the bodies and shared the peaches and water while looking south. No river in sight. Exhausted from almost three days of constant activity with little sleep and less food, they tried to get some rest in the shade of the trees.

A few times during the day they heard trucks on the road below. They seemed to be heading south so they were not American. They could hear artillery fire off in the distance ahead of them. That meant the North Koreans were still pushing south. It was doubtful any rescue force was headed their way just yet.

That night they waited until it was good and dark and headed out again. They weren't about to walk down any roads and found crossing them was riskier than the night before. North Korean columns continued to move south during the night, but the vehicles drove with lights off. A couple of times they spotted trucks headed their way before they heard them. They worked out a system where they would find some bushes near the road and one would sneak across to check out the other side. If it looked good, he would then wave the other two across. As dawn approached, they found a road in front of them with thick woods on the other side that would be great cover during the day. They moved down the hill using a large wooded gulley. The tree line ended but there were some bushes in the open space. The three crawled out to the bushes closest to the road. It was Morgan's turn to cross first. He disappeared into the thick cover on the other side while Swede and Parker got ready to move on his signal. A minute later they saw him step out of the bushes and wave them over. Just as they were about to scoot across, he snapped his head to look down the road and slowly backed into the brush. When they could only see his head and shoulders, he gave them a hold sign and was swallowed up by the foliage as he backed away.

Swede and Parker looked down the road. Troops were coming up from the south! They were used to only looking north before crossing roads. As the troops got closer Swede saw a column of prisoners behind the soldiers. It was too late to move across and there wasn't enough cover behind them to move back into the trees without being spotted.

"Our goose is cooked, man," whispered Ray. "What the hell do we do now?"

"Get on the other side of these bushes but move slowly," Swede whispered back. "Maybe we can play dead and they will ignore us."

When the guards were about thirty yards away, there was an obvious command of some kind yelled out and they moved off the road and filed up into the trees. Swede didn't know how they missed the two of them because he was pretty sure his body jumped at least three feet off the ground when he heard that shout. But the guards were moving into the trees to form a perimeter as the prisoners came forward another ten or twenty yards before they began moving off the road. Which meant the first prisoners passed between Swede and Ray and the guards who had moved into the trees. The rest of the column practically walked right over them but quickly hid any reaction. Without even thinking, the two of them just stood up and moved into the trees along with everybody else. The first guards were still moving farther back into the trees and had their backs to them. Other guards were on the opposite side of the road watching the column. Swede and Ray simply blended in with the group and sprawled out on the ground like everyone else. Within seconds two Americans squatted down next to them and just looked them over for a bit.

"Where the hell did you two come from?" asked one of them. The other seemed to be looking around to see if we were drawing any extra attention. There was a lot of low conversation going on throughout the rest area, so it was apparent it was okay to talk.

"We left Japan as part of the 3rd Battalion, 21st Infantry Regiment, but I don't know who we were with when we got captured north of here two days ago," Swede answered. "They just sent us up some hills in platoons to reinforce other units. We've been working our way south hoping to run into our guys. But you aren't the guys we were hoping to run into."

"You gotta be two of the luckiest bastards I've ever seen. Why in the hell were you layin' out on the road like that?" asked the talker. "I'm Randall by the way. This is Charles. I only know that because it says so on his uniform. He hasn't talked since he joined the column, probably because of that nasty bruise on his neck. I call him Charlie. You two just sit here like you belong. I gotta check in with the captain." Randall had six stripes to their none and moved off without waiting for a reply, so they sat right there. Charlie just nodded at them as if to say he agreed. His head was wrapped in a blood-stained bandage and the left side of his neck was a very dark purple color.

The guards started some small fires by the side of the road and sat down to smoke and chat among themselves. There seemed to be about thirty guards, all armed, all carrying small packs. Ten of them kept watch over the prisoners who were sprawled on the ground under the trees. The other prisoners were dressed like Swede and

21

Parker, just boots and fatigues. Some had caps. A few were barefoot. When Swede looked closer, he noticed there were some wounded in the group. Any bandages appeared to be sleeves cut from fatigue shirts. Everybody, guards and prisoners, seemed to be waiting for something.

Sergeant Randall sat down next to them. Soon another man moved closer but kept his back turned. All Swede could see was that he was tall, slim, and red-headed. Without turning around, he began speaking.

"Randall, were you able to make a count?"

"Sixty-three, captain. We left six behind."

"That's sixty-nine. Yesterday we had sixty-seven. Not likely we have more this morning. Go count them again." The captain continued to talk without looking at them.

"These two clowns enlisted a little while ago, sir. They were tryin' to cross the road when we came up." Randall was also talking without looking at anybody. The captain turned his head to look down at Swede and Parker and then casually looked away.

"Welcome aboard gentlemen. Nice of you to join our little circus. You can fill me in on the details later. Sergeant Randall, I think I hear the chow truck. See if you can find out what happened to our missing men." The captain walked away and stretched out on the ground under a tree.

Swede heard a truck, an American deuce-and-a-half from the sound of it, coming up the road. A canvas tarp covered the back. As it pulled up to the waiting guards the driver seemed to choke it to bring it to a stop. Four of the guards took down the tailgate and grabbed some kettles out of the back. They rolled a barrel to the edge and filled the kettles with water. The guards set them over the fires and went back to smoking and talking. Randall walked out on the road and looked in the back of the truck. He said something to the nearest guard. The guard simply pointed his rifle at Randall and yelled something at him, gesturing that he should get back in the woods with everybody else. Randall walked past where Swede, Parker, and Charlie were sitting. He looked down at Charlie and shook his head. He continued over to where the red-headed captain was now sitting up.

Randall and the captain were involved in a conversation when one of the guards looked their way and yelled. Two guards ran over and backed the two of them up against the tree with their bayonets. Some of the prisoners started to get up and yell in protest. A shot rang out. All the prisoners froze in place. Every single guard had their weapon pointed into the mass of men. Without another sound, the prisoners all sat back down. Except for Randall and the captain. They remained against the tree with two bayonets resting on their shirt buttons. A Korean officer held his pistol in the air as he walked over to the captain.

"What have I told you about giving orders to these men, captain?" the Korean asked in almost perfect English. "These men are now guests of the People's Army. They are free men and no longer have to obey your capitalist orders." He walked up to the two men and placed his pistol a foot from the captain's forehead.

While looking straight into the Korean's eyes the captain said, "You know what you have to do, Mike." A shot rang out and the captain toppled to the ground. Sergeant Randall looked as if he was going to attack the Korean, who simply swung his pistol into the sergeant's face.

"You may bury him, then we must feed the men and put out the fires." The Korean holstered his pistol and walked away as if nothing had happened. Randall walked back over to where Swede and Parker sat with Charlie and slumped to the ground. He put his head in his hands and didn't say a word. Four men picked up the captain's body and carried him off to the side, but not before a guard reached down and yanked the dog tags from the captain's neck. Another prisoner got a shovel from the back of the truck and started to dig the last resting place of the red-headed captain. Swede didn't even know his name.

"What did we get ourselves into?" Parker whispered to Swede.

The guards and prisoners all acted as if this was a normal morning for them. With a yell from one of the guards, the POWs lined up and filed past the kettles to receive one rice ball each and one dipper of hot water in small wooden cups. Swede and Parker joined them, all the while hoping no one was counting cups. They sat back down with Randall and Charlie and ate in silence. Finally, Swede asked, "What just happened?"

Randall looked up with empty eyes. "That bastard just murdered Captain Winslow is what just happened! Weren't you paying attention?" Charlie reached over and put a hand on Randall's shoulder. The sergeant sighed deeply and went on in a more normal tone. "They've been shooting our wounded. Every night for the past three days anyone who can't stand up on his own is held back. We can help them walk once they are up, but they have to be able to get up on their own. That's his rule." Swede knew who he meant. "They tell us the truck will pick them up. But we never see them again. When I asked after the first night's march, I was told they were sent to a field hospital. Then I was told never to ask again. Last night they didn't bother to wait until we got down the road before we heard the shots. From the sound, I think that damned Major does the shooting himself with that fancy pistol of his."

"What did Captain Winslow mean when he said something about Mike knowing what to do?" Swede asked. "Who is Mike?"

"Captain Winslow is - was - our company commander. We've worked together for two years. Our wives take turns babysitting our kids. Before we started our march last night, he brought up the wounded again with the Major. He asked if we could leave some people to help take care of them. That's probably why they made sure we could hear the shots after we left. I think that's why the Captain was killed this morning. And I think he knew it was going to happen soon. We've been keeping track of who gets left behind. The Major spotted us adding to the list and destroyed it. Then he gave a speech to the column about not obeying any orders from the officers or NCOs. He said any officer giving orders would be shot. When he spotted us talking together again this morning that was his excuse." The sergeant had to pause for a while before he could go on.

"I'm Mike. Mike Randall. Captain Winslow meant I was supposed to take care of the men. Most of these guys are from our company." Randall looked as if he had aged twenty years since they had met him a few hours ago.

"We found a couple of GIs on a hill two days ago. Their hands were tied behind their backs with commo wire and they'd been shot in the head. I figured that was just a one-time thing," said Parker. "We need to get outta here." He looked at Swede for his approval.

"I don't know. What should we do, Sergeant?" asked Swede as he looked at Sergeant Randall.

"Go where? How did that work out for you? Where are we? We've been moving more or less to the north but sometimes we are going east and then sometimes west. Korean columns keep going south.

We can't hear artillery anymore. That means we aren't very close to our lines," replied the sergeant.

"I don't want to sound negative. I am impressed as hell with you guys for escaping like you did. I even think we might be able to rush these guards and kill them all. But I'm not completely sure about that. Even if we could pull it off, then what? A lot of these guys are in tough shape. Some are fine physically but have tuned out mentally. There is no way we could move a group this size south to our lines without being spotted. If we split up it would be every man for himself. Not one of us has any food or water stashed away. No, my job is right here trying to take care of these guys. And I'm fairly sure the Major thinks he needs me to keep things organized. I'm the senior NCO in the column. There are two second lieutenants, but they don't have the moxie to help themselves, let alone help this column." Sergeant Randall sat back with an exhausted look on his face, but determination in his eyes.

That's how Swede and Parker were captured a second time. Swede knew they were in no shape to try another escape, certainly not then. The rice ball they had that morning was the most food they had seen in three days. Their efforts in the last few days had come at a cost. They really weren't in any better shape than most of the POWs around them. They had another lesson in survival when there was no rice that night before the column set out. Just one cup of water each. At that rate, it was going to be a while before their next escape attempt.

For the next week there was little change in their routine. March all night-whatever the weather, try to rest in the woods off the road during the day - whatever the weather. A rice ball and warm water in the morning, sometimes the same at dusk before they set out on the night's march, but sometimes just the water. One cup.

One morning the prisoners watched as the guards filled a large cauldron with water and started a fire underneath. A couple of heads of cabbage were thrown in the water. The prisoners were lined up and given what was nothing more than a cup of warm cabbage-flavored water from the cauldron. Then the cabbages were broken up and more greens of some kind were added along with some fish. The guards then had their meal, which by that time was both hot and nutritional.

Swede wasn't crazy about the warm water they were served. Everybody called it "tea." Although every now and then it was hot, it never tasted like any tea he had ever had. He would have much preferred a nice cold drink of water. He learned why that was a bad idea when they came to their first stream.

Crossing a shallow stream at night some of the men started to scoop the water in their hands and drink it. The guards and Sergeant Randall started yelling at the men, even kicking them to get them out of the water. "Goddammit, I've told you people about drinking the water. You have to boil it! They do the same here as in Japan. They put their shit on their fields. You drink that and you will get sick. Get sick enough and you will die. I know you're thirsty. I'm thirsty! But if you don't boil the water before you drink it, you'll end up puking your guts out and dehydrate yourself. It isn't worth the risk." Randall stood right there in the stream until the rear of the column passed. He wasn't able to stop everybody from drinking, but he tried. It was July and it was hot. Most of them were dehydrated to some degree. Their food and fluid intake did not even come close to making up for the calories they spent every night on the march.

Swede approached Randall the next morning after the night's march. "Sergeant Randall, I want to apologize for last night. I was one of those trying to get a drink from the stream. Back home I spent a lot of time swimming in the river. When I was thirsty, I just put my face in the water and drank all I wanted. I never thought things might be different here."

"If you want to survive, if you want to help others survive, you're gonna have to think differently, kid." Randall waved his hand towards the men sprawled out under the trees. "This isn't the army anymore where somebody else takes care of your three hots and a cot. The rules from back home won't work here. These people don't care if you live or die. You have to do what it takes to survive. And you have to help your buddy survive. Because not one of us will survive on our own."

By that morning some were already suffering from their thirst of the night before. If they were lucky and healthy, they only developed mild diarrhea. And if they were able to drink lots of fluids. That meant being very lucky. Those who were unlucky quickly became too weak to keep up. Keeping them clean and helping them maintain the pace of the column could lead to sickness for those willing to help.

Not all were willing. As a result, more died - or were executed. Swede began to understand what Sergeant Randall meant by the rules not working.

The Major and his pistol were gone a week later. They still had to leave some sick or wounded each night before they set out on the road, but the number got fewer each day. Maybe all the really sick and wounded were gone, or maybe the men were simply choosing life over death and forcing themselves to get up off the ground each night. Then one morning the chow truck pulled up and out crawled the two men who had been left behind the night before. That was when they knew the Major would not be back. Even the guards were afraid of him.

The food improved a little. Sometimes their "tea" was more of a soup with a few vegetables added to the kettle. But there were still days when they had only one meal. And days when they had none. Randall continued to try and keep a written record of who died and where. The guards continued to beat anyone suspected of trying to keep any kind of record. Swede finally came up with a method that was almost impossible for the guards to discover. Five men were chosen to memorize the names of the dead and the date they died. Five others were tasked with remembering the date and the estimated number of miles they had marched from the beginning. Every morning and every night those men would sit down and repeat the names and numbers to each other to memorize them. They hoped to write it all down and hide it when they found paper and pencil. The count so far was twenty-three dead out of one hundred forty-nine.

There was no hint of any kind of rescue in their near future. They didn't see any American planes and didn't hear any artillery fire that might suggest the good guys were going to come riding over the hill. The only Americans they saw were prisoners like themselves. Their group grew larger when some smaller columns of POWs joined theirs. A larger column appeared one morning but they weren't allowed to mix with the new guys - instead marching each night right behind them. During the day they rested about 100 yards apart.

No medical care of any kind had been provided since their capture. Wounds that hadn't already killed were full of pus and foul odors. Charlie did what he could. He organized the healthy into teams. Two men would support a less able man in between them. The few they had to carry were sometimes allowed in the truck. The teams also made sure the sick got fed. There were people who would take the food right from the bowls of the weak. Teams of men were organized to deal with that problem. And still Charlie never spoke a word.

One morning Swede noticed someone at the rear of the column ahead of them staring back down the road towards his group. He scuffed around in the dirt while looking at them and then to the side of the road. Swede mentioned this to Mike Randall as they rested during the day. They both noticed the same thing again that evening. They tried to mark the location in their heads and watched carefully as their column moved down the road. Charlie was the one who spotted it. There was part of a torn uniform sleeve on the ground just off the road. Charlie pretended to drop down and tie his boots and scooped it up. Underneath was a small note.

The next morning Randall opened the note as others sat around him to block any curious eyes. It read, "153, 25 ID, no mdcl, 17 dths, orgniz yr troops, LtC GR." He ripped the note to small pieces and pushed them into the dirt. Whoever Lieutenant Colonel GR was he had taken a tremendous risk. "Organize your troops" was an order that would get him shot if his guards had found the note. Randall passed on the information during the day to his small command group. One hundred fifty-three prisoners from the 25th Infantry Division were ahead of them. Their lack of medical care and death rate was about the same. Randall wasn't sure what he could do with this bit of intel, but he had it memorized by his recorders.

His command group was small. It had to be since he was not supposed to be giving orders and therefore should not have a command group in the first place. Swede and Parker had proved their ability to think on their feet, something Randall could see little of in his column. Charlie had a calming influence on the group and helped decide many issues with a simple shake of his head. Swede guessed he was an officer. The fifth man was Jack Usury, an older corporal. His uniform sleeve suggested he had been a staff sergeant in his recent past. Usury seemed to defer to Randall in a way that suggested more than the difference in their rank. But his suggestions for dealing with their captors were well thought out, and he had a knack for keeping the men in the column in line - whatever their rank. He and Charlie were keeping most of the sick and wounded from joining the death list. The guards paid no attention to either Swede or Parker as they were young. That meant they were able to both collect and distribute information for Randall.

Any leadership had to be carefully disguised. The guards constantly made it clear there was no rank among the POWs. They made a habit of forcing officers and NCOs to conduct menial tasks. This usually meant scooping out the day's rations for both the POWs and the guards and cleaning the pots after. They felt this would cause them to "lose face" with their men. The few young lieutenants in the column had abandoned their authority from the moment of their capture. Too many of the enlisted men showed little, if any, spirit. Few of the Americans were even aware of the concept of "losing face," so who doled out their meal made no difference to them. Some of the dim bulbs were impressed their leaders would go to the trouble of helping to serve meals. Most importantly, the lieutenants and NCOs were able to give Randall any information they gleaned from being around the guards while they cleaned the pots.

They were moving now during the day and resting at night. The nights were getting colder as August gave way to September. Spending cold nights on the ground was a problem. Marching all day took more energy than their diet provided. It was hard moving along dirt roads full of ruts and holes when dry, and thick with mud in the rain. Most of the time they followed simple cart trails through the hills. If they were fit, this would have been a breeze. But they were not. Pain from untreated wounds sapped their strength. Something as simple as a blister became a major problem. They all looked miserable and felt miserable. The only baths came from splashing water on themselves when fording streams. No one had brushed their teeth since capture, used any soap, or had a shave or a haircut. Diarrhea was a constant problem. Even those without diarrhea were in a constant state of dehydration. Uniforms were filthy. Many had given parts of sleeves or pants legs to be used for bandaging wounds. Some were bare-footed, others had no shirt. The few days they were allowed to rest kept more than a few alive.

Since their capture in mid-July, they had been sleeping on the ground. No sleeping bags or ground cloths. Just find a soft spot and try to sleep. When they came near villages, the guards hustled them right on through with a lot of yelling and pushing. The guards were more likely to become violent during those times than any other.

Either they were afraid the South Koreans would try to help the Americans, or they wanted to show the villagers how powerless these big Americans were. Whatever the reason, the column had not slept in a building since most of them had left Japan. Rain or shine, the forest floor was their bed, the stars above their blanket. Uncomfortable at times, but something most could handle. Until the temperature dropped. Then men whose health was poor even in warmer weather began to decline.

About the first week of September, the column, by then numbering one hundred and nineteen men, approached Seoul. For a crow that was about eighty miles from their point of capture six weeks before. Their estimate was they walked more than three hundred miles, just not in a straight line. At times they traveled south. It was common for the guards to stop a column of North Korean soldiers heading south and spend time waving their arms and pointing in various directions as they talked. Then they would turn the column of POWs around and march back in the direction they had just come. The guards were North Korean themselves and simply didn't know the territory. Ray Parker claimed they had marched through one village four different times in just two weeks. The guards seemed to have no real plan other than to keep the column moving.

Swede noticed a difference in houses as they got closer to Seoul. At first, the villages were huts randomly thrown together with a path wandering through them. The huts were wattle and daub with thatch roofs. Some had mud-brick walls that reminded him of the old sod shanties pictured in books at school. Then they marched on a road - a dirt road, but a road. Villages looked more organized. Homes had more wood in their construction, with real windows and doors. The better the road they were on, the better the homes. He saw some cement block walls. Once they could see Seoul in the distance, the roofs changed from thatch to tile.

Many of those villages were in ruins, with the debris of war scattered about. Overturned carts with the contents thrown in the dirt. Dead cows. Dead Koreans. The living, pushed aside by the guards, stared at the prisoners as they marched past. Some looked at the soldiers in disbelief, others with hate, but most seemed too exhausted to care about anything except their own survival.

They crossed into Seoul on a railroad bridge, as the main bridge was full of North Korean military traffic moving south. Once into the city, the guards stopped the column and formed them into four rows. With shouts and slaps, they made it clear their prisoners were to be quiet and look submissive. The prisoners were about to be put on display as proof Americans were weak and North Koreans strong. It wasn't hard to look weak. They were. Most of the civilians simply looked on with little interest as the guards strutted their stuff moving the captives through the city. A few civilians tried to give food or water to the prisoners but were kept back with curses and rifle butts.

This was Swede's first good look at a Korean city of any size. There were obvious signs of destruction from whatever fighting had taken place here, but parts of the city were untouched. They marched down some main streets with trolley car tracks in the center and all kinds of electrical wiring overhead. Around the main intersections were brick buildings of three and four stories. Smaller buildings lined the side streets. Some buildings had a distinctly Asian look to them, while many others reminded him of the banks or courthouses back home. He was surprised to see a fair number of churches. He hadn't thought of this part of the world having churches. A shrine or pagoda or something, but not churches. The column marched farther away from what he figured was the city center. It moved through some neighborhoods of almost complete destruction, only tall, thin, brick chimneys poking out of the debris. It was in one of these areas they stopped.

Being in the city meant they got to sleep under a roof rather than in the woods. The column halted on the edge of an area of ruined buildings, most of which seemed to be two stories high. One side of the street was a mess, the other almost untouched. Their new home was probably a schoolhouse. There were two buildings with three equally sized rooms on each side of a central hall. The POWs were kept in one building and the guards used the other. The interior doors were missing, as was any furniture. Some windows were intact, others gone. Each room had straw-covered floors. The two buildings were separated by a small courtyard, with the entire area enclosed by a six-foot wall. Immediately on arrival shovels were provided and they were directed to dig two slit trenches off to the side of their new barracks. One for them and another for the guards. One room in the guard's barracks was the kitchen. The men filed past to get their food and then ate sitting on the ground in the open courtyard. Those prisoners new to Asia were given a lesson in agricultural methods when some locals came into the compound every morning and scooped the mess out of the trenches to be carried away in buckets.

Instead of sleeping on the ground they were sleeping on the floor, but at least they had a roof over their heads and some protection from the cold, as temperatures at night were getting noticeably cooler. They were still fed only twice a day, but a few vegetables were added to their morning cup of rice on some days. Those in the know explained to the others the connection between the bucket brigade and the newly available vegetables.

Little else changed. They still wore whatever was left of what they were captured in. No haircuts, no baths, no blankets. Each day was the same as the one before. Rice or some kind of beans for breakfast, out on work parties cleaning up rubble, back for their evening rice or beans, and then crowded back into their barracks until the next morning.

Seoul

September 1950

New problems soon outweighed the improvements of being in Seoul. First came lice. The general mood their first night had been upbeat as the POWs looked around at their luxurious accommodations. The next morning Swede woke up to an itching he figured came from sleeping on straw. Parker was the first to point out their new friends.

He sat on the floor in their crowded room, scratching his armpit. Then he got a puzzled look on his face and held up something between his finger and thumb. "Where did these little buggers come from? They're all over me."

Jack Usury was already busy picking the bugs from his hair and crunching them between his fingernails. "Lice, boyo. You've got lice. We all have 'em. We aren't exactly livin' in the Ritz here. Best you get busy pickin' 'em off. One more thing to add to your morning bath." He chuckled at his own humor. "Get used to it boys. These lousy bastards are gonna be our constant companions for a while," grumbled the old hand.

Another problem was how crowded they were in their new sleeping quarters. With twenty men to a room, they couldn't all stretch out at the same time when sleeping. Randall came up with a system. Half the men would sleep sitting down against the walls while the others stretched out on the floor. Each night the groups switched. Those in the center slept with their feet to the outside so they didn't get kicked in the head by the men in the outer ring. Nobody had a solution for the many interruptions during the night by those with dysentery trying to make it to the latrine trench. Especially since they had to get permission from the guards to leave the building. This all meant men were not only stepped on in this process, but often were shit on. And still no water for bathing. The only positive about the close quarters was the body heat that helped with the cooler nights. Some of the men tried sleeping on the floor in the hallway running down the center of the building. When the guards didn't react in any way, more joined them, easing the cramped conditions in some of the rooms. Randall then had each room assign men to a rotation: hall, center of the room, the outer ring against the wall.

Living the good life in Seoul brought other problems. Columns of vehicles and soldiers passed through the city every day heading south. When they noticed the American POWs, they sometimes stopped to get a close-up look at their enemy. Some liked to show how tough they were and how weak these Americans were by knocking them around. Others liked the look of American boots and "traded' for them. The Korean took the GI's boots and in exchange left his, more of a tennis shoe than a boot. If the ugly American couldn't fit his new shoes on his big feet that was his problem.

The good news didn't stop there. Certainly no friendships had been formed with their guards, but at least their time together had brought both sides to a mutual tolerance. The POWs had learned to interpret the grunts and yells and gestures. Now a prisoner getting clubbed with a rifle or poked with a bayonet only happened a few times a day. The same morning the lice arrived, a column of Korean troops marched up the street and waited while the old guards fell into formation and marched away. This new group brought another piece of bad news - the Major and his pistol. Their new guards quickly rousted everyone out of the schoolhouse. The Major stood up in his American jeep and raised his arms like a pastor about to begin his sermon.

"I am glad to see you my friends. I have been busy planning for your stay with us. Soon you shall enter the People's Paradise as guests of the People's Army. You will be taught how your capitalist rulers have mistreated you and made you slaves in their factories. You will learn the way of Marx and Lenin. You will be taught to be happy. You will be good students, or perhaps you will stay in Korea forever." At this last statement he gave a little grin, as if he was looking forward to fulfilling that bit of prophecy. "Perhaps we will meet again. I have other guests to attend to now." With that he dropped into the back seat of his jeep. The picture he probably hoped to convey was ruined when his driver ground through the gears as the jeep popped and jerked down the street, dust and exhaust everywhere. The new guards did some more yelling and herded the POWs back into the schoolhouse. Swede stood staring after the Major until Ray grabbed his arm and pulled him off the street.

The change of guards brought on a problem that desperately needed to be solved. When the old guards left so had their truck. The truck that carried the cups had been parked inside the compound. For some reason, the pots had been taken into the designated kitchen area but not the cups. And now the truck was gone. That evening the guards lined the men up for their food only to find none of the POWs had anything to hold their rice and tea. The first man in line just stood there. The guard commander looked down the line and saw no one had any kind of container. He shrugged his shoulders and made a motion for the prisoner to hold out his cupped hands. One rice ball was dumped into his hands. The next guard held up a dipper of water for the man to drink. Some men used their caps as bowls, but not everyone had a cap. This process took a long while and the guards were not happy. The next morning the rice was again dumped into cupped hands, but no one was offered the dipper of water.

Right after chow Randall approached the guard commander. He asked for permission to search the nearby buildings for containers they might use for eating and drinking. They got so little in the way of fluids as it was, being cut off completely was going to be deadly. Whether he was able to get his message across or not didn't matter. The prisoners were lined up and marched off.

Their part of Seoul was in ruins. Rubble blocked many streets. Some buildings still smoldered from fires that had broken out. Most of the buildings seemed to be factories or warehouses for light industry. The prisoners were put to work cleaning things up. They were in no shape for hard labor, but the guards seemed to have orders to just keep them busy. The first few days they cleared a path down some of the streets. Then they were sent into the buildings to salvage what lumber and metal they could. Some men worked in the open, sorting that material into piles. They soon realized they only had to look busy to keep the guards happy.

Swede and Ray Parker were assigned to the salvage crew. No guards followed them into the buildings. They seemed content to watch over the activity in the street. Taking the opportunity to look around, Swede checked some small rooms at the back. One must have been a kitchen or pantry of sorts. There were some tin cups and bowls scattered about, so they picked them up and stuffed them in their pockets. Shouldering some pipes, they walked back outside and dumped them in the correct pile. Swede wandered over to where Sergeant Randall was working and with a smile showed him what he had in his pockets. The word was passed around to gather any small containers that could be found. That night at chow the guard commander noticed some of the men had cups or bowls or even tin cans. He seemed to approve this initiative on the part of his charges. The men in the front of the line ate quickly and passed their cups and cans to those farther back. Within a few days, every single prisoner in the group had at least one small container that would hold liquid. When nothing was said about the cups, Swede decided to push his luck and brought back an old coat he found on a work party. He wrapped it around his waist under his fatigue shirt and then stashed it in the wall where he slept. The nights were already getting cool. He figured if his captors didn't care if he got enough to eat or drink, they weren't about to start handing out blankets.

A few days later the POWs were not called out for evening chow. After an hour or so of waiting, Randall sent a young kid named Rafaldano out to ask the guard commander when they would eat. The guards had a hard time with Rafaldano's name. When they stumbled over the pronunciation, they sounded like they were barking - Raf, Raf. Teased often enough as an Italian kid in his Irish neighborhood, Rafaldano wasn't about to let some people he couldn't even understand do the same. He started barking back at the guards with the same sound. (Which of course, earned him the nickname Bowser among his fellow POWs. And led his captors to think he might not be right in the head.) Rather than admit there was a problem, guards simply ignored him as much as possible. Sergeant Randall figured Bowser could complain about food without getting much of a beating. He was right. The guards simply yelled at him and made it clear he needed to return to the schoolhouse.

The next morning they noticed tables being set up in the street in front of their building. They were called out as if for morning chow, but no food was in sight. The guard commander waved what looked like blank postcards at them and shouted, "You ri, name, numbah, you sahjunt, you pryvet. Give me." The POWs looked around at each other and started talking in low voices about what they should do. Some had no idea what they were being told. The commander yelled out again, "You no talk! You ri! No ri - no eat!"

The reason for the missing meal now became obvious. The men were hungry. They could "ri" and eat. Or not. The commander came up with one more incentive. "I send Red Cross. Give you name Red Cross." He even followed that up with what he probably thought of as a friendly smile. Then he pointed to Randall and said, "Rennel, you say," motioning for the sergeant to come out in front of the formation.

Randall looked at Swede as if to say what do we do now? Keeping his voice low Swede gave his opinion. "What do we have to lose? Maybe they really will turn our names over to the Red Cross. At least the folks back home will know we're alive. And we can't afford to miss any more meals."

Randall walked to where the commander stood. Facing the prisoners, he spoke slowly and clearly, more so for the commander than for the prisoners. He knew this was risky. Giving orders could get him shot, but he understood the commander depended on him to help keep the troops in line. He took the risk.

"I can't order you to fill the card out or not, but I don't see we have much choice. This might be the only way to get our names to the Red Cross." Randall checked to see how the guard commander was reacting to his statement. Then he looked out over his men. For many of them the Red Cross meant packages of food and warm blankets. That was the way they understood it had worked in the last war. Randall turned and took a card from the commander. He printed his name, rank, and serial number, handed it back, and returned to his position in the formation. The men slowly broke ranks and lined up in front of the tables. As they did so, the guards started setting up the kettles for their morning tea and rice. Little did the prisoners know this was just the beginning of many such cards they would fill out.

Later in the day, while working on a cleaning detail, Randall said to Swede, "There is one thing you have to lose by filling out that card. Now they know you are here. They have your name on a list. That might make it a little harder to disappear some night."

Swede nodded his head in agreement. "I thought of that as I handed my card over, but I don't think any of us had much choice. I doubt we were going to get fed until every last man filled out a card. And there is the hope he was telling the truth."

Randall smiled and replied, "Then let's hope so."

Seoul Searching

September 1950

Swede and Corporal Usury were assigned to the brick cleaning crew that day. Tedious, but not difficult. They each found a short piece of pipe and used it to knock the mortar from each brick. They put just enough effort into their task to keep the roaming guards in the area happy. After a while Usury told Swede to keep an eye out for any approaching guards. He quickly jumbled together a pile of bricks they hadn't touched. Then he had Swede help him stack their clean bricks neatly around it. The effect was a large, neat, stack of clean bricks. He told Swede to look busy but slow down and save his energy.

"I don't intend to help these bastards any more than I have to," he growled. "Remember, our job is to screw with these people as much as possible. Right now, we do that by lookin' like we're busy followin' their orders but accomplish as little as we can." Usury had gotten to like this kid in the past two months. He proved he had a level head on his young shoulders and could be counted on to make sound decisions. And he cared about his fellow soldiers.

"Let me tell you a story about a guy I was stationed with in Hawaii. He had been a Marine during the war, but I didn't hold that against him. He joined the Army later, so you gotta forgive his temporary insanity." Usury looked around to check on the guards and settled back against the stack of bricks.

"This guy was stationed in China before the war. He was with the embassy guard detachment in Peking, so they had to look sharp all the time but never had to polish or clean a thing except their rifles. Chinese coolies, or house boys, did all that crap. They had to look sharp and train hard, but he said duty there was better than even Hawaii.

"Anyhow, they were all captured the same day the Japs hit Pearl Harbor. There were about two hundred of them in three different locations and thousands of Jap troops all over the place. The day before they had crated all their weapons and sent them to the coast where they were supposed to board their ship the next morning. Wrong place at the wrong time, I guess." Usury gave Swede an ironic grin.

Just then Swede noticed one of the guards headed their way, so he nudged Usury and started working more energetically. For a few minutes, the two cleaned a few more bricks and generally pretended to be good little prisoners.

Usury picked up his tale. "What I remember most about his story was what they did when they were sent to Japan and put to work in steel factories and shipyards. They would grind the heads down on rivets in the hulls of the ships they were workin' on to make them weak. They would loosen the caps on barrels of fuel and tip the barrels upside down in the storage shed. One guy ran a crane loadin' cargo on the dock. He pretended he wasn't very good at it and kept runnin' the pallets of cargo into the side of the ship and eventually overstressed some seams in the side. When they came back to work in the morning, the ship had sunk right there at the dock. They threw one-of-a-kind tools into fresh cement they were pourin' for foundations. Every time they did somethin' like that, they took the risk of bein' shot."

Usury looked Swede right in the eye. "The point is they never gave up. Maybe those rivets never popped and the ships never sank. But they tried. When they took a beatin' for not bowin' low enough to the guards they felt pride because they had done what they could." He pointed at the pile of bricks that wasn't really a pile of bricks. "It isn't much, but it helps. We need to save our energy as much as possible. These bastards don't feed us enough to do the work they expect us to do. So, we save some calories and screw with 'em at the same time. It isn't sinkin' a ship in the harbor, but it's a start."

"Does escaping count in this game?" Swede asked with just a hint of a smile. He still wasn't sure where he stood with Usury.

"Damn straight! Sure, you got caught again, but even there you outfoxed the little bastards," Usury laughed. "They probably don't know you escaped in the first place and they sure don't know they caught you again. Or you surrendered. Whatever that was on the road that morning." Usury laughed again.

Swede laughed with him. "That was no surrender! We were just reporting for duty." Then he lost his smile and got a faraway look on his face. "We were lucky that day." He looked over at Usury tapping away at some mortar on his brick. "Do you think we'll get lucky again? Do you think a rescue is possible?"

Usury stacked his brick neatly on the pile and picked up another. He looked over at the young private, all thin and scraggly haired and grimy with just a hint of a beard - those blues eyes almost begging for the answer he hoped for. "I have to be honest with you, kid. I think we have a better chance of bein' stood against a wall and shot than we have of bein' rescued. You've seen how they treated those who couldn't keep up. I think if these gooks ever thought a rescue force was anywhere near, they would shoot us all. Not that I think a rescue force is much of a possibility. I haven't seen any of our planes for a couple of weeks now. You can tell by the troops we see headed south there must still be fightin' goin' on, but it sure isn't anywhere near here.

"Let me explain somethin' about the Army. The people who run the Army don't see us as individuals. They see us as numbers. They make decisions based on big numbers and what they think will happen in the future.

"Maybe it will make more sense if I tell you about our guys captured in the Philippines in the last war. Sooner or later, the Japs started sendin' them to work in their factories back in Japan. They crammed them into the holds of their troop transports or cargo ships, the same ships our subs were huntin'. Sometimes the generals and admirals in Hawaii and the politicians in Washington knew that a Jap convoy was carryin' our guys. But they sent the subs anyway. It was more important to them to sink a ship carryin' Jap troops or Jap tanks than it was to save a few American prisoners. Those troops and tanks were goin' to kill even more Americans. Maybe they were right, or maybe they were wrong. The point is, we don't count for much. We aren't high on anybody's list of concerns. There aren't enough of us to be on that list. That is just a reality of war.

"Most of these guys think their war is over, that all they have to do is wait it out. But we have to live with ourselves, have some pride in ourselves, so when this is over, we can say we kept up the fight. We are gonna have to let some hate into our hearts, let that hate burn at us, let that hate drive us. We need to remember what they did to our buddies so we don't give up. Some days we will lose but we never give up. That's how we win in the end; we never give up.

"So, we do what we can to make things better for ourselves and screw with these bastards when we get the chance. We do what we can to stay alive and keep our people healthy. Remember, the end game is to survive, but with your pride intact. Know that survival won't be as simple as movin' from point A to point B. There will be lots of twists and turns. Comin' to get us will be the last thing the Army will do. In the meantime, remember that it's up to you to look out for number one." He grinned at Swede again.

"You've got guts, kid. And brains. You just listen to your old sergeant," he looked down at his sleeve and chuckled. "I mean corporal. And we'll be alright."

The two continued to pretend they were working hard for the rest of the day. When a guard got close, they showed every sign of being productive. When they could, they slowed their pace and talked. Swede grew comfortable with the older man and eventually got him to explain the missing stripes on his sleeves. This happened when he brought up the fact he had been promoted to PFC, but the only one who knew was his Platoon Sergeant. He hadn't seen him since escaping from the column.

Jack Usury enlisted in early 1940 to get away from the hopelessness of the family farm in Kansas where the Depression was still very much in control. He landed in Africa in November 1942 as a corporal. He hit the beach again in Sicily as a sergeant and then at Salerno in September 1943 as a staff sergeant. Shortly after the Salerno landing, Mike Randall had come into his unit as a transfer 2nd lieutenant. He had received a battlefield commission on the beach at Salerno for running an entire company as a master sergeant when the command post took a direct hit from German artillery. The practice was to transfer newly commissioned officers to another unit. Randall became Usury's platoon leader. Over the next eighteen months, they moved up the Italian peninsula and up the rank ladder together. When the Germans finally surrendered in May of 1945, Usury was a master sergeant and Randall a captain. The two had worked well together over that time and had become good friends. They returned to the US from Marseilles aboard the *Wakefield* in September 1945.

It was in Marseilles that trouble started. Jack had found that he did not like the drudgery of the peacetime Army. He replaced the adrenaline of three years of combat with drinking. He got drunk and started a fight that got them both thrown in a French jail. Randall talked them out of jail and got a hungover Usury to the gangplank just in time to make the departure for home. Jack sobered up on the way, but he had lost a lot of Mike's respect.

Then more trouble hit. The bean counters were practically waiting for them on the dock. Washington had decided to drastically reduce its military forces. Soldiers were being discharged left and right. Both Usury and Randall had been part of the pre-war Army, so were given a choice. They could take a reduction in rank and re-enlist or take a discharge. Both decided to stay. The Army had too many master sergeants, so Usury was reduced to staff sergeant. Because the pencil pushers didn't consider Mike Randall a "real" officer, they used his last enlisted rank. So he also ended up as a staff sergeant. It was a slap in the face for both, but neither had a desire to return to civilian life. They liked the Army and were good at soldiering, so both took the chance and signed the papers.

Jack got a handle on his drinking when he transferred to the MPs, getting more of the adrenaline he was used to. He was assigned to the security company of an engineer battalion in New Mexico. He enjoyed the work at first, but the constant travel began to wear on him, not to mention the slow promotions. In early 1950 he asked for a transfer back to the infantry and found himself assigned to Japan. When he arrived at his new unit, he found Master Sergeant Mike Randall as his first sergeant. Seeing the progress Mike made over those few years got him thinking about his career since the end of the war. A weekend of drinking resulted in some damage to government property. With Mike Randall's help, the damage to Jack Usury was limited to the loss of two stripes. Jack had been sober since and the two worked well as a team once more.

Jack admitted to Swede losing the stripes had been his own fault. Now that he had a war to fight again, he felt like his old self. He ended his history lesson with the comment, "This is a different kind of war we have for ourselves. We don't have any training or manuals to fall back on. It's goin' to be OJT all the way and the price we pay will be high if we don't learn fast." He noticed Swede's puzzled look. "On the job training?"

They continued to be sent out each day on work parties. They went to the same general area of the city but not to the same buildings. They never really finished cleaning up a building. Mike Randall thought the guards might be selling their services to the highest bidder of the day. If the building owner came up with the right bribe, he got cheap labor for the day courtesy of the US Army. In fact, Randall was curious as to why his group of POWs had not yet been sent to a permanent camp. Some in the command group thought they were being kept as a bargaining chip for an exchange of prisoners. Usury explained their being in a kind of limbo as a bureaucratic foul-up. Nobody knew what to do with them because nobody was paying any attention. The North Korean Major in charge of the column in the beginning wasn't around anymore. According to his brief visit when they first arrived in Seoul, he was on to bigger and better things. But no one had replaced him. They were being used as cleanup crews simply because no one high enough up the chain of command knew of their existence. This led to more discussion about escaping. But before he let any of his people start planning an escape, Randall needed more information.

"I want you to have a look around. There may be other prisoners around here, but we don't know if they are just passing through or are being kept in the city like we are. See if you can find any groups and get an idea of their size. If you think you can get away with it, make contact. But don't take any unnecessary chances." Mike Randall looked carefully at the young soldier in front of him. "Don't go wandering too far off. Stay near your work party so you can tell a guard you are lost. Be careful. Any questions?"

"No sir. I figure this should be no different than dodgin' cops back in the neighborhood," replied Bowser, trying to look braver than he felt.

Randall was sending Bowser out on this mission because he figured the kid could bluff his way back if any guards spotted him. He was hoping the guards had told stories about the crazy American who thought he was a dog.

Tony Rafaldano did come from a tough neighborhood, but there was no way he was going to admit it wasn't the cops he used to dodge. His problem had been the other kids in the neighborhood. Tony was thin, shy, and liked school. Not qualities that earned him any points with his peers. But his biggest fault was his audacity to live in South Boston with an Italian name and face. When that face started getting attention from the local girls it made his life even worse. Tony became very good at moving around the neighborhood without attracting attention. To be noticed meant a beating. So, Tony developed the ability to move from A to B without being noticed. If his Irish buddies were looking for him. they could find him, but most of the time they had other things to do. Still, getting knocked around once or twice a week was a pain. When he decided the only way to defend himself from five or six Irish lads out for a good time was to bring a gun to a knife fight, Judge Michael O'Reilly decided the Army needed another Italian kid.

Bowser slipped away from his work detail by walking in the front of the building he was assigned to clean out and climbing out a back window. He picked up a mangled piece of pipe and carried it across the street and into the next building. Once inside, he took his time and carefully watched the street and buildings around him. They were working in a large area that must have been light industrial or maybe storage warehouses. Artillery rounds and fires had pretty much made a mess out of the mostly two-story buildings. There was block after block of utter destruction. Crumbling walls had dumped debris into the streets. He could not see a complete structure for half a mile or more. Some areas were just blackened skeletons of timbers poking randomly into the sky. In one building, only a lone staircase survived. Bowser couldn't see any people in the area, Korean or American. He moved out the back of that building and into the next. Doors and windows were missing from the few remaining walls, making it easy to move from building to building. Finding an interior staircase mostly intact, he was able to climb to the second floor. There was no roof, but parts of the walls were still standing. He kept low and took a good look around the area. Korean civilians were moving around on the streets four or five blocks away to both his right and left, but none ahead. He kept moving like this until he spotted what could be another work party a block or two away. Carefully, Bowser worked his way closer until he heard Americans talking in the building just ahead. He picked a window to a room that looked empty and crawled through. He had abandoned the pipe because it made too much noise for someone sneaking through a building, so now he picked up a large board, put it over his shoulder, and walked into the next room.

Two skinny Americans were trying to pick up a large beam, so Bowser dropped his board and jumped in to help. With all three of them cursing and stumbling, they managed to get it out the door and into the street where others were stacking various boards and pipes.

"Thanks, man. I didn't know you were in there or I would have asked for your help sooner," the bigger of the two said. All three stood for a minute wiping sweat out of their eyes. His new friend took a longer look at Bowser and asked, "How *did* you get in that back room? I swear nobody was ahead of us." The man stood in worn and ripped fatigues, dirty face, shaggy hair, and a poor excuse for a beard. Bowser was thinking how bad the soldier looked until he realized he was probably looking into a mirror. He had long adjusted to his own stink but suddenly noticed this guy smelled worse.

Realizing the three of them might attract attention standing there gawking at each other, Bowser replied, "Let's get back in there for more stuff and I'll explain." He turned and walked back into the building. His new friends followed. Once inside, Bowser led them into the back room and turned to them. "I'm not with you guys. I'm with a column being held about a mile back that way in an old schoolhouse. I'm supposed to contact any Americans I can and find out what I can. So, what can you tell me?"

After staring at him for a few seconds both men spoke at the same time. "Holy shit!" Then they went right back to staring at him with their mouths wide open. Bowser was beginning to think he might have stumbled on to prisoners from a mental ward when the big guy spoke again. "You wait here. I'll get the Sarge and you can talk to him." Big Guy nudged his partner, who was still staring gap-jawed at Bowser, and the two hurried out. They disproved his mental ward theory when they stopped to pick up some more broken timbers before they exited the building at a casual pace.

Big Guy came back a few minutes later with a sergeant who looked upset and came in at a pace sure to attract attention. The first thing he did was yell, "Who are you? Why are you here? You are going to get us in trouble!" He got louder with every word.

"Jesus Christ, Sarge! Calm down. Your yellin' is the only thing that's gonna get us in trouble." Bowser tried to keep his voice down. This wasn't exactly what he expected.

"Don't tell me to calm down, Private!" the sergeant practically screamed. "Stand at attention! Now answer my questions. Who are you and why are you here!"

Bowser could see out into the courtyard where POWs were not so busily sorting through the rubble. The only guard in sight was headed in their direction, undoubtedly to see what all the yelling was about. Bowser reached down, picked up a piece of lumber, and whacked the sergeant as hard as he could on the side of his head. The man dropped like a brick. Bowser reached over and grabbed Big Guy by the arm.

"Start yelling for help and drag this dumb bastard back out there. Keep yelling all the way. Convince that guard he fell and hurt himself. When things calm down you get someone in here who can put me in touch with your commander - and knows how to be quiet. Now move!"

Big Guy proved once again he had a brain. He started yelling for help as he grabbed the sergeant under his arms and quickly dragged him into the next room and out the door before the guard got close enough to come into the building. He continued pulling him towards where the bulk of the prisoners were working, yelling all the way. Bowser retreated to the back room and got ready to jump out the window and get to an adjoining building if any guards decided to head his way. Fortunately, Big Guy was doing a good job of causing a scene out in the courtyard. Everybody's attention was focused on him and the sergeant who had 'fallen' and hit his head.

About an hour later things were back to normal and three prisoners headed in Bowser's direction. It was Big Guy, his original partner, and a Staff Sergeant. When they came in the building, Big Guy and his buddy grabbed some boards and left. The new sergeant stayed and walked into the back room where Bowser waited.

The sergeant took a good look at Bowser and then spoke in a low voice, "I'm Staff Sergeant Howard. Do you want to tell me why you are bashing my people around?" His tone was more one of curiosity than concern.

Bowser stood at attention just in case this guy was another asshole. "Private Anthony Rafaldano. I'm part of a work party about a mile away. My commander ordered me to contact any other POWs I could find and exchange information with them. Your sergeant wouldn't listen, and his yellin' attracted the attention of the guards. I had to shut him up before they came in here. Is he OK?" Bowser wasn't all that concerned but thought it might help if he asked.

Staff Sergeant Howard gave a slight grin. "He'll be fine. I must admit there have been times I wanted to hit him alongside the head myself. If he can't do something by the book, he can't do it at all." He looked out into the courtyard to see if everything looked normal. Two more soldiers came into the building and left with some broken lumber on their shoulders without paying any attention to Howard or Bowser.

"Relax, Private. Tell me about your unit. We didn't know there were other Americans in the neighborhood."

Bowser briefly explained who they were, where they were, and what had happened to them since their capture. Randall had told him to get any info on where American forces were and to set up a time and place to exchange lists of deaths - if that was possible. He and Staff Sergeant Howard spent about twenty minutes talking. Howard explained that if the major with his column knew Bowser was there, he would turn him in to the Koreans. The major was afraid to do anything that might upset their captors, so Bowser would have to watch for the guards and even other Americans when he came back with Randall's list of deaths. Howard also explained he had no list because his major had made it clear no such list was to be kept. The Koreans were having no trouble getting the major to cooperate. Howard would be able to give the exact number of deaths and the total of prisoners in the column because he had kept track of them himself.

The two decided they would try to meet in two days in the same area. He was to look for either Howard or Big Guy and get their attention. Both would be watching for him over the next couple of days. As two prisoners came into the building, Howard shook Bowser's hand, wished him luck, and walked out carrying some boards on his shoulder.

Bowser had no trouble getting back to his work party. He decided it might be better to look normal instead of sneaking from building to building. Once he got a few blocks away from Howard's group he simply picked up some pipes and picked his way through everything in the street until he came to the area where his buddies were sorting rubble. There he dumped his pipes and joined the group like he had been there all day. The guards usually did a head count in the morning before they headed out with a work party and didn't bother again until they locked them up in their barracks. Even his buddies hadn't noticed his absence. That evening he gave Mike Randall the details of his meeting with Howard. Randall asked Bowser and Swede to get a few men together on the next day's work detail and find some paper. He wanted to write out the information to pass on to Howard. If he had time, he would make another copy and figure a way to hide it for use later. That would also mean those men who memorized names and dates could start over at zero.

Deciding to keep things quiet, Bowser and Swede only let Ray Parker in on their search party the next day. Parker found a couple of sheets that were probably from an inventory of some kind and only used on one side. Bowser found some sheets of cardboard and peeled off the thinnest layer he could. All three of them found pencils of various sizes. Getting all this back to Randall was no problem. The guards had never bothered to search anyone who didn't have something obviously stuffed in their shirt or pants. Still, all three knew paper and pencils were forbidden as they meant someone was trying to record events. Swede found some cloth bags, what he would call gunny sacks, and stuffed them up one pant leg. Like he expected, the guards noticed them, confiscated them, cuffed him on the head, and passed everybody behind him through without another look.

When they were back in their barracks for the night, and before it got too dark, Randall sat down with his recorders and wrote out names and dates of deaths for the day. They had given up trying to memorize how far they traveled each day. Without a map that became pointless. He included information on when and where most of them had been captured and noted the date they arrived in Seoul. Then he made a duplicate and hid it in the lining of his boot. At some point he hoped to find something waterproof to wrap the paper in.

The next morning Randall sent Ray Parker with Bowser to locate Staff Sergeant Howard. When the work parties went out, they moved a few blocks down from where they had been the last few days. As soon as they could, Bowser and Ray disappeared out a hole blown in the back wall of a building and scrambled over the debris to the building next door. Bowser figured to simply head out in a straight line for a few blocks and then find a high spot to start looking for the other Americans. There seemed to be a few more Korean civilians in the area so they each threw one end of a large plank on their shoulders and walked at a normal pace from one building across the street. Once inside they moved to the far side of the building and checked to see if anyone was close by. If not, they repeated their move across the street. Their theory was if anyone noticed them, they would only see two American prisoners on a work detail. If they spotted any civilians closer than two blocks, they simply hid until the coast was clear. Twice they found their way to a second floor and checked carefully to see who was around. On the third try, they saw what Bowser figured was Howard's group in the same area he had found them two days before.

As they were approaching the area, Ray grabbed Bowser's arm and yanked him back. He pointed to the building they would have entered once they crossed the street. It had been a two-story structure, but the second story on the side facing the street was gone. The exterior wall on the far side of the building was still mostly intact. A guard stood on the second floor looking out a broken window over the prisoners working below, his back to Bowser and Ray. As they watched, he turned from the window and began climbing down a ladder. They quickly backed up further into the interior of their building, still watching the guard, who was now casually strolling around the first-floor level, kicking and poking at the mess inside. Ray motioned to a large timber and whispered, "Should we just fake it and carry this out of here?"

Bowser had given that idea some thought on his first visit over this way, but decided it was too risky. Too many chances a guard or a prisoner would realize they didn't belong. He shook his head and motioned to a pile of stone and timber in a dark corner. "You crawl in there. I'll do the same in the other corner. If he comes in here and spots one of us the other flattens him." In seconds, the two men were pretending to be invisible.

The guard did wander out into the street. He came across to poke his head into their building but then moved on. Bowser came out of his corner to watch where the guard went next. They didn't want to come out of hiding to find him standing just outside. The guard eventually wandered back in the direction of the POW work party, where he lit up a smoke and sat basking in the sunlight. After deciding they could breathe again, Bowser and Ray moved one building down to their right. Then they moved across the street into a building they hoped would give them a spot to contact Howard. It took about an hour, but they finally spotted Big Guy going in and out of the building next to them. They moved to the far back corner of the building they were hiding in. That hid their movements from any guards or prisoners in the work party. When things looked good, they crawled out a window in their building and through a hole in the wall of the building where Big Guy was working. Staying hidden, they kept watching until Big Guy came in the building alone.

In a whisper, Bowser hissed, "Hey! I'm back here. Come on back when you think the coast is clear." Big Guy didn't miss a beat. He grabbed some boards and carried them out into the sorting area. After dumping them, he wandered from their sight for a while. Soon he headed back with Staff Sergeant Howard by his side. They both came into the building and headed to the back. Big Guy stayed just long enough to be sure everything was OK, picked up a beat-up chair, and headed back out.

Bill Howard reached out to shake Bowser's hand. "Private Rafaldano, good to see you made it back OK. I see you brought a friend."

Ray reached out his hand, "Private Ray Parker." There was something about this guy that reminded Ray of Mike Randall. That was a good sign.

"Like I said, I can only give you totals," said Howard. "Do you have something to write with?" Bowser took a piece of cardboard about the size of his palm out of his pocket. He gently pulled the layers apart without separating them completely. Then he pulled out a stub of a pencil. "OK, what do you have?"

"When we took our first count, we had two hundred sixteen men," Howard said. "We've had forty-seven deaths, nineteen of those were shot by guards. The others died from their wounds, or exhaustion, or starvation. Who really knows? Their bodies just quit. Most of us were with the 3rd Battalion of the 24th Division. We were rounded up on 18 July."

Bowser wrote on the inside of the cardboard paper - 3of24 7/18 216/47/19.

Then he pushed the cardboard paper together again so a casual look would only see a dirty piece of cardboard. From his boot he pulled out a torn yellowed sheet of paper covered in small print. "Our sergeant was keeping his copy of this list in the lining of his boot. Now he hides it inside the collar of his fatigue shirt. It should stay dry there. We talked about trying to find a Korean to give it to, but we have no way to judge if we can trust the few civilians we see."

"My theory, for what it's worth," replied Howard, "is that we will either be exchanged or end up in a permanent camp soon. If it is a camp, we can hide these somewhere until they do a prisoner swap. But that doesn't mean I know anything you guys don't. I just don't see things working out any other way. Once our boys get here in force this little war is over. We were unlucky. Not enough of us and not enough equipment. Hell, at the end, I was shootin' at tanks with my .45," he laughed.

"How did that work out for you?" asked Ray.

"Oh, I was hittin' 'em, but I don't think I got their attention." The sergeant had a strange look on his face.

"Do you have any idea what might happen next?" asked Bowser. "We haven't done anything but clean up the neighborhood since we got here."

"Same here," Howard replied. "We did have one squad that was taken away for a few days. Turned out they were used to unload railroad cars. Crates of mortars and small arms ammunition. Not exactly by the book but they did eat better for a couple of days."

"Sergeant Randall says he thinks we are being sold to the highest bidder every day to clean up these buildings," Parker offered.

"Mike Randall, Master Sergeant Mike Randall?" Howard asked.

"Yeah, that's him," answered Bowser. "Do you know him?"

"Sure do," said Howard. "We were on the Post Mess Board back in Japan. You're lucky, he is a good man. Say, is there a Staff Sergeant Usury in your column?"

"We know a *Corporal* Jack Usury," Parker answered.

"Corporal? Dummy got busted again, did he? You tell him he owes Bill Howard two hundred bucks from our last card game. He bet against my four of a kind and lost what he didn't have.

"But enough of this chit-chat. We should all get out of here before some guard wanders this way." Bill Howard reached out to shake their hands again. "Good luck, gentlemen."

Bowser and Ray waited until the sergeant was out of the building and everything looked normal in the street out front. They re-traced their route through the narrow street and into the adjacent building. They paused to be sure they hadn't been seen. Then they began carefully working their way back toward their own people, street by street, building by building.

While moving slowly from one building to the next, Bowser asked Ray about Swede. He was a little curious why Randall and Usury, with their rank and age, seemed to let Swede have input to their decisions. "I know you guys escaped and all, but Swede's younger than me, and I don't think he's been in the Army even a year. What gives?"

"Swede is one of the smartest people I know. He's a country kid from the middle of nowhere Minnesota, so city life throws him some, but he figures stuff out real quick. And he's tough. I don't just mean physical tough, he is that, but he doesn't let what he calls 'stupid crap' get to him. He told me his dad's farm is just half a mile from town. All the country kids went to one room schools through eighth grade. Then everybody went to the same high school in town. So there was country kids and there was town kids. Which do you think he was?"

"He lived on a farm, right? So he was a country kid."

"Nope. Their farm was close enough to town that he had to go to school there. The town kids picked on him 'cause he wasn't one of them. When he got to high school, the country kids picked on him 'cause they thought he was a town kid. He said he never threw the first punch but learned to throw the last one. That and bein' on the basketball team got him respect from both sides. He told me that experience bein' the outsider made him dislike bullies. Maybe that's why problems don't seem to bother him. He figures out the answer, one way or the other, and solves the problem. Some people are just better at stuff, and Swede is one of those.

"And on the hill, before we got captured," Ray went on, "I saw a different Swede. It was like he threw a switch. If he was afraid, he didn't show it. I was ready to jump up and run back down the hill the way we had come up, and I think some of the other guys were too. But Swede just kept talking to us normal like and tellin' us how to get ready. When the North Koreans came at us, he kept yellin' at us to watch that way or shoot this way. When grenades dropped near us, he just flipped 'em away. He must have jumped out and piled dead bodies in front of our foxhole because they were there when it was over. I sure didn't do it. I heard a rumor they were goin' to write him up for the Silver Star. When it was all over there was this look in his eyes for a while. Sometimes I see that look in the older guys like Randall and Usury.

"And I think that's why Sergeant Randall seems to treat Swede as an older NCO. He asks Swede for his opinion on things. Swede just has this thing about him. Rank never seems to bother him. If a guy knows what he is doing, Swede pays attention but doesn't bother with a lot of yes sir, no sir. You and I couldn't get away with that, but like I said, there is something about Swede that is different."

The conversation ended there as they stood just inside a building facing a main street. They needed to be careful crossing over. It was more open than most and they had no choice but to move across in full view of whoever might look their way. They each poked their head out as little as possible and checked in opposite directions. Then they heard the sound of approaching trucks.

"Deuce and a halfs!" Parker exclaimed. "Those are American trucks! I can tell by the sound." He started to lean out of the window to look at the Americans coming to rescue him.

Bowser reached out and grabbed Parker by the collar. "Americans, my ass! There aren't any Americans around here but us." He continued to pull Ray as he headed as far back into the building as he could get. It was the least damaged structure on the block, with two floors mostly intact. The doors and windows were toast, but most interior and exterior walls were sound. The lower walls were brick and cement with the second floor all wood.

Two trucks growled to a halt out front. They were American deuce and a halfs, with South Korean markings painted over. As men started casually getting out and stretching in the street, Bowser pulled Ray into a small closet in one of the back rooms. The door was gone. Holes exposed floor joists above. Bowser pointed and they both pulled themselves up to the next floor. As quietly as they could they moved back into the corner and pulled some rags and boards over themselves. Then they tried not to breathe too loud, not an easy task for two guys who were in no shape to be doing pull-ups.

Ray Parker was jammed against the wall with Bowser backed up tight against him. "Jesus, Bowser. You stink!" Parker complained none too quietly.

Bowser jabbed him with an elbow. "We all stink. Now shut up," he whispered.

The men from the trucks were stomping around in the front room of the first floor, just off the street. Then came the rattle of what sounded like pots and pans. They were speaking a language that was not English and not Korean. Next came the smell of a fire.

"They're havin' lunch," whispered Ray. Bowser's only response was a slight nudge of his elbow.

For the next hour, Bowser and Ray tolerated body odor and muscle cramps without another word. At one point, Bowser watched through the floor as one of the men came into the back room, dropped his pants, and squatted. A couple more came in after him and urinated into the mess while making what were probably crude jokes about each other. Finally, the group packed up and climbed back in the trucks. Bowser and Ray waited for a few minutes after they drove away, then crawled out of their corner to stretch before dropping back to the floor below.

"Jesus," complained Ray. "I don't know what stinks worse. That mess they left in the back or whatever it was they were cookin'. Who do you think those guys were?"

"Russians."

"Russians? What makes you say that?"

"There was a Russian family in our tenement back home," replied Bowser. "Those guys were definitely Russian."

"You speak Russian?" Ray asked in amazement.

"No, I don't speak Russian. But those guys sounded just like the Andropov family. And they had red stars on their hats. Russians."

"What are Russians doing in Seoul?" wondered Ray.

"I don't know, and I don't care," responded Bowser. "We gotta move our asses and get back."

They weren't exactly sure how far it was back to their guys, but they didn't want to get caught in the open by any more Russians, or Koreans, driving around. That caution led to them spotting movement in a building one block over just before they reached the work party. Ray tugged on Bowser's sleeve. "Down! Somebody is over there. Must be one of our guards," whispered Ray.

They were in a brick building that had taken a lot of damage. Crouching down, they peeked carefully through the gaps in the wall. The street outside was almost impassable, but they could see into the remains of the building next door. Somebody, or some*thing,* was moving over there. As they continued to watch, they saw an American peek out from what used to be a door and then dash across to the next building. He was heading in the same direction they were.

"That's Page. I know him!" Parker stood up as if to yell out to Page, but Bowser yanked him down.

"Quiet! We don't know who else is around. I think we're close to our guys. The guards might hear you."

"What's he doin' over there?"

"Probably takin' a crap, just like the Russians. Let him get a couple of minutes ahead and then move out." Bowser picked a spot where he could see out into the street and sat back.

Once they were all back home and eating their 'supper' in the courtyard area, Bowser and Ray reported to Randall. They could easily gather without being noticed as the men sat in groups all over the courtyard. Randall made sure the group did not sit in the same spot every day and they did not all get together every day. It was easy enough to pass on any info to those who weren't involved on any particular day.

To look as inconspicuous as possible Swede sat with his back to the group. When Bowser mentioned they had seen Russians, Swede noticed an older private, Henry Page, reacted to the word "Russian." Page seemed to be around at the end of the day when events were being discussed. Bowser and Ray did not mention they had seen Page after their encounter with the Russians. Had they done so, Swede would have been more concerned about his reaction. As it was, he soon forgot the incident.

Henry Page, the man Parker had seen in the ruins, had a complicated background. In fact, he wasn't even Henry Page.

Alex Haynes was born Aleksandr Goremykin in Kursk in 1920. At age eighteen he entered the Soviet Navy. Both his parents were killed during the Battle of Kursk in 1943. When his mother's tank was disabled, she advanced on foot, letting German Tigers drive over her as she attached magnetic mines to their underbelly. She destroyed four Tigers before being killed as she attacked a fifth tank. For those actions, she was rewarded with the Order of Lenin. A year later a team of naval personnel was put together to be sent to the United States as part of the Lend- Lease program. Dock authorities in

Murmansk were complaining convoys were arriving with critical supplies distributed incorrectly throughout the holds of the ships. That led to problems with off-loading and transporting those supplies to where they were most urgently needed. The team would see to it this problem was solved on the docks in New York. The team members didn't necessarily need to know anything about cargo distribution - they would be given instructions. But it was to be an all navy team. The newly promoted Junior Lieutenant Aleksandr Goremykin, son of a recipient of the Order of Lenin, was assigned to that team.

The journey to New York took the team across Russia by train to Vladivostok and then to San Francisco by boat. From there, it was the train again to New York. By the time they arrived on the east coast, twenty-four-year-old Aleksandr was learning English.

Within a week of his arrival in New York, Aleksandr initiated a change of citizenship. He asked the American who was assigned to guide him through the maze of warehouses and dock machinery what he should do. That man led him to a brother-in-law who was a policeman. The policeman led him to an acquaintance in the FBI. Normally, the FBI would have grave suspicions about any Russian walking in the door asking for help, but Special Agent Larkin had a different idea. Larkin in turn walked Aleksandr right back out the door, into a cab, and across town to a building where they entered the office of Meyer Merchandising. They walked through a room filled with people at desks and the clattering of typewriters. A door marked STORAGE opened to the world of the OSS, Office of Strategic Services.

Jacob Meyer opened his business in Vienna, Austria in 1925. He intentionally limited the business to handling small, but high-end goods. Clothing, jewelry, tobacco items, exotic weapons, intricately carved chests. Anything there was a demand for and could be easily stored and shipped. He relied on a vast network of family and friends to discover various little-known products around the world.

Betar, a Zionist youth movement, came to Jacob asking for his help in moving information, and sometimes more tangible goods, to units in Europe and Palestine. He readily agreed and soon became aware of how dangerous Europe was becoming for people of the Jewish faith. Just months before the 1938 Nazi annexation of Austria, the Anschluss, Jacob moved his family and business to New York City.

Since the Meyer name was German enough, and not all his associates around the world were practicing Jews, most of the Meyer Merchandising offices remained in operation. Most of those offices were a second or third listing on an office door and easily operated under the political radar.

In 1941, Bill Donovan, the head of the newly formed OSS, remembered the help given him by a Meyer representative in Shanghai years earlier. A visit with Jacob in New York led to willing cooperation between the two organizations.

Once he understood what the OSS was, Aleksandr set to convincing the men in the room he was just what they needed. So, Aleksandr Goremykin died, and Alex Haynes was born. Aleksandr remained working with his Lend-Lease team to the day they were scheduled to leave New York to join their convoy to Nova Scotia and then Murmansk. Each member of the team was to board the ship containing the cargo for which they had been responsible. Alex boarded his ship in full view of his team commander. That night he went over the side to a rowboat. The plan had been to announce he was lost at sea in a storm. That plan became unnecessary when the ship was torpedoed a week later in the North Atlantic. No one survived.

Alex Haynes remained in New York and was put to work interpreting documents. Some in the OSS knew the Soviets were going to be the next enemy and people like Alex were going to be needed to fight that enemy. The OSS was dissolved in September of 1945, but certain components were kept active. Alex spent time with one of those components in Turkey and Japan over the next few years and went to work for the CIA when it was formed in 1947. A year later, he returned to Vladivostok, ironically as a representative of Meyer Merchandising. In 1949, Alex was assigned to Japan to help set up a team of agents to obtain information about Soviet military aid to North Korea. In early 1950, he was temporarily pulled from that project and put to work on a possible espionage case. An individual with potentially dangerous information seemed to be trying to contact the Russian government. The case led to Alex Haynes becoming Captain Patrick Murphy reporting for duty with the 24th Infantry on 1 June 1950.

When everything fell apart and Alex understood he would be captured, he took the fatigue shirt from a dead GI and got rid of his own. There was no official record of a Captain Patrick Murphy with this unit. If he was captured as Captain Murphy, the North Koreans might notice. The problem was solved by taking a uniform shirt from a dead private, leaving the dog tags so Private Page's parents would be notified. Later that day, he was captured as he tried to work his way south towards US lines.

Private Henry Page could easily see Master Sergeant Mike Randall was the key to this column surviving as well as it did. But he didn't think the Korean guards had figured out the extent Randall was controlling the men. His "staff," as Private Page liked to think of them, did well at hiding their existence. The only time they gathered as a group was in the evening, not all evenings, and seldom the entire "staff." When they did meet, they didn't follow any obvious pattern. Except to Private Page. Clandestine activity was his profession. It would have not served any purpose for either of his missions so Private Page did not make his real identity known to anyone. He simply sat back and observed. This new mention of Russians had him interested. He was looking for information on Russians in Korea.

Marching North from Seoul
Sep-Oct 1950

The next morning they were sent out as usual. But a few hours later the guards started waving their arms and shouting. They lined everybody up and double timed them back to the barracks. They forced the prisoners into the rooms rather than allow them to sit in the courtyard. It was obvious the guards were upset about something.

In the middle of the afternoon the guards started their shouting again, shoving the men out of the barracks and into the street. Once Randall saw what was happening, he yelled out that they should grab everything they had, not leave anything behind. With all the noise the guards were making he was sure they wouldn't notice him yelling out directions. Swede managed to grab his bowl and ragged coat he had stashed in the wall before he was forced out into the street. As before, he wrapped it around himself under his fatigue shirt.

With even more yelling, they were formed into a column of twos and set off at a pace the guards had not used before. Within an hour, they were out of the city and headed north. The hills they could see ahead were either hills or mountains, depending on where in the states you lived. Most of the men thought of them as mountains. By evening they were marching through a valley with steep slopes on either side. Anyone looking around would have noticed the quilt of early fall foliage painted on the hills.

Only a few noticed. The pace slowed some but was still faster than the men were accustomed to. Mike Randall began worrying about how this pace would affect some of the men. As they continued into the night without any breaks, he knew they were in trouble. Men began slowing down and falling back in the column. Charlie and his crew were doing what they could to help the weakest. Guards reacted to stragglers with shouts of "kwiggly!" or "Bali, bali!", whichever seemed to work best. A rifle butt in the back or the threat of a bayonet got most to pick up the pace. This continued throughout the night. The pace was eventually dialed down a little and the prisoners seemed to catch their second wind. After a while, the column arrived at a village. Up to this point they had marched right through villages. That was before. Dawn was approaching, but they were about to experience darkness.

The village was small - twenty or thirty houses. Each was the typical Korean farmhouse with a simple "porch" structure made from the roof overhang and a couple of poles. The houses were built on a stone slab or pad. Most had a simple door and one visible window. Roofs were of thatch. The structures themselves were wood framed with mud adobe-looking walls. In a few places, sticks, or wattle, could be seen beneath crumbling adobe. A stool or two were on most porches. These were homes to the villagers but considered "huts" by American standards.

The guards went into the nearest three homes and started shouting and yelling. Then the prisoners were shoved in. Each hut had three rooms divided by a door frame and maybe a blanket or cloth of some kind. The two main rooms were the same size with the kitchen on the end a little smaller - slightly lower than the other two, with a small fireplace and a few cooking utensils. Twenty men were forced into each of the two larger rooms with the Korean family left to peer out from their kitchen at the loud, foul-smelling, American invaders. Once the prisoners realized what was happening, there was a lot of pushing back and cursing. "Like goddam sardines" was a common phrase yelled at the guards. Rifle butts were used to get the last of the prisoners in the door and guards posted directly outside.

Mike Randall had made it a practice to try and spread his people out along the column whenever they were on the march. No one person could see what was happening in a column spread out over half a mile or more. When they were rousted out of their barracks in Seoul, Swede and Usury and the others had gradually spaced themselves throughout the column. That meant they were separated from Randall when the guards forced everyone into the huts. Randall didn't have a chance to give orders or advice about who should be in charge of each hut. The men respected him and would have accepted anyone appointed by him to make decisions, but that did not happen. Randall quickly took charge in his hut and got the men mostly quiet. Their yelling was making the guards agitated. He was afraid of what they might do if the prisoners continued yelling. That was not the case in the other huts. Being crammed into a space half the size of the rooms in their schoolhouse in Seoul was too much for many to accept. They continued yelling and started pushing and shoving to claim a space of their own. The guards yelled back and started to threaten the men near the door with their bayonets.

In Japan, Jack Usury had a reputation of being a drunken lifer but had become more professional in his approach to the men since capture. He had started acting like an NCO again and the men had started accepting him as such. When the men in his hut would not settle down, he grabbed a man who was screaming at those next to him. He shook him hard and backhanded him across the face. "At ease, soldier," he yelled. "That goes for everybody else in here. AT EASE, RIGHT GODDAM NOW! You're supposed to be soldiers, ACT LIKE IT!" It was too dark in the huts for most to see who had shouted the command, but the ring of authority was clear. Those close by either saw or heard the slap given to the soldier. The noise dropped to just a few mumblings.

"You people need to maintain some personal control! Some of you are about to go off the deep end. Those guards out there look like they might start crankin' off rounds if we keep this up. Get it quiet and let's think about what we need to do. My guess is if they won't feed us until we settle down." Usury gradually brought his voice down. He could see he had their attention, but it wouldn't last long if he couldn't get them working as a military unit.

"We are all tired and need to get some rest. We can't stand forever so we are goin' to try sittin' down. Everybody sit down with your knees pulled close and your back against the person behind you. Back to back. Let's see how that works for a while. We can try something different in a little bit. Now, sit!" Usury started gently pushing men near him down and getting them positioned back to back. Gradually both rooms followed his commands.

The third hut had no one the men saw as their military superior. Many of the prisoners were starting to buy into the guard's constant reminders that they were all equal. No one could give them orders nor should they take orders from anyone. Officers and NCOs were no longer to be obeyed. The noise got worse and worse. Men were trying to fight their way out the door and the guards were clubbing them back in. Finally, one guard fired his rifle into the hut over the heads of those near the door. All yelling ceased instantly. For about thirty seconds. Then the hut returned to bedlam. Guards approached the door and window and started yelling into the rooms.

At that point, Swede Larson decided he needed to try something or people were going to get shot - maybe himself. He had heard somebody in the hut next door yell "At ease!" and the noise level had dropped and stayed down. As loud as he could, he bellowed out "AT EASE! At ease, people! The guards are going to start shooting at us if we don't settle down!"

For a second, all noise in the hut stopped. Some were probably trying to figure out who had just given a command and if they should pay any attention. From the back room a voice called out, "Why should we listen to you?"

"Because you're gonna die if you don't. Look out there. Those guards already shot at us once, and they are getting ready to shoot again." Swede had seen the guard deliberately shoot over everyone's head but was sure someone stuffed way in the back hadn't. "We can yell and scream and fight with each other and get shot, or we can try to figure out the best way to get some rest in here. They aren't about to let us out just because we yell louder." Swede was still raising his voice so everyone could hear, but just loud enough for that. "Each room try a different way to get people as comfortable as they can. If one plan doesn't work, try another."

Then a voice from the back called out, "Listen to the man. Things are bad enough without us acting like animals. I've slept in tighter quarters back on the block. Course, I got to check out my cousin's ass when she changed clothes, but don't nobody in here get no ideas." Swede recognized Bowser's voice. A few of the men chuckled. Others seemed to mumble in at least partial agreement.

Since nobody was openly challenging him or offering any other ideas, Swede decided to keep pushing his luck. "Everybody in here face the back wall and sit down. You can put your legs around the guy in front of you. It's tight in here, so we are going to have to get to know each other pretty well." Then he sat down. Men around him started to follow his example. Soon all those in his room and then the back room were on the floor trying to get as comfortable as they could.

Almost immediately, a guard pushed into each hut and handed a sack to the family in the kitchen with directions as to what they should do. Soon they could hear the family moving around and smell something cooking. The sacks contained rice the family was supposed to prepare for the prisoners. Once it was ready, a bucket was handed out with exactly forty small balls of rice in it. In each hut, the command from those near the kitchen was the same. "Take just one and pass it on." When the empty bucket came back, the guards yelled something into the kitchens again One of the family members came out, grabbed the bucket, and trotted away. They returned with a bucket of water which was set over the small fire in the kitchen to boil. If the directions from the guards had been to make tea for the foreigners, none of the families did. They weren't about to waste their supplies on forty Americans. When the water reached a boil, it was passed around again, this time with a small dipper. Breakfast had been served.

With some food in their bellies the men started to fall asleep. They had been marching for almost twenty hours. Cramped conditions and all, they were exhausted. As the morning went on, problems arose. Legs cramped and men tried to stretch. Those with diarrhea felt sudden urges to run for an outhouse - if there was one. They had to crawl or stumble across their mates to get to the door and then found they had to get permission from the guard. If the outhouse was occupied, the unfortunate POW squatted on the ground nearby. The guards didn't like it, but the alternative was to foul the homes of the villagers.

Once it started getting dark, the morning meal ritual was repeated, and the prisoners were called out to line up for the night's march. The guard commander was back, the one who had them fill out cards with their name and rank. He explained as best he could with the little English he knew, they would be divided into squads of ten men. Four squads per hut. They were to remain with their squad. Each would be given a sack of rice to carry. The guards knew how much rice was in each sack. If the rice ran out before they got to the next supply point, that squad would go hungry. To enforce the point, the guards carefully weighed each bag on a crude scale before giving it to the squad.

Then the commander brought up one more point. "You no esskay. One man esskay, two mans shotted." There were no smiles this time. There was no call for "Rennel" to explain. Escape and two men in your squad would be shot as punishment.

When each squad had their rice, the guards appointed a squad leader. Every one was a private, no matter the rank of anyone else in the squad. That meant Swede, Ray Parker, and Tony Rafaldano were among the squad leaders. That also meant the men in his hut accepted Swede as the hut leader. His actions of the night before and appointment by the Koreans as a squad leader cemented his role.

And so, the POWs were brought to their new reality. Because they were marching at night again, they assumed the Koreans were afraid of being spotted by planes. The quick pace since the rush out of Seoul probably meant American forces were on the move north again. For those few, like Swede and Parker, who thought now was the time to try an escape, reality dashed their hopes. There were more guards than before, and they were usually shut up in huts when not on the road. With the squads of ten men, it was simpler for the guards to keep track of them. And they had been told what would happen if they did escape.

For the next week, the routine did not change from that of the first day. One morning they did not reach a village before it got light, and they spent the day on the ground under the trees again. They were not fed that day. For a few in the column the pace became too much, mostly because of diarrhea. These men were left behind in a village when the column moved out. The commander said they would be given time to rest and then brought north at a slower pace. No shots were heard as they left the village each morning, but the men were still doubtful as to what happened to those left behind. Charlie and his "medical" team did what they could, but not enough volunteers came forward to help support all the weak during the march. Any hint of an order to help carry the sick quickly led to loud complaints from those prisoners who liked what the Koreans said about not having to take orders. Using shame as a motivator worked in some cases, but still not enough.

Swede Larson had a problem. He had been appointed squad leader and was so far successful at keeping the men in his hut cooperative. The third day into the march two men complained they had not received their rice ration at the morning meal. That night, as they settled in to their new village, Swede changed the way the food was distributed. He had all the men in the hut stand up when the rice was ready. He took the bucket and personally doled out the rice balls. When a man received his ration, he sat down. The first time he did this, Swede gave the last man standing his rice and found he had one left in the bucket. Thinking he had somehow missed someone Swede looked over both rooms to see if anyone was still standing. Noticing Swede's confused look, a young private named Torkle said to him, "You forgot to take your ration, Swede."

Feeling a little foolish, Swede took out his rice ball and returned the bucket to the family in the kitchen. A simple thing, but it did not go unnoticed by the men around him. They realized he was so focused on everyone else receiving their fair share he forgot to feed himself. Over the next few days, Swede realized the men in his hut were treating him more like a senior NCO than the private he was. He was beginning to better understand what both Sergeant Randall and Corporal Usury had said about these being unusual circumstances and the need to help others get through it all. Sergeant Randall had even said he felt it was more important for him to stay with the column than it was to escape. Swede knew he was doing something worthwhile with his squad and with those in his hut. But his desire to escape was eating at him. He saw nothing good ahead and was sure that behind them American forces were once again working their way north. Now was the perfect time to escape. He could either hide in the hills until he was rescued or work his way south to friendly lines. However, there was the little matter of the threat any escape would mean two men would be shot. Swede tossed the problem around and around in his head. He wanted to try again, felt like he should, but was it a good idea?

A few days later the column once again didn't reach a village before dawn. The group had started the practice of picking lice off each other when they had the chance. It was easier than trying to find them all yourself, especially on your head. As they rested under the trees, Swede noticed it was quiet, almost peaceful, in the early light. He looked around to see men sitting calmly, searching the shaggy head of the man next to them. It was a scene right out of *National Geographic*, but with people, not apes. Swede moved behind Sergeant Randall and began picking lice from his hair. He knew this way they could talk quietly without attracting attention from the guards.

"Sergeant Randall, I have a question. What do you think about me trying to escape again?" Swede kept his voice low as he crushed one little bug between his fingernails and looked for another. He had no idea how this conversation was going to go.

Mike Randall grunted. "I figured you might be wanting to duck out again," he said. "But I'm afraid I have to say it's a no-go. They said they would shoot somebody for every escape. This bunch of guards is different than the ones we had before. You saw that when they shot into the huts a while back."

"What if I have a way to guarantee they won't shoot anybody - at least almost guarantee it?" Swede asked. "What if there is a way for me to escape without the guards knowing it?"

"And how the hell are you going to escape without the guards finding out? They count us every morning and every night."

"If I get sick, they'll leave me behind. When they leave somebody behind, they don't leave any guards with them. I counted the guards the last three times we left people in the villages. The count never changed. They don't have any radios, so there is no way to check on what happens after we move on. I think they really are leaving them to catch up somehow."

"How do you know the villagers aren't killing them once we leave?"

"Because the guards leave some of our rice with the village every time one of our guys stays behind. I've seen the guards leave a small sack of rice with the family of the hut our guy is in when we leave. We've left five guys behind so far. I watched carefully the last four times. My squad is always the last one out of the village. A small sack of rice is left if one of our guys stays, nothing if we all move out. The villagers aren't killing anybody. They are getting paid to take care of them." Swede moved in front of Randall so he could be 'groomed' of his little friends.

Mike Randall sat destroying lice for a while, snapping them in two, and then grunted again. "You might be on to something there. I've been trying to think of how we can get a message to our guys telling them where we are and that they need to come get us before we disappear too far up north. If you can get to our lines, they might be able to send a rescue force. But you will have to make sure you don't join up with some other column, if you know what I mean."

Swede gave a little chuckle. "Yeah, I don't want to get a reputation for that." He sat in silence for a minute. "I think I can manage to look sick enough in three days to convince them I'm too weak to go on. I wait a day after you guys move out and I escape from the village."

"OK. Nobody else knows about this. We can't take the chance of the guards finding out. Make it look real. Make it back to our guys and get a rescue party on the way." Randall gave Swede's shoulder a little squeeze instead of a handshake and moved away without another word.

It took Swede five days to convince the guards to leave him behind. His biggest problem was the way men in his hut reacted to his apparent "illness." As he seemed to grow weaker, they grew more concerned - and tried to help. Without the classic signs of diarrhea, he had no chance of being left behind. That meant he had to look bad and smell bad. Somehow, he had to fake all that. Swede knew just the man to ask.

Charlie was known throughout the column as one to always help the sick and wounded. People trusted him, even though he never spoke a word to any of them. His wounds were still not healed, and he could only make faint grunts. Swede and Charlie had spent many hours during their march helping others and formed a bond along the way. Swede was sure Charlie wasn't a private and also figured his name was not Charles, as the tag on what was left of his fatigue shirt identified him. He had asked once if his name was really Charlie. The man simply pointed to his name tag and motioned to the others around them, as if to say, that's what they call me. Then he pointed to his head and shrugged his shoulders. Swede understood Charlie was telling him he didn't know his name. His throat wound was obvious. The ones in his head were not.

Swede knew Charlie could be trusted, so he explained what he had talked with Mike Randall about. He knew he could count on Charlie to help in any way he could. He also knew when people in the column saw Charlie helping him, it would add credence to the story that Swede was sick.

The day Mike Randall gave his OK, Swede started showing signs of getting weak. He managed to stagger off to the bushes and came back with his pants fouled. Nobody noticed another soldier had just used the same bushes. On the march that night Swede dropped out numerous times and re-joined the column looking and smelling worse. The next morning, he turned over the job of watching the rice distribution with the excuse he shouldn't be handling food. Later that day, he asked Charlie for his help in getting out of the hut. He picked up a stick along the way. Once in the outhouse, he proceeded to use the stick to wipe the fresh fecal matter contributed by his fellow prisoners all over his pants. This chore caused him to vomit, and he had the sense of mind to get most of that all over his pants and boots. Charlie almost contributed to the picture but managed to hold it down. Four more days of that and the men in his hut experienced more than a little guilt when they didn't feel as bad as they should when he was left behind.

Getting left in the care of the villagers worked better than Swede thought it would. As the column moved, out one of the guards came to the hut Swede was in and handed a small sack of rice to the family still hiding in the kitchen. His tone was not at all harsh as he pointed back and forth to Swede and the family. Then he hurried off to catch the column as it marched away. Family members came out of the kitchen and went about trying to clean up their home after the invasion of the smelly foreigners. For a while they ignored the especially rank one left on their floor. The mother and the toddler stayed in the kitchen and began cooking their evening meal. The father, grandparents, and two older children removed the straw floor mats from the back room. Swede fell asleep, as his nerves had allowed little rest in the past few days.

Swede woke with a start when four adults came in the room. The men surrounded him as he lay on the floor, expressions of distaste on their faces, talking and pointing at him. He began having doubts about how the villagers might treat him. Then they all reached down, grabbed the mat he was on, and dragged him none too gently out of the house. Just as Swede was about to jump up and defend himself, the men walked away, and two grandmotherly looking women approached with a bucket and some rags or cloths. Wrinkling their noses, but speaking in calm voices, the women began undressing him and washing him down. They made motions he should try to sit on a stool nearby as his clothes, the old jacket he had found in Seoul, and the mat were taken away. Before he could react, a knife appeared, and the women began hacking away at his hair, at the same time deftly picking the lice from his head. When they were satisfied with the results a blanket was wrapped around the now civilized American. The two older children came out of the house and handed the women some bowls. They handed Swede one of the bowls, making it obvious they wanted him to eat. One held her bowl to him to show it was rice, then grimaced as she rubbed her belly and pointed to him. She motioned for him to look at his bowl, which had a soup of some kind. Then she smiled and rubbed her belly again and pointed at him. He understood all the grimacing and smiling to mean they would eat the rice left by the guards, but the soup was better for a sick person like himself. They both broke into broad smiles as he took a sip and realized it was hot and tasty. After eating nothing but poorly cooked rice for months, anything hot and flavorful was a delight beyond expression. The women sat back on their heels and began puffing away on their tobacco pipes. They smiled and jabbered as they watched their patient polish off two bowls of soup and one of hot tea.

Two clean mats and his freshly washed clothes were brought in and Swede allowed to dress. He was made to understand he should sleep, using the blanket to warm him as the wet clothes dried. The family slept in the back room. Clean, warm, and full for the first time in a long time, Swede nodded off.

Sometime in the night, Swede woke and realized he should leave while he had the chance. He quietly pulled on his boots and picked up the old jacket. He was sure he could find some food in their kitchen but could not force himself to steal from people who had just treated him so well. When he left the hut, Swede was frightened to see someone sitting there on a stool. When he jumped back, one of the old women looked up at him and grinned. Talking softly, she held up the sack of rice the guards had left them, motioning for Swede to take it. Then she made shooing motions with her hands as if to say get on out of here now. Swede took the sack, handed her the old jacket, and whispered she should take it in return for the rice. Then he took both her hands in his and bowed to her, an image of his own grandmother appearing in his head.

Grandmother pointed the direction he should take, and Swede left the village.

Swede had put a great deal of thought into exactly how he would travel once he escaped. About the third day's march out of Seoul the guards had taken the column off the main road and headed almost straight north on an unpaved road that was more cart path than anything else. The constant military traffic headed south had caused too many delays when the column had to wait for convoys to pass. Since taking the unpaved road, they had not seen any military vehicles or troops. Swede thought about moving cross-country after his first escape, and how much steeper the hills and ridges were in this area. He decided it would be best to travel at night on the paths and roads between villages. US forces should be heading north, so the quicker he moved south, the better. If convoys did come up the road at him, they would be easy to spot. Columns of troops would be a danger, but he could simply keep to the edge of whatever path he was on. If he listened carefully and kept an eye out for hiding spots, he should be fine. At the first hint of light he found a steep hill to climb and crawled into some thick bushes. He gathered leaves in a pile and crawled in.

According to the sun, it was about noon when he woke. He could hear noise coming from the road but was sure no Americans were this far north already, so he sat tight. Opening the sack of rice, he discovered it was cooked and included some vegetables and tiny bits of meat or fish of some kind. He molded some into a fist-size ball and ate slowly. It looked like he could eat two servings a day about that size and have enough for four more days. One serving a day would double the days but leave him too weak to be as alert as he needed to be. It would help if he spent a little time looking for wild plants he could eat. But drinkable water was going to be the biggest problem.

Swede slept some more that afternoon and carefully checked the area for any plants he could add to the rice. He found some past-their-prime berries but nothing more. Wandering around in the woods in the daylight was not a great idea, so he didn't spend much time foraging. Just before full dark, he moved carefully down to the road and ate some more rice before he set out. He was sure he would run into a village during the night. When he got to it, he would have to decide to go around or through. After a few minutes of looking and listening for any sign of trouble he started south again. It was getting cold and he needed to move to warm up.

Sure enough, a few hours down the road was a village. By the time he got there, Swede had a plan. When he saw the first house he stepped further to the side and looked carefully around. Close to the house was a pen of some sort. Against the simple wooden pole fence was exactly what he was hoping to find. Just about every Korean farmer he had seen in the past months had been carrying something on his back, usually on an A shaped wooden frame. Next to the carry frame were some bundles of rice straw. He had spent hours in the fields at home tying wheat into bundles to be thrown on the wagon and taken to the thresher. They were just what he needed here.

Swede did not want to be stealing from some poor farmer, but hoped he had a solution. He tossed a couple of straw bundles on the carry frame and hoisted it all on his back. Bending low and moving slowly, he walked right on past the village and dropped it all just beyond the last house. If his theory was correct, the next morning farmer Bob would say to farmer Joe, "Why is your carry frame sitting outside my house?" In any case he did not steal anything, just moved it a little. He wasn't sure about the plan, but it was all he had. But it worked, and he was safely past his first village. As dawn approached, Swede again took to the high ground and found some thick bushes. Another tasty rice ball and he tried to sleep, which didn't happen until the sun warmed him enough to stop the shivering.

Swede woke twice during the day to the sound of motors out on the road. The first seemed to be going south and the second north. Once again, he just ignored them. When it was dark enough, he headed back to the road. If he remembered correctly, there would be no village. Three days back the column had spent the day sleeping in the woods along the road. He was right about the village, but twice had to run off the road into the woods when trucks came down the road. They were using black-out-shades on their headlights, but he heard them in plenty of time. Realizing truckloads of soldiers were driving down the road at high speed made Swede more than a little uncomfortable. While it was still dark, he settled down in a hiding spot for the day. He felt good about how he was doing so far. But he also knew he needed water and would need more food soon.

Swede lay looking up at the night sky. Here in these woods, on this hill, in this so completely foreign place, he began to feel an overwhelming loneliness. Randall and the column of prisoners who were his friends were miles away by now. His family was thousands of miles in the other direction and probably thought he was dead.

People here had tried to kill him. He did not speak the language and understood only a bare minimum of their culture. Was he going to end up dead in some woods like this and never be found? Would he ever see home again? But as he looked at the sky, feeling overwhelmed by sadness and self-pity, he realized it was more than twinkling lights he was looking at through the web of tree branches. It was more than a foreign moon shining down on a foreign land. This was his sky! He had looked at this same sky night after night on hunting trips with his father and uncles. He could see the Big Dipper, the North Star, Aquarius, and Pegasus. The same constellations his father would quiz him on. The same moon they would fish under on summer evenings along the South Branch. He might be here on this strange hill in this strange place, but the sky was not strange. Looking at the moon and stars he knew so well began to give him a sense of home.

Swede thought about what his family was doing right then, but he thought about them with a feeling of warmth, not sadness. He felt a certain strength, a strength that seemed to push away the loneliness. He was here because he made the decision to leave home and experience more of the world. As messed up as his circumstances were right then, he was handling them well. He had survived combat and months of captivity with little food. He had escaped from the enemy - twice. He was going to survive this. He was alone on this hill, and yes, he felt lonely. But that could be set aside. He fell asleep then, thinking not of home, but planning what he was going to do in the next few days. But if ever thoughts could be bounced off the moon to someone thousands of miles away, it would have happened that night.

The next night went smoothly right up until he had his new pack of straw on his back in the next village. A few steps later and the dogs started up. Swede kept to his plan and just kept walking. Then a voice grunted out from one of the huts. "Eh?"

Swede responded with a grunt of his own. Just a grunt, and then he spit. And kept walking. He had noticed there was a lot of grunting and spitting in Korea. The dogs barked some more but nothing else happened. He kept the load on his back as he passed the last of the huts, waiting to drop it a little further on in case anyone was watching. Once he figured he was out of sight, he ran as quietly as he could for twenty or thirty yards and dodged off into the trees. There he waited to see if anybody came running down the road after him. If they did, he planned to move away from the road for a while and find a place to hide until the next night. After waiting what he thought was a good half hour, nothing happened so he moved back to the road and continued south. He had noticed a well in the last village and then remembered the women who had cleaned him up using a bucket of water. Did every village have a well? Could you drink from the well or did you have to boil it first? He could understand boiling water from a river, but how about a well? Another thing to put on his list.

When he got to the next village, Swede did not pretend he was a farmer out on a stroll in the middle of the night. Instead, he found a place to hide where he could watch the village in the morning. He needed to see if people drank directly from the well and if anything edible was left outside of the huts.

When he woke to the sounds of the village, he sat and watched carefully. People drew water from the well frequently, but he did not see anyone drinking right there. He did spot vegetables of some kind left on stools outside some of the huts. Then he tried to sleep the rest of the day. He was glad he was sleeping during the day and walking at night. Temperatures at night were dropping. Since he had given up the coat, he had little to keep him warm when he wasn't moving. Once the village got quiet that night, he had another rice ball and headed out. He planned to try for some food at the next village. It would be darker and less chance of someone being awake that late.

It was near dawn when he came up on the next village. Here Swede changed his tactics. The houses were all on one side of the road with fields on the other. He crawled on his hands and knees along the edge of the field. The closest hut had some plants hanging from the support posts. Crouching low, he moved quietly across the road and approached the hut. It was too dark to tell what was hanging there, but it looked and felt like carrots. Making as little noise as possible, Swede took a handful of those and some of what he was sure were cucumbers. Then he reversed his steps and moved back to the field. Keeping low, he moved beyond the huts and then back out on the road. As he passed the last hut before coming up out of the field a dog started barking. The noise seemed common in the villages, but he hadn't noticed any reaction so far.

It turned out he had some radishes of some kind and some

cucumbers. He ate a few of each right then as he walked along and saved the rest to add to his rice ball in the morning. Swede figured he would get some liquid from the vegetables but still needed to get some real water soon. But dawn was approaching. He needed to hide and get some sleep.

Then his luck ran out. It rained most of the day, so he managed to find some clean puddles to drink from. Just before nightfall the rain turned to snow. Swede was soaking wet and very cold. The little body fat he did have was long gone. He was also much weaker than he thought. The pace he kept every night was difficult, and his calorie intake was not enough to balance what he was burning. The cold bit deeply. He had no choice but to keep moving in the snow to try and keep warm. There was no village along the way that night or he would have simply crawled into any shed he might have found. Before morning he was feverish and barely stumbling down the path. Little did he know, but with all his tripping and falling, he was now heading north. Swede had no idea of the trouble he was in. His feet kept moving, but everything else was just a fog. Finally, even his feet quit. He stood swaying in the road, dreaming once again of pancakes and sausages. Then the light came towards him out of the darkness and the cold.

Swede was not aware of how close to death he was. His fevered mind saw only a warm and welcoming light. He opened his arms to wrap them around the dazzling light - to soak up its warmth. He had nothing left. And then there was darkness.

North Korea

October 1950

Colonel Li Chen Hong simply could not believe what his eyes were seeing. Here he was, a Chinese officer, on a back road somewhere in Korea, in the middle of a snowstorm - and a madman was attacking his jeep. What next?

The colonel was not on that back road by choice. First, he was lost. Second, he had not volunteered to come to Korea. Neither had the majority of the 'volunteers' in the Chinese People's Volunteer Army, which were then pouring into Korea. Li and the three men with him had come across a week before the main army with special electronic monitoring equipment in their two jeeps. Their task was to get as close to the US forces pushing north out of Inchon as they could and then stick to them "baochi hen jin" - like glue. Their equipment was for monitoring communication networks between air or artillery units and the troops on the ground. At key times they were to break into those networks and issue conflicting orders, or at the very least, cause confusion. To that end, all four of them spoke excellent English.

Li's parents had died on the Long March in 1936 as the Chinese communists traveled 6,000 miles to escape the Nationalist forces. Because of his parent's rank in the party, and the heroic circumstances of their death, Li was selected to attend UCLA, earning a degree in electrical engineering in 1944. When he returned to China, he was sent to covertly join the Nationalist forces. There he became an expert on American radio equipment and carried that expertise back to the People's Army in 1949 when the Nationalists fled to Formosa after losing the civil war. And now he was on this Korean road to nowhere in the middle of a snowstorm.

His task was so important they did not even have drivers for their jeeps. Drivers would have been a security risk. The jeeps, the equipment, even their uniforms, were American. For now, they were wearing Chinese uniform jackets, but they would be hidden once they were close to US forces. If they met any American units, the plan was to act like an American special ops unit until they could escape. And they may have just gotten too close to American lines. They had almost run over what seemed to be an American soldier.

But some things about this soldier were a little odd. After appearing like a mad man in the middle of the road, this American was now draped over Li's right headlight - apparently unconscious. The left headlight had quit working shortly after leaving the barge that brought them across the Yalu. The man's uniform looked ragged. He had no weapon and no web gear. Li motioned to the driver to stay put. He got out to check on the mad man. He didn't think they had hit him; it was more like he had attacked the jeep - and then passed out. With one hand on his .45, Li grabbed the man by the collar and pulled him off the jeep to fall in the snow. In the light of the headlight he bent down to get a good look at his hood ornament. And turned white as a ghost.

Li had been a tall, slim, twenty-one-year-old when he arrived in California to begin his studies at UCLA. During his first week on campus, he had made the trip downtown to visit the world's longest lunch counter in Woolworths. He was not yet fluent in English and thought out loud in Chinese as he tried to come up with the correct words to order his thirty-nine-cent super jumbo banana split. His choices for topping were strawberry, pineapple, cherry, or hot fudge. The man next to him leaned over and said, in perfect Chinese, "Get the strawberry. It is the best."

Simon Bishop was born in Shanghai, the son of Methodist missionaries. His father, an American, met his mother there, the daughter of Polish emigres. Simon was fluent in English, Chinese, and Polish by the time his parents left China in 1937. The Japanese had invaded, and life was becoming difficult for missionaries. He was in his second year at UCLA when he met Li that day at Woolworth's. The two became good friends. Li appreciated the help in learning how to navigate university life and a foreign culture. Simon appreciated being able to talk to someone who shared his background. In China he was considered a foreigner yet saw himself as more Chinese than anything else. In the states he did not feel like an American, even though everyone accepted him as one. Spending time with Li made it easier to navigate that mental torment.

During the next three years they became like brothers, sharing academic studies on campus, and other studies off campus. Those investigations were not just of the female persuasion. They also read de Tocqueville's *Democracy in America* and then set out to discover the twentieth-century version. Those studies meant lots of time in various Los Angeles neighborhoods and bus trips to places as near as San Francisco and as far as Chicago.

Both men had grown up watching the Communists and Nationalists fight over China. They agreed the country had problems and neither of the two political factions tried very hard to solve those problems. People still died on the streets, regardless of who was in power that month. The Japanese were even worse. The bodies in the streets when they took over were from bullets, not starvation. That background allowed them to see beneath the surface of life in the states. They came away from their adventures with a love of America and Americans, and hope life in China might someday be the same. Their friendship continued even after Simon finished school and went to work for a government bureaucracy.

Li Chen Hong was looking down at Simon Bishop, lying in the snow at his feet, looking just as he had that day in Woolworths. His mind raced! That was ten years ago. How could Simon's twin be here in front of him in the middle of this snowstorm in the middle of Korea? Paranoia set in. The Party knew about his friendship with an American. Did they know what the two friends thought about politicians and governments? How much did they know? His behavior right now was going to determine his future!

Then logic kicked in. Li realized there was no way any Party official could have arranged for Simon's twin to pop out in front of him. Even the Party had limitations. That meant he had much less of a problem than he first thought. His secrets were safe. Bent down as he was looking at this American, his men would not have been able to see any reaction on his part. The name on the fatigue shirt read "Larson." He could toss him aside and continue down the road to what was supposed to be a North Korean army unit just a few miles away. Or he could throw him in the jeep and turn him over to the Koreans when they got there. Since he could never casually toss aside someone who so much resembled his brother, "Larson" was thrown in the back of the jeep and covered with a blanket.

By mid-morning, Swede was in a warm hut under some warm blankets, alternating between bouts of shivering and sweating from his fever. The North Korean unit had a medic, probably with no more than a few week's training, but Colonel Li was sure all the American needed was rest and food. He had made it clear to the Koreans they were to take care of the American until he returned. He might even have information Li and his men could use. If nothing else, Li was warmed by the memory of his good friend. They wrote a few times a year, but he had not seen Simon in six years.

Over the next few days Colonel Li and his men managed to begin collecting information on the American units pushing north. When they finally rolled into the village the Koreans holding Swede had re-located to, Li sought out the officer in charge. It was clear the Korean thought Larson was being treated too well but was deferring to his Chinese colleague. He did make it clear this American was probably an escaped prisoner and would not be placed in the custody of the Chinese. Instead he would be remaining with the Koreans and put on trial for crimes against the Korean People's Army.

Li had the Koreans set up a table with a chair and a small stool in the hut where Larson was held. The fact the stool would make the American sit lower than the Colonel was not lost on the Koreans, which was the Colonel's intent.

The youngest of his men, Lieutenant Bo, questioned Larson first. The American claimed he had gotten separated from his unit when he was out on patrol. His men left him when he got sick. He refused to name his unit or give any other information. Bo was sure he was lying but could not get anything further out of the American without resorting to threats or more. He was also sure the Koreans had tried questioning Larson and had limited his rations after failing to get answers beyond his name and rank.

Li didn't think the American had any information that could be of real value, but he was almost a perfect twin for Simon as he had looked ten years ago. If nothing else, he was a young kid far from home and among strangers. Simon had helped a young kid far from home and now he would do the same. Li didn't see him as an enemy yet - his only contact with the Americans so far had been through his headset. He decided if he could make this Larson's situation a little better without jeopardizing his own mission, he would do so. He asked for some tea and two cups and took them into the hut.

"Private, I am Colonel Li Chen Hong of the Chinese People's Volunteer Army. Please call me Li, or Colonel Li, if you must. My men and I found you in the middle of a snowstorm about a week ago. We turned you over to this unit to get you the care you needed. Have they been treating you well?"

Swede had risen when the tall officer entered the room. He had noticed the lieutenant who had just questioned him didn't look like the Koreans he had seen so far. He also noticed the lieutenant was wearing a strange jacket over what could have easily been an American uniform. Now an older man, also speaking perfect English, and wearing the same uniform, was telling Swede he was Chinese.

"Aren't we on the same side, sir? I thought the US and China were allies." Swede was more than a bit puzzled by the fact the two officers who claimed to be Chinese had turned him over to the North Koreans.

"That was the last war, Private," Li chuckled. "We defeated the Nationalists a year ago and drove them out. Your teachers didn't bring that up in your history classes?"

"I've been a little occupied with other things lately, sir. Exactly when did this happen?"

"In December of last year. But didn't your officers explain that to you before you landed at Inchon?"

"What's Inchon?" Swede asked, completely puzzled.

"You didn't just get separated from your unit, did you, Private? You're an escaped prisoner, aren't you?" Li sat back and poured tea into the cups, sliding one over to Swede. "You have no reason to believe this, but I don't intend to tell the Koreans anything about our conversation. When I leave here, they are going to charge you with crimes of some kind, probably escaping. You didn't kill anyone when you escaped, did you?" Li had a look of genuine concern when he asked that last question.

Swede knew he had only two choices, trust this guy or not. Something in his gut said he should trust him and see how all this panned out. And he was positive no one on the other side knew about his first escape. The second time hadn't really been an escape. He decided to take a chance.

"No, I didn't kill anyone or hurt anyone in any way. In fact, I didn't escape. I was left in a village because I was too sick to keep up. The guards limited how much we could help the sick on the march. Those who couldn't keep up were left behind. The last thing I remember is the column pulling out without me." That wasn't the complete truth, but it was the truth as far as the North Koreans knew. The guards had believed he was sick. If there had been any doubt, they probably would have shot him.

"When were you captured?" Li asked. "You didn't come ashore at Inchon, did you?"

"I have no idea what Inchon means. I was captured in July, about two days after we got here."

"July? You've been a prisoner since July? That explains why you don't know about Inchon." Li looked at Swede carefully. "You have been honest with me, so I'll be honest with you. I don't think I am giving away any secrets. The North Korean Army almost threw yours out of the country. Your army managed to hold on to a little piece of South Korea called Pusan. Then a month ago, your people came ashore at Inchon, south of Seoul, and have been pushing north since. That won't last long because my people came ashore, so to speak, on the Yalu, and will soon push everybody back south. To be honest, Private, I think we'll be at a stalemate in a few months."

Li put his hand on Swede's shoulder. "Maybe then you will be able to go home." He looked at Swede in a way that had a strangeness to it. "What's your name? Private doesn't seem right."

"Swede. I mean Paul, Paul Larson. Can I ask you a question?" Li nodded his head and took a sip of his tea. Pointing to Swede's cup he said, "Go ahead. I don't imagine you get a whole lot to drink around here."

"Why are you telling me all this? You're a colonel in the Chinese Army. I am either your prisoner or a prisoner of the North Koreans. In either case, we're supposed to be enemies. Why not just shoot me and be on your way?"

"What makes you think I would shoot you?" Li asked, mostly in amusement, thinking to himself, this kid has seen too many movies.

"Fifty of the men in my column were either shot or left to die, that's why." Swede was staring at Li with a look approaching hatred.

"Shot? Why? Were they trying to escape?" Li wasn't sure he could believe this latest statement. "How many were in your column?"

"Just over two hundred. And nobody was trying to escape." Swede growled at him.

"That's one-fourth of your men! Just shot for no reason? I don't know if I can believe that." Li sat back, looking at Swede.

"Believe it! The first I saw was a captain on the day I joined the column. He was just trying to take care of his men and was hoping the wounded could ride in the truck rather than have to walk. The major stood him against a tree and shot him right between the eyes with his fancy pistol. Every day for the first couple of weeks men who couldn't get up on their own were left behind. We could hear the shots as we marched off. We had no way to care for the wounded and the Koreans didn't bother to try. So sooner or later, they couldn't get up on their own." Swede was gripping the table so hard his hands were white. "After that major finally left, the guards let the sick ride in the truck. He was a real bastard. He liked to strut around in his tailored jacket with a .45 on his hip. I think he enjoyed shooting our captain! Believe me, it happened!"

"If the guards were shooting those who couldn't keep up, why weren't you shot," Li asked, not sure if he should believe what Swede was telling him.

"I told you. Things changed after the major left. And that was before we got to Seoul. We saw the bastard again just before we left Seoul. He told us he had others to "attend to. "It sounded like he was looking forward to "attending" to them. After we left Seoul, the guards left the few of us who were too sick to march in whatever village we were in at the time. That's what happened to me. I didn't escape. They left me behind."

Li wasn't sure if Swede was telling the whole truth, but there was no doubt he was sick on the night they had found him. Li looked Swede right in the eye. "Tell me, is what you just told me true?"

"Absolutely." Swede looked right back at Li and held his gaze. Then he explained in detail about the march to Seoul, how they were treated there, the quick rush out of Seoul, and how he came to be left behind. He left out the fact he had faked his illness and didn't mention walking away from the village he had been left in. When he was finished, Li made it clear once again the Koreans were going to charge Swede with something and probably send him on to a POW camp. There was nothing he could do about that. He also gave Swede some advice about answering questions.

"You claimed you had gotten separated from your unit. When you were rushed out of Seoul you figured your army must have been getting close, but you didn't know the details. When I asked about Inchon, you asked, "What's Inchon?" That was a give-away you had not been separated from your unit. The only Americans near Seoul would have come from that landing at Inchon. If you are going to lie, make sure you have all your ducks lined up to support that lie. And I'm pretty sure you will be asked some questions. The Koreans think you escaped." Li stood up and put out his hand to shake with Swede. "Good luck, Paul Larson. I hope you make it home soon. I hope we all do.

"Now I am going to slap you hard on the face and call you names in Chinese. Fall on the floor and stay there until the Korean guards come in. If they think you didn't answer my questions, it will make them feel better that you didn't answer theirs. You will just be an ignorant American."

With that, Li backhanded Swede across his face, knocking him off the stool. Then he kicked his chair across the room while yelling loudly in Chinese. He gave a smile and slight bow and left.

Buddha and Confucius
Oct-Dec 1950

As Li was leaving a guard rushed into the hut and pointed his rifle at Swede. Seeing the prisoner on the floor, face bruised, blood dripping from his mouth, the guard relaxed and started laughing. Colonel Li was still outside yelling, apparently about how useless the American was. Within minutes Li and his men were gone and Swede was shoved into the back of a small truck. Two guards climbed in the back with him and the truck headed north. The guards handcuffed Swede's left wrist to the frame of the truck. A tarpaulin covered most of the back, keeping out the sun and some of the wind. Keeping out of the wind was a good thing but sunlight would have been welcome. The ground was snow covered and the temperature was dropping. After shackling Swede, the guards got out a very raggedy-looking set of cards and began a game he couldn't figure out. It seemed to involve a lot of yelling and pounding on the pack between them that was acting as their table. For a while, watching the two try to keep the cards in place as the truck bounced down the road was entertaining. That didn't last long as the cold and constant jarring began to numb his body and mind.

The first night the guards stopped in a village. Swede spent the night handcuffed in the back of the truck. Before the guards bedded down in a hut, they threw him a blanket. It was olive drab with US stamped on it. Their remarks and laughter probably meant, "Here, we found something of yours." In the morning they sent out a bowl of rice and a bowl of tea. He gulped both down before they turned cold. That meal lasted him until the next morning after another night in the truck. Late on the third day, the truck entered a broad valley and

approached the first real town Swede had seen since leaving Seoul. There were a lot of one-story wooden buildings and piles of dirt or gravel under decrepit looking conveyor belts. The truck drove past all this and stopped in front of a concrete block building. The building was on a small hill looking back south at the town. The guards dragged him out of the truck and pushed him towards the big wooden door. The door had bars in a small window.
Noticing the bars, Swede took a better look at the building. There was only one other window he could see. More bars.

Once through the door, Swede found himself in a large room with a pot-bellied wood stove giving off a very welcome warmth. The room ran the width of the building. There were two desks and a couple of chairs along the wall. As he stepped into the room, Swede saw another door directly opposite. This one had a small window in it at eye level. More bars. The wood stove was off to his right. Three bare light bulbs hung from the ceiling beams.

Swede was pushed toward one of the chairs against the outer wall and the handcuffs removed. Other than his guards, there were three men in the room. They were wearing uniforms but not the North Korean army uniforms he knew. One of them had a star sewn above the shirt pocket and a pistol on a belt around his waist. Watching his old guards and the new ones chat as they filled out papers at the first desk, Swede managed to pocket an orange from a bowl on the desk next to him. He didn't know how oranges came to be in this cold, miserable place, and he didn't care.

All the paperwork and the accompanying gossip took a while. As he warmed up Swede noticed a foul smell, then realized he was the source. The heat from the stove was revealing he had been chained to a truck for two days. Despite the smell, Swede dozed off until the guards opened the door to leave. The cold draft brought him back to reality. He had an idea of what was going to happen next and wasn't sure if he liked it. One of the three "jailers," as he had come to think of them, growled something at him and pointed to the door leading into the next room. Swede grabbed his blanket and headed through the door.

This room was much darker, so it took a bit for his eyes to adjust. It didn't take any time at all to recognize the smell. It reminded Swede of walking into the barn at home on a cold winter morning. A lot of smell and little warmth. Inside the door was a hall that ran the width of the building. There were three cells, maybe eight by eight feet in size, separated from the hall and each other by bars from floor to ceiling. From the smell, Swede guessed there was a privy of some kind on the far end of the hall. The only light came from a small window high on each of the side walls. The cells each held five or six people, all squatting or sitting against the walls of their cells. The floors of the cells were covered in straw. The yellow straw was the only color in the otherwise depressing cell block.

Swede was led to the farthest cell and stood while the guard unlocked the cell door with a large skeleton key hanging from his belt. As the door swung out on massive hinges, Swede was reminded of westerns at the movies - minus the black and white hats. He was shoved inside the cell. The guard locked the door, said something to his new roommates, and left. Swede stood just inside the door, looking at the inhabitants as they looked back at him. It was cold in the room, so he shook loose his blanket and settled it around his shoulders.

With that move, one of the figures at the far wall stood up and approached Swede. This guy was big, not tall, but heavy and wide. His hair looked like Swede's had before the village women had cut it. His face and hands were dirty, his shirt and pants of a color that would never be determined again. He pointed to Swede's blanket and said something that Swede was sure meant "give it to me."

Swede had only seconds to decide what to do. There was no way he could let somebody bully him into giving up his blanket. That would only be the beginning. As the unfriendly Buddha reached out to grab the blanket Swede moved towards him and brought his knee up as hard as he could into the man's groin. "Right in the twins," as his drill instructor used to say. Then he grabbed the man's shirt and kneed him again. Reaching up to grab the man by his hair, Swede brought his knee up once more as he pulled Buddha's head down to meet it. Then he pushed him as hard as he could to the back of the cell. Buddha's head slapped hard against the wall and he slid down to collapse in a heap on the floor. There was a collective intake of breath from every man in the room as they looked from Buddha to Swede and back.

Swede knew he couldn't beat this guy every day. Sooner or later, this guy would sneak up behind him and crush his skull. He walked over and crouched down in front of Buddha. He gently shook the man's head and waited until his eyes cleared. Pointing to his blanket, Swede said, "This blanket is mine. You can't have it. But I'll share it with you." He pointed at the blanket and then the man and shook his finger back and forth. He pointed to the blanket and then both himself and the man and nodded his head up and down. Then he sat down next to the man and wrapped the blanket around both their shoulders. He reached into his pocket and brought out the orange. He broke it in two and gave one half to his new friend. "I'll share, but I won't let you take things from me. Understand?" Swede pointed again to the blanket and then to the orange, moving his finger back and forth between himself and Buddha. Then he held his hand out, smiled, and waited for Buddha to shake it. Or rip it from his arm.

Buddha's eyes were back in focus by then. He looked into Swede's eyes for a long while, then smiled himself, shook Swede's hand, and popped his half of the orange in his mouth. Every man in the room went back to breathing again.

A voice from the nearest cell said something in Korean and then, "I tell him he has made a good friend. It is not so warm in here. And you should eat all your orange, both the insides and the outsides. Then the guards will not punish you for stealing."

Swede peered through the dim light to see who had spoken. He noticed an older man, very thin, the exact image of a Chinese wise man, standing in the next cell looking at him. "You speak English?" Swede asked in complete surprise.

"Did I not just do so?" replied the man. "I am Kim. And you are?"

The Chinese wise man named Kim was fifty years old. Kim had been raised at the local Presbyterian mission as an orphan. He had no family name - he was simply Kim. Giving him a family name would have required a search for his parents, and that would have embarrassed the missionaries for they were sure the mother was not married. So, he was Kim. He had spent his entire life at the mission doing whatever needed to be done. As far as he was concerned, Jesus was his father and Mary was his mother. The missionaries were, of course, shocked by the sacrilegious connotations of such a notion, so Kim never mentioned it but the one time. He came to understand he would never be the equal of any of the missionaries. Not only was he

Korean, but a bastard to boot. Still, he was content with his life and held them no ill will. After all, they had given him his life. The Bible says to bear with each other and to forgive one another.

Kim had become essential to the smooth running of the mission. Missionaries completed their service of trials and tribulations and returned to the States. Newer and younger versions looked to Kim for help. He was especially good with the children and gradually became the de facto headteacher at the mission school. "Oncle Kim" was known and liked throughout the area as he was now teaching grandchildren of his first students.

This explained his presence in the cell next to Swede. Anyone who is well known also has enemies. Since Kim was a young boy the Japanese had occupied Korea. They had built the town of Toha-ri to take minerals from the earth and send them back to Japanese factories. They had built this jail to house those who did not cooperate in those endeavors. When an individual was brought in for questioning, it was easy for them to point a finger at Kim in the hope they could strike a bargain for their own freedom. It was known to all he taught the children to read and write using the Korean Hangul alphabet. During the last war, the Japanese had outlawed such teaching. Kim spent two years in this jail during that war. In the cell next to him were the two who had pointed their fingers at him this time. Kim suspected as much, but the Bible says to bear with each other and to forgive one another.

When the Japanese were defeated at the end of the war, Kim was freed. Eventually, the new government considered him to be tainted by his imprisonment under the Japanese. Once again fingers were pointed at him, this time for being a Christian. Back to jail he went. The men who ran the jail were, of course, former students. He was still their "Oncle Kim" and they tried to make his life as comfortable as possible. The oranges were part of that attempt. Kim was regularly allowed out of his cell to perform odd jobs in and around the building. The oranges were there for him to take. He could share once he returned to the cells, but no other prisoner was given such privileges. Had Swede not eaten both "the insides and the outsides" he would have been punished when the rinds were found in his cell. You didn't steal "Oncle's" oranges.

Buddha, on the other hand, had a darker past. His father had been killed by the Japanese. A wealthy businessman wanted to build a house in the country to entertain associates. His father would not sell the family land so one day some soldiers came into the village, shot his father – for trying to evade arrest, of course – and took Buddha's mother away. He was raised by relatives who had little enough for themselves. With no family land, he became a tenant farmer. He married and started a family but often drank too much. One night Buddha got drunk. His wife made him leave the house to sleep it off somewhere else. The fire was not his fault, but his wife and son died. He was found drunk, so he was also found guilty. It was expected he would spend the rest of his life in that cell. Buddha was not normally a bully towards his cellmates, but given his size and quickness to anger, none dared deny him any request. Except Kim. He was making progress in teaching Buddha to bear with others and forgive one another. Along comes Swede, a complete foreigner, who manages in his first minutes in his cell, to make two new friends. One by beating him up and then sharing all his worldly goods with him, the other because Swede was a Christian who spoke English. Over the next months, the two became his friends and taught him skills he never realized he was learning. At one point, Swede wondered if his mother would forgive his being in jail when he told her Buddha and Confucius had been his cellmates.

Kim was able to learn from the jailers that Swede was there only temporarily, just until the North Korean Army was ready to put him on trial. He was being held at Toha-ri to keep him away from the Chinese. It was a matter of saving face for the Koreans to put him on trial themselves. What the jailers didn't know was what the charges were going to be. Until the Koreans were ready, Swede would remain in their custody. He thought it ironic the North Korean Army had the same basic policy as the US army did - hurry up and wait.

That meant many hours of sitting in their cells talking. Many hours of many days which then turned into weeks. Swede and Kim spoke English while Swede and Buddha spoke mostly pantomime. From Kim, Swede learned the history of Korea under the Japanese, the similarities between the Japanese and the Communists, and what to expect from the Communist political commissars when they questioned him. He also learned some French and that the Bible teaches you to bear with each other and to forgive one another. French, because Swede could not learn even the simplest of Korean phrases and French was the only other language Kim knew. Kim felt any hour of the day was wasted if he could not impart some of his knowledge to this boy. He found Swede to be a good person, but ignorant. He spoke only one language and did not know his Bible verses.

Buddha taught Swede to meditate and Swede taught Buddha to leg wrestle. The antics between the two as they tried to communicate became a source of amusement for the other prisoners. Swede had tried arm wrestling, but it was like wrestling with a tree. Buddha would hum songs or pretend he was sleeping, then finally slam Swede's arm to the ground. Swede decided to try Indian leg wrestling in the hope he could win a few rounds. Trying to get across the concept of Indian to Buddha was what their cellmates most enjoyed. Swede would whoop, dance, pretend to shoot a bow, smear dirt on his face for war paint - anything he could think of at the time. In the end, he was sure no one ever made the connection between his antics and the actual leg wrestling. They seemed to think of his efforts as a warmup show for the wrestling - vaudeville Korean style. Given the conditions in the cells, especially the floors, the wrestling only happened twice a month on the day the straw on the floor was replaced. Now there were two reasons to look forward to that day.

All the above was able to happen for only a few hours in the day, if that. Most of their time was spent being cold, hungry, and sitting at attention in their cells. There was no heat in their part of the building. Some warmth came through the wall from the office. Every now and then the office got too warm. The jailers would then open the door leading to the cells to lower the office temperature. The prisoners were fed twice a day with food brought from outside. That meant their meals were often cold. All prisoners were required to sit at attention and in silence after the morning meal until early afternoon. They did the same after their evening meal until two of the three jailers went home for the night. One stayed to monitor the fire and the prisoners. That individual usually slept through the night. During the day, the guards would check on the prisoners during their morning meal, mid-morning, mid-afternoon, during the evening meal, and before the night guard went to sleep. Any time a guard came into the cell area to check, he carried a bamboo rod. Should anyone be taking too long to eat, not sitting at attention, or talking when they shouldn't, they were introduced to the bamboo rod. The greater the perceived offense, the better they got to know the rod. The Korean jailers had learned their methods from the Japanese.

The concrete blocks of the outer walls of the cell area were frost-covered in the winter. When temperatures dropped below zero outside, those walls were ice-covered. To bring heat into the cells the prisoners resorted to theft. On the really cold days, a few prisoners would periodically cause a ruckus of some kind to draw the guards into the room. When they came in, they left the door open to their office - and their wood stove. The prisoners would take their time settling down, usually getting to know the bamboo rod better, and some heat would be stolen from the next room. They got to know the rod frequently on those really cold days. Once Swede caught on to the system, he earned the respect of his cellmates by pretending he did not understand what the guards wanted and then rambling on in English. Sooner or later, the guards would get tired of trying to explain the rules to the stupid American and whack him a few times. They spent more time arguing with him than with the Korean prisoners and usually gave him fewer whacks. They never noticed that when Swede was the one they needed to discipline, he had his blanket doubled up over his head and shoulders. When they left, he went back to sharing with Buddha.

As the temperatures dropped below zero, the guards brought in a few old overcoats and moth-eaten blankets. Not enough for everybody but enough to share. Kim was proud of Buddha because he typically bullied the others to get the best blanket or coat for himself. This winter he just took a regular blanket and continued sharing with Swede. Once the blankets and coats came in the other prisoners began using Swede's idea. They placed their coat or blanket over their head and shoulders when it was time to create enough noise to bring in the guards. If they did not raise their arms as if to fight back, and yelled as if in pain, the guards were more quickly satisfied. If they looked like they were fighting back, the guards hit harder. Swede figured it was close to Thanksgiving when the coats and blankets were given out. By then, temperatures seemed to have dropped below zero and stayed there.

In the morning and evening the prisoners could use the attached outhouse, a simple wooden structure with a hole in the floor. Each cell had a wooden bucket for the rest of the day. Kim was in charge of seeing each prisoner had a few minutes to use the outhouse, one at a time. The first from each cell carried the bucket to empty it. Kim tried to rotate which cell went first and who from the cell went first. Being first meant staying cleaner through the whole process. No paper of any kind meant you were never really clean. The buckets in the cells were not large, so the cell floors were sometimes messy. The only positive about winter was the cold kept the smell down.

Every two weeks, the prisoners could bathe from a small wooden bucket. A pipe came through the wall from the office into the outhouse. Each prisoner would take the bucket, hold it under the pipe, rap on the wall, and one of the jailers would turn a lever for a few seconds. The bucket held a gallon at best. Some prisoners simply dumped it all over their head while clothed. Others stripped down, washed themselves, and then used what was left to rinse their clothes. A rag was supplied but no soap. In the middle of winter many simply wiped off their face and hands with the dampened cloth. The guards knew exactly how many times they could expect to hear a rap on the wall, so no one could go through the line twice. Some bargained their bath away for extra food or a warmer coat from their fellow prisoners.

During the afternoon break from sitting at attention, Kim and Swede would talk, with Kim doing most of the talking. Most of what he said came in the form of lectures on the Bible and the history of Christianity. Once he found Swede could parrot back simple phrases in French, those lessons took up part of that free time. After the jailers had settled down for the night, Kim would sometimes tell about growing up in the mission and the many foreigners he met there. During his afternoon Bible lessons, he would often repeat himself in Korean in the hope Buddha was paying attention.

Buddha taught Swede a form of meditation by example. The long periods of the day the prisoners were supposed to sit at attention were difficult for Swede. He was constantly moving around trying to find a more comfortable position. He would drum his fingers on his leg, he would sigh, he would look around to see how everyone else was doing, even stand up to stretch. All this made it hard on Buddha, especially since they were sharing a blanket. He began nudging Swede and then pointing to himself as if to say, "Look at me, foreigner, and try to do as I do." He would close his eyes, place his hands on his knees, breathe deeply once or twice, and then sit without moving for an hour or more. Now and then he would gently shrug his shoulders and move his arms around, then go back to being still. The fact they were allowed to sit with their backs against the cell walls made it easier. At times, new prisoners would be brought in and a cell would become crowded. The new people had to sit at attention in the middle of the cell without the support of the walls or use the cold outer wall.

Swede began to mimic Buddha, simply because he needed to find a way to make it through the day. When he would get fidgety, Buddha would simply nudge him again, maybe a little harder, and go through his routine. As time went on, Swede found he could spend hours focusing on something pleasant from the past or trying to solve a problem in the present. Which is how he almost saved Buddha's life.

Outside the Cell
Christmas 1950

Christmas came – and went. Swede wouldn't have known it was
Christmas had not Kim brought it up. He mentioned it was his
father's birthday. That was when Swede heard most of the story of
Kim's life with the missionaries. Kim was proud of what he had
accomplished with his life, but not to the point where his ego took
over. Swede was impressed with Kim. He was a man most people
would think of as a common, uneducated peasant. Yet his intellect
and understanding of the world and its people was beyond that of
most people Swede knew. Much of Kim's life had been a struggle,
but he had chosen to focus on the good, to share that good with
those around him. He especially enjoyed sharing his knowledge of
Bible verses.

It was just before Christmas that Swede noticed Buddha having
problems. Everybody was cold more often than warm and everybody
had a cough most of the time, but Buddha seemed to be getting
worse. Then he developed a fever that would come and go. He grew
listless and didn't even bother to try and wash on bath day. Swede
waited until everyone else had used the bucket, including himself, and
then filled it for Buddha. He managed to clean the big man up and
then kept the rag. That night the fever came back, and Swede used
the rag to scrape ice from the wall and hold it on Buddha's forehead
to provide some relief for his friend. Each time the fever hit, it
seemed to be worse. Kim explained others had died this way before
with no reaction of any kind from the jailers. They were on their
own.

Kim and Swede thought hard to come up with any solution other than cooling Buddha when the fever hit him. And the fever was getting extreme. Swede practiced meditating, trying to come up with something that might help. His only medical knowledge came from first aid in basic training and memories of what his mother and grandmother did when someone in the family got sick. He had no actual memory of this himself, but there was a story of his grandmother using hot peppers in a broth to break a fever his father had as a teenager. He remembered conversations among his fellow POWs about different foods – and a mention of Koreans liking hot spices in their food. As soon as he could, he asked Kim if there was a way they could get some spices for Buddha.

"Peppers do not grow well in jail cells," was Kim's response. But Swede would not give up.

"Who cooks our food every day? Can we get a message to them asking for peppers?"

"The head jailer's wife cooks our food. But the head jailer does not like the Buddha. He caused problems when he first was brought here."

"What about when you do work around the jail? What about the storehouse where you get the fresh straw for our cells? Can you look for peppers somewhere?"

"Peppers do not grow well in snowbanks either." Kim was annoyed that Swede, who said he lived on a farm, did not know when and where to find peppers. Then his face lit up with a smile! Maybe the farm boy was not so ignorant after all!

"The rice the jailer's wife cooks for us is stored in the shed with the straw. Our jailer stores many things in his shed. He lines his pockets with dealings outside his duties as jailer. Sometimes he has me carry the rice from the shed to his wife. He gives me a key and I open a small room inside the shed. I think he uses some of the money he is paid to feed us to buy food he does not feed us. Then he sells that food to others. When I am in that room, I can smell gochu. Gochu is red pepper. There must be gochu in that room. He could sell it for a good price in the late winter when people have used up their supply. We can get hot peppers for the Buddha in that shed! You are becoming a wise man for an American." Kim's smile grew bigger, as he thought of how they could help their friend at the expense of the man who was cheating at *their* expense.

"Don't you bring in new straw for our cells soon?" asked Swede.

"You can get the peppers then."

"I bring in new straw in three days. But that does not mean I can bring in any peppers. The storehouse is not locked, but the small room where the rice is kept, is. The jailer gives me a key for the lock, but I think he keeps the key in his desk in the office. I cannot just ask for the key."

"Explain to me exactly what you do when you bring in the new straw," demanded Swede. "Go through it step by step. Maybe we can come up with a plan."

Kim explained he was responsible for some of the menial tasks the jailers didn't want to be bothered with. Exchanging the old straw for new was one of those tasks. The old straw would be swept from the cells and down to the latrine. A small door in the wall of the latrine opened to the outside but was kept locked on the inside. The jailers were more concerned with someone breaking in than breaking out. They would have to break out of the cells first. Kim would get the key from the office and open the door. The old straw was swept out to fall a few feet to the ground. People in nearby houses usually took it away to use as bedding in the animal pens. Kim would then go through the office and out to the shed where the straw was stored. Making a few trips, he pushed new straw through the door into the latrine. Then he would close the shed and return to the cells. He locked the door on the latrine wall and returned the key to the office. The new straw was spread throughout the cells and Swede and Buddha would spend that evening entertaining their cellmates with games of strength.

Later that day Swede spent the time thinking about what they needed to do for Buddha. By the end of the day he thought there might be a way to get to those peppers.

"What else is kept in the shed with the straw?" he asked Kim. "Are there any tools?"

"Yes, there are tools. But we cannot break the lock on the room in the shed. The jailer will see it right away. And besides, how do we get to the shed in the first place?"

"I know how we get to the shed," replied Swede. "And we don't break the lock, we pick it." Swede made little twisting motion with his hands.

"What is pick?" asked Kim, repeating Swede's little hand motions.

"We open the lock without a key. Except it won't be we, it will just be me. Here's the plan. During the night when the jailer in the office is sleeping, I pick the lock on my cell. Then I pick the lock on the door in the latrine wall. I slip outside and go into the shed. I pick the lock on the room where the rice is stored. I find the peppers and grab what I can. Then I lock up the room, sneak back in here through the door in the latrine, lock it, get back into my cell, and lock that. When our food is brought to us in the morning, we mix some peppers in Buddha's bowl. Lots of peppers. Then we do it again that night. And the next day if we have to." Swede grinned at Kim in the dim light. "Simple."

Kim sat in thought for a while. "That could work. But what about your tracks in the snow? The jailers will notice."

"We wait for a snowstorm. If Buddha gets too bad and we can't wait I'll just have to cover my tracks somehow," answered Swede.

"How will you see in the room to find the gochu? You will have no light," came the next question.

"You said you didn't see the gochu, you smelled it. That's how I'll find it. But there are two other important questions," said Swede, smiling.

"What are those questions?"

"Do I know how to pick a lock, and what are we going to pick the locks with?"

"Do you know how to pick a lock?" asked Kim.

"No."

"If you knew how to pick a lock, what would you need to do so?"

"That's why I asked if there are any tools in the shed," answered Swede. "I need some heavy wire or thin nails. Is there anything like that in the shed?"

Now Kim smiled. "There are those things, and more. I can get them when I bring in the new straw. I can hide them in the straw. And so now I know your plan will work!" Kim continued smiling.

"Except I still don't know how to pick a lock," replied Swede.

"No, but he does," said Kim, pointing at one of the men in Swede's cell. "His crime is burglary. He robs rich people. People who hide things behind locks. He can teach you." Kim folded his arms, as if no more questions were needed, and smiled.

The next morning Kim talked with Sook the burglar. He and Sook had spent a lot of time together in the cells. Even better, Sook and Buddha got along well. Kim first talked to Sook about helping

Buddha get well. Sook could see Buddha was sick and could guess at the eventual outcome. Once he got Sook's promise to at least listen to a plan as to how they could help Buddha, Kim explained in general what he and Swede wanted to do. All Sook had to do was teach Swede to pick a lock. All three of the locks were of the skeleton key type, just different sizes. Kim did not tell him all the details about the storage shed and the peppers.

Sook was both very smart and very clever. But he was also very lazy. He would rather con his way to money than work for it. His life had been easy when the Japanese occupied the country. Many wealthy Japanese had come to Korea to run their businesses and build vacation homes. Those wealthy men, and their wealthy friends, liked to gamble. Sook liked to supply them with opportunities to gamble. When he found a businessman who seldom lost or who cheated more than Sook, he got their money by breaking into their fancy vacation homes. He often found himself in jail because the Japanese suspected him of something but could seldom prove anything. The new Communist government was different. They did not care if they could prove Sook guilty or not. They simply arrested him and threw him in jail. Sook had many friends in the black market. When he got out of jail this time, he planned to call in all his debts and move to Japan. He knew lots of wealthy people there who liked to gamble. So when Kim approached him with the idea of teaching the American how to pick a lock to help Buddha, Sook readily agreed. When Buddha was better, he would feel obligated to Sook. Kim would think better of him and maybe quit telling Sook he should not steal. And finally, if he hid the lock pick wires carefully, Sook could escape if that ever became necessary. Sook was glad to help.

Kim was able to bring Sook four long, thin, nails with no problem. Sook said he needed two to pick the locks but wanted four in case he broke one or two. That night, when everyone else, including the night jailer, was asleep, Sook demonstrated for Swede how easy it was to pick the lock on the cell doors. Using the metal frame around the latrine bucket in the cell, he had bent the tip of two nails and made an L shape of the others. Inserting one of each type in the lock and giving a few simple twists, the cell door was open.

"Zhe shi!" smiled Sook, obviously pleased with himself. "Voila!"

translated Kim. With Kim helping to explain the details of Sook's instructions, Swede was able to catch on quickly. The next night they left the cell and practiced on the door in the latrine.

Two days later the next snowstorm hit. There already was a foot or more of snow on the ground and this storm looked like it would last a while. Swede told Kim he would go for the peppers that night. They would hide them in the latrine itself, as the jailers never went back there. When Buddha's fever hit again, and they knew it would soon, they would be ready.

It was well into the night before Swede moved to the cell door. He knew at least two sets of eyes were paying close attention. It took a few minutes, but he finally heard the slight click and was able to push the door open. Swede could tell the temperature was well below zero, so he borrowed the heaviest coat in the cells. He still had his original boots but no socks, and his pants were very thin. The heavy overcoat had a thick collar he could use to protect his ears. But the howling of the wind told him he was going to be cold.

Moving to the latrine, Swede managed to get the next lock open but took even longer than on the cell door. Then he encountered his first problem. The wind was so strong it almost pulled the door from his hands as he started to open it. He caught it just before it would have slammed into the side of the building. It would have made a noise loud enough to wake the jailer. Swede realized he could slip out with no problem but had no way to keep the door from slamming back and forth from the wind. Not wanting to lock it again, he just hung on and whispered loudly.

"Kim! Pssst, Kim!" Swede hoped Kim could hear against the howling of the wind outside. He waited.

"Pssst, Kim! I need help here." Finally, he could feel someone next to him. A hand grabbed the latch on the door. It was Sook! He held the door with one hand and whispered "Waiting." Swede nodded his understanding.

Sook returned in a few minutes with Kim. He had picked the lock on Kim's cell door to let him out. They both grabbed the door to help Swede control it. Kim whispered, "Sook will go with you to help with any other problems. I will stay and hold the door. First, he needs to put on a warmer coat."

Sook left and returned to the cells. Swede and Kim heard some loud whispering about a disagreement of some kind. Then Sook returned wearing a larger coat. He nodded his head at Swede and motioned out the door. Swede slid out into the snow and wind. Sook followed and then pushed the door closed for Kim to grab. It was cold! Swede had been out in wind and temperatures like this before, but only to go from the house to the barn while wearing clothing made for Minnesota winters. The snow was deep and blowing in waves away into the dark. Sook pointed with one hand in the direction they needed to go and held his coat closed with the other. Neither had gloves of any kind. Sook led off into the dark and Swede followed. He realized he hadn't asked Kim where the storage shed was in relation to the jail. Without Sook, he would have wandered around until he spotted a building and hoped it was the right one. And you didn't want to wander far in this wind.

A building took shape in the darkness. Sook huddled up against the wall. Looking back, Swede could not see the jail and their tracks were already disappearing. He realized he better pay close attention so he could find this spot when they were ready to head back. With his back to the wall, he could see they needed to head towards 2 o'clock to get back to the latrine door. Sook moved around the corner on their left and Swede followed. He stumbled into Sook as he stopped to open the door to the shed. The two slipped inside and pulled the door shut behind them. There was instant relief from the stinging snow.

Kim had told them there were carts and tools on the right as they came in the door and straw stacked on the left. When they moved forward to where they could no longer feel the straw, they were to turn left and once again follow the straw on the left. If they moved slow, they would feel the door to the food storage. Once there, Sook nudged Swede aside and went to work on the lock. It was so dark they could not even see the door, let alone the lock. It was miserably cold inside the shed. Sook worked on the lock for a minute without success. Then he was forced to bury his hands in his coat to try and warm them. He grunted something at Swede. It was too dark to see the details of the lock, so Swede brought out the picks he had used and slid them in by feel. Almost instantly his fingers started growing numb. Then Sook put his hands over Swede's and guided him as he moved the picks. Sook's fingers felt colder than Swede's. He closed his eyes and tried to picture Sook guiding his fingers as he had done when they were practicing. It was far too windy to hear any click and his fingers were too numb to feel movement, but he was sure they had done everything just right. He tugged on the lock and it slid open. Being careful to keep the lock from falling to the ground, Swede pulled the door open and the two shuffled inside. Kim had said the bags of rice were on shelves directly in front of the door. There were boxes and barrels to both sides, but he had no idea where the peppers might be.

Swede wasn't sure if Sook knew what they were looking for, so he said, "Gochu. Find gochu." Then he took a loud sniff with his nose.

"Ahh, find gochu, pepper!" Sook moved straight ahead to sniff what Swede knew were bags of rice. He moved to the left and began feeling for a box or barrel to sniff himself. He was hoping gochu smelled like the peppers he was familiar with. As he moved from object to object, he could smell only dust and wood. He felt up higher to see if there were more shelves and sniffed some more. He didn't want to move anything as that might make the jailer curious if he noticed something out of place. Swede bumped into Sook as he worked his way left also. The room wasn't very big. Swede moved around Sook and sniffed his way to the right. About that time, he got an image in his head of the two of them sniffing around in the dark and almost laughed. But laughing would have brought too much air into his lungs and it hurt to breathe as it was. Then he got a whiff of what might be pepper. He had his hands on a small wooden keg, about the size of a barrel of blasting powder his father had in a shed at home. He bent closer and took a bigger whiff. Reaching back to his left he grabbed Sook's arm and tugged. "Gochu?" he asked. He guided Sook to the wooden keg. He heard Sook inhale loudly and grunt something. He could hear Sook working the cover off the keg.

"Gochu, peppers!" Sook practically yelled. Swede moved closer and reached out his hand. Sook took it and guided it into the keg. Swede could feel a powdery substance, but not the pepper shapes he expected. Taking some in his hand, he brought it carefully to his nose. He remembered his high school chemistry teacher showing the class how to smell substances they were unsure of. He would take his hand and wave it over a flask of some chemical, bringing a taste of the odor to his nose without sticking his nose right in the flask. That was just about the only thing Swede remembered from his chemistry class. He did the same thing now and was glad he did. The smell was almost stinging. This must be powdered pepper.

Now he had to find something to carry the powder in. He could just put it in the coat pocket, but he wanted to be able to hide the pepper in the latrine until they needed it. He felt around some more until he came up with a cloth of some kind. He took a whiff to see if it smelled clean. Hoping it wasn't the jailer's favorite rag, he took three handfuls of the powder and wrapped it up in the rag. He could hear Sook rummaging around in the corner and tugged on his arm again. "Time to go. I'm freezing and we need to get back before something goes wrong."

They moved out of the room and put the lock back in place. Swede tucked his rag in a pocket and slid back towards the door. He could feel Sook following. Reaching the door, Swede opened it just a crack and peeked out. Then he realized what he was doing and stepped outside. No one was going to be able to see them in the blowing snow. If anybody else was crazy enough to be out in this weather, they would bump into him before they would see him. Remembering to turn to his right Swede moved around the corner. When Sook followed, Swede put his back to the wall and pointed to his 2 o'clock and asked, "We go that way, right?" Sook nodded.

The two had been out close to half an hour by now and were feeling it. There were no tracks, but they pushed their way through the drifts until they could see a shape looming up in front of them. Swede was careful to approach the building without making noise against the walls. He followed the wall to his right, feeling for wood rather than concrete block, his hand completely numb. Wood meant they were at the latrine area. He continued moving his hand to the right until he felt a frame. His hand was almost too numb to grasp the frame and tug. Nothing moved. He brought his other hand out of his pocket and tugged again. This time there was a little movement. With the wind howling like it was, Swede wasn't too worried about what little noise the door might make as it scraped open. He used both hands to grab the bottom and yanked as hard as he could.

The door flew open and something came with it, falling on top of Sook. Swede grabbed the door to keep it from banging around and looked down to see Sook buried in the snowbank with Kim on top of him. It would have been funny if he wasn't freezing to death. With one hand he reached down and grabbed Kim's shirt. He tugged him upright and started pushing him back into the latrine. Then he helped

Sook out of the snowbank and through the door. Swede himself couldn't climb back in until one of them got off the floor and held the door for him. He finally got Kim's attention and motioned to keep the door steady while he climbed in. Kim quickly put the lock back and all three lay there, brushing snow off and shivering.

The three eventually got off the floor, kicked all the snow down the latrine, tucked the rag with the peppers behind some boards, and got back to their cells. All three were shivering badly. Swede was afraid to join Buddha in the blanket because he didn't want to make the big man any colder than he already was. Instead, Sook and Swede huddled together, rubbing their hands and legs to warm them. When Swede finally fell asleep, he dreamt he could reach his hands through the wall and hold them near the fire next door. When he woke, he was still cold and hoping their morning meal would be warm that day. He thought about getting some of the peppers and adding them to his rice in the morning to help warm up but couldn't bring himself to use Buddha's medicine that way.

Buddha died that afternoon. Swede had joined him in the blanket and felt his breathing get slower and slower. There was a final breath and his head fell on Swede's shoulder. They didn't even have the chance to use the peppers to help him. Swede was crushed. Some of the other prisoners saw Buddha's death as a way to steal some heat and yelled for the jailers. They knew the process would take a while and the door to the next room would open quite a few times as people moved back and forth. Swede sat slumped over all the rest of the day. The jailers didn't say a word or use the bamboo rod. That night Swede ate his rice and drank his tea and sat back in the corner with the blanket wrapped around him. That went on for three more days. The jailers decided his period of mourning was over and began yelling at him to sit at attention. Then they started beating him with the bamboo rod.

Kim finally got through the fog Swede was in. "You are not the only one who has sorrow. The Buddha was my friend also. Maybe you think you should have tried to save him sooner. Maybe then he would still be alive. But I knew the gochu was there. I should have thought of it long ago, even before the Buddha was sick, when others were sick. But I would not think beyond what my eyes can see.

"You looked beyond your eyes. Your idea got us to work together to help the Buddha. He is gone, but others are still here. Others will be sick. We have gochu that might help them. Now I know we don't have to sneak through the cold. I can bring the gochu in with the new straw, I don't have to bring it in with my pockets. Maybe there are other foods we can use. Some extra flavor in our food will help all of us. All these ideas only because you could see beyond your eyes. You will probably leave here soon. But we will stay. And your ideas will stay. Your ideas to help the Buddha will help all of us. If we see you sit in pity, then soon others will follow your example. And then your ideas will be left sitting. Everything you did to help the Buddha will be lost. You must show strength again."

Kim's words began to make sense to Swede and reminded him of something Jack Usury had said. Survival would not be a straight line. There would be lots of twists and turns. It was up to us to survive and be alive when it was all over. Kim was right. They had tried with Buddha. It just took too long for them to get out of their rut, to "look beyond their eyes." He had to be ready for the twists and turns. The fact he was here in this miserable place was not his fault. Yes, he was a foreign soldier in this land, but he had come here to help the South Koreans. It was the North Koreans who had started this war, and it was the North Koreans who refused to follow the Geneva Convention. It was the North Korean Major who had murdered Captain Winslow and others on the march. It was these jailers here who mistreated these men. Swede began to realize he had tried all along to help the people around him. He was not at fault here, but somebody was. For the first time, he found himself wanting to make someone pay, to get some small measure of revenge for all the Captain Winslows and all the Buddhas. The next day the North Korean Army came for Swede. As far as he could tell, it was the first day of 1951.

Agony on the March

Winter 1950-51

Mike Randall was tired and worried. It was fear that was bothering him, but he just didn't recognize that yet. His men were in trouble. Two days of gun powder, oil, and sweat from combat back in July had become the foundation for months of marching through dust, rain, mud, and snow. No change of clothes, no baths, no toothpaste or brush, no haircuts or shaves, no toilet paper but sticks or leaves. Throw in a starvation diet, inadequate clothing, diarrhea, deadly dysentery, and untreated wounds, and the result was beyond understanding. People just don't live like that. People *can't* live like that! But these men were. They had been for five months now. And there seemed to be no end to their ordeal. It never got better, it only got worse.

Food and water were down to a bare minimum. Instead of rice, they now had corn or beans of some kind. When it was cooked, it was never cooked well enough to digest easily. Sometimes it was just raw corn, a handful of kernels you tried to chew without breaking your teeth. They were marching during the day now and being pushed hard by the guards. At first, these marches were difficult, but not impossible. But there were men without boots in the column. No one had any clothing other than the summer uniforms they had been captured in. No one had any coats or blankets. Then the snow came. By November, the temperatures dropped below freezing and then below zero-and stayed there. All these factors started to have a drastic effect. Men were finding it harder to keep up. The column was in serious trouble.

More men needed help. Fewer men were willing to help. Randall and his command group tried, but they became weaker themselves. Smaller columns of POWs had joined theirs and those men had no idea who was in charge. According to the guards they did not have to take orders, so they didn't. Men without boots might make it through the day, but at night, with temperatures well below zero, crammed into huts, they needed help. Someone had to be willing to gently massage their feet or use their armpit or crotch to warm them. Others needed help to keep up during the day. But the prisoners had been worn down to the point where many could not think beyond their own misery. Others who could - would not.

Every night Mike Randall was tormented with the sounds of those around him. The sounds of constant moaning. Some men moaned from the pain of untreated wounds, although most of those men had long since died. Some moaned from the pain of frozen feet, others from the loss of all hope. They moaned out of shame as they erupted into their pants for the second or third time that night, adding another level to the overpowering stench in the hut. Every night those sounds echoed through Mike Randall's head, bringing a pain of their own.

Randall was a professional military man. He would give his last breath to help one of his men. Nobody really knew who Charlie was, but he refused to give up. He was one of the healthiest men in the column and he gave everything he had to help those who needed help. Ray Parker and Tony Rafaldano did everything that was asked of them. A Private Henry Page had become part of Randall's "staff" once they left Seoul. Randall wasn't sure how that happened, since Seoul he was just there. But the column had become bigger. Too few were willing to put out much effort to help those who needed it. Henry Page finally brought up a topic Mike Randall did not want to think about. The fear he had been trying to ignore for the past month.

"Sergeant, you need to ease up a bit. Let me help you." Randall had just helped a man back on his feet. If you got a man back in the middle of the column, he seemed less likely to fall and stay down. Once he got the man moving again, Randall himself stumbled and almost fell. Page had been helping Charlie carry another prisoner, an arm over each of them. He tugged the man next to him over to take his place. Page was older than the average private. There was something about him that made most men do what he asked.

Page moved over to help Randall steady his pace. After a few steps, he removed his arm but stayed by the sergeant's side. "You might consider this out of line, but I am going to say it anyway. You are jeopardizing your own health trying to keep everybody in this column on their feet. If you keep this up, you won't be able to help yourself, let alone the rest of us."

"I appreciate the concern, Private, but I have an obligation to these men. As far as I know, I am the senior man here, at least the senior man who gives a damn. The few officers in the group gave up a long time ago. I promised Captain Winslow I would take care of these men. And that is what I intend to do." Looking over at Page, he continued with no disapproval in his voice, "Under normal circumstances I *would* consider you to be out of line, but these aren't normal circumstances." Glancing at Page's sleeve he said, "You're a little old to be a private, but I see you trying to keep these people in line, trying to get them to act like soldiers."

"I understand and agree with what you are trying to do," said Page. "But you are exhausting yourself trying to take on everybody's problems. Frankly, you look like hell. I can tell you feel worse than you let on. When you run yourself into the ground, when you can't get up out of the ditch, who takes over? There isn't anybody else the men will listen to. As it is already, the new men pay little attention to you. Usury is going to get himself shot if he keeps knocking people around to get them to help. But he will keep it up just because he knows you expect him to give his all. The same with Parker and Bowser and Charlie and a fair number of other men.

"But when you go down, what happens to them? What happens to this column? Yeah, men are dropping out, men are dying, but more will if you aren't here to keep us together. And to be completely honest with you, I'm not a private." Page looked Mike Randall right in the eye. "I can't tell you more than that right now, but I want you to know I'm speaking from a background beyond your standard US Army Private." He gave a slight grin, something Randall hadn't seen much of lately.

Master Sergeant Mike Randall, formerly *Captain* Mike Randall, had been to more than one rodeo. He was a good judge of character. There had been lots of opportunity to work on that skill even before he left the orphanage. Joining the army in 1936, he found himself serving with the 15th Infantry in China at age sixteen. Six years later, he went ashore with the 15th in North Africa, then Sicily, Italy, France, and finally Germany. What he saw in this "not" Private Page reminded him of men he had come to trust over those years. This one had more hair and grime than normal, but the eyes looking back at him reflected a wisdom beyond his age.

"What would you suggest? That I just give up and shuffle along like a zombie, just worry about myself?" Randall did feel lousy and knew he couldn't keep this up much longer. If this guy had some good ideas, he wanted to hear them. They could work out the not-a-private business later.

"Delegate more. Let others move up and down the column. And I've seen you sneak from hut to hut at night when the guards aren't paying attention. How long does it take you to warm up again when you get back to your own hut? The Koreans don't seem to care much lately who the squad leaders are. We can put more effort into seeing we have enough guys we can trust to help in the huts at night and on the march. We can keep you informed. You can focus just on the big problems that come up.

"And there is another problem we should talk about." Page looked at the sergeant as if he was afraid to bring up this other problem.

"Well, you're makin' sense so far, so don't stop now," growled Randall. He was unhappy somebody who wasn't even a private had to point out what he should have admitted himself.

"We won't be able to keep this up much longer. All of us are in bad shape. We burn more calories every day than these bastards feed us. This is only November, so it's going to get colder before it gets warmer. If we run ourselves into the ground much more, who will be left to help? Even Jack Usury can't force enough men to help with the sick. We might be able to get more men to help if we really work at it. But we will have to use a lot more sugar and less vinegar." Page knew there was a bond of some kind between Randall and Usury and didn't want to seem like he was criticizing the Corporal. He quickly continued. "We can spread ourselves up and down the column. When somebody needs help, we step in for a bit and then try to hand them over to people nearby. Show we are willing to help but also expect others to pitch in."

"You have a good point there." Randall interrupted. "I've noticed the men are becoming more tribal. They stay in groups of five or six, kind of like they have formed little gangs. Maybe we can encourage them into taking care of their gang, their tribe. Less vinegar, like you say."

The sergeant looked around as the column moved through the snow. He could hear the crunch of men's feet in the snow on the road, moans from the sick, and the murmuring of those encouraging their buddies. But far too many simply trudged along with their heads down, paying no attention to anything other than their own feet plodding through the snow. Not that he could blame them. It was easy to think keeping your arms close to your body kept you warmer than reaching out to help somebody else. Looking down at your feet kept you from looking at those around you and seeing a reflection of how bad off you really were. But Randall knew working together was going to keep more of these men alive than blocking out the reality around them. Page seemed to have given the situation some thought, more than he himself had.

And then Page brought up the point that neither of them wanted to consider. "But unless there is a town over the next hill with warm houses with food and doctors with medicine, we can't keep this up. At some point we are going to have to start a form of triage - we will have to leave people behind. If we try to help them, we will burn the last of whatever energy we have left and become helpless ourselves. And I think that point will come soon. We have to talk about it before we get there." Page looked at Randall hoping he wouldn't think less of him for bringing the subject up.

Randall was quick and forceful in his reply. "No! That's not what soldiers do! We don't leave our people behind!"

"The soldiers we knew six months ago don't leave people behind. But we do! We have almost from the day we got captured. The North Koreans have shot our wounded since we started on this miserable trek. They shot Captain Winslow!" Page saw Randall flinch at that memory. "Why didn't you go after that man who shot him?"

"Because you knew he would have shot you. What would that have accomplished? Who would have been leading these men since then? You made the decision not to get killed so you could take care of the living. That's the kind of soldier we are now! The kind forced to make decisions that leave a shitty taste in our mouth. We can blame the North Koreans, or we can blame this ungodly cold, or we can blame some generals back in Japan or the US. But we can't blame ourselves! We do what we have to do to keep as many of these men alive. Maybe at some point we might have the chance to get revenge on whoever we want to blame, but it sure isn't now. Now we survive!"

Mike Randall looked over at Page. He knew Page was more right than wrong. He realized he had been deliberately ignoring the reality around him. It just kind of hurt his professional pride to have this "private" shoving that reality in his face.

"Just who the hell *are* you?" he asked. So Private Henry Page explained about posing as Captain Patrick Murphy, who was now posing as Private Henry Page. He left out his real name and substituted Military Intelligence for the CIA. It was best no one knew he was CIA. The fact he was a POW in North Korea didn't mean he was in the lion's den yet, but he was sure enough somewhere in the zoo. He also failed to mention the person he was investigating was in Randall's unit. By the time he finished, they had arrived at a village. The guards gathered the men on the road while they forced enough families out of their homes to make room for the prisoners.

Randall brought Page (they agreed it was best to keep calling him that) over to Jack Usury and gave a summary of what they had discussed on the march that afternoon. He left out Page's background. Mike knew that with the three of them, he had the most experienced men in the column. He needed some professional opinions.

Jack Usury looked at Randall. "He makes sense, Mike. We are in a world of hurt. Last night one of the huts threw a man out in the cold because he was too sick and smelled bad. He froze to death. We need to get better control, but we sure can't hold a formation and order these guys to shape up. They won't listen and the Koreans just might shoot us. And we can't carry everybody that needs help even if we had enough people willin' to do that. We don't have the strength.

"I can't tell if these bastards are deliberately tryin' to kill us off or if they just don't care. I have to believe they are takin' us to some kind of camp or they would have shot us all a long time ago. We just need to make it to that camp. They aren't goin' to all this bother just to get us somewhere else and then kill us. Wherever they're takin' us, there should be some kind of barracks and some regular food. So, we start to talk to the men about gettin' to that camp. 'Just a few days more and we get to that camp.' 'Not long now, hold on just a bit more, and we will be at that camp'. Give them some hope. Too many of these guys seem to have lost hope.

"But we also have to start with that "triage" you mentioned. Only we don't decide. We make them decide."

Both Randall and Page looked puzzled at that remark. "What do you mean, make them decide? They take a vote as to who dies?" asked Randall.

"No. We help those who help themselves. If they can't make it out of the hut in the morning to get their chow, we bring it to them. But when they refuse to eat, we make it clear we won't go out of our way the next morning. If they won't use a sleeve or pant leg to cover their own feet, we don't rip off part of our shirt to give them." Randall noticed Usury was missing both sleeves up to the elbows. Usury continued, "We help them walk, but we don't carry them. I think once the men catch on, they will put out more effort. Maybe more of the healthier ones will pitch in.

"And one more thing. We need to strip the dead. We need the clothes and boots. Too many of our guys are half-naked. I can't believe some of them have made it this far. I think we should have Charlie strip them and hand stuff out to whoever needs it most. Lots of the guys treat him like a chaplain anyways. He can make it like a ceremony for the dead or somethin'."

They slowly spread the word over the next few days about the new policy. Only those they trusted were given the details. Gradually more men did start to help. Most of them had bought the North Korean babble about not having to take orders. However, they still considered Randall and the others to be their leaders. They were willing to follow their leader's example, just not their orders. More sugar. Less vinegar.

Just when Mike Randall thought things might be improving, things got worse. The temperature dropped and the wind kicked up. The column got hit by a blizzard. By the time they reached a village, it was almost impossible to see more than a few yards. The snow was thick and stung their eyes. Drifts made it harder to walk. He didn't even realize they were in a village until the guards started pushing them towards the huts.

At least the huts were warm. The villagers had been preparing for a nasty night and had built just the right fires in their stoves to stay comfortable all night. The standard procedure was for at least one guard to sleep in the kitchen with the family of each hut to prevent the prisoners from using any firewood the villagers had brought in for the night. But this night the guards forced the civilians from the huts they needed, shoved the prisoners inside, and took over two huts for themselves. They didn't come out until the storm was over, not even to feed the prisoners.

Bowser was not used to being warm at night and woke up several times. At one point he looked out and saw two American looking jeeps parked in front of his hut. He nudged Parker awake and pointed outside. Whispering, even though the wind was making so much noise he could have been singing and the guards wouldn't have heard him, he asked Parker, "Are those our jeeps? Did Swede finally get here with a rescue column?"

Parker looked at Bowser in disbelief. "The Swede is a pretty sharp guy, but I don't think he could find us after bein' gone for almost three months. They do look like American jeeps, but let's just watch for a bit. If some GIs show up and start to drive away, we can run out and stop them."

After a while, a group of men approached the jeeps. Parker recognized the uniforms of the Korean guards, but the people getting in the jeeps were wearing a different uniform. The Koreans saluted and the jeeps drove away. Parker couldn't hear any of their conversation or even the noise of the jeeps as they drove away. Both men looked at each other, shrugged, wiggled around to get as comfortable as they could in the crowd, and went back to sleep.

The storm continued through the morning. No guards came around, no food either. Most of the men knew how the heating system worked in village huts from their early experience after leaving Seoul. They had watched the families in their tiny kitchens when the Americans were shoved into their homes. The Koreans built only a small fire to cook, but that fire heated the whole home. A vent went under the floor from the kitchen to the far wall and out to a chimney on the outside. Some of the older soldiers explained how the vent was covered by the mud floors of the huts. Heat from the fire was transferred to the floor of the whole house. The ondol system, the old-timers called it.

But some of those who had joined the column later in the march only knew they had a tiny fireplace and it was cold outside. In two of the huts, they ripped up what they could find and stuffed the little kitchen stoves again and again. In a few hours, men in the center of the room, directly over the heating vent, were complaining about the heat. More and more started to yell as the floor became too hot to touch. Even standing was unbearable. They ended up pushing their way out into the storm to get away from the heat. The floors didn't cool off enough until early the next morning. Some men tried to get into a nearby hut. The men in there had no idea what was going on and refused to let them in, there simply was no room for extras. A few men got lost in the blizzard trying to find some place to get out of the wind. Some ended up huddling with the animals for the rest of the night. Others stayed awake all night, bunched just outside the doors of the huts. They would step in for a minute and then step out again when the heat burned right through their boots. By taking turns, they were able to keep warm enough to survive to dawn when the floors finally started cooling. Nobody fully understood what had happened until the storm died down. Seven men froze to death. Charlie removed their clothing before they were buried in a nearby snowbank.

When the column was forced back on the road the next day, Randall noticed a difference in the way the guards handled the POWs. There was more yelling and clubbing with rifle butts. The pace was faster than usual. He thought it was because of the delay caused by the storm, or maybe even because the seven men had died.

It was not until that evening Parker and Bowser had a chance to tell Randall what they had seen the first night of the storm. The command group gathered while they waited for the villagers to clear their huts. Parker gave a detailed report about the "American jeeps" and the men they saw.

"Could you see who got in those jeeps?' Randall asked.

"All I could see was people about the same size as the Koreans, but their uniforms looked different," replied Ray.

"Explain different."

Bowser chimed in. "They looked stiff and padded. Their hats had some kind of emblem, but I couldn't see well enough to be sure what it was. Oh, and one jeep had a star on the side. But not like the American star on our jeeps."

"And the Koreans saluted the guys who got in the jeeps?" asked Page. He looked at both Randall and Usury. "Russians?'

"Or Chinese," said Randall. "Stiff and padded uniforms remind me of what I remember from when I was in China before the last war. Either one would explain the salutes, and maybe why the guards have acted so different today. Meaner. Maybe somebody else just took charge of their little war. Either way, it probably won't be good for us."

And it wasn't. The next day the pace was even faster. Five prisoners were shot because they couldn't keep up. Charlie was not allowed to recover their clothing. And then things got bad.

The guards pushed hard. Any prisoner who fell and could not, or would not get up, was shot. The snow and the temperature continued to fall. It was twenty and thirty below during the day. All the events of the last five months caught up with the POWs. Every single problem was magnified by the cold. They were severely malnourished and underweight. Their clothing was inadequate even for good weather. Their food, what little they got of it, was making them sick. Every night they did not sleep in village huts, more froze to death. Every night they waited for the guard they called Tail End Charlie to herd stragglers in from the day's march. If a friend had dropped back and was not with the stragglers, he would not be rejoining the column. Tail End Charlie had two jobs.

Ray Parker knew very well what happened to those who could not keep up. He and Bowser had helped many of their fellow POWs over the past months as they struggled to maintain the pace. He had become good at judging who just needed help for a while until they caught a second or third wind. He had also become good at recognizing those who were doomed. It looked like Bowser was now in that category. Three weeks ago, he and Bowser had been two of the fittest men in the column. Then diarrhea hit them both and would not go away. They just barely could help each other stumble through the day, let alone help anyone else. That was probably their downfall. They depended on each other rather than ask somebody else for help. To all appearances, it seemed as if they were managing to make it through each day without too much of a problem. But Ray knew he was almost to the end of his endurance and Bowser was beyond that. He could barely help Bowser get his pants down when he fell out of the column. Getting them back up and then Bowser on his feet was taking longer and longer. Taking any time to clean themselves up was out of the question. When you stopped moving the cold attacked and you could not warm up. Then it became too much to even try to get to the side of the road and their pants down. When one stumbled and fell the tail end of the column would be moving past before they got back on their feet. Each would throw an arm around the other's shoulder, then use precious energy to catch up. Ray mostly dragging Bowser through the deep snow.

Then Bowser stumbled again and pulled them both down. Ray heard the snap just before Bowser yelled out in pain. They looked at each other, knowing this was the end. If Ray stayed, they were both dead. To survive, he had to leave Bowser in the snow for Tail End Charlie.

Before Ray could say anything, Bowser grabbed his shirt and pulled Ray's face close to his. "You make sure you live. You make sure you get home. Find my family and tell them I love them and was thinking of them at the end. Anthony Rafaldano from South Boston, West Broadway and F Street, Tony's Pizza. Remember my name. Tell them." He gave Ray a quick hug and pushed him away. "Now get up and get back to the column! You make sure you live. Go!"

Ray Parker left his friend in the snow, tears freezing in the matted tangle of his beard. He looked back and raised his hand in goodbye just before the wind erased Bowser forever. He put his hands over his ears in the hope he would not hear the shot. It didn't work.

This went on for two more weeks. They were pushed beyond their limit each day. A thick fog of fatigue, hunger, and cold covered each man. Some fought to make it to the end of the day. Others had to fight to make it through the next step. For many it was beyond their limit. Each time that limit was reached, their friends wondered which was more painful—to be left behind to die or to leave someone behind to die.

The guards started promising a camp soon. A few days later the column crested a hill to see a town in the valley ahead. The guards broke into smiles and laughter. There were ninety-three men in the column when it crested that hill. When they left Seoul three and a half months before there were one hundred men in the column. One hundred and four had been added to their number in the weeks just after Seoul. Of those two hundred and four men, ninety-three made it to the town in that valley.

Many of those openly wept as they stumbled over the hill and into the valley. They wept for all those who had not made it. They wept because now their ordeal was over. They had arrived at a prisoner of war camp. They would have food, blankets, beds, doctors. They wept because they would survive. They were wrong.

Caged

Winter 1950-51

Swede was in his mother's kitchen eating pancakes when Ray Parker started kicking him again.

"Oh, come on, man. You never let me finish my breakfast!" grumbled Swede. Ray just kicked him again, only this time with a meanness to it.

"What the hell is wrong with you!" yelled Swede, ready to jump up and smack his best friend. But when he looked up, Ray was not there.

It was Cheechee instead. That was what Swede had come to call the guard who woke him up every morning since arriving at his latest accommodations. He was in another cell, much smaller than the one he had shared with Buddha and the others. There was just barely enough room to stretch out on the floor to sleep.

"Yeah, I know. 'Cheechee not here.' I wish I was not here. What's for breakfast this morning, Cheechee?" Swede jumped up and stood at the back of the cell, something he had quickly learned to do after a few 'instructions' from the guards. "Cheechee not here" was Swede's interpretation of what the guard growled at him every morning. He assumed it meant get your ass out of bed. As often as possible, Swede talked to his guards as if they knew what he was saying. It made him feel better, and it gave him a chance to hear a voice speaking English rather than Chinese. The guards didn't seem to mind as long as he kept his tone neutral.

His guards were all Chinese, at least they all wore the same uniform as Colonel Li and spoke a language that sounded different than the Korean he was used to. So - Chinese. Cheechee seemed to be in charge of his guards. He was bigger and appeared more intelligent than the others. Most of the time he seemed content with his job, as if there were worse places he could be and more hazardous tasks than watching over one scruffy American. At his most negative, he might growl at Swede and give him a good shove. Happy was the second in command. He had big ears, smiled a lot, and said little. Happy had second shift. When Swede got something to eat at the end of the day, Happy was the one who delivered it. He was older than any of the others and had a little of a grandfather's approach towards Swede. The other two guards were the nasty ones. They provided the stings when it was decided Swede needed his attitude adjusted - or when they had nothing else to do. He referred to them as the Goons, a term his grandfather used when talking about his days working for the Great Northern Railroad.

Individually, Swede thought of them as Harry and Norm, two drunken layabouts, his mother's phrase, from back home. They spent most of their time drinking and arguing with each other. When that wasn't enough to make them happy, they picked fights with the nearest person they figured they could beat. Swede had only seen the Minneota version of Harry and Norm once or twice, but when he met the Chinese version, he recognized the type.

Harry was fat, not just heavy, but fat. Any effort made him sound as if he had run a mile. The few strands of hair that poked out from under his ever-present wool cap were greasy and black. His permanent frown and drooping mustache made him look angry. Harry seldom smiled, but when he did, Swede paid the price. Bellowing and waving of his arms followed the smiling. Then his buddy Norm, with his bushy eyebrows and yellow-gapped teeth, stepped in and commenced with the punching and beating. Luckily for Swede, Norm was thin. He never did the damage somebody of Harry's size would have. Both men smelled so bad it was impossible for them to sneak up on Swede in his cell to catch him disobeying their latest order. He always knew if they were in the room. Even so, they managed to get in a fair amount of bellowing and punching.

Swede had been informed the day he arrived he was a *guest* in his new home. He had been so informed by a man speaking almost perfect English, a man who identified himself as Major Han. "You are now a guest of the Chinese People's Volunteer Army. You will conduct yourself appropriately. You will follow all the rules and regulations. You have been sent here to face a court martial for your conduct while with our brothers in the Korean People's Army. We will give you time to think of your crimes. My name is Major Han. I will speak with you again soon." Han was the picture of a professional officer in any army, slim, neatly groomed, erect posture, and just a touch of gray in his close-cropped hair. His comment about Swede facing a court martial apparently meant the North Koreans had decided to let the Chinese have him after all.

Swede tried to ask what his crimes had been and what the rules and regulations were, but he was immediately knocked to the ground by his guards. By the time he came to his senses, the major was gone. Apparently, the Chinese definition of soon was different than Swede's. It had been at least two weeks since he arrived, and Major Han had not come around since.

Swede had no idea where he was. When they left Seoul, he thought they had gone north and a little east. He was fairly sure the two-day trip from his jail cell in Toha-ri had been to the northwest. If he had to guess, he figured he was well across the border in North Korea. His guards certainly weren't very quick to answer his questions, except for a rifle butt to his head or stomach when he asked. He knew they didn't speak English, as he had insulted them with some pretty choice phrases while using a normal tone of voice. Not one of them had given even the slightest hint they understood him, even when their mothers were involved in the insults.

Swede called his new home Cheechee's Palace. He had his blanket, a wooden floor, three walls with iron bars, and a fourth of a very tough wood. His cell was small. There were other cells like his, each separated by a wooden wall. Directly across from him were five small animal cages of some kind. There was another room attached. The room his cell was in had one small window high on the wall. When the guards came in, he could hear them open a door and tromp across the wooden floor of the outer room to enter his cell area. There were no other prisoners in the building, Korean or otherwise. In his cell, there was no straw and no bucket. Just Swede.

Every morning he was expected to be on his feet at the back of his cell before Cheechee came into the room. He would approach the cell and place Swede's morning meal on the floor. Both his meals were the same - a metal cup of half-cooked grain and one of tea. And they were always cold. Cheechee would return shortly after delivering the food and escort him to an outhouse nearby. Mountains stood all around. He could see a large village with what seemed to be a small river running to the south and west. Everywhere he looked. the view was depressing, dirty gray snow and dirty gray buildings. The building he was in was of wood construction, as were a few small buildings nearby. They seemed to be unoccupied. Just beyond them was a two-story concrete block building in which he had met Major Han. Smoke curled up from just about every building he could see on his short walks to see Major Han except his building and those few nearby. When he was escorted to see the Major, they went in the back door of what was probably the headquarters building. The guards seemed to live in there or somewhere on the other side.

For a few hours each morning and afternoon, the guards would have him sit or stand or kneel at attention. The Goons liked to have him stand on one leg. They would show him the position of the day and leave. Then they would try to catch him relaxing. When they did, Norm reached through the bars with his club and jabbed or hit him, while Harry yelled insults at him. It was their way of passing the time. Since they weren't very bright, Swede would hear them or smell them trying to sneak in to see if he was in the correct position. But twice they had come in drunk at night and left him unconscious on the floor. Happy caught him relaxed once when he was supposed to be at attention and just wagged his finger. But then he waited until Swede put himself back at attention.

Not knowing what was going to happen next and not having someone he could talk with made the days long and worrisome. But the worst was the cold. Swede had never experienced cold like this before. The term bone-chilling became his reality. His building was not open to the wind, but he had no heat of any kind. There were some nights he was afraid to fall asleep with the worry he would freeze to death. He had no choice but to burn calories stomping his feet while thumping his body with hands and arms.

Whatever happened, Swede had promised himself he would survive. The circumstances around Buddha's death had hardened him more than any other experience since arriving in Korea. Uncle Kim had made him see he had strengths he had not realized were there. Kim had also given him some insight into both Japanese and Korean treatment of prisoners. He figured the Chinese would be much the same. They would use his own fears against himself. A trial for his crimes, Major Han had threatened. The worst would be a firing squad, unless the cold got him first. So, he would survive, if for no other reason than to show that he could. They might win some battles, but he was going to win the war. He was going to survive. Unless they shot him, or he froze to death.

On his second meeting with Major Han, he was brought into a room in the headquarters building with a chair in the middle and a long table near the far wall. Four men sat there, Major Han and two others in Chinese uniforms and one Korean officer. To the left was a small table with a bowl of steaming rice and a pot of tea. The Goon Squad positioned themselves just behind the chair. Swede immediately felt the warmth of the room and a burning hunger in his stomach.

Major Han shuffled through some papers in front of him. "Your name is Pole Lawson?"

Swede was aware the Geneva Convention said a Prisoner of War was only obligated to give his name, rank, and serial number. He and Master Sergeant Randall had talked about it at length. They had both filled out cards with exactly that information months before in Seoul. He was also aware the Convention had strict guidelines on how prisoners of war were to be treated. So far, those guidelines had pretty much been ignored. He now had to start considering just what information he would give his questioners, more importantly, what information he would not give them. There was no one in this room who was going to offer him unbiased advice. He was on his own.

"Yes, that is correct." Swede decided not to volunteer anything beyond answering the question. And he sure wasn't going to correct the Major's pronunciation of his name.

"You are a private?"

"Yes, that is correct."

"You are an escaped prisoner. You are a spy?" The major did not change his expression when he asked the question.

Where the hell did that come from? "I am a soldier in the United States Army." Swede tried not to show any expression himself. Try not to show any weakness, he told himself.

"You were captured all alone, with no other American soldiers, and you were attempting to find the location of a Chinese column you knew was in the area. Are you not a spy?" Han did not seem to be making an accusation, just asking a question.

Swede decided to tell only what he had already told the Chinese colonel who had talked to him when he had walked away from the village. He explained he had not escaped; he had been left by the guards because he was sick. He was still sick when he was found on the road but had no recollection of the events from the time he was left in the village until he came to in the North Korean army medical tent. He ended with, "I am grateful for their treatment."

Major Han looked down at the papers in front of him again and said something to the others at the table. "Do you admit to theft of property of the Korean People's Army?"

Swede realized the wording of the question meant the Major was not asking about taking the packs or the vegetables from the villages. There had been only villagers there. He could only imagine the reference was to his blanket.

"This blanket is marked property of the US. It was given to me by a Korean guard when we left the medical tent." Everything he had said so far was true.

For the first time the Major raised his voice. "You must confess to your crime! You will return to your cell and consider. Then you will confess because you wish to remove your guilt."

Back in his cell Swede understood the whole thing had been a sham. They kept him in the room just long enough to begin to feel warm and just long enough to smell real food. But he had no idea if he was really supposed to confess to something or if that was just an excuse to make him worry about what was next. A week went by before he was brought before the officers again. This time they gave him a small cup of tea before asking if he was ready to confess. The tea was hot and rich, its warmth and flavor almost overwhelming. Pure pleasure spread to every cell in his body. He tried not to show any expression as he drank but knew it was impossible. They hadn't decided to treat him better; it was just part of their game.

The Major smiled and showed Swede a paper, written in Chinese, and asked him to sign as his confession. He had been willing to fill out the card with name, rank, and serial number, but he didn't think signing something written in Chinese was wise. So back to his cell he went, the warmth from the tea disappearing before they got halfway there.

Another week, during which it got even colder (something Swede didn't think was possible) and he was back in front of the Major. This time he tried to draw out the process. He took his time drinking the tea. When presented with the paper, Swede asked if the Major would read it to him in English. Instead of the Major responding, another of the Chinese spoke to him. He was small and unhappy looking. Swede took him for a clerk who was waiting to have the paper signed so he could make copies and file it away.

"You shurd not be impurdinint! We only try to help you. Do you like live in cell? Do you like smell like pig? Why you do not take best care of you? Do duty of shoulder and confess!" This officer seemed puzzled by Swede's lack of enthusiasm in the whole process.

"Of course I smell like a pig! I haven't been given any soap or water to bathe in since I was captured! You keep me in a tiny cell with no heat! The Geneva Convention says I only have to give you my name, rank, and serial number. It's not my duty to sign a paper I don't understand." If the bastard was going to talk about how bad he smelled, Swede was going to make sure he knew why he smelled. Maybe these men didn't know how he was being treated.

Major Han looked beyond Swede and gave a slight nod. Swede came to as he was being dragged out of the building, wondering why his head hurt. On his next trip he, confessed to stealing the blanket.

"You lie! You do not confess to real crime. Maybe we treat you too well. You must consider on your crime and remove your guilt." The Major threw the papers on the table in front of him and left the room as if he was disgusted with this smelly American.

By then the smelly American had been in his cell a month. The Goons had gotten a little meaner each time he refused to confess whatever he was supposed to confess. Then somebody decided a little extra effort on their part would help the smelly American "consider his crime."

Harry and Norm came again that night. It was pitch black, but he recognized their smell. They shoved him out of the cell, tied his hands behind his back, threw a noose around his neck, and tossed the rope over a beam above. Norm dragged a chair in from the outer room and made it clear he expected Swede to stand on it. When he refused, both guards started pulling so violently on the rope he had no choice but to step up. They wrapped the end around one of the bars in his cell and began pulling again. When they had Swede standing on his toes, they tied the rope off. Then they left the room, laughing. There had been no smell of alcohol. This wasn't their standard drunken behavior.

After only a few minutes his calf muscles started complaining. He relaxed a little to see if he could use his neck muscles to support himself. He found the guards had placed the rope so that a knot pressed against his throat when he relaxed. It looked like these guys were serious. Hopefully, he could hold up for the thirty minutes or so before they came back and asked if he was ready to write whatever statement they had in mind.

The thirty minutes was tough. Then he had to hold out another thirty. His muscles were no longer complaining; they were screaming. His legs were shaking violently. *The only way he was going to suffocate was if he gave up. There was only his will between life and death.* Relaxing one foot to give the other leg a break worked, but only for a few minutes. Then he had to switch or go back to standing on the toes of both feet.

These guys are more than serious. This is bad. They are going for an hour or more before they come back with their offer. But they didn't come back. He was drenched in sweat, his whole body shaking. He could not relax his body, so he tried to relax his mind by focusing on a spot on the window. It was too dark to see anything. Swede was left with just the voice in his head telling him to stay awake, stay upright. *Don't quit.* Had the guards taken his shoes, he would not have made it through the night. His shoes gave him just enough support to keep from collapsing.

Sweat dripped down into his eyes, then down to his beard where it froze. Swede had been asleep when they came for him, so he had no idea what time his ordeal had started. He just knew he would have to make it to morning, however long that would take. Twice he fell asleep and was forced awake by his own gurgling. He thought about trying to get his feet on the back of the chair but realized he would only knock it over. He tried getting at the knot to untie his hands but had no luck. That effort at least took his mind away from constant thought about the time. That realization led him to doing simple math in his head.

Dawn finally poked its way through the window, but it was still a while before the sun came up. People woke up then. *They would come for him soon. Only a minute more, then another.* He had no legs, just pain.

His body shook from the cold of his sweat-soaked clothes. Just one more minute. When Swede finally heard the outer door open and the clump of boots on the wooden floor, he almost cried. He recognized the sound of Cheechee's boots on the floor. *It was over! He had made it!*

Cheechee let out a roar when he came into the room to check on his prisoner. He ran over to Swede, grabbed him by the legs, and lifted him up, all the while yelling for help. Then Happy and finally the Goons came running in. Once they had the rope untied from the cell bars and got Swede down, Cheechee noticed his hands tied behind his back. He apparently thought Swede had attempted suicide, but you don't tie your own hands behind your back. He looked at Harry and Norm and started asking questions, his voice getting louder as they refused to answer. Cheechee finally chased the two out and yelled some commands to Happy. As Happy left the room the Goons returned - with Major Han. Cheechee started complaining to the Major but was himself ordered out of the room.

Turning to Swede, still on the floor, Major Han said, "I must ask your forgiveness. I did not realize my men had treated you so terribly. Can you accept my apologies?"

Swede managed to give a hint of a nod.

The Major continued, "But I think perhaps you also owe me an apology. You make my task here difficult. Sometimes the guards see my frustrations and act unwisely. I am responsible for their actions. When you are foolish, you bring problems like this upon yourself and I feel great discomfort. Do you think you might offer such an apology for bringing me this discomfort?"

Without any hesitation, Swede managed that nod again.

"Perhaps you would be willing to remove your guilt" Again, a nod.

"I will return, and we will discuss this issue." With that, Han walked out. The Goons dragged Swede back to his cell and locked him in, hands still tied behind his back. He curled up on the floor and fell asleep from exhaustion.

When he woke, Swede wasn't sure how long he had been on the ground. From the angle of the light rays bouncing off the dust, it was probably near noon. His legs were still cramped and painful. He stretched out and worked on loosening the muscles. The Goons came into the building, followed by Major Han. Han walked in and stood in front of Swede's cell. His look was clear. 'I am in charge. You can't win this fight.'

Seeming to notice Swede's hands still tied behind his back, the Major turned to the guards and started yelling. They hustled from the building.

Han turned back to Swede. "I must apologize once again. I did not realize they left you tied and did not bring your morning meal. I will give you time to eat. Then we shall talk." Then he walked out again.

Swede was left with his hands still tied behind his back. When the guards returned, they placed a bowl of rice and a bowl of tea on the ground in front of him. They made no move to untie his hands. It took Swede a while to understand what was going on. He didn't believe for a minute the guards had done any of this without Han's specific orders. He got down on the ground and proceeded to eat and drink like a dog - an animal. Han was making sure Swede understood his situation. When he was finished, the guards picked up the bowls, untied his hands, and left the room laughing. As Swede picked himself up off the floor, beard full of rice kernels, Han returned. He brought the chair over to the bars and placed a paper and pen on it.

"Perhaps your signature would ensure no further mistakes by my guards. It would cause me great pain to see harm come to you because they interpret your attitude incorrectly."

Swede had no idea what was written on the paper. It could be a proclamation that Harry Truman was Hitler's sister. He didn't care. He knew he didn't have the strength to survive the consequences of not signing. Swede signed, but spelled his last name with an e instead of an o. It gave him only a tiny bit of satisfaction. The Major smiled, but his eyes still said, 'I am in charge.' Swede's day returned to normal, almost as if nothing unusual had happened.

The next few days and nights Swede spent his time shivering almost uncontrollably. He could feel the weakness increasing every day. And he knew it was more than a physical weakness. Self-doubt was becoming his biggest enemy. *He had failed. He had signed a confession, maybe a petition. He didn't know. They never really intended to let him hang himself. They had been waiting outside to release the rope if he started choking. He should have lasted longer! He had failed himself, Mike Randall, the Army, his parents! He could have lasted longer! He should have lasted longer!* Then reality would come back into focus and he knew better. In the end, he found some comfort in the fact he had not quit, they had taken him down.

Something about the whole situation made him think he was an experiment for the Chinese. It was the Chinese who seemed to be in charge now, not the North Koreans. Maybe the Chinese would never be satisfied with whatever he confessed to. Maybe they wanted to see how far they could push him. That might mean they were willing to let him starve, or freeze, or hang, whichever came first. And if they didn't start feeding him better, one of the first two was going to happen soon. They might be able to find a way to force him to sign one statement or another, but that didn't mean he had to give up. That night Swede escaped again.

When he had first arrived at Cheechee's Palace, Swede realized two of the lock picks Sook had made were still in his pocket. There was a space of a few inches between the bars on the back of his cell and the outer wall of the building. He had tucked the picks into the far corner of that space. Unless someone came into his cell, went to the very back, and ran their hand along the floor of that tiny space, they would never notice the picks lying there covered in dust. The day he realized he might die soon got him thinking about his need for food. That got him to thinking about the storage shed he and Sook had broken into. There had to be food stored here too. Then he remembered his lock picks - and Kim's comment about looking beyond what his eyes could see. It might be a good time to dig out the picks and see if he could look beyond. As far as he knew, except for the one time, the guards never came in his building late at night. The picks meant he could get out of his cell and see if checking other buildings for food was possible. He waited until he was sure it was after midnight, recovered the picks, and with just a few tries, had his cell door open.

There were six more cells like his along the wall with a narrow corridor running in front of them. All six were empty. In the space opposite his cell stood the five small cages. To the left and between his cell and the cages, was a door leading to the other room. That room was small, dusty, and dirty like his cell area, with a small table and chair. The door leading out was not locked, but Swede didn't plan to leave just yet. He assumed he needed a snowstorm to cover his tracks, like the night he and Sook had raided the shed. He did spend time looking out the window to see if the area was patrolled at all.

Two days later, a snowstorm hit and lasted well into the night.

Swede left his cell and quickly made his way into a building directly across from his. Once he adjusted to the dark, he found himself in a tool shed of some kind. A quick search for food was a bust, but he did find some rags and a small knife. Figuring he had pressed his luck he made his way back to his cell and locked himself in. He hadn't seen a soul. The next trick would be to check when there was no storm to see if guards wandered around at night. But first, he had to hide the knife and rags.

The next night Swede set about fashioning the rags into foot wraps and crude mitts. The wraps went under his boots and pant legs and would be hard to spot. Even if the guards did spot them, they had no real way to know they were new. They hadn't done any kind of inspection when he first got there, thus he still had the lock picks. The mitts he could keep in his pockets and simply shove his hands in them. Keeping his hands in his pockets would be normal in the cold. The knife went into the dust at the back of his cell and the picks back in his pocket.

With the blanket over his neck and head and the new socks and mitts, Swede was a little more comfortable at night. Still cold and shivering, sometimes uncontrollably, his heart was warmer knowing he managed to outwit his captors just a little bit. During the next two nights he got out of his cell but did not leave the building. He wanted to be sure the guards didn't move through the area when it was not storming. As far as he could tell they did not. He saw no movement of any kind. The only light he could see came from beyond HQ. Every now and then he heard a vehicle. He also realized he did not have to wait for snowstorms to leave the jail. There were worn paths in the snow leading up to every building he could see. His tracks would just blend in.

On the third night, he went looking for food and hit the jackpot. The second building he tried had sacks of rice from floor to ceiling. Swede wasn't sure how healthy it would be to eat uncooked rice. He knew rats and mice were probably running around, but getting sick was a better alternative than starving. He plunged his hand as deep into a bag of rice as he could and pulled out a fistful. The hole in the bag was probably made by rats, but by digging down he hoped there would be no contamination. One fistful would increase his food intake by a third, so he didn't push his luck. Eating raw rice was a risk, but a fistful of any food in the middle of the night would warm his core and help him fight off the below zero temperatures. He planned to return every night he could.

Major Han had other plans. The next morning Swede found himself in front of the major and his friends, this time wanting a detailed description of Swede's unit in Japan, including names. Swede said he had only arrived there two days before coming to Korea. He knew only his corporal's last name. The major looked at him and said, "Perhaps you need more time to consider your attitude." Swede was returned immediately to his cell building and forced into one of the small cages instead of his cell. His blanket was yanked from his arms and tossed into his old cell. The cage did not have enough room for him to stand up or stretch out. He knew he was in trouble when the guards didn't bring any supper that evening. The next morning, after bringing his meal, Cheechee didn't take him to the outhouse. And Swede had thought it couldn't get any worse.

With only one small meal a day and no blanket to help with the cold Swede knew he would not last long. He wasn't new to extreme cold. Twice a day, all winter long, he had helped with the milking and care of the livestock at home. But he went out in the cold wearing long johns, woolen pants and shirt, heavy coat, gloves, and a thick woolen hat. When he got too cold, he would go in the warm house for a steaming mug of hot chocolate. Now he found himself in a different universe. There was no wool clothing, no long johns, no hot chocolate. Any pain he had experienced before came from cold fingers or toes. Now his entire body felt that way.

The cold was a living creature. Each night it worked its way quickly into his cell and sank its icy fangs into him and wouldn't let go. Everywhere his clothing touched his skin brought burning pain. Then he began to lose feeling in his hands and feet. Shivering set in as the fangs moved to reach every muscle, every nerve, in his body. When he couldn't stop shivering, the creature sent icy fingers deeper to crush his soul.

At that point, Swede had two choices. Curl up as best he could and let his brain shut down or get up and move. Curling up was easy. Getting up was painful. Movement simply reminded him of how cold he was. But if he got off the floor and moved, he could eventually feel the creature withdrawing its fangs. If he was in his cell, he could walk in place, three steps one way and three steps back. He could march in place while swinging his arms. He could get down and do push-ups. In the animal cage, he tried what he called camel push-ups, as it was impossible to stretch full out. All of that burned calories which he couldn't afford. Burn calories he did not have or let the creature squeeze him into an endless sleep.

It was not easy. Choosing to live took energy he did not have. That made him sleepy, which made it harder to know when he needed to get up again and move. Swede would find himself dreaming of warm clothes and hot chocolate and feel warmer. Then he would realize he was dreaming and force himself to get up and fight. Sooner or later he would start to fall asleep and the whole sequence would repeat.

The second night in the cage Swede realized he had little choice but to find more food and even a blanket. If they caught him, they might shoot him, but without more food and a blanket, he was dead in a few days anyhow. He was sure his toes were frost-bitten or worse. His ankle and ears were almost numb to the touch. The rest of his body just hurt. The movement of his clothes felt like a knife dragging across his skin. No matter what he did, parts of his body were up against the cold steel bars of the cage. He needed to do something while he still could. He had to take risks while he was still able.

The picks were still in his pocket. He opened the cage door, grabbed his blanket from the other cell, and headed for the rice storage shed. A fistful of rice and his stomach was full. Then he set out to find other food or something to use for an extra blanket, staying in the area behind HQ. There was no smoke coming from any of the small buildings around the jail, which should mean there were no people in them. He just had to hope no one came wandering through while he was wandering about.

When he opened the door of his third shed, Swede thought he had made a major mistake. As soon as the door opened, he figured he was in a barracks. He could *smell* the guards. As he started backing out without waking anybody up, he realized the door of a barracks would not be locked from the outside. It smelled like the guards because the shed was full of garlic. He grabbed a handful of cloves and ate them right there. The guards would not notice the smell of garlic on his breath because they themselves smelled so strongly of garlic. And eating garlic should be healthier than eating raw rice.

There were no more sheds or buildings near the jail to check so Swede moved beyond the headquarters building. He had never gone that far before. There was no choice but to walk out in the open on the paths made by people moving about during the day. Sneaking along the edge of a building would leave obvious tracks that might arouse suspicion. There were several vehicles parked in front of the larger building. There was also a light above the front door. Swede checked carefully to see if anyone was nearby and then crawled under the closest vehicle and waited. Laying in the snow wasn't how he wanted to spend his time, but he was sure there would be guards in this area. There might be no reason for guards to patrol in front of his building. He was locked in. But this was in front of headquarters and he was sure there would be guards somewhere.

In just minutes he could hear and then see two guards approaching down the road, one from each direction. As they met in front of the building, they each performed an about-face and retraced their steps back down the road. Swede stayed put as they marched away from him and counted to himself to estimate how much time it would take for them to reach the end of their posted area and return. It took them close to ten minutes to meet again in front of the building. When they were out of sight again, Swede looked in the back of the three trucks and found nothing. Next, he looked in the two jeeps. Jammed behind the back seat of one, he found a blanket. Grabbing it, he crawled under the nearest truck. The guards were due back. This time when they met in front of the building they did not immediately about-face and continue their post. They stood quietly talking and sharing a cigarette, almost as if they were waiting for something. Swede didn't smoke, but if they had offered him one, he would have started right there just for the warmth.

Just as they finished the cigarette and flicked the butt away, they both popped to attention and saluted a third figure approaching through the dark. The three exchanged some remarks and the two guards hustled off in the direction the third man had come from. They each returned carrying some kind of bag over their shoulder and approached the truck Swede was hiding under. One of them climbed up into the back of the truck and the other handed the two bags up to him. Then both went to the front of the vehicle and opened the hood. The third man jumped into the driver's seat and all three jabbered back and forth. They were either stealing the truck or there were no keys to start the engine. Finally, one of the men tinkering up front yelled something to the driver and the engine cranked slowly to life. The guards closed the hood and stood saluting as the driver backed out. Once he was gone, they walked to the middle of the road and marched off into the dark.

Swede crawled out from under the next truck. With all the noise of opening the hood and poking around in the engine, no one had noticed him rolling out from under their truck to the next one. Even wrapped in his new blanket he was cold. He stood up and marched back to his building like he was on guard duty himself. Sneaking around would get him noticed sooner than walking calmly down the path.

For the next few days Swede stuffed himself with rice and garlic each night, sometimes adding a few handfuls of snow to increase his liquid intake. Every morning he was awake before the guards came in. His original blanket was back in the cell and the new one stuffed down between the back of his cage and the outer wall. He was standing at attention as required. That meant standing bent over at the waist in the three-foot high cage.

The extra food and a blanket at night made his life a little better. The fact he was using the front of the cage as his toilet didn't help much, but they still weren't taking him to the latrine. The cold meant everything froze and kept the smell down. But he still needed to get back to his old cell and routine. When he finally was taken to the headquarters building again, he was hopeful they would ask for something he could give them.

There was no tea or rice in the room when he was taken before the Four Stooges. As soon as the Major asked if he had considered his attitude Swede asked if he could have pencil and paper to write out his thoughts. This request brought a smile to the face of even the small Chinese clerk. Paper and pencil were quickly produced. Swede was given a chair and led to a table on the other side of the room. He scrawled out a few words and then apologized for not being able to write.

"My fingers are cold, and I am weak because I have not been taking care of myself lately," Swede said to the Major with a straight face. With a snap of the Major's fingers hot tea and rice were produced from the next room. It was the good stuff again and Swede drank slowly. He was forced to use his fingers to eat the rice but was sure that was deliberate. The tea and rice had been ready before he even came in the room, just in case he was ready to "consider his attitude."

Swede tried to lay it on thick enough to make the Four Stooges happy without being too obvious. He apologized for not seeing the truth earlier. He admitted to having a poor attitude but blamed it on American schools for not teaching their students properly. He hoped he could do better in the days ahead as a guest of the Korean people. Perhaps he could learn more about the Korean people and their ways and come to see how American capitalism was not good for the world. He confessed to being ignorant and apologized for being so stubborn. Swede hoped they were looking for something along those lines, because if not, he was screwed.

Of course, all that writing required two more cups of tea. The Major even threw in a small cookie. After translating his writing for the other Stooges, Major Han gave the guards some instructions and then said to Swede, "Lawson, return to your cell now. We will consider your thoughts."

Swede wasn't sure if he had won that round until Cheechee opened his cell instead of the cage. He quickly wrapped himself in his old blanket and stretched full out on the floor. When Happy brought in supper he knew he was good, at least for a while. After his food run that night, he retrieved his other blanket from the cage. He wasn't warm, but the blankets meant he slept without the worry of freezing to death. Every time the cold forced him awake, he readjusted the blankets and went back to sleep, hoping to dream of warm clothes and hot chocolate.

The Chinese Way
Winter 1950-51

Two days later, Cheechee escorted him to HQ again. Only three Stooges sat at the table. The Korean officer was gone. There was no tea or food on the small table to the left, but there were two chairs there. Major Han stood. Swede figured he was about to hear a verdict of some kind or maybe how unhappy they were with his confession from a few days before. Maybe they knew he was sneaking out at night and the Major was about to drop the axe. At least it was warm in the room.

"Lawson, perhaps it would be good for us to talk, to get to know each other better. Perhaps we have some things in common. Tell me about your life." With that, the Major picked up some papers and motioned Swede towards the table and two chairs. "Please, sit." No mention of any confession, his crimes, breaking out of his cell. Just, 'let's chat.' Swede had no idea what was going on, but maybe he could get some more tea and rice out of the deal. He would have to be careful. Nothing was free around there.

It didn't take long for the conversation to turn sour. When he said his parents owned eighty acres Major Han didn't believe him. "You mean they helped work the fields for the village." When he said they owned a tractor and a truck the Major interjected, "You mean they used the village machinery when it was their turn to do so." He couldn't tell if the Major was serious in those remarks. *Apparently,* Swede meant the village allowed them to keep some money when the crops were sold in the fall. *Apparently,* he meant his father was forced to leave school by the "committee" when he mentioned he had an eighth-grade education. *Apparently,* his mother never went to high school but stayed home to help her parents work the fields.

As the Major went on correcting him about life at home, Swede noticed an odor in the room. Then he realized he was the source. The Major inched his chair further away. The other Stooges began wrinkling their noses. Even Cheechee seemed to betray him as he moved to the other side of the room. Finally, the old clerk growled out, "You are mistaken in your memories. Remain here and write. Tell us about your village. We will have tea and rice brought to you to help improve your memory." With that, all but Cheechee left. He grinned at Swede and followed the Stooges through the inner door only to return with the promised tea and rice.

Swede decided to simply explain life at home without trying to change details to fit the image of the Stooges. Hopefully, any disbelief on their part would lead to more discussions in a warm room with plenty of tea and rice. Cheechee didn't seem to be in a hurry to lead Swede back into the cold, so the story of life on the farm took the rest of the day. Only the one bowl of rice appeared but his bowl of tea was kept full. When they finally got back to his cell, Happy brought in his supper. It wasn't hot, but it wasn't cold. It had been a good day.

Over the next few weeks life went up and down. When he would not describe his life the way the Major wanted him to, he was sent back to the cage for being "impurdinint."

When asked to write about "the Negro race in America" he explained where he grew up there was no one of the "Negro race." Major Han asked instead for information about the "Red man in America." Swede wrote about his friend Jimmy Eagle. Before he was old enough to help much on the farm, Swede spent lots of time hunting and fishing with Jimmy. It was because of Jimmy that Swede first looked at his father as someone other than his father. Jimmy told Swede he was allowed to spend so much time around the Larson home because his father, Gray Eagle, trusted Swede's family. Whenever they hired him as an extra hand, he was expected to sit at their table for meals. They never cheated him on his pay. He was treated as an equal. After hearing that, Swede paid more attention to how his parents and uncles treated those around them. He became aware of prejudice. But he wasn't about to explain that to the Major, so he wrote about throwing stones at rabbits. Swede got the feeling Major Han was disappointed with the lack of information on how terribly the "Red man" was treated in America.

When Swede admitted he was brand new to the Army and knew little beyond his corporal's name, the Major seemed downright despondent. From that point on, Swede played the ignorant farm boy. He wrote pages on how to plant and harvest corn and even more on cutting trees for firewood. Some days he spent in the cage, other days in his cell. After a while it seemed he was forgotten. He was in his cell most of the time and back to two meals a day with a latrine break in the morning.

Swede wasn't sure if he was winning the game or not. He hadn't told the Chinese anything important, mostly because he really didn't know anything important, but wasn't sure what if he had told them too much about Americans in general. He had played the game as well as he could. He was getting regular meals, as meager as they were, twice a day. But he was still stealing food at night and still hiding his extra blanket during the day. He still had lice, and still no bath. Stalemate was probably the best he had managed so far in this game.

Boredom and loneliness became new problems. To help, Swede spent more time at night exploring the area around his building. He was sure he could steal a truck or jeep if he wanted, but then what? He had no idea where he was. What direction should he drive? And exactly how far would he get? He did loosen a few oil plugs. He tried dumping dirt in gas tanks but couldn't scrape up enough dirt from the frozen ground. He was careful on his night excursions, but soon realized no one expected him to be wandering about, so no one bothered to check.

During the days he wasn't called to the headquarters building to write about the Negro race or the red man or how much money factory workers earned, Swede took to carving a design on the wooden wall of his cell. It was what he remembered from some scrimshaw given to him by Mike Finnegan, a family friend - an island scene from the South Seas.

Mike Finnegan came to the US from Ireland in 1877 at age twelve, the oldest of five children. His parents thought they had paid their fare from Kilrush to Milwaukee. Upon arrival in New York aboard the *Devonia*, they found they had been cheated. There were no train tickets to Milwaukee. Both Hugh and Bridget Finnegan had grown up during the Famine. They understood the pain of losing family members. They understood sacrifice to benefit the family. Hugh and Bridget sold their son Michael to the shipmaster of the *Devonia*.

Robert Munro saw a way to help both his family and the Finnegans. He and his wife had no children of their own, so she often traveled with him on board the *Devonia*. Having a young boy capable of working as a cabin boy would help make the long days easier for Mrs. Munro. The money he gave the Finnegans was just enough to get them to Milwaukee where they would stay with a cousin. He thought of the transaction as hiring a servant for a period of time. His understanding was he would correspond regularly with the parents about their son. They would make arrangements for the boy to join them when the *Devonia* next docked in New York. So young Michael Finnegan went to sea.

Bridget Finnegan had taught Michael to read and write. Robert Munro gave him an education. Munro loved to read and carried on board a variety of books, adding more at each port. Michael was expected to carry out his duties as cabin boy, and eventually seaman, but also attend 'school' by reading and discussing the books assigned by Munro and his wife. He excelled at both tasks.

For the next fifty some years, Mike Finnegan traveled the world from New York to New Delhi, from Shanghai to San Francisco. He sailed up the Amazon and down the Nile, eventually becoming a master mariner. Mike had no formal education but spoke four languages and could fluently discuss the world's politics, religions, cultures, authors, and artists. His last voyage in 1930 had taken him up the St. Lawrence and through the Great Lakes to Superior. From there he made his way to Minneota to live with Hannah, his recently widowed sister. (Given the mystery and allure of his past there were those who said she wasn't a "sister" at all.)

Swede's mother had become good friends with Hannah from church activities. As a result, Mike Finnegan became a familiar face to the Larson family and a frequent visitor to their home. Having no children of his own, Mike took on the role of extra grandfather to Swede and his brothers and sister. He encouraged their youthful curiosity about everything, never too busy to explain where the sticks they threw in the river ended up or where robins went in the winter. It was probably Mike Finnegan's stories of adventures around the world that planted the idea of joining the Army to see the world in

Swede's head.

Mike was too beat up from years at sea to help much with physical labor, but he could fix just about anything. And he could play cards. Any game you knew and plenty you didn't. He never played for money, but it was obvious from his stories he had in the past - successfully. Many winter evenings Swede's father and uncles would gather in the kitchen to play. Mike often just watched and told stories but every now and then pulled up to the table himself. When that happened, the cry went up from the others, "Uh oh, Finnegan's in." Or, "The Finn's in." Meaning look sharp, you're in trouble now!

Carving Mike Finnegan's South Sea island scene gave Swede something to occupy his time and helped keep positive thoughts in his mind. The wooden wall he was using for his canvas was hard enough to require some effort. That helped keep Swede warm without using too many calories. Either because they didn't care or because it was a simple carving the guards never seemed to notice. When he finally finished his two-foot by three-foot masterpiece he signed it "Finnegan was here."

A few weeks later Swede was back in the cage because he had used the term "South" Korea when explaining what he knew of how the war had started. He didn't even get to the part about the north invading the south before the Three Stooges threw a fit and sent him away to "think on the truth." By this time, he figured it was late February or even March and the below zero temperatures were behind him. Nothing else had changed but at least he didn't worry about freezing to death as he slept. He wasn't warm, but he only woke up two or three times a night from the cold.

On one of his late-night scouting expeditions, Swede noticed some different looking vehicles parked outside a small building just down from headquarters. They looked like delivery trucks, all closed in. One had some pipes or tubes on the roof that looked like they could turn. The markings weren't American and didn't look like Korean or Chinese. The next logical choice was Russian, so he decided to limit exploring at night. The Chinese had never noticed he moved around a limited area at night, but if Russians were in the neighborhood, that was a new factor. They might have a whole different idea of posting guards. So, he limited his nightly excursions to getting extra food.

After a few days of "thinking on the truth" Swede was called back for more discussion. He continued to get the feeling he was being used in an experiment. Would he say what the Stooges wanted him to say? Was he more agreeable after freezing or starving? Could the Goons change his mind? Major Han introduced the latest topic for discussion in the experiment.

"Why did you invade the Democratic People's Republic of Korea?" No good morning, no would you like some hot tea, no why don't you sit next to the fire. Just a quick question as all three Stooges sat there with scowls on their faces, as if Swede was responsible for the whole war. Swede had a sense of being on thin ice with his answer.

"When I was captured, I was far south of the city of Seoul. I was brought to the Democratic People's Republic by Korean soldiers. I did not invade anyone." Swede understood this was not the answer they were looking for and didn't intend to try to come up with the right answer, whatever that might eventually be.

"You came to Korea! You shot Korean soldiers! They did not go to America and shoot American soldiers! Why did you invade the Democratic People's Republic of Korea? You must speak the truth!" By this time Major Han was standing up and waving his arms. "Always you have an excuse! You must speak the truth! If you cannot speak the truth you will never return to your home!"

That night the Goons came for Swede again. He was asleep when they slammed through the doors and dragged him from the cell. When he realized what was happening, Swede assumed he was about to be strung up by his neck again. Then they dragged him outside and tied his wrists to a beam overhead. It was very dark, and very cold. Once they had him tied securely, one of them picked up a bucket of water sitting nearby and dumped it over Swede's head, laughing all the while. Then they both walked away.

Even the Buddha's meditation lessons didn't help that night. The pain from constant shivering and the chattering of his teeth was too much to focus on a warm memory. The only thing that saved Swede was his habit of wrapping his smaller blanket around his torso under his uniform when he slept. The blanket was wool, and even with ice forming in his hair and on his uniform, it kept his core temperature from dropping too low. Had the Goons noticed the blanket and taken it away, Swede would not have survived. Especially when they returned later and threw a second bucket of water on him.

Swede had no idea how long he was out in the cold that night. It was dark when they dragged him out of the cell, and dark when they finally took him down and dragged him back. As soon as his fingers could function, he took off the wet blanket and wrapped himself in the larger, dry blanket. The wet one he placed over the top and then curled himself into a fetal position.

Before they dumped him back in his cage the Goons had taken quite a few whacks at him with their clubs. When he finally started to feel a little warmth, Swede thought he was blind in one eye until he realized his hair was matted to his face with blood from his forehead. He managed to get his eye open by using saliva to wipe away the blood. One of the Goons had hit him hard enough to open a slice on his forehead. He knew he needed to clean it up to keep infection away but spitting in his filthy hand to clean the wound probably wasn't such a good idea. He had been lucky so far that using his fingers to eat hadn't gotten him sick. There was only one way to get any water to clean his hands. So Swede peed on them. Once he had them clean, he wondered why he hadn't thought of that before - and how he was going to explain it all to his mother.

'How did you get that nasty scar on your head, dear?'

'Oh, that's nothing, it would have been a lot worse if I hadn't pissed on my hands before I cleaned it up.' But urine and spit did the job. The blood matted in his hair was nothing to worry about.

For three days he was pretty much ignored. Maybe the Stooges didn't want to see the results of the beating. He was only given some tea and rice for breakfast and allowed a latrine break once a day. On the third day, Cheechee escorted Swede back over to the headquarters building. No one was in the interrogation room. Cheechee led him to the desk and chair and motioned for him to sit. On the table was some blank paper and a pencil. At that point Major Han came into the room with something in his hand.

"Read this newspaper clipping about the United Nations invading the Democratic People's Republic of Korea. Read how the Chinese People's Volunteer Army has come to their aid. Then write your feelings. Be sure to speak the truth."

Then both the major and Cheechee were gone. Swede didn't know how many more hangings, beatings, and nights strung up as a human popsicle he could survive. He knew if he wrote his true feelings, they would stand him against a wall and shoot him. But he wasn't about to roll over and play Commie.

The newspaper clipping came from the Saturday March 17th edition of the Manchester Guardian. Other news had been trimmed off. Swede had only the article he was supposed to read with an article on the reverse side about the bell ringers of Oldham.

####

UN Forces Invade the Democratic People's Republic of Korea

The imperialistic actions of Truman, the man who dropped two atomic bombs on innocent civilians in Japan, carried out by the notorious General MacArthur, have led to the United Nations illegally and immorally sending armed forces across the border into the Democratic People's Republic of Korea. It is well known that puppet leader Rhee and his army have long desired to occupy and control the People's Republic. This desire led to his forces openly invading the peace-loving Democratic People's Republic of Korea on the 24th of June 1950 and then appealing to their unwitting friends at the UN in New York for help, claiming they had been the victims. The Imperialist Truman sent his large army and air forces across the border into the Democratic People's Republic of Korea, a clear violation of UN resolution 112 from 1947. In truth, Truman was simply acting on the desire of his puppet Syngman Rhee to rule all of Korea.

Peace-loving people across the world quickly saw what was really happening-the puppet Rhee and imperialist Truman were attempting to take by force what they had been denied at the end of the war in 1945. These peace-loving people have appealed for

help for their brothers and sisters in the
Democratic People's Republic of Korea. Soon
village after village in China offered
volunteers and the People's Volunteer Army
of China has been formed. In November this
army crossed the Yalu River and successfully
forced the foreign invaders to retreat. When
the Chinese Volunteers and the Korean
People's Army had bravely thrown the foreign
invaders out the Yankee dominated UN
convinced a few other countries to foolishly
offer their armies and only with the help of
these new warmongers were the Americans able
to once again threaten invasion of the
Democratic People's Republic of Korea.

The brave men and women of the People's
Volunteer Army of China and the Korean
People's Army will never allow this to
happen again. They will prevail against the
imperialistic actions of the unlawful body
formed by the colonial efforts of Roosevelt
and Churchill with their plans to control
peace-loving people across the globe.

"Write your feelings and be sure to speak the truth." Swede could
see he was going to have to be careful here. The *Guardian* seemed to
be a paper that supported China and North Korea. He had no idea as
to who invaded who, or even whom. He didn't doubt the North
Koreans had been in the wrong but could never back that up with
any facts. He had no idea who this Syngman Rhee was but guessed
there had been a United Nations resolution to divide Korea and Rhee
was the leader of the South. He now knew the US had crossed the
border into the North and was pushed back by the Chinese, just as
Colonel Li had told him so long ago. And it looked like the whole
UN was pushing the Chinese back north again. It also seemed there
were a lot of peace-loving people in the world. Probably just as
peace-loving as his friends the Goons. Most importantly, Swede now

knew it was some time after March 17th.

Now what? It was obvious to him the part about the South invading the North was a lie. He had arrived in Korea just three weeks after the supposed invasion and the North Korean army was pushing everybody back with ease. If the South had invaded, they surely hadn't planned well. His unit had been rushed there with no preparation. That all seemed more like a reaction to being invaded than being the invaders. How was he going to "write his feelings" without hurting the feelings of the Stooges? He was only getting one meal a day and the Goons had apparently been told to quit pulling their punches. How many more beatings could he take from them without getting a serious injury?

Swede read the article a few more times, looking for information about the status of the war he might have missed. He sat back and thought about how he might call himself "peace-loving" without seeming to call the US a "warmonger." Then he realized he could smell food. He decided looking for food was more important than "writing his feelings." Opening the door used by Cheechee to bring in tea and rice, Swede found himself in a hallway that led only to the left. Following his nose, he found Cheechee and a kitchen. Cheechee was drinking tea and watching the cooks when Swede walked in. Seeing the look of total surprise on Cheechee's face, Swede quickly made warming motions with his hands as if he could not write with such cold hands. Without a word, Cheechee pushed Swede out of the room and back down the hall to the interrogation room. There he rattled off what sounded like "Idiot, are you trying to get me in trouble?" He pointed to the chair and said, "Zoo ah! Zoo ah!" Swede figured that meant sit! or stay! so he did both and went back to pondering the article. In a flash Cheechee was back with a pot of tea. Then he jabbered at Swede some more while knocking on the door. He made drinking and eating motions and knocked on the door again. Swede nodded his head and replied with, "OK, OK." Maybe his day wasn't going to be so bad after all. It took a few hours and a few knocks on the door for more tea, but Swede finally came up with what he hoped the Major and the other Stooges would accept as "speaking the truth."

"People across the world should come to understand that violence is bad. Violence causes pain and suffering. Violence seldom brings positive change. And there is much to change in the world. Children live in poor houses with little food or water. Children are separated from their families by wars. They are left with no news and wonder about their families. All people should hope all invasions and wars can be stopped.

I cannot tell from only one newspaper article what is right and what is wrong. But I know all countries and all leaders should be brave and come together to talk, not to fight. A poet said we should take the road less traveled. The road to war and suffering is well traveled. Peace-loving people should take a different road, a road to peace and happiness, where we treat all others like we want them to treat us. Peace-loving people around the world should bear with each other and forgive one another."

Swede knew Uncle Kim would approve of his last sentence. Cheechee either highly approved of the document or was happy to get Swede out of the building without him roaming around anymore hallways. In any case it earned Swede two meals a day for the next few days. On the third day he was brought back to the interrogation room.

"Poetry poisons the mind. I have a book for you to read that will free your mind. You must learn the truth." Major Han pushed a thin book across the table to Swede.

"Read. Perhaps I can also find more newspapers so you can know right from wrong." Then he repeated himself, "You must learn the truth."

The book turned out to be *The Communist Manifesto* by Karl Marx. Swede would have read it, out of boredom if nothing else, but it was in French. Uncle Kim had taught him a little French but that didn't mean he could read it. More newspaper articles came, but they were all from the *Guardian*. Swede read all the articles and any other articles on either side of the page, hoping he would find something that would tell him how the war was going. All he noticed was there were no articles talking about victory of any kind. Which he considered to be good news.

Swede had the feeling he was being ignored or that Major Han and his Stooges had more important things to do. No one asked for his reaction to the book or the newspaper articles. Swede also noticed some differences in his nightly outings to the food shed. He got the sense the camp was busier. He saw and heard more vehicles. He began to feel more uneasy about leaving his cell and cut back to a few times a week. With two meals a day again, and the nasty cold mostly gone, it wasn't necessary to take the risk.

But what goes up must come down. Swede was finally brought before the Stooges and asked about the book and the newspaper articles. The Goons had been restless, and Swede had been the means for them to work off their excess energy. They hadn't left any new marks but had gotten in some heavy blows. The day before they had come into the cells just after his food was brought in. In the process of swatting him around, they had kicked his tea and rice all over. Swede's foul mood clouded his thinking as he was brought over from his cell to the interrogation room.

All three of the Stooges were there. Major Han asked Swede to give his opinion of what he had been given to read. Swede explained the book was in French and all the articles were from the same newspaper. He could not form a valid opinion with such limited information. The unhappy looking clerk immediately jumped up.

"Always you uncooperating! We give information, you do not read! Always you refusing to learn the truth!"

Swede immediately barked back, "Learn the truth! You don't care about any truth except for your version of truth. The truth is you starve me, freeze me, beat me, treat me like an animal, just so you can hear me agree with your idea of the truth. I don't know who started this war, I don't know who Syngman Rhee is, I don't even know who prints the *Guardian*! You want to hear your truth? Fine. South Korea invaded North Korea and the UN is not peace-loving enough. There! You have your truth!"

The little guy practically jumped across the table at Swede. "No South Korea, there is only Democratic People's Republic of Korea! You are ignorant stooge of Truman and MacArthur. We will not waste time on one so ignorant." With that, the little clerk stomped out of the room. Swede was still steaming, but he did notice the other two officers jumped to attention and remained there until the little guy was out of the room. Uh oh, it looked like the unhappy little clerk wasn't a clerk after all.

Major Han and the other Chinese officer looked more unhappy with the whole situation than they were upset with Swede. Major Han barked something at Cheechee, and Swede was soon back in the cage, not his cell. And then - nothing. No Goons, no loss of meals, not even a loss of his one trip a day to the latrine. He was just ignored. The Goons seemed to disappear. Happy seemed a little less happy than usual but that only lasted a few days and he was back to his normal self. But that was it. Was the experiment over? Were they giving up because he wouldn't give them what they wanted? Or had they gotten everything they wanted and now he would be left to rot? Or worse, shot?

After getting the newspaper article with a real date in it, Swede started keeping a calendar by scratching marks in his cell wall. He added two weeks on to the 17th to compensate for the time it would take to print a newspaper and then get it here, wherever here was. Thirty days has November, April, June, and September. All the rest have thirty-one except for February at twenty-eight. So he figured it was now the 10th of April. Since he was in the cage, he started a duplicate calendar on the floor so he could keep track wherever he happened to be.

With nothing to do and warmer weather, Swede had time to think about other things. Thinking of home did him no good, but he did often think about Ray Parker and Mike Randall and the others he had left behind in the column quite a few months back. The thought they had been in a real POW camp all winter made him feel less guilty for not getting through and sending a rescue force their way. At least they had warm beds and real food. And probably mail. Which brought him back to home and that didn't help. So, when Cheechee and the Goons dumped somebody in his old cell late one day, Swede welcomed the change of pace.

It had been a cold and wet couple of days. Shortly after dark one night, Swede heard some noise outside the building and then the door opening and people thumping across the floor towards the cells. Cheechee came first with the two Goons dragging someone between them. They opened Swede's big cell door and dumped their package on the floor. None of the three paid any attention to Swede all comfy across the way in his cage. The guards locked the cell door shut and left. Swede just sat and watched to see if his visitor would introduce himself. In the back of his mind, Swede wondered if this new person was a plant of some kind, placed in the cell to get information the Three Stooges could use against him. He let that thought sit in the back of his mind.

Happy came in later with Swede's supper. He also left a bowl of rice and a bowl of tea inside the new guy's cell. But the new guy never moved. Swede could hear him breathing, and sometimes maybe a moan, but other than that, he didn't move. Waiting until he was sure the guards were done for the night, Swede let himself out of his cage, wrapped both blankets around himself to ward off the chill, and moved over to check on the new prisoner. There was enough moonlight to see the new guy didn't look so good. His hands were wrapped in bandages and his face looked like he had gone a couple of rounds with Joe Louis. One pant leg was ripped from his knee down and it looked like he had a wound of some kind on the leg. The uniform looked a little off to be American. The stripes on his sleeve had a crown of some kind above them. Swede could tell by the man's face, beat up and swollen as it was, that he was not Chinese or Korean. American? Russian? The Chinese were in the war, maybe the Russians were in too. But would they be a US ally or a Chinese/Korean ally? If they were working with the Chinese or the North Koreans, why would the guards just drop him and leave like they did?

Swede knelt next to the cell to get a better look. Just then the mystery man opened his eyes. He jerked back in surprise and that brought a loud moan from his lips. That movement had hurt him somewhere.

"Hey, are you OK? Do you speak English?

The man moaned something. Swede pressed his face right up to the cell bars to hear him better. What he finally heard was a mumbled, "Bloody right, I speak English! What the hell are you?"

Camp 1 Reunion

April 1951

Master Sergeant Mike Randall had been in the army for fifteen years. He believed in the army. He believed in what it could do for the individual, what it had done for him. The army had given him a purpose, a life that had meaning. And he believed in what it could do not only for the country, but the world. He had seen what it could do for the world during the last war. He had seen the shadow lifted from Europe. He had seen the light in people's eyes, in their smiles, in their voices. He believed in the machine and in its purpose. After the war, he worked hard to keep that machine trained at the level necessary to fight the next war, because it was obvious there was going to be a next war.

The politicians didn't view the world through the same glasses as Mike Randall. In the years immediately after the end of World War II the US military was seen only as a budget item. Washington didn't see a need to spend money on equipment and training in a part of the world where there was absolutely no threat to Americans. Even the generals viewed the Japanese as defeated and China destroying itself in a civil war. "Relax, First Sergeant. Give the troops a break. There's no need to train so hard. The troops complain to the folks back home, they complain to their congressman, and they complain to the us. It always comes back around to us."

It came back around to us all right, thought Mike as he stood looking out over the camp. Understrength, underequipped, undertrained, and tossed into a war in just hours. In just a few more hours he and what was left of his men were prisoners. And then he had to watch as his army fell apart. Officers and NCOs just quit. His friend and commanding officer, Captain Tom Winslow, was executed for trying to do his job, trying to care for his men. In the seconds before his execution, Tom Winslow had passed that torch to Mike.

That had been ten months ago, ten long months. Every time Mike had thought things couldn't get worse, they had. Every time. But maybe this was the end, maybe this was where they caught a break. Maybe this camp. Maybe now the dying would stop. But he had to be honest. The only thing that looked better here was the weather. It was finally warming up.

His men still weren't all here. Seven hundred had left the last camp about four weeks ago. After three weeks on the march, just over two hundred had arrived at this place, wherever it was. In the past week, groups of ten or twenty had straggled in, often in carts pulled by oxen, but sometimes by their fellow prisoners. That is why he stood where he was. From there, he could see a mile or so back the way they had come, hoping to see another cart or another group of men limping their way into camp. Less than half had made it so far, less than half!

They had buried about three hundred men at that camp. The three-week march from there had killed more and the dying continued in this new camp. Camp 1, it was called. Did that mean there were more, or was this the one and only camp? Mike Randall didn't know and didn't really care. He only had energy left to care for his men, those still alive here in Camp 1 and those he hoped would arrive soon. Less than half of the seven hundred were still alive. Less than half after all he and others had done to keep them alive! How much more could these men take? How much more could he take? He felt he was in a cloud of some kind, a fog that was draining what strength he had left. Depression, despair, utter defeat, all the above? He knew physical exhaustion was part of it, but he was supposed to be a leader and he couldn't find what was necessary to stand up and lead anymore. So, he sat, looking out over the dreary camp and to the still snow-covered mountains beyond, hoping to see four hundred men coming down the road. All he saw was Jack Usury coming up the path from their hut.

"Mike, who's that comin' down the road?" Jack nodded his head behind where Mike Randall was sitting. "I didn't know they took any of our guys out of camp. Those two are our guys, aren't they?"

Standing to see what Usury was talking about, Randall saw three men walking down the road that ran past the British compound and on to the American huts. It was obvious they were coming from what appeared to be the Chinese barracks on the hill. But they weren't American, or at least two of them weren't. The big guy in the back was a guard, the rifle and the uniform stood out. The man on the left might be American, but the one on the right wasn't. His clothing looked newer, cleaner, and different. He was also a big man, the biggest of the three. He walked with a severe limp, helped by the man on his right. There was something about that man that seemed familiar. Before it came to him there was a noise from the British huts. Men were running for the rock wall on the British side of the road, cheering. The big man waved, and the cheering increased. British troops lined the wall and reached out to touch him.

The man had some rags wrapped around both hands, and his left leg was bandaged with more rags. Looking back to the smaller man, Randall saw where the rags had come from. Both sleeves were missing from his uniform. What remained was filthy and torn. A blanket covered his shoulders. His hair and beard were wild, his face dirty. The three stopped at the entrance to the British compound. The guard stepped back while the other two stood looking at each other and then hugged. The big man stepped in to be swallowed up by the noisy Brits. The guard spoke to the remaining prisoner and pointed towards Randall and Usury. That man continued down the road to the American compound, stopping in front of the entrance to the huts. There was a fresh wound on his forehead and pain and loneliness in his face.

"Jesus, you guys look like hell," he said, and gave a hint of a smile. His blue eyes did not reflect that smile. What was left of his uniform did nothing to hide how thin he was. Then he looked directly at Randall. "Mike, I'm sorry I couldn't bring help. I just wasn't strong enough." Tears streaked the grime on his face.

Jack Usury caught on first. "Goddam! Swede? Swede, is that you? *We* look like hell? Christ, kid, you look like death warmed over." He reached out, put his arm around Swede's shoulders, and led him through the gate. Mike Randall stood there as if in shock. Swede? This stick figure wasn't Swede. Swede was healthy-looking, young, with an easy smile. Swede had escaped and was in a hospital in Japan or even the states. He looked again at the two men standing in front of him and realized they both looked like hell. And then the confusion lifted, and Swede was looking back at him and the three were wrapped in a hug and doing some cheering of their own.

Jerry Trigg, nicknamed Trigger by Mike Randall, had stepped out of his squad's hut to get some fresh air. With twenty men packed into two rooms, it got ripe in there, especially now that temperatures were warming up. To put it mildly, the huts were filthy and they stunk. To add to that problem, some of the guys were really sick. When you had a nasty case of diarrhea you got weak. When you were that weak you sometimes crapped your pants - just a fact of life in the camps. So yeah, the huts smelled bad.

Trigger's hut held twenty men, ten per room. But Trigger knew they were going to lose at least two of the guys, maybe more. The really sick guys tried to hide how bad they were. The guards came through once a day for a headcount. They sent the extremely ill to a temple of some kind they were using for a hospital. No one had come back from their hospital yet. Trigger had helped Charlie carry a man up to the hospital a few days back. They had managed a quick look inside and saw nothing but men lying on the bare floor, covered in flies and feces. Some were dead or just minutes away. There were no doctors or nurses in sight. When they tried to turn around and take the man back, the guards forced them to leave him there.

So when the guards came around, the guys who were sick tried to sit up straight and smile. If there was somebody so sick they couldn't get up, the guards focused on them. But there was no morning sick call and no medicine of any kind. No doctor came around with the guards to check on the prisoners. Those who were seriously ill either died in the hut or were sent to the hospital - where they died. Some huts kept the dead in the hut for the morning headcounts. When they were successful, there was a little more for the living to share that day. The warmer temperatures meant that trick wasn't going to work much longer. Trigger had stepped out for some fresh air, but he didn't breathe in too deeply. The warmer temperatures also meant you could now smell the whole camp.

Henry Page ducked through the door of the hut. "Cooper isn't going to last much longer, and he knows it."

"I hope we don't have to send him up to that death house," replied Trigger. "I hope he dies here first. If I knew I was goin' up there, I would just give up on the spot." He looked over at Page. The man seemed to understand the world better than most in their hut. "Why do you think so many seem to do just that, quit? It just seems like they quit. They just give up and die."

"They don't give up. It just looks that way. There were two doctors with us in Bean Camp. They weren't allowed to do anything except help wash the sick guys with the crappy water we had. I said the same thing to one of them. 'Why do these guys give up so easy?' He told me it was all part of a disease, pellagra, or something like that. The little food they gave us was just barely cooked, so the vitamins weren't released. The first step in this disease is diarrhea. Then you get dementia, so you don't know what's happening anymore. That's why we think they give up. Then you die. If it hits you hard, it can all happen in a month. I heard him complain to the Chinese and ask if we could cook our own food. All he got from the Chinese was the butt of a rifle in his gut."

"What's this place called again?" asked Trigger.

"Camp 1."

"Are those doctors here in Camp 1? Have they seen that death house on the hill?"

Page sighed. "I haven't seen them yet. Maybe the Chinese kept them back at Bean Camp, maybe they wore themselves out helping people between Bean Camp and here. I've seen that happen too many times. That's why I'm worried about Ray Parker. He hasn't shown up yet either."

"Who's Ray Parker?" Trigger asked.

"Oh yeah, I forget you weren't part of Mike Randall's original column. What did they have you doing again?"

"On the second day they asked if anybody could drive a truck. They said they needed drivers to haul the wounded, and trucks have heaters, so I raised my hand. They put me in the driver's seat with a guard next to me. I spent the next three months haulin' supplies, mostly ammo, but never any wounded. I wrecked three trucks and killed one guard in the process, so they dumped me off here a few days before you guys came in. I still haven't seen anybody from my unit. So, who is this Ray Parker guy?"

"About the third day on the march after we were captured back in July these two guys who had escaped from their column ran into ours, literally. They were trying to cross the road early in the morning and got caught up in our column. Swede and Ray Parker. That was the day they shot the captain. This nasty bastard up and shot him right between the eyes. They shot most of our wounded and anybody else who couldn't keep up. They did the same thing after we left Seoul and started for Bean Camp. Before they started shooting our sick, they were leaving them in villages along the way to get picked up later. That's what happened to Swede. He and Ray were close. Then Ray teamed up with Bowser. They worked hard helping guys keep up on the march to Bean Camp. They wore themselves out. Bowser fell and Ray couldn't get him up.

"That was only a couple of days before we got to Bean Camp. But Ray never really recovered. When he had to leave Bowser, something broke. He was in bad shape when we left Bean Camp. I keep hoping he comes in on one of these buffalo carts soon." Trigger could see the worry in Page's face.

That was why he had attached himself to Master Sergeant Randall and the others. They seemed to care more than most of the other prisoners he saw here, and they seemed to have a direction. Too many in camp did as little as possible, just enough to get by, and that meant they didn't have time to help anybody around them. Trigger knew he had been lucky so far. From what Page had just told him, drivin' a truck hadn't been as bad as he thought. Sure, he hadn't seen any other Americans for three months, and he had been treated like a slave. But he ate the same food as the guards and got to sleep in the cab of his truck. When it got cold, he was able to run the engine to keep it from freezing up. That meant he also got to run the heater. They chained him to the steering column, but he stayed warm.

The chains had bothered him. Jerry Trigg was from Alabama, the son of a sharecropper and the grandson of a former slave. His daddy had told him the stories *his* daddy used to tell. Being chained in that truck brought those stories back. And now this camp, where it felt everybody was a slave. Randall and his people seemed like the best way to deal with this new slavery. They had accepted him as an equal from day one. In fact, he was standing there looking out over the camp because his job was to come up with an accurate count of how many POWs there were in the camp.

Using the marker of two squads of ten in each hut, Trigger put the American side of the camp at about six hundred prisoners. The guards didn't like people wandering about, but he had managed to count every hut that held POWs. There were thirty huts holding Americans. About three hundred British prisoners had marched in a few days before. He knew they were British because they had told him so by yelling across the two stone fences that bordered the road between them. The guards quickly put a stop to that. But the American numbers were falling every day. Jerry had helped the burial crew so he could count the graves up on what they called Boot Hill. He had been in Camp 1 a little more than a week and there were already ninety-seven graves on the hill, almost all of them American.

Just then Page nudged him and asked, "What's all the noise about up there?" He pointed to the stone fence where he could see Mike Randall and Jack Usury watching some people come down the road from the Chinese barracks area.

"Looks like a guard bringing some new prisoners down. I never seen any prisoners come into camp from that direction." Trigger had noticed his eyesight seemed to be better than most in the camp. He wondered if eating better than they had during the winter had anything to do with it.

"One of them must be British cuz they are makin' a racket over there. The guy in back is a guard. I don't recognize the other guy. Looks like he's comin' into our side."

"Let's wander up there," Page said. "I need to talk with Usury anyway." As the two got closer, they saw Mike Randall and Jack Usury grab the stranger and start laughing and yelling.

"I'll be damned!" whispered Page, almost as if he didn't believe himself. "That's Swede! I'll be damned."

After their initial reunion celebration, Mike Randall got everybody moving back to the huts. The guards hadn't paid much attention yet as to who was in what hut. He and Jack Usury were in separate huts, a habit left from the road marches. Mike tried to keep people he could depend on scattered along the column. He kept up the practice in Bean Camp and was trying to do the same here at Camp 1. It was obvious Swede was going to need somebody to watch him while he gained his strength back. Mike had come to trust Henry Page, so he decided to put Swede in his hut and hope the guards didn't say anything. He didn't think Swede knew Page very well, but he did remember him from Seoul. Later he could try and get both Trigger and Swede into different huts. He had the feeling the relaxed attitude the guards seemed to have would change soon, but until then, he would try to maintain some kind of order.

Swede had mixed feelings that first night at Camp 1. He wasn't used to such crowded conditions, yet it felt good to be around Americans again. The body heat while sleeping was a bonus. It was almost too warm for him. The next day he rested. Page and the new guy, Trigger, were in and out of the hut throughout the day. He appreciated the fact they checked in on him so often. Too many others in the hut seemed to be in their own strange world, making no effort to interact with anybody. It was clear they had been through a lot since he had left the column five or six months ago.

After a few days rest and better food than he had been getting, Swede felt better. He joined Mike Randall, Usury, and Page as they sat in the sun looking out over the camp and down the valley to the south. He explained in general what had happened to him since being left in the village. He continued to give the impression he had been sick, and Randall didn't contradict him. The others then gave their story. The march had turned mean and the guards went back to shooting those who couldn't keep up. Bean Camp was little better than the march. They were crammed into some old school buildings in an abandoned mining town. Most windows were missing and no fires were allowed. Still no clothing or blankets were supplied, still no medical care provided. The only well was contaminated because the prisoners kept washing their shit-covered clothes in the same bucket used to pull up water. What little food they were given was hard to digest. Chinese supply convoys sitting in the middle of town were a clear target for American planes, and the town had been strafed several times. At the end of April, seven hundred prisoners were marched out of Bean Camp, headed for Camp 1. So far, only three hundred had made it.

"Where are Ray and Bowser?" asked Swede. I haven't seen them yet. What hut are they in?"

"Bowser didn't make it to Bean Camp," Page explained. "He and Ray wore themselves out helping others along the way and we didn't notice. They fell behind and Bowser broke his leg. Ray had to leave him. He barely caught up to the column himself. Most of us were walking dead by the time we got to the camp. Ray never really recovered. On the march here, they started putting the sick in buffalo carts. Some of those carts are still showing up. That's why we sit here. We can see the road that comes into the valley. When we see a cart, we go down to where Charlie and his crew meet them. We're still hoping Ray is in one of those carts."

Jack Usury had spent more time with Swede than the others as they had been paired up on work parties in Seoul. When the guard brought Swede into camp, Jack was struck by the change he could see. This was no longer the kid asking if they were going to be rescued. This was a much older version of that person. When Page explained about Bowser and Ray Parker, Jack saw a change in Swede's eyes. They grew angrier, meaner. Ray had been like a brother to Swede.

"When we see a cart come down the road we'll head down to see if Ray is there. Sit with me for a while and we'll keep a look out," said Mike Randall. The others seemed to understand Randall wanted to talk with Swede alone, so they wandered off.

Mike put his hand on Swede's shoulder. "I noticed you let everybody think you were left in that village because you were too sick to move on. And I'm guessing you didn't give us the real story about all you've been through since then."

"I don't know why, but it just seemed right at the time. I know you and Jack, but Page is different. There is something about him that I can't figure out. So, I thought it best not to go into too much detail. In fact, seeing him here reminded me of something back in Seoul that I was going to mention but never did. Remember when Ray and Bowser came back from meeting up with the column near us just before we left Seoul? They mentioned seeing Russians. Page was sitting near us. When he heard the word 'Russian' he reacted, not much, but I could see he was interested. And he always seemed to be nearby whenever we talked as a group. It seems a stretch, but could he be a Russian, a spy of some kind?" Swede shrugged his shoulders as if he knew the idea was a little much.

Randall laughed. "You are closer than you think. Yes, Henry Page is a little different. But don't worry, he is definitely one of us. I'll ask him to give you his story. Now, why don't you tell me what you didn't want to talk about in front of him."

Swede filled in the blank spots. He explained about the Chinese colonel, Uncle Kim, Buddha, questions from the Chinese that had no right answer, the possibility of Russians being in the camp. He explained about the confessions he had signed when he saw no way out short of starving or freezing to death. The fewer people who knew he had escaped twice the better he felt. And he explained his feeling the Chinese were going to start putting the whole camp through a version of what he had experienced.

"I was just an experiment. If I died, the experiment would not have been a failure, it would have been one of a couple of possible outcomes. They really didn't care. I was just a rat in a maze. But I set up some experiments of my own. I learned to use their ideas to make them think I was 'learning the truth.' Two plus two doesn't necessarily equal four to them, so you have to be careful. But if we are willing to take the pain when the answer is five, we can beat them at their own game, or at least break even." There was almost an eagerness in Swede's face as he looked at Randall.

"The trick will be to get everybody on board, but we can do this," added Swede.

"No, we can't," responded Mike Randall. "Get everybody on board, I mean. Too many have bought into not taking orders anymore. If we push them, they will simply complain to the Chinese. The Chinese will remove anybody that even looks like they are giving orders. In Bean Camp they kept the officers separate. I think they'll do the same here, and probably the NCOs too."

Randall looked at Swede. "But I tell you what. You hit the nail on the head with that experiment theory of yours. Maybe you haven't noticed yet, but there are some guys here who have new clothes, hats even. They were captured near the Chosin Reservoir when the Chinese first came in and taken to a place called Kanggye, or something like that. The Chinese gave them haircuts and warm clothes. Supposedly the clothes are what students in China wear, blue padded pants and coats. They were told if they cooperated in their "re-education" they would be sent home. From what they tell me, it was pretty much what you went through. Lots of lectures and threats and lots of writing their opinions on who started the war. Most of the guys went along enough to keep the Chinese happy, but some tried too hard. When the experiment was over, they sent most of the guys here. A few were sent off somewhere else, so maybe they did send them home.

"There are still empty huts, so they are probably waiting until everybody headed this way gets here. Once that happens, they will start in with their games. There are some guys from Kanngye that I trust. Maybe we can hold some 're-education' classes of our own and give some of our guys an idea of what will happen and how to handle it. But we will have to be careful about what we say and who we say it to." Randall pointed down the valley, "But right now I see some carts coming in. Let's go down and see if any of our guys are in them."

By the time they got down to where three carts had come into camp, the sick had been placed on wooden stretchers made from doors. Somehow hot tea was available and those among the sick who could drink were doing so under the watchful eye of Charlie and his crew. A few were too far gone to even drink on their own. A couple of Americans had walked beside the carts to help with the sick on their journey. One of them was arguing with a Chinese officer about getting IVs for the prisoners that were barely alive. The Chinese officer simply folded his arms across his chest and looked away. The American noticed Randall and Swede and came over.

"So, things are no different here, Mike? This is just another temporary camp? I hoped we would be done with marching around the countryside and be in a permanent camp with a hospital."

"This *is* a permanent camp, Captain. Welcome to Camp 1. But so far things are no different. Pretty much the same food and I haven't seen even a bandage or aspirin given out to our sick. They call a building up that way a hospital, but so far nobody has come out of there alive." In a lower voice Swede heard him say, "Sorry, Joel."

The man Randall called Captain, and then Joel, slumped back against one of the carts. "Two weeks ago we had ten carts and twenty-four patients." He pointed to the three carts and seven people being tended to. He couldn't bring himself to say any more.

Swede noticed Usury and Page were kneeling next to one of the new patients. Hoping for the best, he quickly moved over to them. On the door was a man he didn't recognize, but the man's eyes lit up when he noticed Swede.

"Swede! I thought you were dead, man! I thought you were dead!" Seeing the blank look on Swede's face he said, "It's me, man, Ray! Don't you recognize me?"

Slowly it dawned on Swede the skeleton on the ground with the whisper voice was Ray Parker. If it hadn't been for the red hair, Swede would never have taken a second look. But gradually his buddy came into focus. And he knew he had to be careful how he reacted.

"You look a little uglier than the last time I saw you, Ray. I leave you on your own for a while and you let yourself go. You're never gonna pass inspection in that uniform!"

Ray smiled. "Yeah, I was kinda sick there for a while. But I'm feelin' better now. Hey, what happened to your head? You look like you picked a fight with a wall."

Henry Page watched as Swede continued to ignore the reality of how bad Ray looked and bantered gently back and forth with his friend. Page didn't know Swede all that well and expected the conversation to be more like "Oh my god, you look terrible! We need to get you to a doctor right now!" Instead, Swede had managed to bring a little light back into Ray's eyes. He hadn't risen like Lazarus yet, but the look of complete helplessness was gone from his face. Ray Parker had just gotten the best medicine possible.

Two of the seven men brought in that day died before they even got to a hut. The doctor that came in with them said he expected the same result for Ray, but if he made it twenty-four more hours, he just might survive. He didn't understand Ray Parker had just received a miracle cure. Swede managed to keep Ray from getting sent up to the hospital and spent most of the next two days by Ray's side. When Ray was sleeping, Swede got to know Henry Page and Jerry Trigg a little better. Page explained how Jerry got his nickname from Mike Randall.

"He claims when he needs something done, he just aims and pulls his Trigger and it gets done."

Trigger laughed. "When he first called me that I thought it was just another way for a white man to call me a "nigger." I came in the army to get away from that kind of thing when President Truman passed that law that said the army had to accept black folks as equals. Not that I expected everything would be tall cotton, but at least I'd have a job. But Sergeant Randall don't mean nuthin' wrong by it. He's a good man. And I'm glad he trusts me to help out with these Chinese. I still get the willies when I think of bein' chained in that truck."

"Speaking of the Chinese, it looks like they are up to something in the British compound," Henry Page pointed across the way. Although there was a dirt road and two low stone walls separating the two camps, it was easy to see what was going on. At times they even managed to shout back and forth to each other, but the Chinese frowned on that kind of behavior. Frowned, as in hit you with a rifle butt if they caught you doing so.

More and more Americans noticed and lined the stone wall to watch the action across the way. The Chinese had set up chairs out in the open and were lining the Brits up for haircuts. Everybody was getting the same style, buzzed down to less than an inch. The idea was kind of appealing, as lice were still a constant problem. From the haircut area, the men moved over and stripped down, tossing all their clothes into a pile the guards were setting on fire. The Americans really started hooting and hollering at that sight. The next step was wading into the river and sharing some bars of soap. That stirred some interest. Nobody had seen soap since they were captured. A delousing station was next, followed by the issue of new clothes. When they saw the result, the Americans were jealous.

Page noticed Swede heading back towards their huts and followed to see if he needed help. When he ducked into the hut, Swede was sitting next to Ray.

"I figured I should check on him. From the looks of it, we might be getting some improvements around here. The clothes they are getting are the same as the guys from that Kanngye camp are wearing. And I bet I know what comes after that." Swede tugged the extra shirt they were using for a blanket up around Ray's shoulders.

"I've talked to some of those guys. Mike Randall says you have some ideas about what the Chinese have planned for us. Any thoughts on what they might put us through?"

Swede still wasn't sure about Henry Page. Randall said he was okay, so maybe it was time to ease up on his suspicions. It wasn't that he thought Page was a spy; there was just something different about him.

"According to a Korean I spent time in jail with, the Chinese treat their own people the same way. They figure the average peasant can't think for himself, so they have to teach him why communism is good for him. Since we have been exposed to the dreaded capitalist way of life, we need to be *re-educated*. Which means we are in for lots of lectures and writing about our understanding of the truth, with some self-confessions thrown in for good measure. Lots of talks on how capitalism is a disease that is the rot of society and we must all work together for the greater good. And they play hard. They will ask the same question twenty times, and when you change your answer just a little bit on your twentieth answer you will be accused of being 'impurdinint' and sent off to some miserable little cage without blankets to freeze until your thinking changes. By then the question will have changed and you start all over. Then you will have to write about how George Washington is a money grubber and Marx is a saint. They will read every word and ask you to explain how you came to your conclusions. But I'm pretty sure that if they wanted to kill me…us, if they wanted to kill *us,* they would have done it by now."

"Is that what they had you doing up there in the jail these past months?" asked Page. "I get the idea you aren't just bein' hypothetical here. You know this firsthand?" He had noticed the scars on Swede's neck and forehead and picked up on the change from *me* to *us.*

"Yeah, I know this firsthand. I suppose it will be a little different with so many of us. They can't take us one at a time. It will have to be done in groups. Probably by squads or huts. What do the guys from Kanggye say about what happened to them?"

"Pretty much what you just said. And you're right. The Chinese worked on them by huts except for long lectures to the whole camp every now and then. How do you think our guys will handle all this? Will they fall for it? Can we do anything to get them ready before it all starts?

Swede thought a bit. "I think we should talk to a few people we know are solid. Maybe find some guys who were at Kanggye who are willing to talk to a few of our guys. But I think we will have to wait and let most people see for themselves. Then we can step in and try to help those willing to fight the bullshit. I'm tellin' you though, these people can be pretty persuasive when they put their minds to it."

And then it was their turn. The barbers made quick work of lice infested hair and the uniforms went into the fire. No one seemed to mind the chilly river water as they tried to scrub away months of grime. Most didn't notice the extra guards with burp guns posted along the river in case anybody wanted to make a break for it - naked, but clean. Two shades lighter and a few pounds less, they waded out of the river to move through the delousing stations and get their new clothes. Their new uniform was a lightweight jacket, trousers, and a cap, all a dark blue color. Some of the guys who had served in China after the last war said this was what students wore in China.

The next day they found out how fitting their new clothes were. The entire camp was assembled in the open and told to sit. A box was set up and a group of Chinese officers walked down the road and entered the compound. Followed by extra guards and their burp guns. Swede recognized Major Han as he stepped up on the box and began to address the prisoners.

"On behalf of Chairman Mao, we officers of the Chinese People's Volunteer Army Camp Number One welcome you. From this day, you are no longer prisoners of war! You are free men, free from the oppression of your war-mongering government, free from the yoke of capitalism!"

A man sitting somewhere behind Swede began to comment on the Major's speech in a voice loud enough to be heard by those around him but not by any of the Chinese. *You thank Chairman Mao for me. I'll be headed home now since you say I'm free.*

"This is all because of the lenient policy of the Chinese people. *I'd hate to see the policy if they were upset.* It is the Chinese people who have sacrificed for you. They send food and medicine and clothing for you. *Could you ask them to sacrifice a little more cuz I only just now got my clothes and the food and medicine must be held up somewhere.* You must show your gratitude and respect by learning the truth. The peace-loving people feel no ill will towards you, even though you have invaded the homeland of their brothers and sisters in Korea. *I was perfectly happy down south, you folks brought me up here.* They ask only that you put aside your imperialist ways and accept the teachings of Karl Marx and Chairman Mao." *I prefer the teachings of Groucho, myself.*

Some of the guards and officers circling the group sitting on the ground began to notice the smiles and chuckles in the area near Swede. They weren't sure yet what was causing the disturbance but didn't look happy. The major simply continued.

"They ask only that you learn the truth and put aside your decadent ways. The sooner you accomplish this the sooner you shall go home to your families. *Would you quit barkin' at us then, so we can get on with it? I told my wife I was goin' down to the corner to get some smokes.*" By that time, some in the area were chuckling aloud. The Major looked right at them.

"But those students who demonstrate a bad attitude will not see their families so soon. The peace-loving Chinese people can only give so much. Those students who demonstrate bad attitudes shall be given special consideration until they learn the truth. Reactionaries who refuse their duties as students shall learn a different truth!" By then the Major was working up to a frenzy and the kibitzer had decided he better lay low. Swede had noticed a lot of giddiness around the camp. The baths and new clothes had given many a sense of relief, the feeling all was now well. The laughter at the sarcastic humor made him realize, new clothes or not, most of his fellow "students" had no idea what they were in for.

After the Major figured he had the crowd all warmed up, he turned and pointed to the officers seated behind him. "Now our camp commander shall say a few words." As the man stepped up to the box, Swede let out a little groan.

Mike Randall leaned over. "You okay?"

"Maybe. That unhappy little guy up there? Our camp commander? I spent the last four months yelling at him on a regular basis. I thought he was a clerk of some kind. I hope he doesn't hold a grudge. Better yet, I hope he doesn't recognize me with my new haircut. I bet you it won't be long before he calls us 'impurdinint!' Seems to be one of his favorite expressions."

"I don't think the new haircut will help. That scar on your forehead is still pretty obvious," Randall offered.

"Actually, the little guy probably never saw this. Swede motioned towards his head. "After the Goons gave this to me, I was never out of the cell again until they brought me down here."

The Camp Commander was well into his speech about the lenient treatment the new students were getting. Just then a man stood up and yelled out, "What about all our buddies up on that hill? Where was *their* lenient treatment? Sure seems like those graves are a truth!" In a flash two guards had the man by his arms and were escorting him up the hill towards headquarters. Hours later he reappeared, the guards leading him with a rope. In full view of the entire camp the rope was tossed over a beam and stretched until he was hanging by his wrists, his toes just barely touching the ground. The next morning he was returned to the huts. Major Han had demonstrated what he meant by students who refuse their duties shall learn a different truth. There was no laughter then.

Repeat Offender

Summer 1951

Along with their new status as "students," the men found they had new responsibilities. Rosters were posted of work parties and which huts were assigned to them. Swede noticed Henry Page headed out with the wood-gathering detail, so he decided to join in. Seeing the look on Page's face, Swede said, "Hey, most of my time for months now has been inside a cell. I could use some exercise in the fresh air."

"You may have a point there," responded Page. "Some simple exercise would do most of us some good. The British are out there every morning doing a short version of PT."

"Actually, Mike Randall says I should talk with you. He's worried the officers and NCOs will be split off from the rest of us pretty soon. He seems to think we should get to know each other before that happens. He says there is more to you than meets the eye, and I should trust you." Swede waited for Page's reaction.

"Yeah, he said the same to me about you. I don't know if you know this, but Mike has a lot of respect for you. He says you've escaped twice and went through some nasty stuff with the Koreans and the Chinese on your own since then. He says he met a guy at Bean Camp who was your platoon sergeant on the hill where you were captured. He told Mike that he intended to put you in for the Silver Star for what you did on that hill. But he is one of those who hasn't shown up here yet."

"Mike says I should fill you in on everything. So, I'm going to take the chance he's right about you. He says you thought maybe I was a Russian of some kind. Well, Swede, you are three fourths right on that. Listen up." Page grinned and clapped Swede on the shoulder.

Being careful no one else got too close, Swede and Page swapped histories as they gathered wood that afternoon. Swede was amazed by the tale Page told him. But he was even more amazed when Page demanded he recall every detail about the English-speaking Chinese colonel and the Russian trucks in camp. The questions he asked about both incidents made it clear to Swede that Henry Page knew his stuff.

"Remember, if the Chinese find out any of this about me, I'm a dead man. Don't mention it to anyone, not Ray Parker, not Trigger, not anyone. Other than you, only Mike knows my story. I'm trusting you with my life here." Page looked carefully at Swede. "Speaking of trust, what did you hide in the wall of your hut the day the British got their baths and haircuts?"

"Jumpin' jehoshaphat! You noticed?" Swede looked at Page with a new respect.

"Jumpin' jehoshaphat? Where did that come from?" Page laughed.

"My mother is pretty strict when it comes to language around our place. My father and uncles learned to watch their language around her and came up with some acceptable phrases to keep them out of trouble. Gadzooks and hornswoggled are two of my favorites. But I gotta admit, this past year has caused me to use language she would not be happy about."

"My English is good, but there are times when I hear something I've never heard before. You just gave me three new words. And I guessed you were hiding something. I saw you react the day the British were getting their new uniforms. When I walked in the hut, you wanted me to think you were checking on Parker. But I saw your hands moving away from the wall. I didn't put it all together until just now.

"And you just proved to me Mike Randall is right about you. When we saw what was going on with the British, you realized we would be next. You needed to hide whatever you have until after we got our new clothes, or it would have gone in the fire with your old uniform. Do you have money, a map?"

Swede told him all about Sook the burglar, the lock picks, and stealing food for Buddha and then for himself a few months back. They agreed the picks might come in handy someday, and the fewer people who knew about them, the better.

The wood-gathering detail wasn't exactly the simple exercise they had envisioned. Within a few hours each, man was carrying about fifty pounds on their back. Then they had two hills they had to climb to get back to camp. They were easily burning more calories than they would get in their skimpy meals that day. But Page had a reason other than exercise to be on the detail. He explained to Swede what he needed.

"When we approach camp, we should pass near some people from the village. They will yell at us for using their firewood and try to take some of it from us. I need you to get involved in the pushing and shoving. Dump your load of wood and make a lot of noise. While you do that, I am going to be passing a message to one of them. Don't hurt anybody. In fact, let them knock you down. Get in a tug-of-war over some of the wood. Make a scene. But don't hurt anybody. If that happens, it will be harder to get them to help next time." As he talked, he looked around to make sure no one was close enough to hear.

"You have contact with our side? Can you get us out of here?" Swede didn't think escape was possible this far north, but with the locals on their side, it was a different story.

"Yes and no. I had a network gathering information for me before the war broke out. I got a message to them when we were in Seoul. They managed to find me in Bean Camp and last week got a sign to me they were here at Camp 1. I'm not going to give you details because what you don't know you can't tell anybody else. I trust you, but if the Chinese catch on, they might start asking questions. Does that make sense to you?" Page watched for Swede's reaction.

"Absolutely. So how big of a group is your network? Or shouldn't I ask that?" Swede wasn't sure if Page would even bother to answer.

"There are no local people involved, except for the little cooperation my guys can convince them to give. And escape is not part of any plan at this point. A couple of us could probably get out of camp easy enough. But then what? Americans are going to stand out even if we use my guys to guide us. And that would just blow the whole network. But I can get *information* out. Information like there are English speaking Chinese units doing some kind of work they don't seem to be telling the Koreans about. Information you are going to help me find on Russian units in this area."

Page had a hard look in his eyes. "Maybe, just maybe, my guys could get me out of here. What would that accomplish? America took me in, trusted me, trained me, gave me a new life. I can't earn my keep back in Japan. My guys can pass information back and forth. But they don't know the kind of information I am looking for. What I was assigned to find is right here. It makes sense for me to stay here and find it."

Swede looked carefully at Page. Here was a guy with a strange story, a guy who was at least ten years older than himself. Here was a guy who had been raised under communism and wanted to fight it. A guy who Mike Randall said he should trust. So, he would.

"So, I'm working for you now?" he asked.

"No. Working with me. And only if you want to. Otherwise, I just ask you don't let any of this get to anybody else. I know Ray Parker is your friend and you might want to share. But that can't happen. Not Trigger either. At some point we might need their help, but they don't need the details."   He paused. "Make a decision. We should see the locals pretty soon." Page shifted his load of wood, trying to make it ride more comfortably on his back.

"Okay. Let's see how good of an actor I am," Swede said with a hint of a smile.

Henry Page got his message out. It said no more than I am here, wait for further information. If there were no problems, his plan was for the next message to be about how the POWs were being treated. Until then, the camp set into a routine. About one hundred Chinese political commissars, instructors, and interpreters had arrived to help their new students "learn the truth," and they set right to work. There were group lectures for the whole camp. Sitting in the open listening to Truman, Roosevelt, and Washington being maligned and Chairman Mao, Stalin, and Marx being portrayed as men of the people was mostly boring under the sun. But the hours long tirades were painful in the rain and mud. The lectures were followed up with visits to each hut by individuals the POWs eventually called instructors. Some people had started calling them teachers, but others felt there was something very wrong about using that term in their current situation.

As Keith Rulstad from Oklahoma put it, "I spent more time in the field than in the classroom, but when I hear the word teacher, I think of Miss Roberts and our one-room schoolhouse at Hickory Grove. And I don't plan to sully her memory by callin' any of these bastards 'teacher.' I ain't gonna let that happen." So, instructor it was.

Along with anything Page had in mind, Swede intended to do everything he could to keep any of his fellow prisoners from buying in to the Chinese efforts at "learning the truth." Whenever he saw a chance to take a poke at their "truth" that two plus two equaled five, especially in front of some of the more gullible prisoners, he took it. Which eventually sent him back to his old jail cell.

Early one morning, Swede had been in line to get his morning rice, hoping maybe they would throw in some cabbage or maybe some dried fish. As he waited, he found himself looking at the hills outside the camp and admiring the scenery. He realized that under different circumstances this would be a pretty view. The grays and browns of winter and spring had turned to colors of summer. He heard some bird songs from the banks of the river and saw flashes of yellow in the bushes. He was sure the colors and the birds had been there for weeks but could not remember seeing them before this particular morning. Life must be getting better after all. His mind was willing to see more than the black and white of the past months. Maybe his study session for the day would be a little brighter.

The instructor assigned to Swede's hut was named Weng. He spoke both English and Russian, a fact Swede made sure Page knew. It was obvious to Swede that Weng was still unsure of how to handle his American students. Although he spoke English well, this seemed to be his first actual contact with Americans. The day before, he had left an article from the 1 October 1950 edition of London's *Daily Worker*. The men in the hut were supposed to discuss the article and be ready to talk about it when Weng returned. Most of the men had read it, but there was no effort to talk about it as a group.

####
ARNHEM HEROES JOIN PEACE MARCH

Arnhem heroes, parachutists and wounded ex-prisoners of war are among the thousands of Londoners who will join in the world peace demonstrations tomorrow, International Peace Day. They are marching in the procession, organized by the British Peace Committee, to place a wreath on the Cenotaph in memory of those who died in the fight for peace and liberty.

Peter Robinson had been wounded and captured at Arnhem.

Two of his brothers were killed in Italy. "I intend to safeguard the future of my baby son and the rest of my family," he told the reporter yesterday. "The people who rejected collective security with Russia before the last war are still at it. We must make sure the same thing does not happen again. We'll only get peace by marching for it."

London's Celebration of International Peace begins tomorrow in Hyde Park at 2:30 pm. Mothers with young children who cannot march all the way are invited to assemble in Mortimer Street (near Oxford Circus) at 3:30.

A statement by the executive of the British Peace Committee last night said: "Now people can see they are at the parting of the roads. One road leads to an increasingly mad armaments race, reinforced with bacterial warfare and other horrors straight to war. The other road leads to disarmament and negotiations for a lasting peace.

"Did you find the article interesting?" was Weng's first question of the day. Both Page and Swede had tried to sit towards the back of the group in these sessions. They could see and hear what was happening without being obvious. They tried to give the impression they were watching over Ray Parker, as he had still not recovered from the trip from Bean Camp. That kept them from getting too involved in any discussions. Page was older than most of the others, so when he spoke, they usually listened. Guys who remembered Swede from the march out of Seoul respected him. Neither wanted to dominate the conversations as that would put them in Weng's spotlight. They hoped by letting others interact with Weng, they would see what he was trying to do.

"I think it makes sense that ex-prisoners of war would want to march for peace," said Bob Torkle. Swede remembered him from their march north from Seoul. "Everybody wants peace, but veterans probably more than other people."

"So, you want peace? How does the world get peace? How can we have peace when war-loving countries use atomic bombs that destroy whole cities?" Weng directed his questions directly to Bob. He had a pigeon in his sights.

"No country has a bomb that can destroy a whole city. Not a big city anyway." Swede could see Bob was serious in his response. How could he not know about Hiroshima and Nagasaki?

"But if a country did have such a bomb and they used it, what should be done about such a thing?" Weng was careful to hide any emotion. He was just asking a simple question.

"No one would ever drop a bomb like that, would they? It would kill everybody, not just enemy soldiers." Bob was serious. He really didn't know! And from the looks on some of the other faces in the room, he wasn't the only one.

By now Weng was showing his delight. He was about to have a roomful of Americans condemn their own government. "Would you write a statement against using such weapons? That would be something veterans would be against, would it not? Writing a statement against using bacterial and atomic weapons, weapons that would kill indiscriminately, should not every person be against such things?" Suddenly, bacterial warfare was part of the equation.

"I don't write very good. I never learned to spell words good." Bob was either finally seeing where this was going, or he honestly couldn't write very well. Swede was guessing it was the latter.

Page leaned over and whispered, "Guess what happens next." Swede just shook his head. He didn't know if he felt disgust or pity for what was happening to the men around him.

Weng offered up the perfect solution. "What if I write the statement? You can sign it. You can all sign it. You can be the heroes who ask the world not to use such horrible weapons. Your actions will help bring peace, perhaps even bring an end to this war, and get you to your homes. Thank you, my friends. I will beg the cook to add some extra flavor to your supper for suggesting such courageous action."

Swede and Page looked at each other. This guy was good. They had no doubt that when he brought his statement for world peace back to the group, he would have no trouble convincing them to sign. A little something extra in their rice that night would convince most of them Weng was a good guy. He was friendly, he talked about world peace, he thought they were courageous, and he was going to beg the cook to give them better food. Finally, somebody was on their side in this miserable camp.

After they ate that night, including the added fish in their rice, Swede asked how many were planning on signing Weng's statement the next day. Fifteen of nineteen hands went up. Swede spent the next two hours pointing out to the men in the hut how Weng had fooled them. It helped that half of them finally admitted they knew the US had dropped atomic bombs on Japan. One of them had even been in Nagasaki after the war and described the city of rubble he had seen. With a lot of talking, Swede finally got most of the men to agree signing any statement would be a bad idea.

Weng was not happy when only Bob Torkle and one other were willing to sign his statement asking for world peace. "Who has told you not to sign this statement? You must remember, you do not have to take orders from your NCOs or officers here in this camp. That is part of your old life, the life that brought you to Korea to destroy our farms and villages."

Bob pointed at Swede. "Nobody ordered any of us to do anything. But he told me the US dropped atomic weapons in Japan and destroyed some cities. That wasn't right. But I still think we should tell people we support world peace."

Weng wasn't listening to anything Bob said after he pointed to Swede. "I can see how you might misunderstand what I was saying yesterday. Perhaps if we spend some time together, we can discuss it further, and you can better explain the need for world peace to your fellow students. Please, come and have tea with me and we will talk more." Weng stood and the guard with him waited for Swede to also stand.

There was no tea and there was no talk about world peace. Swede found himself occupying one of the regular cells he had spent most of the winter in. There were other occupants, so he had to take a cell further down the darkened row from the cell he had called home just a few weeks back. He was only asked for his name and shoved into the cell. The Goon Squad was still there, along with some new faces. And they still liked to poke at the animals in their cages when the animals didn't sit up straight. They hadn't changed any of the rules. Which meant no guards were around late at night. Over the next few days Swede got to know the other four men, each in a cell by himself. He erased any doubts he might be a stooge of some kind by describing the island mural carved in the first of the cells. Once the others realized he really had been there before, and long enough to carve such a complicated picture, they accepted him. When he told the man in the first cell he could probably find the knife he had used in the dirt at the back of the cell he was practically their brother. When he realized one of the men was in the animal cage he had once called home, he described the calendar he had scraped onto that wall. That was the end of any distrust.

Swede knew he would be there for at least a week before anybody came to check on his understanding of the truth. When he found the man in the animal cage was only getting fed one meal every two days, he knew how he would spend part of his time. Rather than trying to explain what he was about to do, he waited until the early morning hours and let himself out of his cell. He then unlocked the animal cage and woke up its occupant. Swede explained what he had in mind and that they needed to watch out the window for a while to see if guards came through or not. After an hour, the two left their building and moved quickly to where Swede had found the rice and garlic. He was hoping maybe now there would be fish on the menu. Once they both had eaten Swede asked the man if he was willing to be his look-out while he checked around. What he wanted to do was see if the Russian trucks were still there. They were. That was more than enough for the night and they returned to their cells.

The next night he got out of his cell, woke all the others, and explained he could pick the locks but wanted to keep that talent very secret. "I can help if they are trying to starve you into giving up, but that is about it. We are going to have to put up with anything else they throw at us. During the day, you have to deal with everything on your own, but know that at night we will all be here to help. We can talk about what they want us to write or what they want us to sign. I spent a couple of months here on my own. Having roommates will make it a whole lot easier. But the Chinese cannot get even a hint we can get out of the cells or that we talk about their demands at night. So, don't give them a hint. Not even after you get sent back to camp. Can we all agree on that?" Swede sat in the moonlight from the window and waited. After a short pause, he heard whispers of agreement from the other four cells. At that point, they began to think of him as Superman.

Frank Pennington, an insurance salesman from Los Angeles, was the man in the cage. Frank referred to the cage as a dog kennel and proclaimed himself as the founder of the Kennel Club. Swede didn't bother to remind him of the calendar on the wall and how it got there. He let Frank out every night so he could stretch all the kinks from being cramped in the cage all day. Swede told the others it was too risky for everybody to be out of their cells. Frank had earned his membership in the Kennel Club by taking a swing at a guard who had knocked a sick POW to the ground. After the guard and his pals knocked Frank around, they threw him in one of the cages. Most nights, either Swede alone, or the two together, made their way to the food storage shed. They would bring back some garlic and fish for the others. Just a handful each, but it made a difference in their ability to tolerate their cells.

Carl Lehman was the oldest of the group. He had a hard time listening to the Chinese talks about "lenient treatment" and the benefits of communism versus the "criminal behavior of the capitalist leaders Roosevelt and Truman." Carl had absolutely no tolerance for any POW who bought into any of the Chinese theories. He grew up south of Jackson, Tennessee, just north of the Mississippi border. The family survived, just barely, on little more than two hundred dollars a year. Franklin Roosevelt and the Tennessee Valley Authority changed all that. Carl Lehman was a believer in the American way.

"If I can't talk some sense into these dummies who agree with everything the Chinese say just for a few cigarettes, maybe I can bash some sense into their thick skulls," Carl would growl during their late-night sessions, almost as if his cellmates deserved some bashing. The instructors had started handing out gum and cigarettes to their class favorites.

"You're probably right, Carl," agreed Tony Shears. "But you can't do much talking or bashing from here. Try being a little sneakier, like you're squirrel hunting back home. When you make a lot of noise, you don't bring home supper."

Tony had been a small-town mayor in upstate New York. Probably a good one, thought Swede. Because he had just come up with the solution Swede was looking for. "Jim, what did you do to get sent up here?" Swede turned to Jim Riordan. Jim was a career Private. He was a good soldier but had no desire to take on any responsibility by getting promoted. He liked to keep his life simple. But he was no dummy.

"I challenged my instructor in front of the rest of the guys. He said South Korea had invaded the north. I asked the guys how many of them had been kept in Seoul and then marched north to Pyongyang. Then I asked what Seoul looked like when they were there. Then I asked what Pyongyang looked like when they got there. I said if South Korea invaded the north how come only Seoul was in ruins? I asked how come I was hundreds of miles south of Pyongyang when I was captured, just two weeks after the war started? I was told I have a bad attitude. That was the only thing that instructor said all day that was true."

"Think about it," said Swede. "We all tried to show how this 'learn the truth' crap is phony. Why did we do that? We know it's phony. But we spoke up because we want the other guys to see how phony it is. We want them to see the real truth. The US isn't perfect, but it's a lot more perfect than what these clowns stand for. So how do we help our guys see the real truth from here? Our communist friends outwitted us. We point out the truth and they isolate us up here while they continue their little education program. I guarantee you every day they convince somebody else to write a letter or sign a statement. We have taken ourselves out of the fight."

"We need to go squirrel huntin', boys!" Swede pretended he was taking aim at a squirrel up in a tree. The rest of them looked at him like he was more than a few cards short of a full deck.

Finally, Carl said, "I see what you mean. The guys that are cooperatin' are the squirrels. We can't shoot 'em out of the trees, so to speak, by yellin' at 'em. We need a better plan."

"Exactly," agreed Swede. "We need to sneak up on them. Try to get them to think about what they are doing and saying. If that doesn't work, maybe then we throw a few rocks at 'em."

"But if our guys are the squirrels, who are the Chinese?" asked Carl.

"They own the land and don't want us shootin' at their squirrels. So we have to be sneaky with them too. When they catch us in their woods, we can't just yell insults at them. That will just end up with the Boston Massacre with us on the short end. We need the Boston Tea Party. Make our point without getting shot."

"So how do we hold this Boston Tea Party?" asked Frank. "We're in the pokey, in case you haven't noticed."

"Eventually, they will come around and ask if we have reconsidered, if we have realized our error. Some of us will say the right things right away. Some of us will have to take more time to think. We can't all roll over at the same time. We have to make them think they are holding all the cards."

"Then what," asked Tony. "What do we do different once they send us back down to camp?"

"Every one of us has other guys in our hut that thinks like we do, right? Maybe only a few, maybe most of them. First, we don't go back down there and talk about how bad it is up here. Don't sugarcoat it but talk about how you have to be tough and pull together. You probably had a DI who was meaner than most of these guards.

"Tell them they might get knocked around by the guards, but if you yell like they are hurting you, the guards will feel good and go away laughing at the weak American. Try to be the tough guy and they will beat you to the ground." There was enough moonlight in the room for the others to see the scar on his forehead when Swede pointed it out. "Tell them you might not get a lot to eat, but you lived on less food this past winter. Tell them if we play the game right, we can win. But try to make all these points to the guys you think will listen, the guys you think will be willing to go squirrel hunting.

"Then play nice with the landowners. Agree a little bit, then have a 'but' to throw at them. But what if. But I also think. But what about. But I need to think some more about this. If they want a statement against American aggression, write one about aggression. Get others in your hut to go squirrel hunting with you. And maybe there will be times we have to give in and sign their paper for world peace. But the next day, we refuse to sign anything. Keep the weather gauge out. How much can we push our luck? When do we back off? Make this a group effort without letting on we are still a group. We can still fight. We can still go home with our heads held high."

"What do we do if we get thrown back in here?" asked Jim.

"We do it all over again. And hope others will take their turn." Swede waited for any arguments. "Now, let's figure out who gets bailed out first and start working on their confession."

By the time Swede confessed how foolish he was and how world aggression was a problem and how Marx had a better mousetrap, others from camp had replaced everybody but Frank. And each one of them had been told how to squirrel hunt. Then they passed the technique on to others. When they finally got back to camp, they continued to recruit squirrel hunters. The instructors eventually heard something was up from their favorite students, the ones who became addicted to the candy, the cigarettes, even better food. But the idea of squirrel hunting came up so often they put most of the rumors down to Americans and their silly folk heroes like Daniel Boone and Davy Crockett. Some of the more astute POWs gave long explanations to their instructors about Dan and Davy. One wrote a ten-page essay in his cell about the life of Davy Crockett before the interrogators finally gave up and let him go back to camp.

The Chinese didn't pay a lot of attention to the black prisoners, so Trigger managed to convince more than a few POWs that being a 'good' student was maybe not such a good idea. He also managed to spend some time on the wood gathering details and left messages for Page's people.

Over the next few months, Swede was sent back up the hill three more times. Page got sent up twice. When Swede was there, he managed to get a good look at the trucks he had seen during the winter. He spent some time under one while soldiers he was positive were Russian went in and out the back loading what looked like large radios. He drew diagrams of the funny shapes on top of the trucks for Page and described the patches on the Russian uniforms as best he could.

In June, the Chinese threw their first curve ball at the POWs. Until then, they had pushed for individuals or single huts to write and sign statements of one kind or another. But an international peace conference was going to be held in Chicago at the end of the month and they saw an opportunity. The prisoners were told they would send greetings to the conference, with all their names attached. A few of the enlisted signed but most officers and NCOs refused. Then the Chinese said the name of the village would be included in the message and that would prevent any more bomb raids in the area. That argument persuaded many more to sign. When the peace message reached Chicago, no village was mentioned.

To prevent further influence on the younger enlisted men, officers and sergeants were moved to compounds across the camp. That lead to Swede's third trip up to the jail to spend time in one of the cages to 'reconsider' his attitude. He wondered out loud at a group lecture why the Chinese were afraid to keep all the prisoners together. Why did they separate the leaders from the men? Swede thought he had been rather tactful with his question but once again found himself being called a bad influence. Not long after being released back to the compound, Swede was given another truck ride. At least this time it wasn't below zero and he wasn't alone. Carl Lehman, Jim Riordan, and Frank Pennington went along for the ride. Two trucks and twenty POWs drove out of the camp early in the morning without saying goodbye. They followed the river to the northwest until they came to what they thought at first was the ocean. Then somebody figured out it must be the Yalu River, which meant they were looking at China on the far bank. Swede began to worry he was about to visit his fourth foreign country. As far as he knew, there were no American troops in China that could come to his rescue. And it was not going to be an easy to swim to get back across the Yalu.

Camp 3
August 1951

It was the end of July or early August when the twenty POWs from Camp 1 arrived on the banks of the Yalu. They knew for sure it was the Yalu when the guards that had ridden with them became excited. One of them had worked with Americans during the last war and spoke enough English to explain that yes, it was the Yalu River. They were excited because they could see their homeland on the far bank. No one had explained exactly why they were escorting the prisoners or exactly where they were going. They simply had orders to reach this point and wait.

That little bit of information worried Swede even more. They had discovered on the way up that all the men in the trucks had spent time in a punishment cell at Camp 1. Some of them had spent time in both areas. Did that mean they were considered troublemakers and were on their way to China? What exactly would that mean? Their fears weren't set at ease when Jim Riordan called their attention to stacks of lumber down on the shore. Further investigation turned up a variety of wood-working tools and nails. Were they going to have to build a boat of some kind and row across to China?

The guards seemed to be in the dark almost as much as the prisoners. Late in the afternoon, one of the trucks sped off back in the direction they had come from. A half hour later they noticed a truck headed north on the far side of the bay that the river they had followed up from Camp 1 emptied into. They had arrived on a point of land that stuck out into the Yalu, like a thumb. To the west was China, easily visible from where they sat waiting. Directly north was the Yalu itself. To the east was the bay or inlet, which pointed back down the river towards Camp 1. Across that bay were the other fingers of the hand, forming the east bank of the Yalu. Up a slight hill from where they stood was a small village.

The truck they could see could have been theirs, but they had no way to tell for sure. An hour later they noticed a truck again, this time headed back down that road across the bay, dust billowing along behind. Soon, a truck rolled up to their little vacation spot, followed by its dust cloud. The men were rewarded for their patience with supper and some old jackets for blankets. They were told they would all sleep there for the night and go to work in the morning, whatever that meant.

In the morning, the men wandered down to the river and proceeded to take baths. The fine sand replaced the soap they hadn't seen since their bath at Camp 1 when they were issued their new clothes. It was a warm morning, all sunshine and shimmering water. The splashing didn't take long to start. Swede felt a repeat of the first time he had escaped. Complete freedom and joy at the world around him. The truck had taken off again, so breakfast was hopefully on the way. The guards were laughing at the antics of the Americans. In that moment, all was well with the world. Swede looked at both groups of men enjoying the day. Could they solve it all right here? Could these men, enemies, sit down and agree to solutions for whatever the problems were? Looking at the smiles and relaxed attitudes right then, the answer was yes. Too bad it couldn't be that simple. Other men in other places would not allow it.

Breakfast rolled in accompanied by another cloud of dust. And a barge. A barge appeared moving its way down the river. As it drew closer, it turned towards their point of land and pushed its nose ashore. The cargo was more lumber and more tools. Then a second barge pulled ashore. Followed by a third, then a fourth. These all carried a different cargo. There were at least fifty men on each of the last three barges. All dressed in student blue.

None of the POWs on the barges made a move to hop ashore. They looked at the men from Camp 1 with suspicion. Who are these guys and why do they look like they are having a picnic? The men from Camp 1 did the same. What was so special about these guys that they were floating down the Yalu like they didn't have a care in the world? Carl Lehman figured it out.

"What camp have you guys been thrown out of?" Carl had put two and two together and come up with his version of five. Troublemakers were sent into the middle of nowhere to build their own camp, a place where they couldn't influence the more 'progressive' students. But apparently, he was the only one to figure it out because still nobody else said anything.

Then came a shout from one of the barges. "Swede! Hey Swede! You made it! I thought you were dead, man!" A figure jumped down from one of the barges and rushed at Swede. Somebody else thinks I was dead, thought Swede. This is getting to be a habit. Who the hell is this guy? Then it hit him.

"Danny Morgan? Morg, is that you?"

That broke the ice for both groups. Here was one of their own hugging one of the strangers. These guys must be okay. Danny Morgan wanted all the details on where Swede had been. Everybody relaxed. Then the guards started being guards again and the men were put to work unloading the supply barge. As they were working on that, two jeeps pulled up. Chinese officers pulled out their blueprints and construction began on Camp 3.

The men on the barges had come down the river from Camp 5, just a few hours or so away. By the end of the first day, most of the details had been worked out. No one from either camp had known the other existed. No one from either camp knew of any other permanent camp. So, there was a Camp 1 and a Camp 5, and now they were building Camp 3. Was there a Two and a Four? It also became obvious that only about thirty of the men from Camp 5 were troublemakers like Swede and his group. The rest were just cheap labor.

For a week, they slept on the ground and got their meals delivered by the "Dusty Deuce," as they called the truck that made the trip north for food each day. The guards that brought the men up from Camp 1 headed back south with one of the trucks. New guards were brought in and slept on the ground like the Americans. Every other night those guards were rotated out, probably to whatever place their food was coming from

After a week, the barracks were complete enough to let the men move inside and sleep on the floor. A kitchen and guard's quarters were finished, trenches dug for permanent latrines. The project was beginning to look like it was meant to be a permanent camp. That began to worry Swede and a few others. Was the war at a point the Chinese felt they were going to be holding prisoners for a long time? Were other more permanent camps being built? Why on the Yalu? So they could move all the prisoners across to China? Nobody liked that theory.

The idea of escape came up more and more often in conversations. There were a handful of POWS who had escaped since their initial capture, but only a handful. Some held them in awe for taking the risk, others saw it as way too much of a risk.

"What makes you say it's too risky?" asked Hank Thompson. He himself had not tried an escape but knew some who had.

"How many guys do you know escaped all the way, got all the way back to our lines?" challenged Herman Vogl.

"How would I know if they did? If they make it all the way they don't turn around and come back up here to tell us. The only way we could know is if somebody here was with a unit when somebody escaped and made it to their lines. Then that person would have to be captured so they can tell us what they saw. Not very likely." Hank's explanation made a few scratch their heads, but he was right. How would any of them know if an escape attempt was successful? They could only see the failures. Herman Vogl was one of those who had escaped. He managed to get away by floating down a river his column crossed during the night. Five days later he tried to steal some food from the wrong village. His argument was escaping wasn't the hard part, finding food and shelter as you worked your way south was. Or did you go east? Or west? Where *was* the American army?

"Too many unknowns," said Herman. "While you meander around out there everybody you run into immediately knows you are a foreigner. How do you get food? Water? Shelter? Too many unknowns. Take a look out there." He pointed at the river. "Can you swim? The Yalu here must be what, half a mile wide? And if you make it, you're in China. On this side, Korea seems to be nothing but up and down. Where I come from, we call these mountains. You climb these and on the other side is a valley and another mountain to climb. Most of us aren't in shape to try it even if we did have food and water."

Most people seemed to agree with Herman. Danny Morgan wasn't one of them. He told Swede how he got to within hearing distance of US artillery when he stumbled into a Korean ambush set up to capture some prisoners. They weren't looking forward to getting into a shooting match with anybody. When he came along, they grabbed him and took off. When their people found out he had been captured a week before in an entirely different sector, they almost shot him out of frustration. Lucky for him they had several other prisoners and threw him in with them.

After spending time in Seoul and then Pyongyang, his column had reached an old mining camp in a place they called Death Valley. They were held there for the month of January. During that time nearly six hundred died. More died on the march to Camp 5. And then more. Bodies were stacked outside the huts until work parties took them to a nearby hill and scraped a shallow grave in the snow. Little food, no medicine, and plenty of cold. Danny had been on a burial detail when one of the men collapsed and died and was buried with the others.

In June, the entire camp had been forced to sign a peace petition. It was a simple request from the Chinese. Sign this or don't eat. Somebody had done the math. There were 1700 signatures on the petition. One from every prisoner in camp. At the end of January, there had been more than twice that number in Camp 5.

Listening to Danny's narrative, Swede thought about something his mother frequently said. "When you start feeling sorry for yourself, remember, there is always someone worse off than you." His uncles, Kurt and Eric, put it a different way. They would all be working in the field in the heat or fixing a stubborn piece of machinery in the cold. Sooner or later one of them would say "Smile, things could get worse." The other would immediately respond. "So I smiled, and sure enough, things got worse." Even though they both laughed, they weren't being funny. They were simply reflecting on what they had learned through personal experience in Africa and Europe during the war.

Danny and Swede talked about their situation. Winter wasn't that far away. The camp they were building looked like it was going to be better than any they had been in yet. But there was no heat system in the floors, no stoves in the buildings other than the kitchen. Nothing that could be considered a hospital. Was the upcoming winter going to be a repeat of what they had just gone through? There had not been any deaths in the last month, but they were eating better, and the weather was mild. What would happen once it turned cold again? Where were their beds, where were the blankets they would need to survive? Swede had no trouble admitting he could almost taste the fear when he thought about repeating last winter's experience. Even POWs who had been captured in the spring could sense the uneasiness of those who had survived the winter.

Jim Riordan brought it right out in the open. "I don't want to repeat last winter. I don't think I can handle that. Why not leave now? I know the arguments for not going, but did you have the Yalu River on your doorstep? We can float down river, steal a boat, and sixty miles later get picked up by the US Navy. No walking up and down these mountains. No stealing food from villages. We can go without food for the few days it will take us to reach the sea. If we go now, the weather won't be a problem." He looked at Danny and Swede as if to say, go ahead, find fault with *that* argument.

They could, but neither wanted to. Simply follow the river right to the sea. Be home before winter came and the dying began. So, they left.

Little planning was required. Sneak to the river, find a log, float silently away. Which is exactly what they did. They kept the log close enough to the near bank so they could swim to shore and hide if necessary. By morning they felt like they had gone at least five miles. They pushed the log into a small bay and hid in the nearby woods. They even managed to find some berries. Once it was dark, they pushed their log back out and set out again. Their hope was to spot a village and steal a boat. Steal a boat and sail down to the US Navy, just waiting to pick them up. They could taste the steaks and feel the sheets.

The village came along after a few hours. They could see the lights and hear the villagers wrapping up their day. They could even hear motors. As they let the log continue on its silent way, they smiled at each other. The lights and noise and motors meant a larger village. A larger village meant a bigger boat. A bigger boat meant sails instead of oars. They would reach the sea that night.

All three stayed in the water and paddled along the bank until they saw a boat. It had a small mast and sail, exactly what they were looking for. Without getting out of the water, they tugged it off the bank and pulled themselves aboard. The current was pushing them close to the bank again, so they felt around for the oars to use as poles to push farther into the river.

Except it wasn't the riverbank they were getting close to. It was a barge alongside the bank. And it wasn't a village they had found. Villages don't have all those lights and noise at that time of the night. Villages don't have motors. But military depots certainly do. And military depots downstream are notified when prisoners go missing upstream. The thumping of wood on wood as they dragged the oars out alerted a sentry on the barge. He had been told to watch for any sign of a small boat going by in the night.

"Ting! Ting!" The sentry flipped on the spotlight and pinned the boat to the river. Danny was in front paddling with his hands, Swede in the back doing the same. Jim Riordan stood using the oar as a paddle. Danny and Swede flipped out of the boat away from the barge and the light. Jim stood frozen and took the full burst of the guard's burp gun, disappearing in a pink mist. The next barge flipped on its spotlights and more sentries appeared, each carrying the same weapon. Since the first sentry was still firing at the boat, others joined in, figuring there must be a good reason. More lights beat away the dark. The splashing of Danny and Swede as they tried to swim away from the chaos attracted more fire. Then a small motorboat approached from downstream and turned its light directly on them. Voices of authority roared out and the shooting stopped. Two days later Jim Riordan reached the sea.

The order had simply been to capture the escapees and return them to the camp they were building. The sentry tried to explain to his commander he had not intended to kill anyone, didn't even plan to fire his weapon. When the light caught the boat, he thought about firing a burst in front of it to get them to stop. But two jumped and the one in the middle raised what looked like a rifle. He pulled the trigger in self-defense.

Danny and Swede didn't give the soldiers any hint they might try to break away. They simply sat in shock. The depot commander felt bad his guard had killed one of them. He ordered the guards not to rough the prisoners up as they were loaded aboard the small motorboat and sent back upstream. Neither of the men realized they had only gone three miles at best in their escape attempt. When they finally arrived at the nearly completed camp they had left two nights before, they noticed two small wooden crates on a slight rise just beyond one of the buildings. As soon as they were ashore, they were led to the crates and told to climb in. The guards forced each man down and nailed a cover over the top. They couldn't sit fully up nor stretch out. With effort, they could manage to curl into a fetal position on the floor. No matter what position they tried it was uncomfortable. Their moans and groans, and then the smells, just added to the message the Chinese wanted everybody to understand. You can't escape, and if you try, this is what will happen.

For two days the men were kept in the crates. Herman Vogl managed to sneak each a cup of cold tea that he poured into their mouths through cracks in the cover to each box. Swede gave Herman the details on what had happened. Herman told him the rumor was they would be sent to Camp 5 sometime in the next few days. From what he had seen at Camp 5, if you tried to escape, they threw you in jail for a while and then sent you to a different camp, kind of like a rotten apple in a barrel.

"I'm done with escapes," Swede told Herman. "I don't think it can be done and I've tried. This time somebody got killed. From now on I'll fight these guys a different way. Maybe somebody is trying to tell me to stay here and help people make it through to the end."

"A guard told me you were lucky," Herman replied. "He said the Yalu is nasty here. Lots of strong currents and really deep."

"Maybe I was lucky." Swede wasn't thinking about the Yalu.

Two days later, Swede and Danny were shoved into the back of the Dusty Deuce for the trip up to Camp 5. They were too cramped from their time in the boxes to climb in themselves. The Deuce headed southeast, turned left, crossed a wooden bridge, then headed back to the north on the other side of the small bay. Just across the bridge they passed through a small village with a few Chinese vehicles parked next to the larger buildings. Twenty minutes more and the truck stopped, the "dusty" part of the Deuce catching up to them and rolling on by. They could see a village to their left on another little thumb of land sticking out into the Yalu.

The driver and guard hopped down from the cab and went into a building, not at all worried their prisoners were going to run off. Even if Swede or Danny had any thoughts of running anywhere, they were incapable of doing so. They could barely unwind their muscles enough to stretch full out in the bed of the truck. When their escorts returned, they tossed each of the prisoners a rice ball wrapped in a cabbage leaf. Whatever their motivation for doing so, the two Americans were grateful. They hadn't eaten in three days.

Crossing another wooden bridge, the truck rattled and bumped its way in a northerly direction, sometimes following the river and other times cutting back inland. Eventually they headed west and drove out onto a peninsula jutting towards the Yalu. By then both Swede and Danny were standing up in the bed and looking out over the cab. There was still this nagging concern in the back of Swede's mind they might be headed across the river to China. He half expected to see a bridge as they topped a small rise and could see the broad river itself. No bridge, the river was far too wide, but there was a village spread out across the tip of the peninsula. It looked like Herman Vogl was right.

The truck pulled up in front of a large building on the top of the hill, their dust cloud catching up one last time. Once inside, it was obvious they were in a new barrel, so to speak, one where rotten apples were kept. They were escorted through a door with a small barred window and then directed to a cell where other apples sat in silence.

"Sit! No talk!" So much for being introduced to their roommates. There were six cells on each side of a narrow walking space. The farther down the row of cells, the darker it got. Swede and Danny were placed in the last cell on the left. Four other men were already there, each sitting in silence, their legs crossed in front of them. Straw covered the cement floor. The slamming of their cell door was a nasty sound. The place reminded Swede of his time with Uncle Kim and Buddha; steel bars, straw on the floor, men sitting in silence. At least this place didn't smell as bad.

The silence continued into the evening when they were allowed out to balance on the pole over the slit trench and quickly down their cup of rice and cup of tea. Once back inside, an English-speaking guard gave a speech about the people's leniency policy and taking the time to consider how foolish they were in trying to escape. It was impossible, and now they must accept their just punishment for their actions. After it grew dark, the two guards watching over the cells withdrew to the outer office, closing and locking the door behind them. Everybody relaxed their posture but remained quiet and sitting. It was another hour before the whispering started.

Camp 5

August 1951

It was very dark in their cell with only a little moonlight coming in the window on the far side. Swede could see figures in his cell, but not faces. The figure next to him leaned in.

"OK, new guys, tell us about yourselves." As dark as it was in the cells, there was a sense of who are you guys, can we trust you?

Danny broke the tension, just as he had done when the barges from Camp 5 pulled up to the shore at Camp 3. "I'm Danny Morgan. I was sent south of here in a group on three barges in early August. Swede and I tried to escape a week ago. They sent us up here as punishment."

"Yeah, that sounds like Morgan all right," came a voice from a cell closer to the window. "What was the name of the guy who died as we were carrying him from Death Valley? We didn't even know he was dead until we tried to get him back up after a break."

"Hey Redmond, is that you? We weren't carrying him. We could barely keep each other up. The two guys ahead of us were carrying him. Lundstrom was his name. He was from Michigan. Clark and Gibson were the two carrying him. They didn't last more than a week after we got here."

"He got it all straight. That's Danny Morgan," the voice that was Redmond declared. "But who is the other guy with you, Morgan? Do you trust him?"

"Swede and I served together in Japan and were captured together in July of last year. We escaped but then got split up. He was with a small group on the beach when we got sent south on the barges. We built a new camp only a few hours from here. Camp 3. And I trust him as much as I trust you."

"What's your story, Swede?" asked Redmond.

"My name is Paul Larson, but they call me Swede. After Danny and I got separated when we were first captured, my column ended up in Seoul for a while. Apparently, our guys landed at a place called Inchon, just south of Seoul, about the middle of September. On the march out of Seoul I got left behind when I got sick. They shot the sick when we first got captured, but on the way out of Seoul they just left us in the nearest village. Then I got a nasty fever and wandered off from the village at night. I got captured again and was sent to a civilian jail for about two months. Then they sent me to the jail at Camp 1, but there weren't any other prisoners there yet. In April, they put me in with the other Americans. There were some British there too, in a separate compound. They sent about twenty of us up to build Camp 3 in early August. And now we're here. I've spent seven months in one jail or another since I was captured. I hope this is better than the other two." Swede left out the parts he didn't think everybody needed to know. Even Danny didn't know about the Chinese colonel or the lock picks. Just because you're paranoid doesn't mean they aren't out to get you.

After that initial conversation, the men in the cells stood up to stretch or lay flat out to relax. The other men in Swede's cell introduced themselves. Billy Beckman was the man who had first spoken to Swede. Richard Shea, Fred Moeder, and Earl Stoneman were the others. Billy and Fred were there because they had tried to escape. They were caught before the next morning. Richard and Earl had the bad habit of arguing with the instructors. Earl told them everybody in the cells had either tried to escape, argued with the instructors, or harassed the people they called Pros. The Chinese called the men who easily cooperated in their own re-education "Progressives." Men who spent time in the cells were called "Reactionaries."

Sitting silently most of the day wasn't the easiest thing to do, but the food was better than down in the camp. The Chinese found it simpler to feed the men in the cells from the kitchen used by the guards as it was much closer than the kitchen used to feed the rest of the camp. Except to punish anyone who fell asleep or relaxed too much during the day, the guards left them alone. Punishment was usually a few sharp jabs from poles the guards kept handy. Every couple of days, they entered a cell and used clubs. Once a day the POWs had to listen to a very boring lecture about how they had been corrupted by the capitalist warmongers in Washington D. C. So far, three different instructors were taking turns giving that lecture. Each of them had his version of the same speech. The men had taken to betting on how many times a certain word or phrase would appear in each speech. Keeping track of the phrases helped the time pass more quickly. A bigger benefit was the obvious pride the instructors took at the attentiveness of their audience. That sometimes got the whole group rewarded with extra tea or more vegetables in their rice for being such good students.

The standard jail time was one month. Then they were either released back into the general camp population or sent somewhere else. Swede and Danny had been placed in one of the last cells because three people from that cell had recently been released. Late one night when most people were asleep, including the guards in the outer room, Earl Stoneman explained to Swede his theory on how the system worked.

"The Commies want to get us to sign statements about how well they treat us or how bad life is in the US or how they are the only ones who want world peace. If they can get confessions about some "war crime" that will really float their boat. They don't want people like us trying to escape from their wonderful 'lenient policy.' They don't want people like us to argue with them in front of everybody else. That makes people think about all the horseshit they are feeding us, and they really don't want that.

"When reactionaries like us stir the pot, they can't let us get away with it in front of the others, but they can't line us up and shoot us like they do with their own people. Instead, they show how 'lenient' they are by sending us up here to this jail. Usually they have us 'confess' to our 'crime' in front of the whole camp as an example to the others. The thing is they don't have enough room in the jail to keep all of us here permanently, so we get a month. When that month is up, they send us somewhere else, like the guys they sent down to build that camp you worked on."

"So, what happens to me when my month is up?" asked Swede. "I've already been to Camp 1, I helped build Camp 3, and now I'm at Camp 5. Where do they send me that I haven't been before?"

"Technically, you haven't been here yet, not to the actual camp. So maybe they just send you down to the main camp. Or maybe when they run out of places to send you, they really do shoot you," he chuckled. "But I think that's just a slim possibility. New guys who have come into camp the last couple of months say there are some kind of peace talks going on. They are gonna need us to trade for their people who got captured. Maybe they will just put all of us who "can't learn the truth" in a camp away from the others. But I got a question for you. What do you think about escaping? Can it be done?"

"How many of these mountains can you climb with no food and no water?" Swede motioned out beyond the walls of their cells. "The first time I escaped was way south of Seoul. Even *those* hills took everything we had. I didn't make it clear before, but this was my third escape. We stick out like giant sore thumbs in this country. We don't know who we can trust. Food and water are a real problem. So yeah, we can escape, but can we get away? I think the answer to that question is no.

"I know I'm a lot younger than most of you, have a lot less experience. But I think we shouldn't try to persuade people not to escape. Who knows? Somebody might make it. More importantly, it shows the Chinese we won't quit, we won't buy into their 'people's paradise.' And *most* importantly, it shows the rest of our guys the same thing. Some of them will think a little harder about what the Chinese are trying to get them to do. And that is where the rest of us come in, the rest of us 'reactionaries.' We stay here and we work on our guys just like the Chinese are doing."

Earl looked at Swede. "Don't worry about the experience thing. Too many people have all kinds of experience and never seem to learn a damn thing. But I don't get what you mean by we work on our guys like the Chinese are doing. Explain that a little more to your elders," Earl said with a grin.

"First, we set an example to the whole camp. We don't buy the Chinese BS, and more importantly, we fight back, even if all we do is argue with them. But the ones who are bending over backward for the Chinese, the 'progressives,' we help them learn the real truth. We talk with them, if that doesn't work, we get a little more aggressive. We let them know we are watching, we make little threats, then we make bigger threats - maybe pay them a visit at night."

"Are you saying we should out-Commie the Commies?" Earl thought about that for a bit. "You know kid, I like the way you think. But we need to be careful. Let me tell you about when they first started this re-education bullshit.

"We had a Major Hume with us when we first got here. The Chinese were readin' some newspaper article that talked about how the US invaded North Korea and started the war. The Major stood up and said the article wasn't worth the paper it was written on. They grabbed him and hauled him up the hill to their HQ, up here where we are now. They kept him up here for three weeks, beatin' on him until he agreed to inform on the rest of us. When he was released, he told us what he was supposed to do and said if the Chinese beat him again, he would tell them anything he had heard. He died a few weeks later.

"And then there was Father Kapuan, our chaplain. He constantly argued with the Chinese to get us better food and medical treatment. He held religious services. He would go down to the river and chop a hole in the ice to get water, bring it back, boil it, and give it to the sick. He snuck out of the officer's section and visited sick in the enlisted huts. The man was a saint, as my mother would say. He gave away his food and used parts of his uniform to help clean the sick. The Chinese instructors hated him. He contradicted their lectures with quotes from the Bible. When he finally got sick, they practically dragged him from his hut and took him to their hospital. I don't know of a single person that got sent to that hospital and lived. The Chinese put him in a room by himself and left. He died a couple of days later.

"Here's my point. If the Chinese think one of us is trying to get others to stand up to them, they will come down on us hard. They seem to be improvin' things a little, apparently because there are some kind of peace talks goin' on. But I'm pretty sure they will arrange for us to get special attention somewhere out of sight if we get too obvious. We are gonna have to be careful, and we are gonna have to be willing to take some licks when we aren't careful enough."

Earl Stoneman never told people where he was from. Not exactly. He would just say West Virginia and move on with the conversation. Earl Stoneman was from Hog Holler, West Virginia. He never knew his father. Apparently, his mother didn't know the man well either.

After Earl was born, his mother took up with one of the local ne'er-do-wells. Most of the local girls wouldn't have anything to do with him, so he was happy for her attention - at first. Then five more kids came along and that meant responsibility and that meant a job. He didn't do well at either. Having to do for his own brats was bad enough, but Earl was the bastard of the bunch and easy to blame for anything and everything. He was barely old enough to walk when he was farmed out to relatives for whatever he could earn. Earl learned to hate everything about Hog Holler, West Virginia. It was a tough place to love under any circumstances.

One day a distant cousin was nice enough to let Earl join the family for supper after a long day of splitting rails. The family had a radio and Earl heard his first song. It was about being stuck in a sad place and leaving for better places with no regrets. Hearing a radio for the first time was a miracle in itself. But the words of the song went through his fifteen-year-old mind like a bolt of lightning.

Earl had never thought about a life outside of Hog Holler. Hog Holler *was* life. There was nothing else. But that song talked about a different life out there, a better life. Two days later Earl Stoneman walked away from Hog Holler and never looked back. He was big enough and strong enough to take care of himself. And he could spot somebody even thinking of taking advantage of him a mile away. The talk on the road was California had the flowers and sunshine he was looking for, hopping freights the way to get there. That was how Earl came to be working in a bar in Sausalito, across the bay from San Francisco, when he heard someone singing the song responsible for him being there.

When he realized the man singing was the same as on the radio, Earl introduced himself and told the man the story of how that song had set him free. That conversation led to Earl's life taking another drastic turn. The singer, Sammy Craig, had been around the world after running off at age twelve to join the circus. Earl reminded him of himself, so he took the boy under his wing. Sammy told Earl about his adventures in the Philippines, China, Australia, and South America. He didn't do so to fill the boy's head full of dreams but to let him know there were lots of possibilities out there. However, it was 1938, and the Depression was in full swing. Sammy convinced Earl his best bet was to enlist in the army. He would get three squares a day and regular pay. If the Depression was still on when his time was up, he could re-enlist. If he was lucky, he could get assigned to the Philippines or China. With his size and Sammy's signature, he had no problem at the recruiting station.

Since then, Earl had taught himself to read and write and was the first to admit he wasn't that great at either. But he was content with his place in life. As a sergeant in the US Army he had just the level of responsibility he felt he could manage. Earl's life in Hog Holler had cut deep into any desire to form close relationships. He made friends easily and left them that way too. Army life meant he had done a lot of both. He had seen many of the places Sammy Craig had told him about. There was much about Earl that reminded Swede of Mike Finnegan.

The night Earl told Swede about hearing the song for the first time, he started laughing. "What do you think was the last song I heard before we left Japan and headed over here?"

"Let me guess," said Swede. "The first song you ever heard."

"You got it. Somebody else was singin' it. But I gotta say I liked Craig's version better. I call it my travelin' tune. Every time I hear that song, I feel good. Every bit of my life since I first heard that song has been good." Swede looked at Earl with one eyebrow up and just a hint of a smile.

"Well, good up until now anyhow. And I plan to get through this and look back one day to see this was just a bump in the road." Swede gave him the same look again.

"OK, so this is a really large bump. But I plan to come out of this alive and more or less well. The army can nurse me back to health and I'll be goin' down the road again. Maybe this time I can get a new car. After the last war I had to settle for a '41 Ford. I sold it just before I shipped out for Japan. Only car I ever owned. Maybe the next one will last until I make my twenty."

Over the next week, Swede and Earl had many late-night conversations with others in the cells. And when new guys came in, they sounded them out. The idea was if they all worked together, wherever they ended up, they could throw a large wrench into the Chinese game plan to convert as many American capitalists as possible. If people wanted to escape, they would help them. If people were willing to listen to reason, they would reason with them. Those who would not listen would be approached a little more firmly.

Their first shot at putting the plan into action came when the Chinese sent an obvious Progressive into the cells to find out who the diehard Reactionaries were. After only one conversation, it was plain why he was there. But the poor guy had a serious medical problem. He was constantly tripping and hurting himself. Way too often he managed to knock others on top of him. Everybody would be concerned and help him get back on his feet. He was removed from the cells only a week after he got there.

The group thought they had put one over on the Chinese until Fred Moeder developed a bad case of diarrhea with a fever to boot. The guards wouldn't let him out of the cell until their regular break in the morning or evening. Two days into Fred's problem, a new prisoner was thrown into the cell next to Swede's. The guards actually threw him in the cell, with the prisoner calling them names all the while.

Al Windorski had been on a firewood gathering detail in the hills east of camp. One of the guards for Al's detail was a hard nose, which is why they called him Mussolini. He kept demanding the men carry more wood, his demands backed up by his bayonet. Al, not known to tolerate the guards on a good day, finally decided he had enough. He threw down the logs he was carrying and told Mussolini he could "damn well carry it yourself." Mussolini didn't speak English, but he got the gist. He lunged at Al with his bayonet. Al sidestepped and grabbed the rifle. With his hands on the rifle, and Mussolini staring at him wide-eyed, Al knew he had gone too far. He let go and began to back off. Outraged by this American trying to take his rifle, Mussolini swung the butt at Al's head, just missing as he backpedaled. What happened next probably saved Al's life. He tripped over the wood he had thrown to the ground and fell down the hill. The hill was steep, and he picked up speed as he rolled, finally coming to a stop against a fallen tree. Somewhere along the way he had hit a sharp rock or tree branch and opened a nasty gash on his leg. By the time Mussolini got there, fully intending to stop this attempted escape by pinning the American to the tree with his bayonet, Al was yelling in pain and trying to stop the bleeding. As much as he wanted to, Mussolini knew killing Al would just cause him more trouble. He figured he could save face by claiming he had thrown the American down the hill. The pain and the blood would be enough for now.

So Al joined the group in the cells. His wound was a long gash below the knee, but not deep enough to cause any long-term bleeding. The Chinese, of course, hadn't treated it in any way. It wasn't until the third day that Al asked the others in his cell what they thought about how the wound looked. The area around the wound was red and stiff to the touch. Al admitted he felt hot. The consensus was he had an infected wound.

"You need sulfa powder and some aspirin," stated Earl Stoneman. When Earl gave advice, it was listened to.

"Just where does he get those?" asked Billy Beckman. "I suppose we could ask whoever comes in to give us the lecture today. But I ain't seen them treat nobody for nothin' yet around here, and I been here since January."

The word was spread to all the cells about Al's problem in the hope somebody might have a solution. Hank Prosser claimed he had seen medical supplies in a hut when he was on a work party earlier in the summer. "There were boxes with red crosses on them. I saw some USA stamps on some of the boxes. I figured they were medical supplies the Chinks grabbed from some unit or another. We were up in this area of the camp digging drainage ditches around the buildings. The shovels and picks we used were stored in the same building. It was about a ten by ten shed just behind a big concrete block building."

"Might as well be on the moon," said Earl. "But we can ask. Anybody want to volunteer?"

Swede spoke up. "I'll give it a shot. It won't hurt to ask, will it?"

"You never know with these guys," answered Billy. "If they decide your question shows you don't understand their lenient treatment policy, they might give you a few whacks."

Later that day, before the lecturer began, Swede called out. "We have a man here who needs medical treatment. Can you get him something for his wound?"

The Professor, as this particular lecturer was called, looked blankly back at Swede. "The Chinese People's Leniency Policy means no one here can have any wounds as none of our soldiers would wound a prisoner. You are here as our guests, to study with us and learn the truth. Any sickness you might have is only from your refusal to take care of yourselves. You simply have to keep yourselves clean and there will be no problems requiring medical treatment."

With that bit of logic, the Professor went right into his version of how the factory owners in the United States had started the war against the innocent villages of Korea just so they could make more profit. Billy leaned over to Swede and whispered, "At least he didn't have the guards whack you around. I suppose because they wouldn't do that to one of their guests. Looks like we need to come up with Plan B."

Later that night, the discussion was Plan B. It was a short discussion as no one had a Plan B. Those who had experience with wounds agreed Al was only going to get worse if nothing was done. Al had been in too much pain to think clearly when he was first tossed into the cell. It wasn't until the next day had used his tea to wash the wound out. By then the infection had already set in.

Swede pulled Earl into the back of their cell and explained that he had a way to get out of the cell but had no idea about getting out of the building to search for the supply shed. Did the guards spend the night in the outer office? Did the window down near the door open? "You come up with how we get out of the building and I can get us out of the cell and into the shed. If we can find it." Then he explained to Earl about the lock picks.

"You are a genuine reactionary, no doubt about it," Earl said with a grin. "OK, I think at least one guard sleeps in the office at night. The window opens. I was here a few months ago for an 'attitude adjustment' and saw a guard open it up to bring in some fresh air. The whole window swings out. If you really are going to try, I'm going with you. And we need to try tonight. That infection is going to be a problem real soon."

The two spread the word through the cells what they were about to do. "We are trusting you guys not to say a word. Just pretend you're sleeping. If they catch us you don't know anything," Swede whispered to the group. He opened the cell door and Earl followed him out. They left the door unlocked in case they had to get back in a hurry. Earl looked through the small window in the door leading to the office. If any guards were there they weren't moving around. The window on the wall was easy. There was no latch. It swung open without a sound. Both men slipped outside, pushed the window shut again, and crouched below.

"I've hid from the cops and the MPs a few times in my life," whispered Earl. "But this seems different."

"Nobody expects us to break out of our cells and go wandering around at night. So, they don't look for it. If we are quiet and slow, we should be OK," responded Swede. "Let's find Hank's shed." He realized his heartbeat wasn't paying attention to his words.

It took about twenty minutes of peeking around corners, but they finally saw a shed that fit the description. Getting in was no problem. Once inside, they found they had to leave the door open to let in enough light to see what they were doing. "This is easier than I thought," whispered Earl.

"Don't get too relaxed. We aren't home yet. What exactly are we looking for? I don't want to start ripping open boxes," said Swede.

"Look for a Carlisle First Aid Packet. That will give us a bandage and some sulfa. And look for a small box of sulfa packets, they come in boxes of eight. Probably cardboard boxes but maybe in a small red or OD metal container."

The more their eyes adjusted to the light the angrier Swede got. "There's a truckload of stuff here! They won't let our doctors use it and their quacks sure haven't. Somebody needs to pay for this! This is wrong."

"You can make them pay for it later. Let's find what we need and get back." Earl continued moving boxes into the light. "OK! This is a Carlisle packet. Now we need to find boxes of sulfa packs. And some aspirin."

"Why the Carlisle?" asked Swede.

"It will have a sterile bandage and one sulfa envelope. The bandage is brown instead of white, so I think we can keep it hidden under Al's pant leg. In fact, we should take a couple of the Carlisle packets and a couple of boxes of sulfa."

"Here we go!" said Earl. "Found 'em. Open these boxes and put the sulfa packets in your pocket. We can get them to our medics to use. If the Chinese find them, we just say we have had them since we were captured. Nobody ever took them away. Or some other lie."

Each man took two Carlisle packets and two boxes worth of sulfa envelopes. They hid the empty containers behind all the boxes of supplies and stuffed everything in their pockets. Checking outside, they closed and locked the door and headed back. Swede had a smile on his face, thinking about how they had put one over on their captors. When he realized he was smiling, a chill hit him. Something bad was about to happen. He pulled Earl back into the shadows between two buildings.

"What's wrong," asked Earl.

"I'm not sure. Let's wait a second and make sure nobody's around."

They sat for a few minutes, checking in all directions. No noise, no movement. "I guess we're good. Let's get back," whispered Swede.

As soon as they stood up and headed between the two sheds, they heard a shout from behind them. Looking back, they could see someone running at them, but still about a hundred feet away. They turned and began to run back towards the jail. They were easily outrunning their pursuer as they came close to the jail.

"Keep going!" huffed Earl. "If we stop and try to get in the window he'll catch up. Turn left here." The two made a quick turn between two buildings. They were closer together and blocked any moonlight. Earl pulled Swede to the right and down. "Let him go by. Then we sneak back and head for the jail."

It wasn't a guard chasing them. He had no jacket on and didn't have a weapon. Just somebody out using a latrine and curious as to why people were wandering around in the dark. Swede couldn't understand why the man hadn't been able to hear the pounding of his heart as he went past. The fact he wasn't fit to be running hundred-yard dashes wasn't helping.

Keeping low and against the buildings, they moved back out and headed for the jail. Just as they turned the corner, they heard another shout. Maybe their little buddy wasn't just a clerk after all! But now they had opened the distance between them. Breaking into a run, they made it to their window before he turned out into the open. The window swung open and an arm reached out to grab Earl. For an instant Swede thought they had been caught after all.

"What are you waiting for? Get in here!" Billy Beckman and Fred Moeder each grabbed an arm and lifted Earl up. Swede flew in after him. The men had just swung the window closed again when the little guy went puffing on by.

"Quiet and slow, my ass," growled Earl. "Let's get back to the cell before that guy wakes up the whole camp."

They hadn't been in the cell more than five minutes when there was shouting in the outer office. The door banged open and two guards came hurrying in. With all kinds of noise and flashing of lights they did a head count of each cell and then did it again. When the count was to their satisfaction, they stormed back into the outer office, banging the door closed as they left. This was followed by more shouting and then banging of the outer door. It sounded like their guards were not too happy some paper pusher had the nerve to accuse them of letting some of their prisoners escape.

Al Windorski slid over so Earl could reach through the bars and sprinkle the sulfa powder on his wound and then apply the bandage. Al swallowed a couple of aspirin. Earl kept any wrappings and managed to dump them in the latrine pit the next morning. Reusing the bandage, they repeated the treatment for the next couple of days. Al recovered nicely but had a nasty scar as a souvenir. Everybody felt good. They had outwitted the Chinese in a big way. If there had been any Doubting Thomases about Swede and Earl's suggestions for fighting back against the Communists, they were now eager converts.

A couple of days later, Swede earned more points with his fellow Reactionaries with his confession in front of the whole camp. Prisoners in the cells didn't mix with the rest of the POWs except when they were stood up in front of the entire camp during a group lecture to 'confess their crimes.' They weren't brought out in front of the group until they looked shaggy and dirty enough. The Chinese hoped their appearance and their 'sincere confession' would convince their fellow POWs to behave. Swede stood in front of the group on a rainy day and read his confession.

"I want to thank the Chinese People's Volunteer Army for giving me this opportunity to confess my crimes. The Chinese People's Volunteer Army has given me many opportunities to think on my errors, but I still tried to escape down the river. I apologize to the Chinese People's Volunteer Army and to all of you for trying to escape down the river. I was wrong to try to escape. I should be grateful to the Chinese People's Volunteer Army for their lenient treatment of me after I was captured. They only punished me for two days and then sent me here to apologize to you for my incorrect behavior. Even after my mistake, the Chinese People's Volunteer Army still feeds me once a day. I do not deserve such good treatment. I hope you also see the leniency of the Chinese People's Volunteer Army in all they do for you. I hope you do not demonstrate an incorrect attitude and try to escape down the river. I promise to demonstrate correct thinking in the future and never try to escape down the river again."

The key words were there to bring smiles to the faces of the camp staff. Chinese People's Volunteer Army, confess my crimes, think on my errors, apologize, lenient treatment, demonstrate correct thinking. When the POWs cheered and clapped after Swede's confession, the camp staff smiled even more. They could see how the prisoners appreciated such a sincere confession. The prisoners themselves appreciated being told not to try to escape down the river and that when they tried to escape in some other direction, they would not be shot if they were caught.

A week later, all the men in Swede's cell were escorted down to the riverbank and loaded on a supply barge. Nobody said anything, but from the looks on the faces of the others, Swede was sure they were thinking the same thing he was. Somebody had talked! Now they were on their way across the river to China!

Then Swede noticed Earl. He was sitting on a crate, leaning back against another, and quietly singing a tune.

The sun came up and I set off
To leave my sadness and woe.
The breeze whispered there was bound to be
Sunshine and flowers where I could go.

I'd had enough and I set off
To leave that life behind.
Knew that I would never go back
And that brought me peace of mind.

3 North

Sep-Oct 1951

As the barge pulled out into the river Swede was trying to tell himself maybe China wouldn't be so bad. He had joined the army to broaden his horizons. China would be another story to tell when he got home, with all his former classmates hanging on to every word. But he wasn't buying his own argument.

Then the barge turned south.

A few hours later, the barge arrived at the point north of Camp 3. The guards had stopped in the village on their way up to Camp 5 about a month before. Danny Morgan looked over at Swede. "Looks like we're headed back to Camp 3. Wonder if they'll send the Dusty Deuce to pick us up?"

Instead of a truck, they were met by two guards who marched them down the road past where they had each been given a rice ball wrapped in cabbage. Then they turned right and moved back towards the river. Swede realized what he had assumed to be a village on the trip up to Camp 5 was a POW camp. There were four long buildings set near the river with two similar, but smaller, buildings just to the south. Scattered between the long buildings, obviously POW barracks, and the buildings back near the road, were several smaller sheds. Closer to the road itself were twenty or so Korean huts.

Swede put his hand on Earl's shoulder. "Looks like we were both wrong. They didn't send me to Camp 5 and they aren't sending me back to Camp 3. I wonder if this is Two or Four?"

Earl grinned back at Swede. "And it looks like they aren't gonna shoot you. Unless this is where they send people to be shot."

By this time, they were walking past a group of prisoners cutting logs into firewood. One of them spoke up. "You're both wrong. This is Camp 3. And they haven't shot anybody. Yet." The man chuckled at his wit. "Where did you fellas come from? I'm Harvey, by the way."

It took the rest of the afternoon to work out the details. Harvey Reynolds argued the place was Camp 3. Swede and Danny argued they had helped *build* Camp 3 and it was south a few miles on another little peninsula like this one. Swede had been in One and Earl and the others had been in Five, so this had to be Two or Four. Later that evening, after the guards were gone, they sat down and drew up a rough map in the dirt. Camp 5 was maybe twenty miles north. Where they were became 3 North, and where Danny and Swede had worked became 3 South. Camp 1 was maybe five miles southeast of 3 South, along the river which flowed into the Yalu between 3 North and South. At the mouth of the river was a village that was probably the headquarters for the Chinese handling both parts of Camp 3.

Harvey and the hundred or so prisoners with him at 3 North had been sent from Camp 1 and Camp 5 at the end of August. A few were new captures. Given the fact there were still empty barracks, Harvey figured more were on their way.

When Swede heard that more prisoners had been sent up from Camp 1 he asked, "Is there a guy here from Camp 1 by the name of Henry Page? How about a black guy by the name of Trigger?"

"From what I hear, all the black guys were put in a separate company at Camp 1. Can't say I know anybody by the name of Page, but I sure haven't met everybody. You can check in the morning. The guards don't like us wandering around at night. If you need to get to the latrine at night, make sure you yell 'da bee in' or 'benjo' as soon as you get outside. Either will work here. Then wait for a guard to yell back or maybe just grunt. If you can't, wait just keep yellin' as you run. Like I said, they haven't shot anybody around here yet, but no point pushin' your luck."

The next day Swede asked around and managed to track Henry Page down. He was at the edge of the camp looking over at the road. Swede came up from behind and growled, "If yer thinkin' of runnin' off, don't bother. Ya won't get very fer."

Page turned to see who was giving him advice. "Swede! So this is where they sent you. How come I haven't run into you before this? I've been here a couple of weeks." Page was all grin.

"This is where they sent me yesterday. I've been in two other camps since we got trucked out of Camp 1. How about Trigger? Is he here? Or Ray?"

"Ray's gone, Swede. He died about a month ago. He just never got any better and then diarrhea hit him again. He died in his sleep. I'm sorry, I know how close you two were."

Swede just stood for a while, looking back in the general direction of Camp 1. Once again, his uncles were right. Just when things were looking better - they weren't. Ray Parker had been his link to life before. Before the war and before Ray interrupting his sleep that morning so long ago. Before he saw up close what some men were willing to do to others. With Ray's death, he felt more than ever he owed a debt to him and all the others who had died. Death on a battlefield is one thing. Death by execution or complete neglect was another. Swede intended to see that debt was paid. He looked at Page.

"I haven't thought about home for months now. What do you suppose that means?"

"It means you're focused on now, so you can survive this mess and get back home. And you do a good job on the now. You help others with the now. I think we have a way to go yet. We just need to focus on the fight we have here. The Chinese think they can bring us to their way of thinking, their *gestalt*. We need to prove them wrong. Squirrel hunting, I think you called it back in Camp 1." Page grinned at Swede.

Swede gave Page a strange little grin of his own. "You're right. And there are some good guys here to help us with that. Earl Stoneman reminds me of Jack Usury. People respect him, they'll listen to him. But before we talk with him, explain something. I'm just a kid from Minnesota. My vocabulary doesn't have words like *gestalt* in it."

"I can see I'm going to have to improve on your education. Like a guy I knew in New York used to say, 'Whatsa matter kid, ya don't got no school housin'? But so far, for a kid from Minnesota anyway, you seem to be holdin' your own." Then he explained *gestalt*.

In the next week, Camp 3 North settled into a routine. The food didn't come close to even one star, but the guys from Five said it was better than what they had been getting. They got two meals a day and some bread for a mid-day snack. The food may have improved a little but the Chinese attitude towards Reactionaries hadn't.

Swede thought he had been careful in how he worded his reaction to an instructor's request that the men in his barracks send a petition to the United Nations demanding they put a halt to the inhumane treatment of Chinese soldiers who were held as prisoners of war. Swede wasn't really aware of the deep anger he felt when he thought of all those who had died - or had been murdered by the Chinese and the Koreans. He had looked right at the instructor and said, "I'll sign that, just as long as it says halt the inhumane treatment of ALL prisoners of war. I owe at least that to all the friends of mine who died under the lenient treatment of the Korean and Chinese People's Armies."

For that he was put on another truck and sent down to the village halfway to Camp 3 South. He was told he was being sent to Regiment, which turned out to be what they had thought, the Chinese headquarters for the camp. It wasn't much, just a small Korean village. The area had attracted a lot of Japanese tourists over the years and some had built vacation homes. Homes that looked like any cottage around lakes and rivers in the states. The Chinese had taken these homes for their headquarters. The village itself was pretty much left alone.

After only a mile or so the truck stopped, and he was taken inside one of the larger homes. He recognized a few of the Chinese in the room, so he figured this was the command post, so to speak, of the instructors and interrogators. His escort handed some papers to a man sitting behind a desk. He was an older man, very fit, and well groomed. After reading over the paperwork on Swede, he gave some orders to others in the room. Looking up at Swede, he wagged his finger back and forth. There was no smile. His eyes were dark and cold.

Swede was pushed back out the door and escorted none too gently to a small building set apart from the others. His hands were tied behind his back and he was shoved into the building. Inside were two other doors. One was opened and Swede motioned inside. As he stepped in, he felt a pain to his side. Then another. His escorts were jabbing him with stout boards that just happened to be next to the door. He was tripped and forced to the floor. The jabs became more forceful. The room was too small for them to swing their clubs, but they put as much force into the blows as they could. Then the door

204

was slammed shut and Swede heard a bolt slam across. He had no open wounds that he could see or feel, but his legs and arms were on fire. Swede realized they had not hit him in the head or face. Was that because of the size of the room, or was there a purpose to their method?

The room was small, but nowhere near as tight as the rooms at the Kennel Club in Camp 1 were. A major difference was how tight the construction was. No outside light came through. After feeling his way around the room to discover any weaknesses, and finding none, Swede stretched out to see if he could sleep.

Swede spent three more days in his dark little room. He could tell night from day more by the sounds of the camp than anything else. And it was during the day that his guards came in to smack him around. After the first beating he remembered his own advice and yelled really loud after the first few blows. It was easy to yell because they were putting bruises on top of bruises. He was sure they were trying not to break anything, just cause pain and discomfort.

Another problem came when he realized they weren't going to give him any latrine breaks. They weren't giving him any food either, so the two balanced out. His pants were loose enough, so even with his hands behind his back he was able to get them down and point his butt at the back corner of the room. The heat during the day caused a definite odor problem, while the October nights kept it at tolerable levels. The strangest thing of all was the guards never said a word to him. Open the door, whack him around, and on their way they went. With his hands tied behind his back, the lice never went away. They bothered him more than the guards.

On the fourth morning, Swede heard the guards come in the building and could feel himself tense up for the coming physical therapy session. Instead, he was dragged out of the cell and then the building. The light hurt his eyes for a while, so he couldn't see where they were dragging him. He found himself at the shore of the bay or estuary. The guards motioned him out into the water. They didn't want to get too close and made their point by holding their noses. Even with his hands still behind his back, Swede managed to roll around enough in the cold water to get reasonably clean.

He was marched back to the command post and presented to the same stern looking man who had wagged his finger at him four days ago. This time the man gave Swede a short speech and waited while an instructor translated.

"The Colonel says he hopes you enjoyed your visit. Maybe next time it will not be so pleasant. You must adjust your attitude." With that friendly bit of advice, Swede was escorted to a truck and driven back up to 3 North. Once there, he was turned over to the camp guards, wet and hungry, hands still tied behind his back.

Swede wasn't the only one to disappear from camp for a while and return noticeably worse for wear. A couple of times a week, a prisoner would be called to the guard shack and a truck would leave camp. Sometimes they went south and sometimes they went north. The men who ended up in Camp 5 for their attitude adjustments said the accommodations were better in Regiment south of 3 North. In Camp 5 they were placed in cold, drafty huts, or even pits dug in the ground and covered with timbers and dirt.

About a week after Swede got back from his time at Regiment, some new prisoners arrived in camp. It was late in the day towards the end of October. Some of the braver men were washing in the bay. A few guards stood by in case anybody decided to take a half-mile swim across the Yalu and escape naked into China. The setting sun was painting the sky before it disappeared for the night. The fall temperatures regularly created an evening mist on the river.

Earl spotted the barges first. They came out of the mist from the north. No noise, just five barges, floating down the river, bringing the night with them. The only sound came when they slid onto the gravel beach. More prisoners from the camp had come out to see what was happening. No one had yelled out, no one rushed around telling people something was happening. They just came down to the shore as quietly as the barges came down the river.

The sun had disappeared, leaving just the dim glow of twilight. There was a rustling from the barges. Figures began stepping down. They moved slowly, almost ghostlike. A handful of guards arrived and began leading the men from the barges into the camp. As they passed through the crowd, they moved like living dead, shuffling along with their heads down. Swede noticed many of them had a look of despair, others were noticeably afraid. Looking closer, it became obvious these men were American soldiers. More obvious was how thin they were, with tired and haggard faces, their eyes haunted.

Almost as if a command had been given, the men from the camp moved in among the new men. They greeted them in soft voices and helped those who seemed about to stumble and fall. Page whispered to Swede, "These guys look worse than we did when we finally got to Bean Camp. But that was almost a year ago! What's going on? Where have they been?"

Harvey Reynolds had been right. The guards led the new men to the empty barracks. Once they realized they were in a regular camp with other Americans, the men from the barges began to smile and relax. Conversations broke out. The old hands explained where they were and how things worked. The new guys offered simple explanations on their background. They had been in "some camps up north." They had been "on the road for a while." It was obvious they were exhausted mentally as well as physically. They were left to settle down for a night's sleep.

Swede noticed none of the old hands challenged any of the new prisoners. There was no demand to prove you weren't a stoolie of some kind for the Chinese. There was something about these men. You just knew they were different. They had gone through something you had not. Gradually, over the next few days, their story came out.

Page and Swede learned the story from a young private by the name of Johnnie Johnson from Ohio ("My name is Wayne, but everybody calls me Johnnie"). He referred to the group as the Tiger Survivors. They were the first captured in the war and had been under North Korean control since that time. Just a few days before they had been turned over to the Chinese at Camp 5 and then sent to Three. There had been 750 of them in the beginning. Only 232 had been on the barges when they arrived at Camp 3. Their initial experience had been much the same as other POWs. Little food, constantly on the march, many without shoes, no medicine. Johnson filled in the details.

"By October, we were far north even of Camp 5, sleeping in holes we dug between the rows of a cornfield in a snowstorm. Then the march began. The Tiger Death March. Eighty of us had died by that time. About a hundred more died on the nine-day march, at least half of them shot when they fell behind.

"We were marched over a mountain pass in a blizzard. On the first day, the North Korean Major in charge shot a young lieutenant, Cordus Thornton, because some men in his section couldn't keep up.

Then he turned the killing over to the guards. They even shot Mother Beatrix, a seventy-six-year-old nun who was part of the sixty civilians in the group. After marching one hundred miles in nine days we were exhausted. The Major told us we were not taking proper care of our health and we needed to exercise. He forced us to perform morning calisthenics for the next couple of mornings. Twenty-four died in the eight days we spent at that village. Then they moved us again. Two hundred more died. It was December and some of us still didn't have shoes. They wrapped their feet in rags until somebody their size died. The "hospital" was a ruined hut with no heat and a sack for a door. The guards weren't shooting us anymore-they didn't have to.

"The Major, the Korean we called the Tiger, was replaced. Beatings became rare, and in March we were moved again. That camp was our best. Still, seventy died there. Then out of the blue, they marched us back to the Yalu and loaded us on barges." Johnnie paused in his story. It seemed as if he went somewhere else for a second or two.

"When we got here the other night, I figured it was just another place for more of us to die. I think a few will, but maybe the nightmare is over for the rest of us." Then he got quiet again. He looked around to see if anybody else was listening. He went on in a whisper.

"I've got a list. A list of who died. Other guys who tried to keep a list died when the Koreans found it and beat them. I'm guessing the Chinese will do the same. Do you guys have any ideas what I should do, where I can keep the list safe? I think it's the only one left."

As they talked about the list, Swede began to realize something about Johnnie's story was familiar. "This major, this Tiger, did he have a tight jacket with a pistol strapped around his waist, with the holster on his right side?"

Johnnie looked at him in surprise. "How did you know that?"

"He's the same guy who was in charge of our column. On my first morning with that column he shot a Captain Winslow for trying to keep track of who had died or had been shot by the guards. We saw him again just after we got to Seoul. He said he had other 'guests' to attend to. I hope we never see him again."

"Amen to that, brother," replied Johnnie.

Gradually, some things began to improve. The lightweight uniforms they had been issued in the late spring were exchanged for a winter version, including hats and gloves. The buildings at 3 North were solidly built and kept the wind out. The larger barracks were given buckets to burn coal or charcoal for heat at night. The huts had the standard floor heating system. A bigger problem was a lack of wood to burn. The buckets weren't the most efficient or healthiest system, but they usually kept the temperatures above freezing. A combination of blankets and large overcoats was issued to each squad for sleeping. Meals improved when Americans were finally allowed to run the kitchens. The Chinese still monitored the process and controlled the menu, but real cooks now did the work. The quantity didn't change much, but the quality was vastly improved. Work details continued. Latrine pits were filled in and new ones dug. Drainage ditches were carved out. What did not improve were the daily lectures and the questions that followed.

The final hint of a better winter came when men were assigned to digging large pits. They were filled with turnips and covered over. The prisoners realized they were to add needed vitamins to their meals during the next winter. Those vitamins would prevent the night blindness so many had experienced in the last winter. Why go to all that trouble if they knew they were going to lose so many prisoners over the winter? And there were more rumors of talks going on to end the war.

But as the temperatures dropped and snow started to fall, more than just a few prisoners worried about a repeat of the first winter. It was not easy to forget waking up to find your best buddy frozen to death next to you. It wasn't easy to forget dragging his body to the hillside and digging a hole in the snow with your hands. It wasn't easy to forget stripping off his uniform because you needed it more than he did. Some men were broken by those experiences. They were so afraid of what the Chinese might do to them, they bent over backward to please the instructors. But there was not one single prisoner who didn't have at least some concern about the coming winter.

Thomas Sedlinski certainly had concerns. Every single person he had called a friend back in Japan was dead. Every single one had died, either on the march after their capture at Kun-ri, or at Camp 5 in the weeks after they arrived. Howard Kastler lasted the longest, but one morning Tom woke up to find Howard frozen next to him. Tom, or Red, as he had been called since before he could remember, had considered himself a good soldier. Waking up to see his friend's lifeless eyes staring at him had pushed all that aside. Staying alive became his only goal. He told himself the army would want him to stay alive. He was no good to them dead. Asking for an end to the war or world disarmament seemed only logical. And it got him the extra blanket or extra food he needed to stay alive. He didn't want to be another Howard.

Red wasn't quite sure how he had become a Progressive. He thought signing a petition asking for world peace was harmless. But Red was no match for the well-educated Chinese instructors sent from Peking. Pai was one of the best.

"Today we will discuss an article from the Daily Worker." Pai began in his usual way, stating exactly what the group would do. Not asking, just telling. "I am sure you will find this most interesting. The Soviet Union has put forward a Ban the Bomb resolution in the United Nations. It is a resolution for peace and disarmament. I am sure you will support such a resolution."

"The resolution calls on the permanent members of the Security Council to conclude between them a pact on the strengthening of peace. Who can tell us the permanent members of the Security Council?"

From the back of the group came a response, "The United States and England?"

"Yes, very good. And China and the Soviet Union and France. Yes, very good. I see you are a most educated group," smiled Pai. "I do not need to read this article to you. I will just leave it. You read it and discuss it among yourselves. I shall return to talk with you on what you have learned." Pai handed the newspaper clipping to the man sitting in front of him, and that happened to be Red.

Red took the clipping from the instructor out of reflex. But then he became responsible for it. No one else in the group reached for the article, no one said a thing. "Well guys, I guess maybe I should read this to you," Red commented, half begging for someone else to take over.

"Go ahead, Red. You go ahead and read to us." The statement came from the back somewhere. It was hard to tell if it was in jest or not, but Red decided to take it as an assignment of responsibility. It was a rather bland article, asking for prohibition of atomic weapons and praising the people of China and the Soviet Union in their desire for world peace. There were also some remarks about some people in the world being more interested in supporting capitalism than peace. There was a pause when Red finished. Then the man next to him spoke up.

"Pai said he will be back. He will ask us what we think about the article. If we don't say anything, will they feed us tonight?"

The immediate look of fear on the faces of many in the group was clear. They knew other huts had missed meals because their instructors were not happy with their feedback. Were they next?

"That's easy," another soldier spoke up. "We say it makes a lot of sense. We might be soldiers, but that doesn't mean we don't support peace." Others nodded in agreement. "They aren't going to starve us for supporting peace." More nods and murmurs of agreement. "You tell 'em we support peace, Red. And we'll all be fine." For the rest of the morning, the guys huddled in their hut, trying to stay warm. When Pai approached later in the day, many of the men looked nervous.

"So how did you find this article? Was it of interest to you?" Pai looked around to see who might respond. It was easy to spot the young soldier he had given the article to. His shaggy red head stood out. The men simply waited for Red to handle things.

"We all agree it makes a lot of sense. We are soldiers, but we support peace." Red simply re-stated what the group had said earlier.

"So, you support the people of China and the Soviet Union in their call for peace?" prompted Pai. "You agree with what the article says?"

Now Red looked around. Nobody had said anything about supporting any Chinese or Russians. He hoped somebody would speak up. He hadn't volunteered for this and didn't feel comfortable speaking for the group. No one said a word. And Pai just sat there looking at Red, waiting for a response.

"Well, we think peace is important, but we can't say about anyone else." Red tried to agree and disagree.

"Do you think only people in America support world peace? Cannot others also support world peace?" Pai again looked only at Red, waiting for a response.

"Well, I suppose they could," responded Red. "But if the Chinese people support world peace, why are we being held prisoners by the

Chinese?" He decided he would match wits with Pai. There were murmurings of agreement from the group.

"Oh my goodness. You are not being held prisoner by the Chinese people! You are students and the guests of the Chinese People's Volunteer Army. Once you have learned the truth, you will be ready to go home to your families. Had you not been used as pawns by your government in invading Korea, you would be home now.

"Perhaps if you would sign a letter proclaiming your support of people across the world asking for world peace, your government would agree to bring you home sooner. How many of you support world peace? Come now, do not be afraid to show your hand." Pai looked over the group with a friendly smile. "Surely you agree the world should have peace? Children should not have to suffer the wars of world aggressors." Again, he looked over the group. "Or would you like to reflect on these thoughts until later?" There was a deliberate hint of nastiness in this last question. And there was no smile on his face.

"I support world peace. I think maybe all of us do." It was the same soldier who had earlier expressed the idea the Chinese would not let them starve for supporting world peace. He raised his hand and looked around at the others. Slowly, more hands went up, until only Red remained uncommitted. Then his hand went up.

Pai was back to smiles again. "Excellent, excellent! You see, the truth is easy to understand. All the world's people want peace. You are no different. Discuss this among yourselves. Tomorrow you will give me your group thoughts in writing. All thoughts will be welcome." More smiles as he reached into his bag and handed Red two sheets of paper and a pencil. "And be sure to put your names on your thoughts so I know which group of students you are. Perhaps you can then enjoy some extra rice in your evening meal."

As Pai left many of the men looked worried again. They had to write their thoughts? They had to sign their names? Writing they supported world peace would be okay, wouldn't it? Rodney Wapner finally voiced what many seemed to be thinking.

"What's the catch here? Do we get to eat tonight? Red, you almost screwed us there. You were the last man to raise your hand. Are you tryin' to get us in trouble? He appointed you as spokesman. Be more careful. Make sure you write out somethin' that will get us that extra rice he talked about."

And that settled it. Red would take care of things and the rest would relax. Just like that, Red Sedlinski found himself walking down the Progressive path. The next day Pai had little trouble getting all to sign up for world peace. And Red had a new article to read to the group. A few days later, Pai made sure he was unhappy with the groups' response to his question on who had started the war. They went hungry that night. The next day's discussion went much better. His students were learning.

By that fall Red was questioning his own actions. The extra favors of candy, cigarettes, warmer blankets, and fewer work details were nice, but was he doing the right thing? He shared anything he got from the instructors but was expected to give them something in return. Adding his name to peace petitions didn't bother him that much, but too often he was asked for information on his fellow prisoners. Was this man saying anything negative about China, was that man telling people not to sign petitions, who was responsible for throwing rocks at his fellow Progressives? His answer was always the same - people didn't talk to him about these things, they didn't trust him. But he also knew many POWs thought he gave answers to those questions. Other Progressives who spent time in the "rec room" that had been set up just for them answered those questions. No one had any reason to doubt that he did the same. The fact some of his fellow soldiers thought less of him made him question all his actions with the Chinese. How could he change that? How could he stop now? Red decided to ask for advice.

Swede had never paid much attention to Red. He knew he was a Progressive but seemed to be a good person. He knew Red shared whatever rewards he got from the instructors. Swede had suggested a few times maybe Red should change his behavior, but he knew fear was a powerful motivator for many Progressives. When Swede returned from his latest visit to the closed-in cells of headquarters, he was assigned to Red's squad. It was common for the Chinese to put a suspected Reactionary in with a bunch of Progressives. It made keeping an eye on them simpler. Many Progressives had no problem reporting to the Chinese on their fellow prisoners. Swede and many of his fellow Reactionaries saw the practice as an opportunity to put subtle pressure on the Progressives. They would ask questions during lectures the Progressives would never bring up. But he never expected Red to ask him for help.

Red brought the topic up when the two were on a firewood gathering detail. Normally he was exempt from the harder work details but told the guards he wanted some exercise. Red was older than Swede and had been in the Army longer. Yet he had a lot of respect for him. Swede was the kind of soldier Red knew he should be. He had seen Swede go out of his way to help others. He heard rumors about how Swede pushed for less cooperation with the Chinese and better conditions for all the POWs. But Red knew his own limits. He wasn't a good thinker. Once he learned something, it stayed with him. But he found it hard to think ahead, to look at a task before he got involved. And he had a low tolerance for pain. He dreaded a repeat of last winter. He knew he would not make it. But if things were going to be better this winter maybe he wouldn't have to cooperate so much anymore.

As soon as he got the chance on the work detail, he just flat out told Swede, "I don't like being like this. The more I saw people die around me the more scared I got. Then the instructors said none of this was my fault. Other people were to blame for the war. Why should I have to suffer? They seemed to make a lot of sense.

"Then I see you and guys like Earl Stoneman argue with them. You get punished and come right back and do it all over again. I know you must be right and I must be wrong, but it's hard for me to change now. I'm afraid if I don't eat better, I will get sick and die. But I look around and notice nobody has died since the end of summer." Swede could see the self-doubt and anguish in Red's eyes.

Red went on. "The army has been good to me but I'm not doing much good for the army. Just last week, I wrote another statement about how our generals are probably at fault for all of us being prisoners of war. I don't like the me I am now. But I don't know how to change. What do you think I should do?"

Swede had often talked with Earl and Page about how to stay ahead of the Chinese. If they knew what the Chinese were going to be asking questions about, they could better prepare answers that would be acceptable. If Red was willing, he could really help.

He looked at Red for a while, trying to assess how honest he was being. This could also be a Chinese tactic to stay ahead of the Reactionaries. "If you mean what you say, I have an idea that you might not like. Are you serious? You really want to stop cooperating?"

"Yes. I want to be a soldier again." If Red was lying, he was good at it.

"What if I said the best thing you could do is not change at all? What if I said the best way for you to be a soldier again is to keep cooperating with the Chinese?"

Red looked at Swede in disbelief. This is the guy he thought could help? Telling him to keep doing exactly what he was more and more unhappy with himself for doing in the first place?

Swede could see the confusion, even a little anger. "Listen. If you just quit cooperating, they will know something is up and come down on you hard. They don't want to lose any Progressives. What I am going to suggest will take a lot of guts on your part. It won't be easy, but you will definitely be a soldier again.

"I want you to be my eyes and ears. What are they worried about? What do they think we are planning? Who are they watching? Who is telling them about escape plans? Who do they have watching us?"

"You want me to spy on the Chinese?" Red looked like he was beginning to understand.

"Exactly. They have spies all over the place. We normally assume most of the guards don't speak English, but lately I'm not so sure." Swede looked carefully at Red. He was ninety-nine percent sure Red was being honest, but, kept that one percent in reserve - just in case. "Are you willing to give it a try? This could be dangerous. If you get caught it will mean time in a nasty cell of some kind. If you make up your mind to do this, you will be helping all of us. But make sure you understand what it is I am asking you to do."

"I used to be a good soldier. I want to be that person again. And it will help make up for what I have been doing for the past months. Yes. I want to do this. What exactly do I do, and how do I do it?" Swede could see a determination in Red's face that hadn't been there before.

"I just want you to listen. Listen to what the instructors ask you or anybody else to do. Listen to other Pros to see if you can find out who they are watching. Listen to learn who is talking about who. Don't do anything different. Just listen better. Once you start thinking about who is talking and what they are saying, it will start to make more sense to you. You'll begin to see patterns. Then let me know what you are learning.

"One more thing. Like I said, this could be dangerous. You can't tell anyone else what you are up to. People will still think you are just another Pro taking the easy way out. But when we get out of this mess, I will be your witness and set the story straight. I will tell only one other person what we are doing. That way, if something happens to me, they can back you up. But I don't think that will be a problem. If I get sent somewhere else, that person will contact you." Swede looked Red right in the eye. "I can't treat you any different. We can't start bein' pals. Everything has to stay the same. This won't be easy. But if you need help, let me know. We can manage some time together, just like on this work detail. Now get to work."

Within a week Red had news for Swede. The Chinese were planning a big parade to celebrate the anniversary of the Chinese Revolution. The prisoners would do the parading. As part of the parade, they would construct large banners to carry. They would wave the banners and shout slogans calling for peace as they marched through the camp. And smile for the cameras. As a reward, the entire camp would be treated to a wonderful feast - after the parade.

Red was one of those in charge of making the banners. He and Swede managed to get a crew into the back of the work area where they came up with some special banners. Somehow the imperialist was left off "Down with Imperialist War Mongers." One banner read "Long live the Chinese People" and another read "Long live Peace-Loving People" but "Long live the Peace-Loving Chinese People" never got finished. They couldn't change all the banners but managed enough to feel like they had stood their ground. Somehow, "Up Mao" struck the Chinese as a good idea and was allowed in the parade. On the day of the parade, those POWs carrying the modified slogans cheered the loudest and smiled the widest for the cameras. The feast was as good as promised, so many felt the day was at least a draw.

The October parade and feast led to lengthy arguments among the Reactionaries. Some said they should have refused to participate. Others said refusal would have led to severe reprisals. Some said now was the time to push for an end to any cooperation with the Chinese and their re-education attempts. Fred Moeder and Billy Beckman wanted a complete halt. "Too many of our guys are writin' confessions or makin' statements that make us all look bad," Billy argued. "Let's show the Chinks we're still American soldiers. I hate these uniforms they make us wear. We aren't students, we're prisoners of war!"

Fred felt even more strongly. "It's time to grow a spine! Too many of these guys have forgotten who they are. Some of these guys will rat you out to the Chinese for a couple of smokes."

"If we try to get everybody to stop cooperating now, I'm not sure it will work. All they have to do is take away our bucket stoves or cut back our food. Within a week they will have all the statements they want," argued Harvey Reynolds. "If we spend the winter working on our guys, we can have everybody ready come early spring. It will take time to get the word out to the other camps. Once we get through the worst of winter, most of the guys who are cooperating out of fear will see the Chinese aren't going to let us die."

Earl seemed to have the last word. "I agree with Harvey. But we need to push hard on the Pros. We can't just wait for spring and hope they all magically turn over a new leaf. We have to be more persuasive than the Chinese and we have to be sneakier about it."

So the sparring with the instructors continued. More and more prisoners seemed to be questioning the logic of the lectures. The biggest change of late fall was the removal of the officers to a separate camp. No one knew where it was, but they noticed the trucks went north out of camp. The rumor was all POW officers were being sent to a single camp to separate them from the enlisted. The rumor was substantiated when trucks from Camp 1 also passed through on their way north. People who returned from Five after time in a punishment hut said the officers had spent about a day there before leaving again. Apparently there really was a Camp 2 or Camp 4 somewhere in that direction.

The firewood crews were kept busy. They were having to go farther from camp to fill their quotas. Page volunteered for as many of these work parties as he could. Swede figured he used some of them to maintain contact with his network. That was something Page never talked about and Swede accepted that fact. If the Chinese caught on, he couldn't be forced to talk about what he didn't know.

Page did ask Swede to volunteer with him on other work parties. They were able to develop detailed knowledge of the camp lay out. A couple of times, they ended up in the Chinese areas of the camp on various projects. Every now and then, a prisoner from 3 South was sent to Regiment or even to 3 North for questioning or time in a punishment hut. Sometimes that person was able to pass on information to a fellow prisoner. Other times somebody just asked a guard what was going on. Some guards could be conned out of information just by sharing a smoke. POWs were often given American or European cigarettes by the instructors or interrogators. Sometimes the rewarded behavior was real, but just as often a prisoner would pretend to be cooperating, so he could get some cigarettes or even some candy. These rewards could be consumed by the individual or used as trade items. Or shared with a talkative guard.

Too many prisoners were unable to control their nicotine addiction. The Chinese used that addiction in their favor. Some prisoners with a real craving would write any statement put in front of them. Others would pass on information about their fellow prisoners. A lot of trips to a punishment hut or pit in the ground happened because somebody was willing to do more than walk a mile for a Camel.

When it became known one of their own had turned against them, the squirrel hunters went to work. Jerry Branigan was visited in his hut late one night. Three men snuck carefully from hut to hut, making sure the few guards who roamed the area were off in the other direction. When the three entered Jerry's hut, they were met by another prisoner. He led them to Jerry's sleeping spot and then went back to watch for guards. Taking a lesson from the Chinese, the men made sure they didn't hit Jerry in the face or head. All the bruises would be hidden by his clothes. Leaving Jerry in pain, they hustled out past the man on watch. He then rushed over to Jerry in an 'attempt' to help him. If Jerry continued working for the Chinese, more visits were scheduled. If Jerry complained to the Chinese and a guard was kept near the hut, he found himself tripping a lot or dropping his rice bowl. One of Earl's favorite tactics for the hard cases was throwing rather large stones at them as they went about their day. Earl had spent a lot of time as a kid hunting rabbits and real squirrels with stones. He was accurate from quite a distance. Eventually, people like Jerry either changed their behavior or were placed with others like them in a special hut close to the guard's quarters.

Earl and Swede put together a small team of what they called night hawks. This particular club began when Earl stopped Swede one day. "Keep your eye on that truck." He pointed to a truck that made a regular supply run down to regiment and back.

"Sometime today, maybe tomorrow, the engine will seize up and quit running." Then he walked away and wouldn't answer any questions.

Swede did keep an eye on the truck, and sure enough, later that evening as it came back from a run, smoke blew all over the place and the engine coughed itself to a stop. Swede watched as the driver opened the hood and more smoke billowed out. Other Chinese gathered around, all shouting advice of some kind. The show ended when another truck towed it away. Swede looked over to see Earl grinning at him.

"OK. How did you know that was going to happen?"

"Simple. I pulled the oil plug last night. Drained every drop out of it. Then I put the plug back in but left it loose. Scooped a bunch of snow over the oil and went about my merry way. Most fun I've had in days.

It was an experiment." Earl looked pleased with himself.

"How was that an experiment?" Swede asked.

"I wanted to see how long it would take before it seized or threw a rod. I needed to know it would take a few miles before it shut down. Now, we could pull the plug on every vehicle in camp, but that would be a little obvious. At the worst we would end up hauling supplies on our backs. But convoys. That's a different story. They pass through. And they carry supplies that are used against our guys somewhere. Ruin an engine on one of those trucks and it makes a difference." The big grin was still there.

"So, we drain the oil from trucks in a convoy, and they break down somewhere on the road. No way to trace it back here to us. I like your idea," Swede grinned back.

"Not exactly like that. We can only hit one, maybe two trucks, in a convoy. And we don't drain the oil. Sooner or later there would be a lot of oil out there. When the snow is gone, there will be no way to hide it when the drivers check over their trucks before they take off. Instead, we loosen the plug. Bring it right down to where it's almost out. Sooner or later it will rattle itself out, and the oil will drain out far away from here. We hit convoys going both north and south and there is no pattern that points back at us."

The two men kept an eye out for a convoy to try out Earl's idea. More often than not, convoys just rolled right through. But a week later a convoy appeared just after dark and pulled over for the night.

The drivers all went into the little restaurant and used nearby huts in the village to bed down for the night. It was well after midnight when Earl and Swede worked their way out of their barracks area and towards the convoy. Earl had "borrowed" a wrench on a work detail and buried it behind the latrine. The two took their time, moving slowly from building to building and then bush to bush. There were guards posted, but they were predictable in their behavior. When they were standing still, they were either smoking or coughing and spitting. Easy to spot. If they weren't smoking or coughing, they marched slowly back and forth on the same route. Once you spotted a guard, you just watched for a few minutes. Soon enough you knew when his back would be turned and for how long. By timing your steps to his you covered any noise you might make.

When the two nighthawks got to the convoy, they slid under a truck. In less than a minute Swede had the oil plug loose. He whispered to Earl. "I've got an idea. We loosen one plug almost all the way out. Then we move down a few trucks and loosen one about three-quarters of the way. Then we do one more about a third of the way. We don't hit any two trucks next to each other. The plugs rattle loose at different times. By then they might even be in a different convoy."

"Jesus, we're gonna need more wrenches," said Earl.

They expanded the club over the next few months. It wasn't a good idea to have ten guys all trying to sneak out to a convoy, so they put together teams of two, which then took turns. The rules were made clear. No more than three trucks in a convoy of more than ten. Five to ten trucks meant only two were hit and less than five meant only one truck. As they got better, they came up with more ideas. Fred Moeder suggested they loosen the tie rods on one truck per convoy. Spin the nut up and almost off and let the lousy roads do the rest. If they got lucky, the truck would run off the road and be wrecked.

Harvey Reynolds suggested they spike the road to catch traffic that didn't stop. "Exactly what do you mean by spike?" asked Earl. "Do we bury spikes of some kind in the road? How do we do that?"

"No, we just drop nails made into jacks or knucklebones. If we have to, we throw them out on the road from behind some huts when no guards are around. Whenever a truck comes along, *pssshh*, flat tire. And we are far away on a work party of some kind," Harvey explained. "We just need some long nails or heavy wire we can bend

220

into the right shape. And maybe a tool to help with the bending."

"Looks like a job for Hardware. Let him know what you need and he'll find it," said Earl.

Sam Hardy loved working with tools. His grandfather had been a blacksmith. Sam spent so much time wandering around in the shop as a youngster his grandfather started using him to help out. Grandpa Herman was one of those individuals who had no problem making the crossover from the horse and buggy to tractors and threshing machines. Sam learned right along with him, without even realizing he was learning. He was just "helpin' Grandpa." It was Grandpa Herman who suggested he open a hardware shop. More and more farmers needed parts and tool they could no longer make on their own. Sam's Hardware was built right next to Herman's Smithy. What Sam couldn't order, Herman could make. Then Herman got too old to handle the work and one of the first Ace Hardware stores opened just down the road in Lewisburg. A year later, Sam was in the army, assigned to the motor pool. He had Grandpa Herman's gift for making something out of nothing, but also developed the skill of 'finding' what he needed to keep his vehicles running. It wasn't long before "Hardware" was the man to see if you needed something you weren't supposed to have.

Hardware had a small network of men working for him in camp. They volunteered for any work party they could. That gave them detailed knowledge of where everything was around camp, exactly what was stored where. They also were very forgetful when it came to returning tools they used on their work parties. Just little things: small knives, pliers, nails, screws, screwdrivers, wire. They bummed a cigarette off a guard and stole two from the pack. The next day they traded all three for a hat or pair of gloves. If Hardware's people didn't have what you needed, they could come up with it in a day or two.

The nail spikes worked well. Almost too well. Harvey dumped a bunch of them in the snow on the road late at night, hoping to catch a convoy coming through. The only truck to come through was the Dusty Deuce early the next morning. One tire blew immediately, and the driver found spikes in another. When he started looking around, he found more spikes. That put the plan on hold for a week.

Harvey's plan B was to sneak out near the road late at night to listen for truck traffic. When he heard more than one truck headed up the road, he scattered his spikes. Once again tires blew. The drivers made a big stink and that brought out the guards. The next day every building housing POWs was searched. A few questionable odds and ends were found, but no spikes.

Earl was not happy. "Now you got 'em nervous and the guards are payin' more attention. We can't get out to loosen the oil plugs. You gotta lay off, at least for a while." Earl was practically begging. He enjoyed messing with the trucks.

"Why don't you try this," suggested Harvey. Take some spikes with you and work them into a few tires. Push them into the sides and they should gradually work their way through. But that should take a couple of days. They won't be able to pin it on us."

Everybody was happy with that idea. The guards settled down and no more searches were made. But when Page mentioned he had a project, Swede figured something else was in the works. He knew Page was in contact with his network but never asked questions. The next day Page convinced him to go out on another firewood detail.

Once they were spread out across a hillside picking up wood, Page answered the questions Swede had not been asking. He had been sent to Japan to set up a network to investigate whether the Russians were helping the North Koreans. They supposedly had sophisticated radar equipment that was more mobile than anything they had come up with before. The theory was they wanted it in North Korea to see how it worked against US planes flying out of South Korea and Japan. Once he got things started, he was to go to Korea and work from there, maybe eventually infiltrating into North Korea posing as a Russian technician. He was pulled from that project to help with a quick investigation in a possible espionage case. That blew up when the unit he was attached to got sent to Korea when the war began. Now his network was telling him they had spotted what they thought were some mobile radar vehicles working in the area. It made sense. US planes were constantly chasing Chinese aircraft along the Yalu. That meant lots of targets for the new radar. If the Russians really did have more advanced equipment, and if it was really in the area.

"That's where we come into the picture," smiled Page.

"We? As in me with you? How do I fit into whatever you are cooking up?" Swede asked.

"You've seen the trucks that I think we're looking for. The diagrams you drew up before seem to match what my guys are telling me. They brought a camera for me to get some photos. And I am supposed to get photos of any manuals I can find in the trucks."

"In the trucks? As in climb inside a Russian van, find the manuals, take pictures, and get out without being caught? And 'we' are doing this?" Swede didn't see anything funny about this plan.

"First, the photos of the inside of the truck and the antennae. Next, we get shots of the manuals. Only if we can."

"Why not just steal the manuals and get out?" Swede asked.

"If we do that, they know we know. Then they modify the equipment and we are back to step one. Nope, we have to get the information we need without making them suspicious we got it. Who is going to worry about a couple of POWs sneaking around and taking pictures of sophisticated radar equipment?" Page stood there with a log on his shoulder, waiting for Swede to say he agreed.

"Being caught in an escape attempt is one thing, but we get caught trying to take pictures of anything around here and we *will* be shot, right there. Shot while attempting to escape will be the story." Swede still wasn't agreeing to any participation on his part.

"And how do we do this, now, in the middle of winter? We can't exactly go wandering around the countryside looking for some trucks. It's cold, we'd leave tracks all over, we could only go so far at night and still make it back before dawn, we'd have to have a way out of and then back in to camp, and did I mention we'd leave tracks all over? This plan of yours seems to be mostly unplanned so far."

"You're right," replied Page. "We can't wander around. What if I tell you there is a way we won't leave tracks and have plenty of time to get there and back at night? What if I tell you this radar unit is only a mile from here? My guys say the unit frequently sets up in a little valley just north of the bridge on the way to Camp 5, the bridge about a hundred meters from our camp. There are only ten of them. When they are there, the crew comes into the village to get some hot food and warm beds. They follow a very regular pattern. Once they set up in that valley, they stay put for four or five days before they move out." Page was serious now, no grins, just the facts.

"So we find out exactly when they will be there. Then what? We crank up ol' Dusty Deuce and drive over? We hike out of camp and walk down the middle of the road looking for trucks?"

"That we need to work out," answered Page. "But they tell me it's no more than a mile. We leave before midnight and get back well before dawn. What do ya think?"

"I think you're nuts, that's what I think." Swede added more wood to his bundle.

"Hey, you're the guy who told me he got out of his cell and wandered around camp on a regular basis because nobody bothered looking for something that crazy." Page was beginning to worry Swede wouldn't go along with the plan.

"I didn't wander around the whole camp, just a small part of it. You want us to sneak out of here, walk a mile down the middle of the road, sneak into another compound, break into some trucks, and then reverse the whole process to get back here. *That* is a whole new level of crazy."

"My guys say there are no guard posts on the bridge or the road north of here. They've watched the radar unit set up. No guards are posted except when they head back here for the night. Then one man stays back. And he sleeps in the generator truck. Sleeps. There is no attempt to guard anything. They drag a big log across the road going into the valley. No Korean or Chinese troops have any reason to be closer than the main road as they head north towards Camp 5. My guys watch from the hills to the east of the valley." Page didn't have much more in the way of an argument and waited for Swede's reaction.

"We'll have to get some kind of camouflage blankets or ponchos, but I guess Hardware should be able to come up with something. And they'll have to be warm enough to keep us from freezing if we have to hide in one spot for a while. Other than that, you seem to have your ducks lined up pretty well." Swede looked over at Page with a little grin of his own.

"You mean you'll do it? Well, you bastard, I thought you were going to turn me down." Page felt much more relieved than he wanted to let on. He didn't have a plan B if Swede had turned him down and didn't want Swede to know that.

"Galoot," said Swede.

"What?"

"Galoot, not bastard. My mother would not approve." Swede just grinned at Page. "You didn't mean 'bastard' in the nasty sense of the word, so galoot fits."

"Galoot? Gadzooks? Jehoshaphat? Where do you get these gems?" asked Page.

"Simple," replied Swede. "I mentioned before that my mother didn't like swearing. A *damn* or a *hell* she would tolerate, but that was about it. My father and uncles really had to be careful around her, and around me, when I was little. I would repeat any phrase I heard. So, they used dime novels to come up with words they liked instead of normal cuss words. There are a lot of galoots in dime novels. And if you say 'jehoshaphat' just right, it feels like you really are swearing. A fella named Mike Finnegan helped me along those lines. 'Consarn those lubbers' became a favorite of mine. My mother couldn't decide if I was breaking her rule or not. But, like I said, lately I've been breakin' her rule quite a bit."

"So, are us two galoots gonna do this or not?" asked Page.

"Do we have a choice?" There was no humor in Swede's tone now. "This is just as important as keepin' our guys from bein' suckered by the Chinese. But I see one problem you haven't mentioned. Something like this would get a stooge a lot of special privileges from the Chinese. We need to make sure as few people as possible know any details. They really will shoot us if they catch us."

Page was just as serious in his reply. "Actually, I have thought about that. Nobody but the two of us will know all the details. Anybody else will only know their part. I have a source that should be able to tell us if the Chinese are suspicious."

Over the next couple of weeks, Hardware scrounged up two large, well-used coats and what looked like a bed sheet. The sheet was cut into smaller pieces and sewn to the inside of the coats. When worn reversed, the coats were effective winter camouflage. Page's sources were able to let him know when the Russians were in the nearby valley. Watching the camp to see if they could pick up any patterns, Swede and Page realized a truck, an old Jimmy, left camp late at night, drove north, and returned about fifteen minutes later. A dozen large men climbed out from under the tarp-covered back and entered the restaurant in the village. Early the next morning, the same truck took the men north and returned empty. As they watched the truck return, Swede and Page turned and grinned at each other.

"Bingo!" whispered Page. They now had a way to get out to the radar trucks and back.

Cookin' with Gas

November 1951

Swede knew Page had Hardware working on another project but didn't know the details. All Page would say was, "Don't you worry. We're gonna be cookin' with gas!"

Two weeks later, Page got the word the Russians were back in their valley down the road. That night he and Swede worked their way past the guards and headed towards the village and the Jimmy. They were wearing Hardware's coats with the "camo" side out. Swede noticed Page had something stuffed inside his coat.

"That must be one really big camera you have there," whispered Swede as they moved from shadow to shadow. Page just grinned. Getting closer to the road, the two began crawling. Once they positioned themselves directly across from the Jimmy parked outside the village inn, Swede whispered again. "Are we just gonna jump in the back?"

Page just whispered back, "Follow me." The two scooted low across the road and Page slid under the truck. "Don't just stand there, get under here." Once they were both hidden under the truck, Page slid closer to the back end. Pulling some ropes out from his coat, he handed one end to Swede. "When this truck starts to move, we jump up behind it. The tailgate has hand grabs on each side at the top. You take the right side. I got the left. Tie a slip knot on the grab handle and hop on. Just keep below the top of the tailgate and try not to make any noise." Page looked at Swede. "You can tie a slip knot, right?"

"Now you ask? Don't you think you could have brought this up a little sooner?" Swede struggled to keep it at a whisper.

"You can, right? Tie a slip knot?"

"Of course I can tie a slip knot. But you could've asked a little sooner. Any other Boy Scout skills I'm gonna need to brush up on?"

Page gave Swede a puzzled look. "What's a Boy Scout skill?"

Just then a door slammed and boots squeaked through the snow towards the truck. With a grunt, the driver swung himself up into the cab. The engine turned over slowly and then came to life with a roar. Grinding into gear, the driver popped the clutch and jerked out onto the road. Two silent shadows jumped up, looped their rope around the grab handles, and hopped into the miniature hammock that unraveled. Swede looked at it in admiration while Page just grinned at him. Slowly, the truck made its way out to and over the bridge. Other than the cold, the snow being thrown at them by the tires, the bouncing and slamming into the frame, and the exhaust, the two hitchhikers had no problem on the way out of town. After less than a mile, the driver slowed, made a right turn onto an even lesser road, and then stopped completely.

Before the truck even stopped, Page was off their little sling. "Release your knot and get under the truck again," he whispered to Swede. The two men slid under and waited while the driver dismounted and walked up to move the log across the road. "When he pulls out, just stay right here. If he stops on the other side of the log, roll off the path to the right and stay still. But I think he leaves the log until he comes back out."

And that is just how it worked. They watched the truck move down the path about fifty yards, turn left, and disappear behind the trees. They could hear it moving for another minute or two and then it stopped again. Swede looked around. There were huge evergreens all around except for the path back out towards the main road. With at least a foot of snow, sounds were muffled. It was a world of dark green and grayish white, all of that shadowed by the night.

"OK, let's move. Follow me." Page moved down the path, staying on the tire tracks. Fifty feet before the tracks turned left, he jumped off the path, landing upright behind a small bush. Looking back at Swede he said. "Don't make obvious tracks moving off the path." Swede followed his example, and the two moved further into the evergreens. They moved up a small hill and turned towards the sounds coming from the camp. They could hear faint laughter and boisterous conversation as the Russians climbed into the truck, undoubtedly looking forward to their night in town. Wasting no time, the driver gunned the engine and headed back out to the path. Page and Swede simply melted into the ground behind low-hanging branches and caught glimpses of the truck as it passed by. After waiting about thirty minutes, the two started moving slowly toward the Russian camp.

They approached cautiously, eventually crawling to the last trees before the clearing where the trucks were parked. It wasn't much, just a small glen surrounded by evergreens, hills all around except for the southern end. Forty yards across at the most. They waited for another thirty minutes to make sure the one guard wasn't wandering around. Page pointed to the truck with something mounted on the roof of the bulky trailer behind it. "That's the one we want. The trailer in the middle should be the generator where the guard is. You keep an eye on the door at the back and let me know if it starts to open. I'm going to take a close look at the antenna and get a picture or two."

They crouched down and moved carefully to the radar trailer. Sliding under, they waited a while and watched the generator truck to see if they could spot any movement or hear any noise. "I'm going to stand up and check out the gear on top. You stay low but hang onto my pant leg. If something happens, you give me some sharp tugs." Swede nodded.

Page could see the gear on top could swivel up and then the dish would rotate. He had been told the film would work even in dim light, so he snapped some pictures from various angles. The camera was no bigger than a pack of cigarettes and made little noise. Once he was satisfied he had enough, he slipped back under the trailer and pulled Swede after him.

"Now we try the door and hope it isn't locked." Swede just grinned. Sliding to the back of the trailer, the two slowly stood up and checked the door. Locked. Page sighed in exasperation, but Swede just nudged him aside.

"I thought this is what you brought me along for." He whispered. Digging into his coat, he brought out his picks and waved them in front of Page. He inserted them into the lock and began slowly maneuvering them. "I've been practicing. Even found a couple of interesting storerooms about a week ago." Gently, he pulled down on the handle and the door opened. Both men squeezed inside.

"Without the generator running we'll have to find a lantern or flashlight," Page said. He pulled some matches from his pocket and scraped one on the wall. The match flared up and sent shadows bouncing around the interior. With no windows, they didn't have to worry about being spotted. Page reached over and pulled a flashlight from a bracket on the wall as the match died.

There were three stools, bolted to the floor, in front of three large boxes on the wall. Below each box was what looked like a typewriter keyboard of some kind, with a series of toggles above the keyboard and below the box. In the center of each box was a darkened window with a line grid built into the window. Nothing was on, at least no lights were lit up and no noise of any kind was coming from any of the machines. While Swede was looking in confusion at all the equipment, Page sat at the middle stool, opposite of the door, and began opening drawers in the desk that held the keyboard and toggles.

"Bingo!" Page held up a thick book and waved it at Swede. "This is what we want. The manual."

"How do you know that," asked Swede.

"Because it says so right here." Swede could see some Russian looking words on the cover.

"You can read that?" Swede asked, and then caught himself. "Oh yeah, I don't usually think of you as Russian," he continued.

"I'm not. I was. But I'm not. And I hope everybody thinks the way you do on the subject. Now, I'll work the camera. You turn the pages. I'm supposed to use one foot as the best distance for print material. I'll hold and click; you turn the pages and position them under the camera. There are a lot of pages here. This may take us a while. It's going to be hard to judge time."

The two worked out a system, but Page was right, there were a lot of pages. Every now and then they would turn off the flashlight, open the door, check for any signs of daylight, and listen for any sounds of a truck. Then back to work.

Finally - the last page. Swede replaced the manual in the drawer while Page carefully wrapped the camera in a small piece of cloth and placed it in his hat. The flashlight was stowed back in its original position and they carefully opened the door enough to peek out. Seeing and hearing nothing, Swede stepped out and down to the ground where he slid under the trailer. He waited until Page closed the door and joined him. Swede was just about to say "let's go" when a door banged open on the generator trailer. Both men froze, looking at each other with eyes wide open, waiting for the yelling to start. And probably the shooting.

The only noise came from the sound of boots on the steps off the back of the trailer and then the crunch of snow as the man stepped away. Still no yelling. Then they could hear the rustle of clothing. Swede peered out around the tire. With a smile he whispered, "He's takin' a leak." Both men visibly relaxed and waited for the guard to climb back in the trailer and go back to sleep.

The two tensed up again as the crunching moved away from the generator trailer. Carefully looking out, Swede could see the man had no visible weapon and just seemed to be checking the area. As he swung near their trailer, both men involuntarily held their breath. Swede first noticed the man's untied boots and then spotted the pistol and belt around his waist. He decided if a hand moved toward that pistol, he would tackle him and hope Page could follow up with a knockout punch, kick, or rock. The man stopped just a foot from the two under the trailer and Swede got ready. Then he heard the rattle of the handle on the door above them as the guard checked to see it was locked. Apparently happy, and without any idea how lucky he was, the guard crunched his way around to some of the other trailers, checking the doors. At one point, he neared the trees where the two men had crouched before coming into the camp. Swede thought he saw some hesitation, but the guard moved on. Eventually he returned to his trailer and stepped back inside, slamming the door behind him. If he had been paying attention right then, he would have heard the collective sigh from both men under the radar trailer.

"Thought we were in trouble there for a minute," whispered Page. "We better wait here for a bit and make sure he goes back to sleep."

They sat for what was probably fifteen minutes but seemed like an hour. Page slid out from under the trailer and stood. As Swede followed, both men froze. They could hear a truck coming! The snow must have muffled the sound because they could see the dim glow of the blackout lights as the truck turned the corner and headed into the clearing.

Page grabbed Swede's arm and hissed, "Move!" He crouched low and quickly headed for the nearest trees, Swede right next to him. As the truck came into the clearing, Page got ready to dive to the ground and hope they wouldn't be seen. This time Swede grabbed him and kept going. "They can't see us yet. Get into the trees!" The two reached the tree line and slid under the low-hanging evergreen branches. Then they slithered further into the safety of the forest. When the truck stopped, they both stopped moving. Once again, they waited for the yelling and the shooting to start.

The tailgate slammed down, but no one jumped out yelling in their direction. The men seemed to be either tired or hung over. They moved slowly out from under the canvas and dropped to the ground. With little conversation, they all disappeared into their trailers. Wasting no time, the driver gunned the truck around in a circle and headed back out to the road. Without a word, both Page and Swede jumped up and moved as fast as they could back towards the log barrier to catch their ride home. They could only hope the snow and dense forest would cushion the noise they made as they ran. They both were silently wishing the driver had stopped this one time to replace the log across the path on his way into the compound.

When they caught their first glimpse of the truck through the branches it was standing still. That meant the driver was either removing the log to get out or replacing it before he headed back down to the camp. In either case, they couldn't go charging out to catch their ride. They moved quickly, but quietly, to the edge of the trees. Just as they came up directly across from the truck, they could see the driver dragging the log back across the path. Then he pulled himself up into the cab, slammed the door shut, ground it into gear, and headed home. Swede and Page burst out of the trees and ran for the back of the truck. They couldn't take the time to try and avoid leaving tracks in the snow. Any delay and they were walking home.

The two were almost out of breath when they caught up just as the driver turned left onto the main road and prepared to pick up speed. Page pulled the ropes from under his coat and handed Swede one end on the run. Swede wasn't quick enough in tying his slip knot and ended up skiing behind the truck as he held on with one hand and attached the rope with the other. Page hung on with both hands and his feet resting on the bumper. As they pulled themselves into the hammock seat, they looked at each other and began to chuckle.

"Cookin' with gas, my ass!" Swede whispered, still smiling.

"Hey, we made it, didn't we? In and out and nobody knows. Couldn't have done it any better if I had planned it that way." Page grinned at Swede.

As they approached the bridge just north of camp Page said, "About fifty yards beyond the bridge we let loose the knots and roll off the road to the right. That should put us right at the path that heads over to our huts. I'll take care of the rope. Then we get back to our huts and pretend we just went out to the latrine."

As they bounced their way over the bridge, Swede found himself grinning. They really had pulled it off. Just as he realized he was grinning, his knot pulled loose. He had just enough time to warn Page and then he was on the ground, rolling and sliding and getting a nose full of snow. When he stopped, he was just barely off the bridge. Looking up he could see Page hanging on with the rope dragging behind. Rolling quickly off the road to his right, Swede knew continuing down the road until the path Page had mentioned was not a good idea. Looking around, he realized he could just follow a path in the snow alongside the shore that would take him to the area where the cooks kept some holes chopped in the ice to get their cooking water. There were plenty of paths through the snow in this part of the village, mostly created by the villagers themselves. He jumped up and forced himself to move at a leisurely pace. There was just a hint of dawn to the east. It wouldn't be long before somebody from the cook shack would head down to draw some buckets of water. That would not be a problem. Running into one of the guards getting water for their morning tea would be.

As he moved along the path, Swede reversed his coat to hide the camouflage. What was left was just another raggedy old coat. He reached the water point and quickly grabbed one of the poles left there to break the ice from the holes. As he was dropping the coat in the snow, he could hear someone shuffling down the path from the camp itself. It didn't matter, friend or foe, he had to go through with his plan. The shirt came next. Then he started splashing very cold water over his head and torso, making lots of noise as he did so. He heard the shuffling stop, then break into a run. He continued splashing and sputtering - and shivering. The water was *really* cold.

"You do? You do?" yelled a guard as he came into view. He carried only a small wooden bucket, no weapon. He was probably no more than sixteen. His face had a look of complete disbelief.

"I wash! I wash!" Swede smiled, splashing ice-cold water in his armpits, as if he bathed that way every morning.

"You wash? You wash? No wash! No wash!" the guard yelled, dropping his bucket and waving his arms. "You do? No wash!"

Swede reached down, grabbed a handful of snow, and began rubbing it all over his face and chest, soaking up the water. All the while he was smiling and jabbering right back at the guard.

"Man, that feels good! You should try this. A nice cold bath and I am ready for the day. Good for what ails ya, my grandpa says."

The guard kept yelling. "No wash! No wash!" and waving his arms about. Finished with the show, Swede slipped on his shirt, picked up his coat, and started up the path as if this was just another part of his day. The guard just stood, finally silent, scratching his head. Then he shrugged his shoulders, filled his bucket with water, and headed up the path himself, mumbling about these crazy Americans.

Once he knew the guard wasn't looking, Swede picked up his pace. He hurried past the cookhouse and headed for his hut, just a hint of dawn in the chilly morning sky. Pushing aside the heavy canvas door, he snuggled down on the floor next to some unfortunate hut mate and tried to rob him of his body heat.

Learn the Truth

December 1951

December came and the temperatures dropped. This was the biggest fear of every POW who had lived through the first winter. The cold. Would the deaths start again? Will we have to carry more friends to the hillside and bury them in the snow? Will it be me this time?

The cold came. But it was only uncomfortably cold, not deathly cold. Meals didn't come from the kitchens of Cordon Bleu, but got them through the day. They had blankets and usually at least a few hours of heat from fires each day. Any of that could be taken away and sometimes was. But only for individuals or small groups and only for a limited time. After all, some people still had not 'learned the truth.' But no one died. As far as anyone could tell, there had been no POW deaths since early fall.

The Reactionaries began to gain ground with their arguments. We can fight back. We don't have to sign every statement they put in front of us. We need to be soldiers again. We are Americans, let's act like it. More prisoners began to push back at the daily lectures.

The daily lectures continued into the winter. If there wasn't a group lecture where the whole company had to sit outside, one of the instructors would sit outside the door of a hut and lecture from there, with the door wide open. Day after day, the message was the same. Communism good, capitalism bad. The problem was the instructors would take an hour or two to convey that simple message. With the door open, in the middle of winter, with fires limited to early morning and evening. The 'communism is good' part was easy to ignore. The constant portrayal of everything in the US being negative got to somebody at least once a week. Swede did not see that as all bad.

"We need to get serious about getting everybody in all camps to quit cooperating with the lectures. We need to agree on a set time and get the word out. We've talked about this. How about April, the first Monday after Easter? Most of us will know when Easter is. We use the day after in case they plan to feed us better on Easter. No point in lookin' a gift horse in the mouth. Winter will be mostly over, and the meek won't be able to use the argument the Chinese will let us die," Swede argued.

"Unless the Chinese let us die before then," Dick Shea offered.

"That's not gonna happen," replied Earl Stoneman. "They need us now because of the peace talks. We are pieces in their chess game. Pawns, but still part of the game. I vote for the day after Easter."

With little more discussion, the group agreed. "Now for some details," added Swede. He was the one who pushed hardest on this plan. The others had just accepted him as the leader. He just seemed to make sense. The number of times he had been sent to regiment or up to Camp 5 demonstrated he led by example. "Talk to the people you trust. Get them on board. Put pressure on the middle of the road guys and the milder Progressives. Hint that the war will be over by fall and they need to think about what happens when we get home. If they come around now, all can be forgiven."

Earl spoke up again. "I'm almost afraid to ask because I think I know the answer. But how do we get the word out to the other camps? Everybody needs to walk away at the same time. If part of a camp or just one camp quits cooperating, but the others don't, the Chinese might just decide they can afford to lose a few chess pieces as an example."

Swede smiled at Earl. "Camp 5 is the key. When was the last time you had the privilege of a visit?"

"Aw hell. I knew you were gonna suggest that. But I suppose there is no other way." Earl didn't look very happy.

"What are you two jabberin" about," asked Fred.

"They mean we're gonna have to take turns gettin' sent to the slammer, you bonehead," said Billy.

"On purpose? Why the hell would we do that?"

Swede looked around at the group in the hut. The flickering of the one candle allowed at the end of the day cast shadows on the walls of the hut in a somber dance. "Camp 5 is the key. We never get sent down to Camp 1. But when we do time up at Camp 5, we see people from Camp 1. By getting sent there, we cover both of those camps. Maybe somebody from 5 can get word to the officers in Camp 2 or 4, or wherever they are. We can talk to guys from Camp 3 South when we get sent down to regiment. The slammer in 5 and at regiment will be our grapevine, or rice telegraph, whatever we want to call it. That is how we get word to all camps about the Monday after Easter.

"I don't know that we have to take turns getting in trouble," Swede continued. "We just keep doin' what we have been. We might need to throw a few more rocks at a few more Pros or call Mao a few more names, but enough of us will get sent to the slammer, I'm sure. Just remember, the Monday after Easter is the beginning."

"The beginning? The beginning of what?" asked Harvey Reynolds.

"Of the end," answered Earl, smiling over at Swede.

"Exactly. And that's how we advertise it. The beginning of the end. We don't play their game anymore!" Swede pointed towards regiment.

They couldn't just run around camp telling everybody about the plan. Only those who were proven Reactionaries were given the details. Even then, it wasn't that simple. The rules still said you could not visit from company to company. But sometimes during group lectures, people could manage to sit next to someone else they didn't see on a regular basis. Work details, especially wood gathering, would often require more men. Exchanging information while scattered over a large hill was easy. Some men became good at pretending they were on a work detail. A shovel and some buckets often went unchallenged as they moved from one company area to another.

Fred Moeder came up with another way to mess with the Chinese. Pai had given them another of his assignments. They were to write their family history - their autobiography. "Take your time. Be complete. Do not worry about politics. Simply write the truth. I wish to learn more about you and your country. To be friends and understand each other, we must know each other better." With that Pai gave each a small notebook with lined paper and a pencil.

"This is my third life history they have asked for," complained Fred. "I'm gonna sign a different name on this one, just to see if they are payin' attention." This brought a chuckle from some of the others.

"What are ya gonna say when Pai comes back and says he can't find your history?" asked Dick Shea.

"Good point," answered Fred. "So, what I'm gonna do is write mine and then make one up for some other guy. Paul Milhouse. That will be the name on the second one. I'll make it short and add it to the pile. If we hand them over as a group, he won't notice until he reads them, and maybe not even then."

"He gave each of us one notebook. How do we get extras for our second guy?" asked Dick.

"Another good point. I'll ask Hardware. If he doesn't have some, he can get them easy enough."

It didn't take much to get the guys interested in an idea like Fred's, especially when they could mess with the Chinese. If Pai realized he had autobiographies with names he didn't recall they would all simply profess ignorance. 'Hey, it's not our job to keep track of everybody here in this camp.' Swede was one of those who went along with the idea. For no particular reason, he signed his second autobiography with the name M. S. Finnegan. A couple of days later, when Pai asked who had his autobiography ready, they handed him a stack of notebooks. Pai was so pleased he didn't bother to count them or look for signatures at the end of each history. That night the hut got more than the normal ration for supper.

The very next day Pai left a flyer with the instruction it would be discussed the next day at group lecture for the company. "You must study and talk about the truth amongst yourselves."

Learn the Truth

On the morning of June 25th, 1950, Syngman Rhee's puppet army attacked the Korean people at the 38th parallel. The Democratic People's Republic police forces beat back the invaders until war mongers McArthur and Truman released their army which overwhelmed the heroic of the Democratic People's Republic forces. DPR was then forced to call on its volunteer army to protect their families. The Korean People's Army pushed

Truman's aggressors and their southern puppets almost to the sea! The families of the DPR rejoiced!

Then the capitalist controlled United Nations illegally entered the scene. When their planes rained death on the Korean People's Army and forced them north of the 38th parallel the Chinese People's Volunteer forces spontaneously rose up to help their neighbors. This defensive action continues today.

You are the victims, just as the tens of thousands of villagers who lost their lives to the aggressor forces. You were lied to.

You were sent to make war on the innocent with inferior weapons and supplies. You were not trained to protect your health and many of your comrades died while guests of the Korean and Chinese people.

And now you have been abandoned! Your own General Van Fleet has said the "US government should delay truce negotiations in order to gain time for creating a situation of strength." Your own generals have abandoned you!

Why are they delaying the peace talks?
Why are you still in Korea?
Why do they want this war to continue?

You can help the families that are suffering in this illegal war! You can help yourself and your comrades get back to your families! Demand peace talks go forward. Demand the invading UN forces be removed from the Democratic People's Republic of Korea.

Demonstrate your gratitude to the Chinese
People's Volunteer Army for your lenient
treatment as their guests while your
Generals delay peace.

Sign the petition to end this war!

Don't let them take away your constitutional
right to free speech.

We must all work for peace. Do your part!

"This one's a doozy," Earl Stoneman exclaimed. "Some of our guys are gonna trip over themselves getting in line to sign this! The poor villagers, we were lied to, inferior weapons, we have been abandoned, get back to our families. We have a constitutional right to free speech. Signing a petition for peace is free speech! Yep, they're gonna line up for this one."

"Yeah, we definitely have our work cut out for us this time," Swede added. "I can see a few days in the slammer coming up. It is good, but they gave us a couple of things we can use. And they should be obvious if we get everybody to pay attention.

"First, did any of us see any North Korean police forces in the beginning? We can point out that one as a lie. And our comrades died because we were not trained to protect our health? That should get some people mad!"

"Guests of the Korean and Chinese people?" Fred growled. "That argument usually riles us up."

Earl was right. The next day many hands shot up when the question was asked, "Will you sign this petition for peace? You have a right to do that." But Reactionaries throughout the company asked questions. And received the same old answers in reply. Swede understood the Chinese would not back down on this. They would not let the Reactionaries question the 'facts' in the flyer. But to *not* question them made it easier for the majority to make excuses for why they would sign. Everybody wants peace! Were you there? Did you see who invaded first? Maybe it was the fault of the South. We sure did have lousy equipment. No general can tell me I don't have the right to free speech!

When he stood up, Swede did so with the knowledge he was probably going to end up in a cold cell for a couple of weeks. He figured he might as well take his best shot and hope that his fellow POWs would see the truth in what he was about to say. So, he stood up and challenged the Chinese on their weakest point.

"You are correct. Many of our friends did die. But they didn't die because we weren't trained well enough. They died because they didn't have enough food. They died because they had no medicine. They died because they had only summer clothing to survive the winter. They died because they had no shoes. They died because they had no shelter and no fire. Half of our friends died. I don't know why I did not die. But our training had nothing to do with how many died.

"What kind of training does a soldier need to survive with summer clothing in the winter? What kind of training does a soldier need to sleep on the ground when it is twenty below? What kind of training does a soldier need to strip his friend naked before burying him in the snow? The Korean Army, and then the Chinese Army, were responsible. You did not supply us with the proper food and clothing and shelter until the winter was over, until the dying was over.

"Sign your petition? Why not? It only makes sense to ask for an end to this war, any war, all wars. I might even sign it myself.

"But not before you admit to and apologize for the deaths of all our friends." Swede waved his hand around at the group. "You guys think about that."

Others jumped up, some yelling in favor and some yelling against signing. The Chinese were losing control. The guards were starting to grip their rifles tighter, nervously looking from the crowd of POWs to their officers standing up front. Pai finally managed to wave everyone back down to their seats in the cold snow.

"It is good that we can discuss these different points of view. Perhaps we need more discussion in small groups first. Return to your huts and continue to talk. We will meet here again in one hour." Swede knew what was going to happen next, so he borrowed a heavier coat and stuffed some rags in his pockets. He wrapped a blanket around his shoulders. Then he waited.

It didn't take long for pairs of guards to show up at various huts and call out names. Swede stood up at the call for "Low-son" and joined others as they followed the guards out of the compound to the road. Some were turned south and marched down the road to regiment. Swede and three others were told to climb in the back of a truck, which then headed north. Five more were in a different truck following them.

After a couple of hours of a cold, uncomfortable ride, the trucks made a hard-left turn. It was now the first week of January 1952 and Swede was back at Camp 5. So were Earl Stoneman and Fred Moeder, both in the truck with him. They had seen Dick Shea climb into the second truck but hadn't been able to see the others. It was dark when the trucks stopped. All nine were herded into a building they didn't recognize. In that building they were shoved into one room, and the door was shut behind them. They were hungry and cold and jammed together in a room too small for a group half the size.

"Déjà vu all over again," muttered Earl. He was right. The circumstances were very much like their first winter, but with some major differences. They were hungry, but not starving. Their calorie intake had been adequate for the last nine months to keep them healthy. They were cold but dressed much better to ward off that cold. Both the room and the building they were in were well built. There would be no icy fingers of wind tormenting them through the night. They simply sat down with knees drawn up and shared their blankets as they tried to sleep.

Morning came with just a bit of light sneaking into their room and the noise of people in the building around them. What felt like hours passed before their door opened. They were all hustled out of the building into a gently falling snow. Each was given a turn in a very decrepit outhouse and then lined up again outside what seemed like the back door to a two-story cement block building. They carried on some quiet conversations but mostly looked at their surroundings. There were identical buildings on each side of the one they were next to, with smaller wooden structures to their left. Five guards stood around the group with occasional figures moving through the snow in and out of the buildings.

Two men were taken through the door before Swede. When his turn came, he was led down a hallway and into a room. On the far side was a raised platform with a large desk. A guard stood off to each side, his escorts took up positions to either side of the door behind him. At the desk sat an older Chinese officer, short gray hair, and a grim look on his face.

"Your name?" asked the officer.

"Paul Larson," replied Swede in as neutral a voice as he could manage. The officer shuffled through a stack of papers on the desk in front of him. He found what he was looking for and set the others aside.

"Pole Lawson, you have been tried and found guilty of crimes against the Chinese People's Volunteer Army. You are sentenced to three months confinement in a punishment camp." With that simple statement, the officer nodded to the guards by the door.

Swede wondered when his trial had been held. He sure hadn't been there. There was no real point in saying anything and he wasn't given time if he had tried. The two guards behind him stepped forward and shoved him towards a door on the right. That led to another hallway which took them to the front of the building. Outside once again, Swede was led to an American jeep and handcuffed to the frame in the back seat. The driver immediately pulled away. Swede noticed there were two other jeeps and a truck waiting, their engines running.

Solitary at 2-3

January 1952

The jeep bounced its way back east, then turned left and headed northeast. The road became narrower and cruder. About half an hour later, Swede could see a small village ahead. They pulled up in front of some small huts just as daylight left. His driver released the handcuffs as two new guards appeared. As they led him off, Swede saw the jeep turn around and head back west.

He spent the night in a hole dug in the ground, covered over with logs and dirt. There was an actual door fitted into the logs and a ladder leading down into the hole. Once he was inside, the guards closed and locked the door with a chain. Then he was left alone in the dark, no orders of any kind. No one had spoken to him since he had heard his sentence back in Camp 5.

What little light was left filtered through the roof in a few spots. Swede poked around until he found a small stick and enlarged one of the holes. He could see some buildings on a little hill to the east. Figures moved around up there, but it was too dark to see who they might be. Every now and then he heard Chinese voices giving commands. Soon it was completely dark, so he found a smooth spot on the ground and let himself drift off to sleep. Maybe the morning would bring some details about where he was. Before sleep came, he had to admit to himself he was feeling a little alone and a little afraid. Three months in this hole in the ground was not an appealing thought. But he had been through this before. He was healthier and wiser now. He could do it again. Keep fighting that fear.

With daylight came a much better look at the buildings on the hill. He was sure it was a POW camp of some kind. Men were lined up for what looked like a headcount and then breakfast. He didn't have long to think about it as the chain rattled and the door was pulled open. This time there was no truck, no jeep. The handcuffs were put back on and two guards motioned him forward. No one had said a word to him since he had been told of his sentence. These new guards continued that treatment.

They walked east, past what he was now convinced was a POW camp. Swede was sure he could hear American voices as he and his guards crossed a frozen little stream and continued down a foot path. They continued walking for a couple of hours, the path wandering more and more between heavily wooded hills that grew larger. Every once in a while, the beauty of his surroundings, the hills covered in snow and evergreens, untouched by the war, made him forget he hadn't eaten in twenty-four hours.

Mid-afternoon Swede noticed a few small buildings ahead. There were five or six standard Korean farm huts and two wooden cottages, each with a little porch. A little farther up the slope on the north were three more huts, each isolated from the other. Footpaths in the snow connected all but those three huts. Smoke came from the chimneys of the two cottages. The well-worn path he and his guards were using went right between them.

The guards stopped Swede in front of one of the huts near the cottage on his left. One guard moved ahead and stepped through the door to that building. The other moved to the cottage on the right and yelled inside. Someone handed out a cup of tea and the man sat in a chair on the little porch and relaxed. After a few minutes he seemed to realize Swede was still standing across the path from him and yelled to those inside the cottage again. A second cup of tea was brought out. The guard got up and brought it across to Swede. He didn't say anything, didn't smile, didn't even frown. His prisoner was standing in the cold and deserved a cup of tea as much as he did. The guard returned to his chair.

As Swede stood sipping the hot, rich, tea he heard a whisper. "Don't turn around. Pretend I'm not talking to you. When you answer me, make sure your cup is hiding your mouth. Don't offer to give the cup back. They might let you keep it."

"Where are you from and why are you here?" the voice asked.

"Camp 3 north." Sip. "They didn't like my response to a petition." Sip. "Said I earned three months punishment." Sip.

"Turn your head like you are looking around the place." Swede turned slightly and scanned both sides of the hill. "Yeah, I know you. I remember you from Camp 5. You're a bit of a troublemaker, aren't you?" There was a hint of a smile in the question.

"Yes, I am," Swede agreed with a little pride. Sip. "And I intend to keep that up." Sip.

"If they feed you tonight, look for a message in the bottom of the bowl. Sooner or later we will be able to fill you in. But it might be later. You'll start out up the hill on your own. As time goes by and you behave, they bring you down and put you with others. They'll take you to your hut soon. Good luck." With those words, the voice fell silent. Swede finished his tea and casually tucked the cup in his coat pocket.

His guards came back across the path a few minutes later and led him up the hill to the nearest of the three isolated huts. Swede took notice as they removed a thick board that slotted across the door. There would be no picking locks here. The first guard looked inside and came back out with a satisfied grunt. He motioned Swede in, and they blocked the door up again. Swede looked around his new home. A worn straw mat on the floor and a bucket in the corner were the total of his furniture. Well, he thought, I've been in worse. There was a small window that looked over the buildings in the valley. The paper over the window let in light but prevented him from seeing out. Once he looked carefully, Swede noticed quite a few small holes in the walls that let in light. He spent the next few hours plugging them with dirt he scraped from the floor, leaving only a few to use as peep holes. If he was going to be there for a while, he needed to keep out the cold as well as he could. He decided not to enlarge any of the peep holes in case the guards looked for that kind of thing when a new guy came in.

Later in the day he heard singing from down below. Someone was actually singing! Using his best peep hole, Swede looked out to see what looked like at least one hundred POWs milling about the huts down near the cottages. It looked like they had just returned from a wood gathering detail. Using a variety of axes and saws they worked at cutting up their firewood. One of them was singing "I've Been Working on the Railroad". Suddenly Swede noticed the crooner threw in a "hey up there on that hill" that didn't belong. After a few verses of the old classic he began a new song.

"Hey new guy up on the hill,
Listen up and I'll give you the fill.
Meals you get only once a day,
Look for news at the bottom of your hay.
Make sure you are nice to the boys
Or they will slam you around like a brand-new toy.
This song won't always rhyme,
But I'll deliver the news when I get the time."

The message was repeated and then 'Bing Crosby' broke in to "The Erie Canal." Every time he got to "low bridge, everybody down" the rest of the workers bent low as they worked. The guards didn't seem bothered by any of this. Swede wasn't positive, but he thought even a few of the guards laughed. In any case, he appreciated the news. The fact his fellow prisoners were taking the risk of helping him made him feel better than he had since leaving Camp 3.

Swede continued to watch as food buckets were delivered to each of the huts below. Then two men began the climb up towards Swede. It looked like a prisoner carrying two small buckets and a guard with a bayonet fixed on his rifle. As they got to the door, the guard yelled "No talk. No talk!" Swede wasn't sure if that was meant for him or the prisoner delivering his supper. When the door opened, the guard took a half step into the hut with his bayonet pointed straight out. He found Swede standing at attention at the back wall.

"No talk, no talk!" The guard punctuated his command with small thrusts of his bayonet. The prisoner reached into the hut and placed both buckets on the floor. He looked carefully at Swede and then down towards the buckets. Swede made sure he didn't react in any way. That was difficult, as the prisoner looking at him was Trigger!

Trigger and the guard immediately withdrew, leaving Swede to wonder how Trigger ended up in this place, wherever this place was. He didn't wonder long as he was very hungry and his food was getting cold. Opening the buckets, he found one with a decent tea, most of all because it was warm, and the other of rice. Taking the cup he had neglected to return earlier that day, Swede poured some tea for himself and quickly replaced the cover on the bucket. He sat on his mat and brought both buckets inside his coat to help keep his meal warm. A small wooden spoon in the rice bucket was a welcome surprise.

As he enjoyed his meal Swede wondered at the appearance of Trigger. He had heard all the black prisoners at Camp 1 had been put in a separate compound in the camp. So how did a black prisoner end up here? Was this an all-black compound? As he ate and thought, Swede also paid attention to the bucket of rice. Both the song earlier in the day and Trigger's look made him suspect there was a message of some kind at the bottom of his "hay." And sure enough, a piece of paper was folded tight at the bottom of the bucket. Swede set it aside until he finished eating.

When the rice was gone, Swede poured the last of the tea into the bucket, swished it around to soak up any nutrition that was left, and drank it down. There had been a bit of fish and greens at the bottom, probably put there on the sly and then covered with rice to hide it from the guards' inspection. Whoever these guys were in this camp, they had their act together. Putting his cup back in his pocket, Swede placed the spoon in the rice bucket and replaced both lids. Then he sat back against the wall and read his note in the last of the days' light.

keep spoon, hide
if u r ok blink 2x at supper
if not look cross eyed
behave, dstry note

Again, the reference to not antagonize the guards. He removed the spoon from the bucket and placed it in his pocket with the cup. He wondered what would happen if he looked cross-eyed the next day when his supper was brought in. Just knowing he was not OK wouldn't do much for the guys down below, but maybe they had a way to talk to him to find out what he might need. He would find out later. What most puzzled him was here, wherever here was. Swede had never heard about a remote camp like this. Where was it and why? Maybe over the next few days he would find some answers. He had the time. Rolling up in his blanket, he settled down to sleep.

In the morning Swede thought about the cup and spoon. Maybe keeping them in his pocket was not a good idea. Stealing was probably frowned on and he had been warned to be careful of the guards. The mystery voice the day before had told him he would be here a while and then move down the hill. So, it would be okay to hide the cup and spoon. He took a large rag from his coat pocket and carefully wrapped them up. It was important to keep them clean. Using his boot and a stick from the wall he dug a hole and buried them.

The prisoners in the lower huts had breakfast and Swede watched as they were marched down the trail to the east. He guessed they were on a work detail of some kind. There were quite a few logs stacked up down there, more than they would need for daily fires. Maybe they harvested trees for some other camp. After the work detail left, a guard started up the hill toward Swede's hut. Once again, he made sure he was standing at attention opposite the door. The guard pointed to the slop bucket and motioned for Swede to pick it up. When they returned from emptying it, the guard picked up the food bucket from the night before, barred the door, and left without saying a word. Apparently, part of his three-month sentence was supposed to be with minimum human contact. Swede was happy the other POWs had already nullified that. He knew from experience how difficult these months would be if he felt he was out here alone.

With nothing else to do, Swede inspected his hut. Dirt floor, wooden beams in the walls with an adobe type material in between, boards covered with thatch for the roof. He could probably tunnel his way out if he had to. Or just kick the wall out. Neither would make much sense under the current circumstances. The door was solid with the hinges on the outside. He looked over the matt, hoping it didn't contain lice. He had been free of them for a while. After the inspection, he paced back and forth and did a few pushups. A couple of months without physical activity would not be good. Since it looked like he might only eat once a day, too much activity would also not be good.

Next, he spent time looking through his peepholes to see what he could learn about the camp in general. A few guards moved around and maybe a prisoner or two, but the majority of both seemed to have left on the work detail. When he got cold from sitting, he got up and paced some more. After a while boredom set in and he took a nap. The noise from the returning work party woke him later in the afternoon. He watched them fill a small trough with buckets of water and wash up. Was the water hot, would *he* get water to wash?

Guards strolled around the area or sat on the porch of one of the two cottages. The prisoners were allowed to talk with each other and go in and out of their huts. Swede was too far away to identify faces or hear voices distinctly. He did notice a prisoner pointing up towards his hut every now and then. It seemed as if they also pointed to the next hut over from his, but he couldn't be sure. As daylight faded, he watched as two men, carrying buckets and followed by two guards, started up the hill. One pair headed off to the left and the other came his way. Apparently, he had slept through the arrival of a new prisoner.

Swede followed the same procedure as before and was standing at attention opposite the door when it opened. The guard didn't bother to come in. Swede made sure he had eye contact with Trigger and gave the two blinks to say he was okay. Trigger looked carefully at the bucket again and withdrew. Once they were gone, he settled down to enjoy his supper.

Just the two buckets this time. No spoon. Swede carefully uncovered his spoon and cup and dug in before everything cooled off more than it already had. First, he removed the new note and tucked it in his pocket. When he was finished, he licked his utensils clean and hid them away. Then he pulled out the note.

new guy says name Earl
was in 5 then 3
older guy
blink 2x if know him
cross eyes if no

It was good to know the guys down below were checking out new prisoners. That meant they were looking for a stooge of some kind to be planted in their group. That meant they were Swede's kind of people. It was also good to know Earl was nearby. He got up and found a small hole in the wall looking toward Earl's hut. He didn't expect to see Earl standing in a window waving at him but wanted to be able to see if he could spot him in the morning. After making two marks on a post to keep track of his days, Swede settled down to try and dream the night away.

With Earl at 2-3

February 1952

Almost nothing changed over the next few weeks. Notes of encouragement appeared every now and then in his rice. Once a week the prisoners below were given a half-day to clean their huts and generally relax. 'Bing Crosby' would entertain the with his songs, interjecting words of encouragement for Swede and Earl. Swede looked forward to meeting these guys who seemed to be so well organized.

Swede's days were spent pacing, doing push-ups, and watching the camp through his peepholes. He began using Buddha's meditation techniques again and practiced the French Kim had taught him. He studied the guards that brought his food and noticed they all had a veteran look to them. Some had scars or limped, but they all had a certain look in their eyes that said they had experienced more than they wanted to. But most of Swede's time was spent thinking.

He went back over his experiences since the day he first met Master Sergeant George W. Tucker. He remembered a few mistakes he may have made. Not making sure somebody kept watch that first night off the hill was one. At the same time, it may have saved their lives. Maybe he could have kept Ray and Bowser alive if he hadn't wasted all that time trying to escape - and then failing. Or, he could have died himself. No sense trying to figure that one out. The more he thought about it all, the more Swede became convinced he had tried hard all along to do the right thing. If it all ended tomorrow, he would go home with his head held high. But it wasn't going to end tomorrow, so he needed to continue to be a soldier, continue the fight. And maybe, just maybe, there would be payback for all those who had died and the way they had died.

All those minutes in his day meant he thought about home every now and then. Not in a sad or homesick way. Just wondering how things were going back there. That got him thinking of what he would do when he got home. What was next? Farming had no appeal for him. He didn't mind the work but couldn't see himself on a farm for the rest of his life. College? Maybe. But for what? The army? The problem he saw with the army was too many people he didn't trust or respect had complete control over his life. Within days of being captured, he saw the army collapse around him. Too few leaders and too many followers who gave up thinking for themselves the day they enlisted.

Men like Randall and Earl Stoneman would be professionals no matter what their work. He respected them, both for their abilities and their obvious concern for those around them. But even if he served in a unit with them for twenty years, there would be others above them who made decisions. Even Jack Usury, a career soldier, said the army saw soldiers as numbers, not individuals. The army was like farming. He didn't mind the work but couldn't see it as a long-term prospect.

Be a sailor like Mike Finnegan? Maybe. He was aware that for every story Mike told of adventure, there were more of the dangers of life at sea. Traveling to far off corners of the world had a definite appeal, but being a sailor probably was much like being in the army. What happened when you were in danger and a Mike Finnegan was not in charge?

The more thought he gave to life after the war, Swede found himself thinking of Henry Page, or whatever his name was. Page was a leader like Randall. He put himself at risk by staying with the prisoner column when in the early days he could have escaped with the help of his contacts. He had given up his entire past life to become an American. What he was doing was important. Finding information on the Chinese and Russians would help his new country for years to come. Swede enjoyed working with Page. It was more than the thrill; it was knowing you were doing something important, something more important than even yourself.

Swede spent a month with little more than his thoughts for

company. Every day was the same boring routine. Empty his slop bucket in the morning, exercise, meditate, daydream, nap, practice French, watch life in the camp through peepholes, supper, sleep. On the thirtieth day, Trigger had signaled another message was in his rice bucket.

be ready
u move tomorrow

Apparently, he had passed whatever the requirements were to move to the next phase at this camp. Swede made sure his cup and spoon were in his pockets before he went to sleep. If they came for him early, he wouldn't be able to dig them up.

The next morning was routine until Swede had emptied his bucket and started back towards his hut. The guard reached out and tugged him back. Then he pointed towards Earl's hut. Was everybody just shifting over one hut for some reason or was he about to join Earl? The answer came when the guard removed the bar from Earl's door and motioned Swede inside. Earl stood at the far wall. Swede could see the surprise and then smile on his face, but neither man said anything. They both stood still as the guard replaced the bar and started back down the hill. Once they knew he was gone, both men broke into broad grins and threw their arms around each other, laughing.

"Jesus, kid. It sure is good to see you!" Earl was about to break some of Swede's ribs. "I was hopin' you were in one of these huts. They shipped out Fred and Dick Shea right behind you, but then kept the rest of us there for the night. I was the first one to leave the next day. It sure has been a long, quiet month. Do you know where we are? I think it might be where they keep the Negro soldiers. At least, the guy who brings in my supper is black as night. Did you know they send messages up to us in our rice and when they sing songs on Sunday?"

Earl was talking a mile a minute, pausing only to give Swede another hug before going on. It was kind of funny to see the older man show this side. A month in solitary had gotten to him. Swede had seen it as fairly easy compared to that first winter at Camp 1. Apparently Earl had never had the opportunity to learn from a Kim or a Buddha. He finally slowed down and the two began to compare notes.

Swede explained he knew Trigger but wasn't sure how he ended up there. His hut was a little closer than Earls' to the huts down the hill, so he was sure Trigger was the only black guy in the camp. Earl said he arrived late at night and had only heard a voice from a hut when he waited for his escorts to turn him over to the camp guards. The voice had asked some questions, but Earl had no idea who he was. Swede told about his arrival and how he had been asked if he knew Earl. Neither of the two knew where they were or anything about the camp except what they could see from their huts.

Earl joked that he was innocent of any charges and any day now expected the Chinese to release him. The morning after they had arrived at Camp 5, Earl had the same experience as Swede and was sentenced to three months punishment. "He asked my name, flipped through the papers on his desk, and pulled one out. Then he said 'Reechar Shee, you have been tried and found guilty of crimes against the Chinese People's Volunteer Army. You are sentenced to three months in a punishment camp.' So, I figure it was all a mistake and I shouldn't be here with you other criminals."

Swede laughed. It felt good to have someone else to share the experience. Especially someone like Earl. They spent the rest of the day talking and watching the camp. That night another message came up with Swede's rice bucket.

Wrk tomorrow
Hard work
3 wks

As far as they could figure it meant they would be sent out with the work details from the lower huts. What happened after three weeks was a guess, but maybe the guys could explain it all to them in the morning.

They went to work the next day, but not with the prisoners from the lower huts. Instead, two guards led them up over the hill from their hut. In the valley on the other side was an area that had been partly cleared of trees. Off to the east there were stacks of logs near a road or path of some kind. They were given axes and a two-man crosscut saw and made to understand they were to cut down a group of trees just up from the bottom of the little valley on the north side.

It was a grove of hardwoods, mostly maple. At the end of the day they understood what the message had meant by hard work. The next day brought another change. Lunch. It was the same as supper, but welcome in any case. Their guards carried four lunches in little boxes, one for each. Playing Paul Bunyan was hungry work.

Over the next few days both men agreed they were working harder than they ever had before. One day they would cut down the trees, and the next they would cut them into logs with the saw. On the third day, they dragged them to the road and stacked them up. On the days they were in the woods, the men from camp loaded the logs onto large sleds pulled by shaggy ponies. The groups were never allowed to get close enough to communicate. Sometimes the ponies pulled their sleds north, other days south. Earl and Swede learned just how fast they had to work to please the guards. As their stamina increased, they were able to slow the pace, but not by much. They burned every calorie they got from their added lunch.

After the first week, they had a little energy to spare at the end of most days and spent time talking before falling asleep. The conversations had no pattern to them. One or the other brought up a topic, and they spent an hour or two chewing on it.

"Have you thought about tryin' to escape?" Earl asked. "There aren't many guards here and I'm pretty sure they don't post a guard up here at night."

"Yeah, I thought about it. We could kick out one of these walls and be gone in no time. But it's the same old problem. Go where? I have no idea where this is or how to get from here to where our guys might be. They would know right away in the morning we were gone and just follow our tracks. They could probably ride one of those ponies they use to haul the sleds. And then what? Just imagine how hard they would work us. They said three months and then I guess we go back to one of the regular camps. We still have a job to do in those camps, remember? If I could get out without them knowing, I might look around to get the lay of the land, but make sure I was back before morning. Otherwise, escape is off my list."

"Do you think there really are peace talks going on?" asked Swede.

"Peace talks, prisoner exchange talks, some kind of talks. We hear the same rumor from the few new guys who get caught. The fact we don't get too many new guys seems to say there's not a lot of movement back and forth on a front of some kind. So, yeah, I think somethin' is goin' on. If they ever deliver any mail from home, we'll know for sure. They aren't about to tell the folks back home how to get letters to us if they plan to kill us. When they let *us* write letters, then there is no doubt. So, short answer, yeah, I do."

"Earl, if you could go back in time, what would you change?"

"Easy. I'd join the Navy instead of the Army."

"That's it?"

"Yep. The Navy eats a lot better than the Army and you don't see many Navy guys around here, do you? What about you?"

"Well, now that you took all the fun out of it, maybe I'd be a medic instead of a rifleman. Maybe I could have saved guys like Ray Parker and Bowser, maybe a lot of other guys too."

"Swede, I think you've saved more guys than you know. I think you are doin' exactly the right thing. What's a Bowser?"

"Are you a religious man, Earl?"

"Well, my momma read the Bible to me a fair amount, so I guess I outta be. What she read to me might have stuck some, but my daddy used the Good Book to knock it right outta me about once a week. It was the only book we had in the house and didn't leave much of a bruise. I really don't think it mattered. I never saw much of what she read to me in the world around me. It seems to me people like to preach the Bible but not practice it. What about you, Swede?"

"I had a history teacher in high school who spent time in the trenches in World War I. He said what he saw there made no sense. People killing each other by the thousands over a few yards of mud. Then he went to college and found out humans have been doin' that to each other since we lived in caves. He used wars as examples. The Christians used their religion to justify killing Muslims. The Muslims used their religion to justify killing Christians. In the Civil War, both sides prayed before a battle to the same god to help them defeat their enemy. In World War I, there were posters that said we should kill the heathen Hun. I can't figure how any God could let us do that to each other. I think somehow, we're all related, all the same. I've even seen that here in these camps. Not often, but I've seen it. But I don't think there is any super person sitting somewhere out in space watchin' all this and picking sides. My mother is a religious person. I think that's a good thing, because it works for her. I pretty much keep *my* religion down to the basics, the Golden Rule."

The second week on the tree cutting detail, Swede and Earl experienced one of those times when everybody was equal. Each day their two guards came up from their cottages in the valley and escorted the prisoners over the hill to their work site. One of the guards was rather elderly, with a peasant face. He didn't seem interested in anything that went on around him, just did what he had to do to get through his day. The other was probably a little older than Swede. He had intelligent eyes, eyes that held a hint of a smile. By the end of the day he walked with a slight limp, as if an old injury got worse with the effort of the day. When the guards decided it was mid-day, they called a halt to the work. They would pull the lunch boxes out of the sack and give Earl and Swede theirs. The two groups would separate by a few feet, find a log to sit on, and enjoy their lunch. One day the guards sat down and pulled out the boxes. They gave the prisoners theirs and opened their own. One was empty. The cooks had tossed an empty box in the bag. Swede could tell by the tone of their conversation something was wrong. Then he realized the problem. He could also tell the guards were trying to come up with a solution. It was a fifteen or twenty-minute hike back to their camp. If one guard went the other was left alone with the prisoners. If they all went, it would mean a lot of wasted work time.

Swede nudged Earl and pointed over to the perplexed guards. He got up and approached them, motioning for Earl to follow.

"If we all share, we can work this out," he said, pointing from his box to the empty one. "Share. I give you," he said again. The older guard simply looked at him with a puzzled expression. Swede reached slowly over and took the empty box from the younger guard. He seemed willing to go along with whatever Swede was trying to do.

Swede grabbed a stick and wiped it clean. He took the stick and moved one-fourth of his rice into the empty box. Then he took Earl's and did the same. Earl had almost the same look as the older guard. Finally, Swede reached for the other box. The guard held on to it for a bit, but Swede gently pulled it out of his hands. Then he scraped one-fourth of that box into the once empty one.

"See, now we each have enough. And we each have the same. Bon appetit." The younger man almost smiled as he nodded his head in response.

As they walked back to their log Earl said, "You did notice we don't all have the same? Their rice had all kinds of goodies added."

"Yeah, I noticed that. But, the Golden Rule, remember?"

"Hey, that's your rule. I didn't say it was mine. But I guess I can live with it. Just try not to give away my rice too often, will ya?"

The guards talked quietly, looking over at their prisoners every now and then. Nothing changed. The day went on as usual. But the next day, the guards didn't just hand over two boxes of rice. They took out all four, set them on a log, and opened them up. They motioned for Swede and Earl to come over and look. All four boxes held the same kind of rice, all four were of the better rice, with 'all kinds of goodies,' as Earl had put it. The guards smiled, took their two boxes, and went off to eat. Every day for the rest of that work detail, Swede and Earl ate the same as the guards. Swede reminded Earl of the Golden Rule once or twice a day for the next couple of days.

As their second month drew to a close, the weather started warming up enough they were able to take off their coats as they worked through most afternoons. They left camp before the prisoners in the valley and returned later, so they had no news of what was going on in camp. A guard brought up their supper instead of Trigger, so no messages appeared in their rice buckets. Then one day, no guards came up to get them. By mid-morning they decided to go back to sleep. Somebody would wake them if they wanted them for work. In midafternoon they heard the prisoners returning to camp below them. A guard broke away from that group and started up the hill.

"My calendar says we're two months into this deal," said Swede. "Looks like we are about to find out what happens in our last month."

"I'm guessin' we join the boys down there," replied Earl.

"I'm *hopin'* we join the boys down there." Swede quickly dug up his spoon and cup and tucked them in his coat. Earl joined him. They stood ready as the guard opened their door.

"Come."

Swede was afraid to smile. He knew things could get worse, but inside he was hoping.

Camp Sunday
March 1952

"Sunday," sighed Earl.

"What about Sunday?" asked Swede.

"That's what I'm going to call this camp. Sunday." Earl answered. Swede chuckled.

The day they had come down from the hill to join the other prisoners turned out to be their Sunday. Nobody was sure if it really was a Sunday, but it was the day they got a break. They only worked half a day. They used the spare time to clean up the huts and themselves. And that meant a bath.

The sixth hut had a large tub. A well was just outside. During the week it supplied water for tea and just enough to do a quick wash of their hands and faces. The work they did was tough on hands, and the guards had decided it was better to allow them to wash their hands on a regular basis than to let the many scrapes and cuts become infected. But Sunday was bath day. On Sunday, they brought extra wood back to heat the tub. It held four men at a time, and the water was almost black by the time the last man was clean. A few braver souls then washed part or all of their uniform, depending on the temperature at the time.

New guys were allowed to bathe first. They didn't get many guys up on the hill. Most of the men in the huts in the valley were sent there as punishment for their poor attitudes or behavior. But not many were sent to the huts on the hill. You had to be a real problem child to get sent up there. The guys in the valley considered themselves Reactionaries. Anyone who spent two months on the hill was a Reactionary's Reactionary. So, they did what they could for them. Gave them advice on what to expect. Sent them messages. Tried to make them feel they were not alone. And let them in the tub first on the day they came down from the hill.

On Sundays they could relax a little. Somehow singing had become part of the Sunday tradition. Whether it was the weekly bath, the half day of rest, or the singing; the day gave Earl the feeling of a Sunday. So, Camp Sunday it was. Not everyone at Camp Sunday was there for three months. Most only spent a month. Their work helped supply firewood for the officer's camp, where Swede had stayed at one night. They also sent logs north to a river which emptied into the Yalu. Those logs eventually were sent downriver for either firewood or lumber.

And there were other small camps like Sunday scattered around the hills nearby. Men on the crews that went with the ponies and the sleds to stack logs on the river said they thought there was another camp farther north. They could see another series of isolated huts and cottages back in the woods off the sled path. Trigger was gone by the time Earl and Swede came down from their isolated huts. He had been sent there for his bad attitude. All the black troops at Camp 1 had been put in a separate compound. Some thought they should just sit back and wait out the war. Trigger thought otherwise.

Several at Sunday knew either Swede or Earl or both. A few knew about the plan, Easter Monday they were calling it, to end all cooperation with the Chinese "re-education" lectures. All the others were brought into the loop. Swede made it clear they needed to spread the word when they left Sunday. Wherever they ended up, they had to spread the word about Easter Monday. People were to either not show up for the day's lecture or walk away when the lecture began.

The work at Sunday was the same as Swede and Earl had been doing. With far more men it was much easier. There was also a breakfast of tea and a handful of peanuts. Their lunch was cooked in the woods in two kettles they carried back and forth every day. With a breakfast snack and a hot lunch, the day was more tolerable. They were expected to meet quotas, but unless more than an axe or two broke on any particular day, the prisoners had no problem doing so. The food and exercise had some of the men in better shape than when they were first captured.

Hank Prosser was the man who had talked to Swede when he first arrived at Sunday. He had been in the cells in Camp 5 with both

Swede and Earl. Hank explained the routine at Camp Sunday.

"The guards here are different. I figure they are all older veterans, either from here in Korea or from their civil war back in China. This might be their reward for the years they spent fighting. They don't hassle us as long as we fill the wood quota they give us. It doesn't seem like any of them speak much English. They've never catch on when we sing messages to guys on the hill."

"Or they don't care," added George Kasprovicz. "We pretty much don't rock their boat, and they don't rock ours. But I bet if we refused to work or somebody escaped, they'd be on us like flies on a dead possum." George had been a real hard nose when it came to the guards back in Camp 5, so when he said something positive about the guards, the others listened.

"Look at those guys," continued George. "It's pretty obvious this isn't their first rodeo. Most have scars or they walk like they hurt. They pretty much let us decide who goes on what work detail. They let us use the bathhouse. Now, I'm not sayin' they're easy on us. I'm just sayin' they seem to figure us workin' our asses off six and a half days a week is punishment enough. As long as we do what they expect us to do, everybody is happy."

Swede thought back to the two guards who gave them better food once he and Earl had shared. For a second or two he felt an anger rising in him. They shouldn't be making friends with the guards! But then he realized they weren't. This was a temporary situation, and both sides were making the best of it.

Over the next couple of weeks, Swede got a good look at the area around Camp Sunday. There was another group of POWs two ridges south. They were never allowed to mix with them but saw them from a distance a few times when on work details in that direction. The one time Swede worked on the logging sleds, he saw another group of huts to the north. The road the sleds ran on paralleled a river that ran north and then turned west towards the Yalu. At that point, the pony crews unloaded their logs on the ice of the frozen river. Swede guessed the logs floated out to the Yalu when the ice melted in the coming spring.

The huts to the north of Camp Sunday were set back to the west of the road up a small valley. One of the huts sat apart from the others and appeared to have a stockade-like fence around it. That probably meant there were POWs there. Hank and George said they were certain they had seen Caucasians outside some of the huts the few times they had worked in the area.

On one of their rest days, George Kasprovicz told a strange tale of his time at Camp 5. He had been the only survivor when his patrol was ambushed in August of '51. By the time he got to Camp 5, his wounds were infected. The Chinese had started to provide slightly better medical care, so George was sent to the hospital to recover.

"By September I was doin' pretty good. Then one day, most of the guys were sent back to their companies in the camp. About forty of us were left. These female Chinese nurses came around and drew up medical charts on each of us. Some of them spoke decent English. They said we were gonna get special care and special medicine. We sure got better food than we had seen up to that point. After a few weeks, we were all feelin' fairly good. Then came the special medicine.

"For two weeks they gave us daily injections of what they said was vitamins. Then a group of doctors came in and told us we were going to have a procedure that would cure any disease we had or would ever have during the rest of our lives. They said it was based on the latest Russian research.

"Now, I know you aren't gonna believe this, but I am tellin' the truth. They made an incision in my left side, slid in what they said was a chicken liver, and sewed me back up. For real! Did the same on every one of us. We watched as they went through the whole room. They didn't use any gas; they just numbed the skin with somethin' that smelled mostly like turpentine. I even watched as they worked on me!"

"You're bullshittin' us, right?" asked Hank.

George laughed. "I know it sounds crazy, but I'm tellin' ya the truth. I don't know if I would believe it myself if I hadn't been there."

"So, what happened?" asked Hank.

"Not a damned thing I could see. They kept us there until the incisions healed over, then sent us back to the companies. As far as I know, no doctor or nurse ever looked at us again. One of the guys crowed like a rooster every morning for about a week, but even he got tired of it."

Pretty soon Hank and George were gone. Their punishment time was up, and they were sent back west to one of the regular camps.

Swede and Earl were now the veterans in Camp Sunday. Satisfied they had done everything possible to spread the word about Easter Monday, they looked forward to the end of their time at Camp Sunday.

When that day finally came, they were escorted back to the west towards the officer's camp the guards called Camp 2. It was chilly and the trail was muddy, but they were anxious to be gone from the work camp and maybe see some old friends. Swede had been held in every camp he was aware of except Camp 2. Where would they send him next? Was there a Camp 4 out there somewhere? They passed Camp 2 around noon and kept walking, the guards setting a rapid pace. A few hours more and they crested the hill on the peninsula that looked out over Camp 5 and the Yalu. The guards stopped in front of the building they recognized as the place where their "trials" had taken place three months before. A truck engine popped to life and they were loaded in the back. Before their eyes adjusted to the dim light under the tarp, a voice welcomed them.

"So, how did you fellas like your vacation?" It was Dick Shea and Fred Moeder. The four of them were jostled around as the driver headed back east and turned right on the main road.

"Looks like we're headed back to Camp 3," suggested Fred.

"Could be Camp 1," offered Earl. "I haven't been there yet."

"Might be our mystery camp, Camp 4," teased Swede. "A new adventure every couple of months, my recruiter said."

As they bounced their way south, the four friends compared notes. According to their description, Dick and Fred had been held with the group just to the south of Camp Sunday. POWs held there called it Camp 2 and ¼. To help make the mental map of camps easy to remember, Swede and Earl decided to refer to Camp Sunday as Camp 2-3. But the biggest topic of discussion was guessing where they were going to end up next. The truck crossed the bridge just north of 3 North and they waited for it to come to a halt in the village. It didn't. Earl whistled a couple of bars of his favorite song and grinned at Swede. Next, they approached Chinese HQ. Once again, the truck rolled on through.

"The turn off towards Camp 1 is just over this bridge," Swede noted to the group as they headed out of Regiment. He was the only one who had already been at Camp 1 and was silently hoping they would take the turn. It would be good to see Mike Randall again. But after the bridge, the driver swung right off the main road on to a less traveled path. All four men looked at each other in surprise.

"We're headed back to 3 South! Maybe they figure we didn't spend enough time there," suggested Dick Shea. "Or maybe they need some lumberjacks to supply more timber to build the camp. I don't think it was finished when I left."

"At least we will have real barracks instead of village huts," said Fred, thinking of the buildings they had put up in early fall. By that time, the men had rolled up the tarp on both sides of the truck so they could look ahead. They were eager to see how the camp had changed since they had been there. The truck was heading up the peninsula 3 South was located on, splashing water and mud from the spring thaw in all directions. Then it slowed and turned on an even lesser path to the left. Once again, the four looked at each other in surprise. The camp was farther up, where were they headed now? Were they about to see the mysterious Camp 4 after all?

After bouncing and splashing a short distance, they crested a small hill and 3 South dropped out of view. They could see the Yalu on the other side of the peninsula, where Swede had attempted the escape that got Jim Riordan killed. The road turned south and followed the river off into the distance. Then the truck slowed even more and turned right to go back north again over another small hill. The driver brought the truck to a halt in front of some huts. They were home.

The road continued down the hill towards 3 South and the Yalu beyond. The driver and guard up front jumped down and opened the tailgate.

With amazingly good English, the guard looked up at the four men and said, "Welcome to your new home. We hope you enjoy your time here." Once the four had dismounted, he and the driver jumped back in the cab and splashed their way down the road towards 3 South. POWs began coming out of the hut, none of them said anything; they just stood and looked over the new guys. Earl realized what was going on before the others.

"OK, take a good look. Somebody here must know us. We ain't no stooges, we ain't no Pros." He knew they had to get this cleared up right away.

Once again, Danny Morgan stepped forward and broke the ice, just as he had the previous August when he recognized Swede on the beach where 3 South now stood. "What took you guys so long? I've been down here a month already. I was hopin' you guys would show up. Hey everybody, these four ugly bastards were sent up to Camp 5 with me three months ago. C'mon guys, fill me in on where you've been."

With the four new arrivals, the population at Camp Hilltop came to thirty-three. Most had been sent there from the main camps at 5 and 3 South a few weeks prior. Hank Prosser and George Kasprovicz had come directly from Camp Sunday. Everyone there was considered a hard-core Reactionary by the Chinese. Herman Vogl hadn't been at Camp Sunday, but instead had been held for a month at Camp 5 in an isolated hut. It wasn't isolated enough to keep him from talking with some other POWs in the outhouse they shared.

"I knew a couple of the guys. They were considered troublemakers. The Chinese decided to keep them separate from the main camp. They weren't being punished, just kept away from everybody else. They got fed enough, they had blankets, they even were allowed fires in the huts every morning and evening," Herman explained. "I think that's what is goin' on here. The Chinese are tired of people like us throwin' pebbles in the pond, so to speak." Then looking at Earl, "or rocks. By separatin' us they make life easier for themselves. Looks like they've given up tryin' to re-educate us."

"Do they keep us from talking with the guys in the main camp?" asked Swede. "I'd like to see if people still plan to stop attending the daily lectures. Easter is less than two weeks away, if I had my calendar figured right. And speakin' of the lectures, do we attend them down in the main camp, or do some instructors come up here just for us?"

"I kinda like the lectures," chimed in Danny Morgan. "They take a little of the boredom out of each day. But we haven't had any speeches since they put us on this hill. You can see the guys in the main camp all gathered around every morning and afternoon and sometimes hear some of the speech, if the wind is right. But it looks like Herman is right. The Chinese have given up on us. I don't think the Tiger guys get any lectures either."

Swede looked confused. "What do you mean?"

"The Tiger guys," answered Harvey Reynolds. "You know, Johnnie Johnson's group, the ones who came in by barge when we were up at

3 North? They sent them down here. They're in those huts about a hundred meters down the hill, between us and the main camp. For some reason, the Chinese separated them from the rest of us."

"Funny thing is, we can wander down and visit with them pretty much whenever we want. Guards patrol around here at night, but during the day, not so much. But I don't know if anybody has gone from the Tiger camp to the main camp out there."

Swede talked it over with Earl. They decided it was worth the effort to see if they could get into the main camp. The day after Easter was D-Day, so to speak, and they wanted to make sure the camp planned to quit attending the lectures on that Monday. Swede and Earl Stoneman had developed a strong bond, starting with their raid on the medical supplies at Camp 5. Earl was impressed somebody so young was willing to take risks for others. He hadn't seen a lot of that in his life. To Swede, Earl was a combination of Mike Finnegan and Henry Page. Earl had the life experience and Swede had the ability to think a problem through to a sound conclusion. The time spent in Camp Sunday had brought them close based on mutual respect. And both men hated what the Chinese had done to so many of their friends.

You Must Attend!

Spring 1952

The morning after their arrival, Swede and Earl stood looking out from their little hilltop. They could see the twenty or so huts of the Tiger POWs. The brown huts stood in contrast to the lush green of the Korean spring. The dirt road ran from their hill down to the Tiger camp, about fifty yards away and maybe a hundred feet lower than the hill. The road skirted the edge of that camp, swung to the left, and continued towards the much larger village that was the home of the POWs held at 3 South. The rectangular buildings Swede and Earl had helped build the summer before stood out on the beach of the peninsula that jutted out into the Yalu. Clear skies high-lighted the green of the peninsula and the sparkling waters of the river. It was a welcome spring day, especially as the two men had just a few weeks before been working in the snow and cold.

They headed down the road towards the Tiger camp, walking along as though they belonged there. It wasn't long before they reached the Tiger huts and found Johnnie Johnson. After exchanging details on the last few months, Swede explained they wanted to get down to the main camp and talk with people there. Then he asked the question that had worried him all through their stay at Camp Sunday.

"Have you heard any rumors about Easter Monday?"

"Yeah, a couple of guys in the main camp mentioned it to me," replied Johnnie. "They said we should help spread the word if we get sent to a different camp. Should be interesting."

Swede and Earl looked at each other and grinned. "Looks like we might be able to pull this off," chuckled Earl.

Johnson explained the Tiger POWs were pretty much left alone. They had been sent down from 3 North shortly after Christmas. "We can wander over to the main camp whenever we want, as long as we go in small groups throughout the day. Nobody in this group has been sent anywhere else since we got here from 3 North where we first met. The Chinese mostly ignore us.

"It's as if we are lepers." Johnson explained. "They just use us to train their new instructors that don't speak English all that well. A couple of instructors will come in and give their speeches. They aren't trying to convert us, just use us for practice. Then they ask us how they did. We tell them their English is very good and give them a few suggestions for improvement.

"The young Chinese are really interested in American slang, American movie stars, American sports, and especially American cuss words. One of those new instructors left here calling everybody a dumb ass. 'You real good dumb ass.' We convinced him it's the latest hip talk in the states. We taught another that whenever an American answers a question, he should tell them, 'You really hit that little weasel out of the park.' And every single instructor that comes in here leaves thinkin' he should call all British troops 'bloody wankers.' One of our better efforts was teaching them all to begin every speech to US troops with the phrase, 'I am speaking American most greatly.'

"The new instructors speak passable English," explained Johnnie, "but only from the book. They really have a hard time with anything a little outside what they were taught back in Peking U. Hot dog and hot rod confuse them. So naturally we taught some of them to say, 'hot dog' when they like something, others to say, 'hot rod.' A couple of the more gullible ones think "shit for brains' is a nickname for people you like. We figure those kinds of mistakes should make it clear to everybody that has to listen to their speeches that the instructors can be easily duped. At least, that's our plan."

"Mess with 'em every way we can, that's my motto," growled Earl.

"Can you get us over to the main camp?" asked Swede, as he pointed to the buildings on the peninsula.

"You wanna go now?" asked Johnnie. "Come on, grab a shovel and a bucket, and let's go."

On the way down Swede motioned to the shovels they were carrying. "So how is it you can just wander over to the main camp? Nobody stops you?"

"No. There are guards that patrol on a regular basis between us and their HQ back down near the bridge. During the day, a few guards hang around our huts and more patrol the main camp here." Johnnie pointed to the huts of the main camp they were approaching. "But they are looking for troublemakers, not another work crew.

"From the day they brought us down from 3 North, my guys have volunteered for work that will give us some physical exercise. We were in pretty bad shape when we got here last October. So most of us took every chance we got to do light work. We weren't strong enough at first to go out on firewood detail. But we could patch up huts, carry water for the cooks, even dig ditches if we went at it easy. Most of us are in good shape now, but we keep our pace slow so they think we're sickly. We're goin' back and forth on some kind of work detail all the time. It's just normal now. We use the work details to keep in touch with the guys down here," Johnnie waved his arm around to include the main camp huts they were now walking past.

"We pass information back and forth. We look for patterns in the behavior of the guards, when trucks bring in supplies, who is bein' held in any of the punishment huts. Sometimes we sneak some food or water to people in those huts. Sometimes we can only manage to whisper a few words to them."

"Those words mean more than you know," said Swede. "When you think you're all alone, it's hard to keep up the fight."

The three men spent a few hours looking for and talking with people they knew. Frank Pennington and Harvey Reynolds filled them in on the plan for Easter Monday

"I think the Chinese know something is up," explained Harvey, "but they don't know what. Some of the Pros are tryin' to ask questions, but everybody keeps tellin' 'em we are lookin' forward to a day of rest after Easter."

"Religion is a big no-no for the Chinese," offered Frank. "But they seem willing to accept Christmas, so maybe they'll cough up some special food for us on Easter too. That way, we'll all be fattened up when they quit feeding us after our little revolution on Monday."

"Hey, you know Henry Page, don't you?" asked Harvey. "He's a couple of huts down this way. He seems to have a better handle on what the Chinese think. Let's go see if we can find him."

Page was glad to see the "lost sheep" as he called Swede and Earl. "Trigger told me he saw you up at that work camp, Swede, but he said he never got a chance to talk with you. Said you were pretty much in solitary confinement. Is that how you spent the entire time?"

After answering all of Page's questions about where they had been and how they were treated, Swede asked Page what he thought about Easter Monday.

"The Chinese know something is up, but they aren't sure just what. Some accept the theory that we are all just looking forward to celebrating Easter and resting the day after. A few of them who understand a little bit about Christianity think we plan an uprising, like the 'uprising' of Jesus Christ, as they put it. The real paranoid ones think it all has something to do with the presidential election back home. Both Eisenhower and MacArthur are running in the primaries, but the Chinese don't understand the concept of a primary. They think it is the actual election. And they are afraid that whichever one wins will decide to use atomic bombs. Some of them think all of us are planning a big demonstration demanding our people use atomic weapons and end the war. So there apparently is a Chinese counterplan. They seem to be asking a lot of questions about germ warfare."

"Germ warfare? What are they gonna do? Put some of these rats and lice in hot air balloons and launch them towards Japan?" asked Earl.

"That's not it," answered Page. "They claim that the US is using germ warfare here in North Korea. I guess they figure if they convince the world we are using germ warfare, we won't dare use atomic weapons. I'm not saying it makes sense, I'm just saying that seems to be their plan."

Swede wasn't surprised to hear this kind of detailed knowledge from Page, but Earl didn't know him like Swede did.

"Just how is it you know all this?" Earl asked. There was more than a hint of suspicion in the question.

"I try to know ahead of time what is happening around here," Page responded. "I know some Progressives who admit they try to make their life as comfortable as possible but will never do anything to harm any of us. They fill me in on what the Chinese are up to. They get to spend time hanging out with the instructors getting free smokes and candy. The younger Chinese instructors, the new ones, aren't as hard-nosed as most of the older Chinese. They enjoy talking with Americans and practice their English with each other in front of these guys. So, these friends of mine hear a lot of talk they probably aren't supposed to. And they are hearing a lot of talk about germ warfare.

"Then there are the enlisted aircrew that have been brought into camp lately. They know all the news from home. And they say they were all asked a lot of questions about what's in their bombs, what kinds of diseases are being used, what aircraft are used to make night drops of germs on villages. They say their pilots get roughed up quite a bit in the questioning.

"This is just a guess," ventured Page, "but I think if we just refuse to listen to their lectures instead of holding a massive demonstration, they won't react much at all. I just hope that all the camps pull this off. We need to prove to ourselves, and to the Chinese, we are still Americans."

Easter came, and with it, sweetened rice with ham and fish, steamed carrots, bread, and hard candies. Supper was more of the same with six American cigarettes each as an extra treat. The non-smokers saved theirs for bartering. Page convinced both Swede and Earl to give him their ration for a special project he was working on.

"First you give away half my lunch, and now he gets all my cigarettes," grumbled Earl. "Next, one of you will want the shirt off my back."

"Just remember what happened to our lunches after I shorted us for one day," grinned Swede. "You called it high cotton."

Page was carefully sliding the cigarettes into a small box. "Hopefully, I won't need your shirts any time soon, but I do thank you for the smokes. When I can finally tell you what they're for, you'll consider it a worthwhile sacrifice."

"Swede says you're OK, and that's good enough for me," Earl replied, rubbing the stubble on his chin. "But you're still an odd duck, and I'm gonna be holdin' tight to my shirt." He smiled to take any sting out of the remark.

That night the reminder went out to every hut. Don't assemble for the lectures tomorrow. In the morning, the normal routine was followed: work details, headcount, a tin of water to wash up. Then the routine was changed. Only Progressives showed up at the assembly area for the morning lecture. Shortly after, instructors came scurrying to the huts to roust people out.

"Why are you not assembled this morning? You must attend! You must attend!" was the half plea, half command from the Chinese.

Herman Vogl gave the answer for his hut, the one Swede had suggested the night before. "You told us yesterday we didn't have to listen to any more lectures. You can't back off that promise now. That would not be correct behavior." Swede's reasoning was to convince the Chinese this was their idea. At the very least, it might confuse the issue enough to tone down any drastic response from them.

More instructors showed up - more questions. A few more guards than normal appeared, but not enough to alarm anyone. The standard lunch of peanuts and a cup of tea didn't show up, but that was expected. Some of the braver prisoners threw it back at the Chinese to make them lose face in a non-threatening way. "First you break your promise about the lectures and now you don't feed us lunch. This is not correct behavior."

When the time came for the afternoon lecture, the camp loudspeaker clicked on. "The camp commander wishes to make an announcement to his American guests. In celebration of the recent agreements at the Panmunjom talks, and in honor of General Peng, commander of the Chinese People's Volunteer Army, and hero of the struggle against the Kuomintang, our guest students will no longer be required to attend lessons on a daily basis." The Chinese instructors and guards snapped to attention as the March of the Chinese People's Liberation Army blared out. There were smiles throughout the American ranks. When word came that the instructors were talking about the same thing going on at 3 North, the smiles got bigger.

Progressives were still invited to the instructor's day room, where they got more treats than normal - cookies, American chocolate bars, cigarettes, and even Chinese beer. Along with those carrots came the stick of continued lectures on the benefits of Communism. A few continued to believe the Communist message. Most just went for the carrots and the comfortable chairs. Less than a handful went for the information they could pass on to Page and the others. Eventually, they heard all camps had refused to attend lectures.

But the Chinese didn't roll over and play dead. More and more men were called down to Chinese HQ to tell what they knew about germ warfare. Since they didn't know anything a lot of them got roughed up and some spent a week or more in the "hole". At HQ, that meant not only isolated huts or rooms, but some actual covered pits in the ground like Swede had experienced at Camp 2.

With the mild spring weather, the cold wasn't a major factor. But the Chinese were trying to save face over the lecture "strike." Two weeks seemed to be the average stay in the pits. An occupant got one cup of water and one cup of rice a day. Unless they were pulled out for additional questioning, they spent the entire two weeks in the pit. The smarter ones used one corner of their pit as a latrine. But good hygiene meant nothing in the spring rains. Soon, anybody held underground was ankle deep in a cesspool. By the end of the two weeks even the interrogators refused to spend much time with them. Why put up with the odors when their questions were getting them nowhere.

"Radio? What radio?"

"The one you used to send and receive orders about no longer attending your lessons!" came the charge.

"If I had a radio, I would be callin' for an airdrop of food and a stove. And some paratroopers with 'em," was a typical answer to that question. That was probably not the smartest response, because soon the questions asked for information on where the radio was that they used to call for "American parachutists." When Swede and Earl were questioned about a radio, they pointed out they had just arrived at 3 South after three months in a punishment camp. They were sent back to their hut and for once became the on-lookers as others were sent off to the hole.

Col Li Chen Hong was confused and worried. He had been in Korea almost two years and was sure his unit had performed its duties well. Then he was ordered home to Shanghai to attend a funeral - his wife's. He had been told she had died of complications from pneumonia. His wife's only surviving relative, an uncle, had given him the real story in whispers over tea just after the funeral ceremony. Her parents were the ones to die - in front of a firing squad. They had been arrested as part of Mao's Campaign to Suppress Counter Revolutionaries. They had been innocent, but Mao had set a number for arrests and executions in Shanghai as a message his brand of Communism must not be questioned. They had died because officials had a quota to be met. With Li in Korea and her family disgraced, his wife threw herself from the roof of the Cathay Hotel to the Bund below. She was not alone in her actions. Pedestrians had taken to avoiding the area as bodies falling from that rooftop were a daily occurrence.

Before he returned to Korea, Li asked questions of people he could trust. Mass executions were being carried out throughout the provinces. Li had seen how the people had turned against the Nationalists when they had done the same before their defeat in 1949. He had come to view the Nationalists as fools, unfit to govern the Chinese people. Now the party was acting like the warlords of old, killing their own people. Mao's revolution seemed to be leaving the people behind. His wife's parents hadn't had a political bone in their bodies. Would he also be accused as a counter revolutionary? He had served with the Nationalists on the orders of party leaders. Was he now to be branded for his loyalty to the party?

A silver lining in the gloom of his visit home was the time he spent with Simon Bishop. Simon was working in Shanghai on trade agreements for the Polish government. The two talked about their years at UCLA, but more importantly about the changes happening in the China they loved, and what those changes meant for the future.

Li's worry only increased when he was given a new assignment on his return to Korea. He would no longer work with his unit to intercept communications between American units. Instead, he found himself working as a special interrogator in a POW camp on the banks of the Yalu. He was told his knowledge of both the language and the culture would be of greater use in breaking the resistance of troublesome reactionary prisoners. Was this true or would accusations of crimes against the state be next? Did they know any darker secrets? Was this work really a better use of his skills and knowledge, or a set up for an excuse to arrest him?

With Lt Bo and the rest of his crew assigned elsewhere, Li had no one he could trust to talk with. He avoided long conversations with his fellow interrogators until he had a better read on who he could trust. Until then, he had work to do. The camp was rather complicated. He had been to what he thought of as the main camp, and the headquarters a mile or so to the south. This third part of the camp was new to him. It sat isolated on a small peninsula another mile from the central headquarters. To make it more complicated, it was separated into three parts, each smaller than the next. The far northern branch of the camp, the one he had been to before, held about three hundred prisoners. So did the main part of his new camp, sitting directly on the tip of the peninsula. About two hundred prisoners were kept in a smaller area halfway up a little hill, with fifty or so more prisoners held in a few huts at the top of the hill, almost hidden in the trees. He had quickly found a small number of prisoners eager to cooperate in any way. Better food, huts, clothing, and cigarettes were the prime motivation. These men were referred to as Progressives. The bulk of the prisoners cooperated as little as possible, hoping for a quick end to the war. The peace talks at Panmunjom were the gold at the end of the rainbow. Do only what was necessary to survive and go home.

Then there were the Reactionaries. Li was told as soon as he understood how to coerce these men into signing confessions or making tape recordings, he would be working in the upper camp. Interrogators with excellent English skills and an understanding of American culture were needed there. Those men were criminals, they were devious. Many had attempted escapes. Almost all of them tried to intimidate the Progressives. The camp commander was sure they were the source of the "strike" by the students at all the camps a few months before. If he couldn't give General Peng the instigators, he would find those willing to confess to being involved in germ warfare. A promotion was sure to follow.

By mid-May, Swede had spent a lot of time on various work details. He and Earl convinced Johnnie Johnson to get them on as many work details as possible. The peace talks had been going on for almost a year with no agreement. What if it took another year - or more? Their work at Camp Sunday had gotten them into excellent physical shape. If they ended up spending another winter as prisoners, they would need to stay healthy. Sitting around in their hut was not going to help. None of the work details came close to the effort required at Camp Sunday. They were also eating better now than when they were first captured. Going out on work details was good for them. A few cigarettes every now and then and the guards had no problem letting some dumb Americans volunteer for work.

Physical activity wasn't the only benefit of work details. Both men took careful note of details as they did odd jobs in various parts of the camp. How many guards were posted where and when? When did guard shifts change? Where were places you could hide if you wanted to move around at night? What buildings held food stores or medical supplies? How close were civilian huts? Where were guard posts on the road back down to Chinese HQ? Any information they could gather was shared with Henry Page. They were sure he had other sources, but they didn't ask, and he didn't offer.

Page did ask if they would go with him on a detail down to Chinese HQ. Once a month, twenty men spent a few days filling in old slit trenches and digging new ones. They were marched down, walked actually, by guards who then took turns visiting with old friends in the Chinese barracks. They slept in an old warehouse and were allowed to bathe daily in the river that flowed into the estuary. The same river that flowed through the village holding Camp 1. Page explained to Swede he was out of touch with his people because few civilians were allowed in the Camp 3 South area. At HQ, he knew he could pass on a message and get back in the loop. Page also asked Swede to explain to Earl they were just getting lists of POWs out to help with the talks at Panmunjom. He didn't want Earl knowing his real background. A couple of days before they were scheduled to work down at HQ, Page got the other two together to come up with a clear map of the existing POW camps as they knew them.

"You guys have been in most of the camps we know about," declared Page. "We need to put that together with what I have been told and come up with a clear picture of who is where." Drawing in the dirt at his feet, Page marked Camp 1. "As far as I know, the Chinese themselves use these numbers to identify their camps. This is Camp 1, with the river flowing through the village and on to where it empties into the estuary down at HQ for this camp. It includes British prisoners."

He drew the river flowing northwest from Camp 1 up the Yalu. "OK, this upside-down horseshoe is where we are, Camp 3. At the left peak is Camp 3 South, Chinese HQ for 3 is here at the river, and the right side of the horseshoe is 3 North. Swede and I were at Camp 1. Swede was sent up here to 3 South about August of last year and I got here in January."

Earl continued drawing a line north from 3 North. "This is the east side of the Yalu. Camp 5 is on this peninsula that points almost straight west towards China. Right here on the tip of the peninsula. I got there in January of '51. Half of us died that winter."

Swede marked an X in the dirt directly east of Camp 5. "This is Camp 2, the officers camp. I spent one night there on my way further east. About a half-day's walk in good conditions from 5."

"The officer's camp has been divided in half. A mile north of Two is the other officer's camp," Page chimed in. "Let's call the one you were in Camp 2-1 and the new officer's Camp 2-2."

"That makes our penal camp from last winter 2-3," Swede continued. "It is another half-day walk from 2-1. Earl and I call it Camp Sunday. There are at least three separate little valleys holding fifty or so guys each. The guards go back and forth. I could never come up with a pattern. But the three valleys are really one camp."

"What about that small camp we spotted when we hauled logs north along that little stream from Camp Sunday?" Earl asked. "The stream that bent west and flowed into the Yalu? I got the feeling it was not part of our little punishment farm, but even more isolated."

"From what I have been told, that is a place where aircrew are held, and a few special prisoners," Page explained. "But I can't find out what 'special' means. In any case, not many are held there. It makes sense to call it 2-4. The original camp at 2-1 seems to be the governing camp for all four of them."

Earl gave him that look again, the one when he called Page an odd duck. "Hey," countered Page, "I ask questions. And American cigarettes make some of the guards talkative."

"Glad to see my smokes are bein' put to a good use," growled Earl.

"So, we have Camps 1, 2, 3, and 5," suggested Swede. "Does that mean there is a Camp 4 somewhere?"

"I have heard of a 6, 7, and a 9," offered Page. "But they all were temporary camps before they opened up Camp 5. The three camps way up north where the Tiger prisoners were held was called 7. But I am fairly sure only 1, 2, 3, and 5 hold a significant number of POWs. I haven't heard anything about a Camp 4."

"That means it is a very secret camp," growled Earl, "or it is sitting empty somewhere waiting for whatever poor saps the Chinese want to hide from the peace talks. Maybe we need to spend a few more of our cigarettes and find out. And, I've been meanin' to ask. What about Camp Sunday and Hilltop? I kinda like the sound of Camp Sunday. Reminds me of that nice hot bath we got when we came down off that hillside."

Swede laughed. "I know what you mean, Earl. But I agree with Page. We need to keep our camp ID system as simple as we can. Not many of us use Sunday or Hilltop. It would be kind of like having a Captain Midnight decoder ring. Nobody else would know what we were talking about."

"Den Up!"

There were twenty prisoners standing in the cool of the early morning. The normal practice was to make the forty-five-minute hike down to HQ and have breakfast there before beginning work on the trenches. All twenty looked around at the noise.

"Den Up!" Louder this time and with a bit of irritation in the voice. Four guards were there to escort the work party. The oldest was the source of the noise. When the group continued to look puzzled, the elderly man threw back his shoulders and straightened his frame in an exaggerated movement.

"Den Up!"

His face lit up with a smile as his prisoners finally caught on and came to attention. He had worked with American soldiers in the war against the Japanese and wanted to show his superiors, none of whom were watching at that time of the day, how well he could handle them.

"Fort! Mart!"

The men obligingly formed into a column of twos and marched out of the camp. A hundred feet down the road their proud drill sergeant visibly relaxed and the men went back to walking and talking quietly. Playing the game put the man in charge in a good mood and cost them nothing.

The trees and brush along the road thinned out as they approached the village used by the Chinese as the headquarters for both sections of Camp 3. Looking ahead, Swede could see people moving about. Seeing an opportunity to earn more points with the man in charge, Swede tapped his arm to get his attention.

"Laoban. Den Up?" Swede pointed ahead to the village.

The man looked confused for a moment. The young American had called him boss. Looking to where Swede was pointing, the guard caught on. With a smile and a nod in appreciation, he called out to the group, "Den Up!" Marching his prisoners properly into HQ would make him look good. Once again, the men played along. They weren't going to win any Regimental trophies but managed to look like they knew what they were doing. Their smiling drill sergeant led them to the center of the village and down a path to the latrine area. Once there, he brought them to a halt with a shouted, "Hart!" Then "Stan on eez!" He had just used up all the English he knew.

As they worked through the day, civilians started to wander through the area. Page managed to get Swede a few feet away from the others.

"Make a little fuss, will you? Not much. Just enough to make people look your way for a bit." Swede nodded in acknowledgement. A few minutes later he was working near the taller grass.

"Snake! Snake!" Swede started swinging his shovel into the grass, as if he was trying to kill something moving there. A few other prisoners joined in, poking around to find the nasty creature. When nobody found anything, a couple of the guys gave him funny looks.

"Hey, I hate snakes." Swede shrugged as if to excuse the uproar. Everybody went back to work, putting enough effort into their task to get the job done without exhausting themselves. They had been told they would remain for two nights in the village and march back up to their camp on the afternoon of the third day. After their supper and a bath in the river, they stretched out on the floor of their temporary barracks. Empty rice sacks were supplied for bedding and pillows.

Looking around in the fading light, Dennis Grafton said, "This reminds me of when we were first captured." Then he looked around again. "For you newer guys, I mean just like when we were first captured, except we had three meals today, it isn't twenty below outside, we have comfortable clothes and some sacks to sleep on, we aren't packed in here so tight we can't move, no guards are shooting at us, we haven't marched thirty miles through the snow, and nobody has shit on me yet. Other than that, this is just like back then. Oh yeah, and I am fairly sure all of us will wake up alive in the morning." Some of the newer guys chuckled, but none of the guys who had been captured before that first winter did.

Page had pulled Swede and Earl to the back of the storage shed when the group first came in at the end of the day. So, when he was nudged awake sometime later that night, Swede didn't overreact. Heeding the tug on his sleeve, he followed two shadows to the back wall. Page and Earl were crouched beneath the window.

"Open that lock, would you Swede?" Swede had noticed the simple locks on the inside of all the windows in the large shed. Since they were on the inside, somebody wanted to keep people out, not in. If they wanted to keep people in, the locks would have been on the outside. When he noticed the rice sacks, he assumed the building had been storage for grain in the recent past. When he got the window open, all three hoisted themselves outside.

In less than a whisper Page informed them, "We're going to burn some buildings down. First, we need to steal some gas."

Earl was better at moving through the night, so the other two followed him. Walking down the center of the path like they belonged was not an option here. They kept to the shadows and moved slowly. Page pointed out some direction changes and they soon approached the motor pool. Motor pools are kept away from the general population due to their noise and smell. This one was no different. There were no walls or fences, so it was a simple task to approach from the rear.

"I need some rags and two buckets. One with a cover and filled with gas. The other with a little grease or oil. Not bottles or jugs, buckets. I'll get the rags. Try not to get anything on your hands or clothes." Page moved into an open shed. Swede and Earl separated and headed into other sheds.

In less than a minute, Swede heard Earl whisper, "Over here." He handed Swede a wooden bucket with a dark fluid. "Oil." He took a second bucket back to the corner of the shed and cranked the handle on a pump. Swede could smell the gas as the bucket filled.

"OK," whispered Page. "Follow me. And be careful not to spill anything."

They headed back towards the center of the village. Page was extra cautious, waiting in the shadows whenever they saw someone moving about or heard footsteps. Finally, he motioned the other two closer.

"We need to get through that window." He licked his finger and held it up. Pointing to the building on his right, he continued, "Then we use the rags and oil to set the roof on this building on fire. We take the buckets with us and hide them a few buildings back towards our barracks. Earl, you stand watch. Stay in these shadows and throw a rock through the open window if someone heads this way. Swede, follow me." With those instructions, Page slipped over to the window and stood up to peer inside. He tugged the window open, pulled himself up, and disappeared inside.

"I hope this works better than the last time," Swede whispered to Earl. Then he moved across to the window and followed Page.

By the time Swede pulled himself off the floor, Page was tugging at the doors of an old wooden cupboard. "Another lock," he whispered.

Swede had it open in no time. Page reached in and started pulling small boxes out and dumping the contents on the floor. "You do the same to the desk." Page pointed at the old office desk near the window. "Put everything just under the window."

In just a few minutes they were back at the window. Page looked across for an OK sign from Earl. Then he slid out, dropped to the ground, and motioned for Swede to wait. There was a generator running off in the distance. Nothing but insect noises anywhere near them. Page motioned Swede out.

"Leave the window open." Page then dipped his rags into the oil in Swede's bucket. Motioning to Earl, he instructed, "Put the rags up in the thatch all along this side of the hut. Swede, keep an eye out for any problems." The two men took turns dipping the cloth rags into the oil and pushing them into the thatch. The smell was obvious. Swede hoped there wasn't enough of a breeze to carry it too far.

When he finished, Page motioned the other two in close again. "We leave the oil bucket right here against this wall. I'll take the gas and stash it on our way back. Then we sneak back through that window and make like we've been sleeping all night. The guard at the front door is probably asleep, but don't make any noise. One more thing here and we skedaddle." He reached into his pocket and brought out a cigarette and a book of matches.

"Huddle around here and block my light." When the other two pulled in close to block the light, Page lit the cigarette and took a couple of puffs. Checking to see it was well lit, he folded it into the match box, reached up, and slid the whole thing into the thatch near one of the rags. "Let's go. Follow me."

About halfway back to their shed, Page slid the bucket holding the gas into a narrow space between two buildings. They continued to their window and carefully crawled back through. Swede tucked the lock in his armpit to muffle the click as he locked it back up. All three resumed their spots on the floor. No one around gave any indication they noticed. Swede knew they were putting time and distance between themselves and the building that was about to go up in flames, but wasn't sure about the papers they had dumped or the bucket of gas. Just another project of Page's. It was better to not ask questions. He fell asleep.

The door slammed open and someone started shouting, "Shing lie! Shing lie!"

Swede knew that sound. Get up! It felt like he had just gotten to sleep. As he sat up and looked around, Swede saw two guards with flashlights moving around the room, pointing to each POW as if they were counting. At least one more stood at the door with another flashlight, continuing to shout. Then they started pushing the men out the door. As they stumbled out, Swede realized it wasn't morning, it was still pitch black out, except for a strange glow off in the distance. So he had only been asleep for a few minutes and their building was burning! Then he realized the guards were herding them towards the fire. As they got closer, they could see figures running back and forth near the flames. By this time everybody was shouting. Even the prisoners were adding to the noise as they realized they were about to be enlisted as fireman to help put out a fire they really didn't care about.

The building they had planted the cigarette and matches in was completely engulfed. The roof of the one he and Page had been in was ablaze, as well as the one next to it. The prisoners were shoved to the head of the bucket brigade. As the buckets splashed their way to them, they tossed what water was left on the flames. Swede heard a loud "wooosh!" and saw Page holding the now empty bucket of gas. He had tossed it directly through the window and on top of all the paper they had dumped on the floor below. Then he calmly handed it off to the line passing empty buckets back to wherever the water was coming from. Other prisoners got in on the act, running back and forth with empty buckets, yelling, throwing water near, but not on, the flames. More and more Chinese soldiers joined the line, but by the time they got organized, four buildings were gone, and more were on fire.

About that time, Page grabbed the head guard and began mimicking using a shovel to throw dirt. The guard yelled at a few others and they ran off to return with all the shovels the prisoners were using on their work detail. Page then tugged on the guard's sleeve and got him to move the group ahead of the flames. With Page yelling directions, all the POWs were soon hard at work throwing dirt on the flames in the buildings that had just started to burn. There wasn't enough water or dirt to save those farther back. Soon they were able to keep the flames from advancing to any more buildings. Finally, they fell to the ground and watched the last of the ruined buildings collapse in a shower of sparks and smoke. The prisoners themselves were covered in sweat and soot. Dawn was beginning to lighten the eastern sky.

As things calmed down, Swede noticed a large group of Chinese interrogators and other officers standing back and watching. Two of them were soon involved in a whispered conversation with the head guard of the prisoner work detail. He was waving his arms in what seemed to be an explanation of how the fire had been stopped. He kept pointing to the prisoners and their shovels and the buildings only partially burned. Soon he came over to the group and yelled, "Den Up!" Slowly, the POWs groaned themselves off the ground and into a column. With "Fort! Mart!" the group headed back towards their barracks. The two Chinese officers followed behind.

Once they were back inside, a loud conversation broke out with the officers and the guard contingent. Someone tugged on all the windows from the outside. Their head guard seemed to be explaining he had counted the prisoners as soon as he opened the door. Again, he was pointing to their shovels piled outside in what was probably an argument that the only thing that had kept more buildings from burning to the ground was the hard work of *his* prisoners.

That seemed to be the end of it. The men were taken back to the stream on the edge of the village and allowed to wash up before getting back to work. During their noontime break, one of the guys summed up the whole experience with the remark, "So that is what a Chinese fire drill looks like!" The whole group burst out laughing, completely puzzling the guards.

When he got the chance, Page explained to Earl and Swede why they had started the fire. "I got word the interrogators down at Headquarters were in the process of gathering all the paperwork they could on anybody here at Camp 3 they considered to be a Reactionary. Anything any of us ever filled out, confessed to, signed, or even refused to sign. They had it all and were about to start working us over. Peking has been yelling at them to find where the radio is that was used to talk to all the camps before we quit attending lectures. Who are the ringleaders? And then there is this new push about germ warfare. They also had a lot of notes the Pros have given them about what we say and do. Too bad a fire broke out and it all went up in flames."

"If we're lucky," Earl added, "we burned up all their pay records too."

Unexpected Ally
Spring 1952

Life at 3 South went back to normal. Earl and Swede continued to go out on work details a couple of times a week. One day, when they were talking with Johnnie Johnson, another Tiger survivor sat down next to them. He had been on the work crew the night of the fire.

"I'm not sure what the other night was all about or what you guys had to do with it, but I'm glad I was there. It felt good to hit back for once. If you ever need any help with anything, just say the word. Until then, I hardly know you guys." With that, he got up and wandered away.

Johnnie looked at Swede and Earl. "That's Bobby Hanley. He's a good troop. And I don't want to know anything about your adventures down at HQ. What I don't know can't hurt any of us."

A few days later, two guards came up to Hilltop from the main camp at South and escorted Swede down the hill. He was led into a small room with only a desk and two chairs. There was a pot of tea, two small cups, and some peanuts on the desk. After motioning for Swede to sit, the guards left the room, leaving the door open. Understanding this to be SOP for interrogations lately, he sat quietly and watched camp life through the door.

In a few minutes, a tall, slim, Chinese officer walked into the room. He carried a well-worn briefcase. As he moved to the opposite side of the table and looked at the American sitting there, he paused and looked at Swede for a bit.

"Don't you rise to attention when an officer comes into the room, soldier?" he asked in a neutral tone.

"No sir. Not when that officer is part of an Army that refuses to conduct itself according to the Geneva Convention, not to mention simple human decency," Swede responded. "Nothing personal, but I am not going to bother with military protocol until China starts treating us like military prisoners."

The officer, Colonel Li Chen Hong, thought there was something familiar about this soldier. His skin was dark from the sun and dirt, his hair was sun-bleached and shaggy. There was a jagged scar on his forehead. But there was something familiar about him, twice familiar, in fact. Then he realized this was the young American who had attached himself to his jeep early in the war, the young man who reminded him of another young man he had known in California ten years before. So far, it didn't look like the American remembered their meeting almost two years prior. He removed some papers from his briefcase and placed them on the table.

"For now, we will set aside your refusal to show proper respect to a superior officer. My name is Colonel Li." *No reaction. But I am almost positive this is the same man from that cold, snowy road.* "Let's talk instead about your claim you are not being treated like military prisoners. Are you not fed and housed properly? Your clothing seems adequate. I do not see any chains on you or any others. No firing squads. What is it about your treatment you deem inadequate?" Li's job was to build a rapport with these men in the hope he could gather information about camp leaders and how they managed to coordinate what his superiors were calling a "strike." He could use threats. He much preferred carrots over sticks.

"I have been a prisoner for two years. I have yet to sleep anywhere other than on the ground. A handful of peanuts," now pointing to the peanuts on the table, "aren't exactly a nutritious lunch. But those are minor issues compared to the executions, lack of medicine, and slave labor I have seen so much of in those two years."

Swede understood he carried a constant anger about the deaths of so many people he knew. The fact neither the North Koreans nor the Chinese seemed to acknowledge in any way their responsibility for those deaths was even more angering. Their callous behavior went against his core beliefs. Not fighting back upset his core beliefs. The longer he was a prisoner, the more anger he felt. He understood that. He also understood standing up and screaming at this Chinese officer, or any other, was not going to be of any help. But a conversation, heavy on facts, was something he was willing to share. Even when the other side ignored those facts. He had refused from the beginning to have anything to do with their version of education, their version of the truth.

Colonel Li was now certain this was the same man he had met before. The topic was the same, the tone much more forceful. He had not really investigated the charge this young man had made about the treatment of American prisoners early in the war. He had not had the time.

"I believe you have mentioned these things to me before. Do you remember our meeting almost two years ago? You were sick when I talked with you in a North Korean medical camp. I told you about your Marines landing at Inchon. You had been captured before that. You claimed to have been left behind by your guards because you were sick." Li picked up a folder and flipped through some papers. "Your record says you were telling the truth."

Swede sat in a bit of shock. He did remember the conversation, if not the man specifically. But he was also shocked by the fact this man was holding up what he claimed to be Swede's record. They had supposedly just burned them all a few weeks ago!

Almost as if he could read Swede's mind, Li went on. "Many prisoner records were destroyed in a fire just a few weeks ago. Lucky for you, I was given records for the men I am responsible for before that fire broke out. I am told your fellow prisoners saved the fire from destroying much more that night. You are to be commended for your community spirit."

He has my records! Is he hinting he knows I had something to do with the fire? This is not good! Swede could feel the fear building in him. He could not let that show.

"I do remember that conversation. I also remember you knocking me to the ground when you were finished asking me questions."

"Do you remember me telling you I was going to hit you and why? The North Koreans were not happy with my orders to get you healthy and keep you that way until I could return to talk with you. You were sick when we found you on that road. I hit you so you would lose face in the eyes of the Koreans and they would not feel it necessary to do the same. What happened to you after I left?"

"You have the records."

"Yes." *He is afraid to give me details in case he tells me more than what is on these papers. I need to convince him I am being truthful.* "There is not much here. You went to a civilian jail and for some reason were not turned over to the North Korean Army until January. Then in April, you were sent to join your fellow Americans in Camp 1 in that same town. You attempted escape that August after being sent to help build this camp. A man was killed. You were sent to Camp 5 for punishment and then to the northern part of Camp 3 up above headquarters. Your attitude during re-education lectures got you sent to a penal camp for three months. Then you were sent here just before the camp strike. Does that all seem accurate?"

"That's pretty much everything in a nutshell." Swede responded.

"Then you could not be responsible for giving orders for your comrades to go on strike and refuse to attend student lectures." Li waited for Swede's reaction to his statement.

Swede put on what he hoped was a serious face. "I'm sure your army is the same as ours. Privates don't give orders to anybody. Besides, according to your own rules, our people are not supposed to give orders, and we are not supposed to take any orders from our people. I wouldn't be a very good 'student' if I did either of those things."

With just a hint of a smile Li nodded. "You are correct. But there are questions I must ask. Even a colonel must follow orders."

For the next hour Swede was asked about how the prisoners at all the camps had quit cooperating on the very same day, did he know of a radio in the camp, had he heard any talk of germ warfare from the newer prisoners, was there a person or persons sending orders to all the camps? The Chinese colonel asked the questions as if he was carrying on a normal conversation. There were no threats and no guards standing behind him. The colonel often asked about Swede's background and at times contributed information about himself. Swede was hesitant to say too much as he knew it might be used against him later, but there was a sense this man was different. Then the colonel asked for his help.

"You talked earlier about prisoners being executed and not enough food or medicine. Can you give me more information?"

"The people you need to talk to about those things are just up the hill."

"What do you mean?"

"In the huts just above here are the survivors of a death march. They can tell you about the man they call the Tiger. They can tell you about the deaths of more than half the men in the column. They can tell you about the murder of nuns on the march. Ask any one of them. You could ask Bowser about the march to Bean Camp after they left me. But he died. You could ask Ray why half of the men who left Bean Camp to march to Camp 1 died on the way. But he died. You don't have to believe me!" At the end, Swede was almost screaming. Li waited, saying nothing, until he was sure Swede was in control again. A guard looked in. Li waved him away.

"Thank you. I will talk to the men in the huts above. You may return to your hut. We can talk again later." The Colonel went to the door and motioned for the guards to escort Swede back up the hill.

Over the next two weeks Colonel Li talked with every other prisoner at Hilltop. Every single one of them reported the same experience as Swede. Some of the questions were blunt. Where is the radio? Who is giving orders? But much of the conversation was about life before the war. Johnnie Johnson gave a different story.

"He talked with a lot of us, one at a time. Each person said his questions were more specific than what the man before him had reported. He asked for details, who was shot, when? How much did we get to eat? Who treated our wounds? How many died? What clothing were we given? What work were we required to do? How many civilians were with us, what were their ages, how many women, how many kids? And he asked for names of the Korean guards. Sometimes the questions he asked contradicted what we had told him the day before, as if he was testing us to see how we responded. And people in the main camp below said he asked questions there about how POWs were treated in other camps. Some of the guys were afraid to answer. They thought maybe he was trying to see who knew too much."

Earl Stoneman summed it up well. "Either this guy is tryin' to put together a list of who knows all the nasty details so they can make us disappear, or he really is tryin' to find the truth about what happened. He seems interested in what we tell him. He is either good at his job and is just settin' us up for somethin' bad, or he's an honest man. We need to be careful."

"I get the feeling he doesn't think paratroopers are coming, or diseased rats either," Hank Prosser offered to the group. "He isn't a dummy. I just can't figure him out."

"For some reason he helped me when he found me in the snowstorm after I left that village," Swede added. "And for some reason I think we can trust him, at least to a point. But let me do the trusting. You guys be careful with him. That way, if he is trying to trick us, he will only have me in his trap. I think it's worth the risk. Besides, as far as I know, there is no radio, and there are no diseased bugs or rats."

"Other than what were already here when we got here, you mean." Earl only half grinned.

Over the next few weeks, Li called down a few of the men from Hilltop just about every day. The questions were different versions of the same topics. He never threatened anyone. He never had a guard in the room while he asked questions. He didn't push very hard for answers. And he frequently ended up talking about life in the US. Where were you born? What did you do? What sports do you like?

Eventually, Li began coming up to Hilltop rather than having the prisoners come down to the main camp. Swede was sure the Colonel wanted to talk with him about something other than radios and rats, but wasn't sure what it was. Maybe that was the reason for him coming up the hill, fewer people who might be listening.

"I have looked into what you told me about deaths among the early prisoners," Li said to Swede. They were sitting in the interrogation hut at Hilltop. The view out the door was of the sparkling Yalu and the green hills on the far side of the river - the Chinese side. It was a pleasant late spring day. Li had asked for some tea from the kitchen. Anything more would have seemed like he was favoring a prisoner - a hardcore Reactionary at that! He was sure that very few, if any, of the guards at Hilltop spoke English. But he knew they reported on anything out of the ordinary. Li read all those reports, but so did others. Any hint he might be favoring a prisoner would be a danger to him. He could argue tea was a tool to soften up a prisoner before questioning him. Anything more could be seen as favoritism.

"I am sorry to have found you are correct. Prisoners were often mistreated in the early months of the war. Executions were not uncommon. Evil does not have to be a tool of war. Apologizing makes no sense, but I cannot stand by and do nothing. However, I am not sure what I can do. I have created a document with the facts I have uncovered." Li ran his hand through his hair. He looked at Swede, sadness in his eyes.

"The man in charge of what the men in the camp below call the

Tiger Death March was a major in the North Korean Security Guard Bureau. He is Korean, not Chinese. He ordered the execution of other groups of prisoners before he took over that march in late October of 1950. His name is Chong Myong Sil. He was reassigned at the end of that year. I was not able to find out where he went but I believe he is now in charge of the unit responsible for obtaining information on American pilots involved in germ warfare. Most of us don't believe those charges, but our political commissars are determined to find evidence."

"So now what?" asked Swede.

"Now I have a document with names and dates and facts. It would probably get me shot if its existence became known. Is there someone in Peking that should see it? Or maybe someone in Washington?" He looked at Swede, waiting for a reaction.

"And exactly what would I do with it? How would I get it to anyone? And if I took it, would I then be charged with spying? Shot? Would that help you get your next promotion? How exactly am I supposed to interpret the fact you're even discussing this with me?"

"I can promise you this, young Paul Larson. I have no intent to trick you or harm you in any way. To help prove that, I am going to have you confined to the punishment hut for a day." Li smiled as he watched Swede's look of confusion. "It will be like knocking you to the floor, do you remember?"

"To prove you don't intend to harm me, you are going to send me to the hole? That sure clears things up for me!" The 'hole' is what the POWs called any place they were confined for punishment. At Hilltop, that was a small shed removed from any other building on the hill. Facing their huts, backed against weeds and brush, it resembled a tiny outhouse. It had only a door, no windows. Its size meant a normal person couldn't stand completely erect. Sitting was only possible for smaller men. Even then their knees were jammed so tight against their chest, breathing was difficult.

"Sending you to the hole will prove you are still a communist hating Reactionary. Those who might be watching, and they are watching, will see that I punish those who do not cooperate. I have 'questioned' you often and have nothing to show for it. It is time for me to demonstrate I will not let your poor attitude go unpunished. Sending you to the punishment hut will do away with any suspicion about either of us. I'm sorry, but it will only be until tomorrow." Li rose and called loudly for the guard. He wanted the anger on Swede's face to be real.

"I hope you learned your lesson, young man." Earl laughed as the guards escorted Swede back to their hut the next day. "Just how did you manage to piss off the Mystery Colonel? I don't think he ever sent anybody for an attitude adjustment before."

"I'm not sure. C'mon. I want to walk down to the main camp and talk with Page to see if he knows what's going on."

Swede noticed something while walking through the main camp with Earl and Page. The camp had changed. Some men were playing basketball, others baseball. Some sat in small groups playing cards. Others were playing volleyball. Page saw the look on Swede's face.

"I see you've noticed the latest improvements. The peace talks seem to be going on forever, but we have gotten a few benefits from them. There is even a library. All the books and newspapers have a definite Party line slant to them. There is even a copy of *Les Miserables* if you haven't read it before. But the sports equipment is the biggest hit. And I'm sure it makes for good propaganda. I've seen them taking pictures. *See all the happy prisoners playing baseball and basketball?* I'll bet they pass out copies of the pictures at Panmunjom. In fact, I hope they do. Just one more way for our guys to identify who is here."

"Didn't you play basketball in high school, Swede?" Earl asked. "Those guys don't look like they are very good at it."

"Hey, that's my team you're talkin' about," Page complained.

"Your team? What do you mean, your team?" asked Swede.

"I'm the manager. And you're right, they aren't very good. That's why I think it would be a good idea for young Swede here to join. There is supposed to be a tournament up in 3 North soon. And maybe then we'll get to visit some of the other camps. I have a couple of ideas that you might be able to help me with. And that includes winning the tournament." Page just grinned at Swede.

With a big grin of his own, Earl asked, "Could you use an assistant manager? I wouldn't mind doin' a little travelin' myself. I'm more of a checkers kind of guy, but an assistant manager mostly just hands out towels. I can handle that. You have towels to hand out, right?"

Over the next few weeks, various teams spent time practicing for the upcoming games. Others spent time watching and calling out graphic suggestions for how the players could improve their technique.

Two years into the war, the biggest problem for the POWs was boredom. There were still work details – especially the firewood detail. The food was still minimal in quantity and poor in quality. They were still sleeping on the ground, but they had fires and old blankets to share when it was cold, and they still had to watch for lice. The peace talks at Panmunjom, however, made the POWs important. The Communists needed them to exchange for their prisoners held by the UN forces. The talks were going slowly, but at least they were talking. The treatment of the POWs hadn't been brought up to anything near Geneva Convention standards, but anything was an improvement over the first year. So now they waited. Thus, the sports equipment and playing cards.

There were a few that weren't content to be bored, basketball or not. With better health and summer weather, a few talked about escaping. Since most of the prisoners knew Swede had tried to escape from this very camp a year earlier, a few malcontents came to him asking questions. He explained why he felt escape was not possible but agreed to give them what help he could. He didn't know the three men all that well, but felt better when they mentioned Danny Morgan had suggested they talk to him. Swede and Earl had helped Page study guard placement in and around the camp. He didn't tell the men how he knew, but offered advice on how to get past the guards.

So, Swede was not bored. He had basketball practice and he had his escape classes. The Chinese hadn't let up on their push for confessions of any kind, so he had that too. Colonel Li continued his work on finding the hidden radio. He considered it a waste of time, but his superiors were convinced there was probably more than one radio with a control network of POWs giving orders to all the camps. They were even sure they had the name of the leader. Li played along, even getting a reputation for sending people to the hole.

But that crazy bunch of Reactionaries held at Hilltop had modified that shed. With their new concern for the welfare of their 'guest students,' the Chinese were slowly making materials available to improve the huts where the men slept. Bunkbeds were being constructed in some of the buildings in the main camp down the hill. The men at Hilltop were allowed to haul boards up to cover the many gaps in the walls of their huts. Swede suggested they stack those boards against their little punishment hut. Anybody paying attention on the days when crews worked on the huts would have noticed a lot of noise and confusion. Much more than what should have been normal. In all that confusion a few men removed the back wall of that little hut and extended it six inches. A board was left inside of the completely dark hut which could be used as a bench for anyone unfortunate enough to spend time there. Colonel Li only sent men to the hut for a night. That meant a man could fall asleep on the bench while leaning against the wall. His buddies made sure he was awake and standing before the guards came up to let him out in the morning. Some men propped the board against the back wall and slept reclined on it. It was still a tight fit, but time in the hole became a lot more tolerable.

Swede got credit for the idea of remodeling the hut. What he did not tell anyone, other than Page and Earl, was the suggestion had come from Colonel Li. He explained he sent people to the "hole" for the good of the Reactionary squad on the hill. He was getting plenty of information from the Progressive POWs in the main camp, most of it useless. That made his superiors happy. Being visibly tough on the Reactionaries made them even happier. But he saw no reason why they should have to suffer a night crammed into an uncomfortable space. He suggested the remodeling project to Swede. He even made some changes in the guard schedule on the days of the remodeling. Some of the men from Hilltop were sent to the main camp to help build a bath house to use in the winter months. Only one guard was left on the hill and he was easily distracted.

Li explained to Swede it was obvious the war was at a stalemate. It might not end for a while, but it was going to end with little change. He didn't care if there was some kind of control network sending orders to all the camps. People were not escaping, at least successfully. Fewer military convoys passed through the camp, so sabotage was rare. He also made it clear to Swede he was taking a risk helping the men at Hilltop like this. After finding out how poorly they had been treated during their first year as prisoners, Li saw no reason to make their life difficult now. If each of them was willing to spend one night in the "hole" every couple of months, the rest of the camp, guards and prisoners, would go on thinking they were being harshly treated because they were Reactionaries.

After the punishment cell remodel was completed, Li presented Swede with an envelope. "I want to give this to you so you understand I am sincere in trying to help you," Li told him.

"There is no way I am going to take those documents on which Koreans and Chinese were involved in killing prisoners. I get caught with those and I am a dead man." Swede held up his hands and leaned back. They were in the interrogation hut at Hilltop.

"This is a different kind of list. These are men you refer to as Progressives. Men who give information to me and others. Not just information about who has a 'bad attitude,' but information that often causes harm to their fellow prisoners. Getting caught with these papers won't get you more than a few months at a penal camp, like the one you were in before you came here.

"Actually, that is not completely true," added Li. "Let me tell you what I know about you. Don't worry, I do not have this information written down. You escaped on the same day you were captured in the first weeks of the war."

Li chuckled at the expression on Swede's face. "Oh yes, I know all about that. After your column left Seoul, not long before I first met you, you escaped again by pretending you were ill. You spent about two months in a civilian jail waiting for the Korean Army to take custody of you. They finally took you to Chongsong. No other American prisoners were there yet. Chongsong was where Camp 1 is located. You were not treated well as you waited to be released into the actual camp in April. In August you were part of the group that was sent here to build this camp. You were probably included in that group because of your 'incorrect attitude' and your' refusal to remove your guilt'." Li smiled as he used the standard charges thrown at the POWs when they were first captured.

"Then you escaped a third time. You were sent to Camp 5 for punishment. There are rumors you were not a model prisoner while at Camp 5. Next you were sent to 3 North. For attempting to influence the thinking of your fellow prisoners there, you were sent to a penal camp, the place you call 2-3. From there you came here, where your behavior, except for a few rumors, has been quite acceptable.

"I only gathered this information after you convinced me to investigate the treatment of prisoners early in the war. Once I found the truth in your accusations, I began to ask questions about you. No one I talked to knows all of what I just related, and much of it was just rumor, but one man told me much more about you than he should have. His name is on this list." Again, Li held up the papers Swede had refused moments before. "I am a Chinese officer, but here, in this camp, I am your ally. I will not ask you for any information about your fellow prisoners or their actions. I will not ask you to do anything that might bring harm to your fellow prisoners or your country. Until you are free, I am your ally.

"I am your ally because the actions of the Koreans and my countrymen in the beginning of this war were wrong. They have improved those actions, but only a little. They are still wrong. Which side is right or wrong in this war is of little importance to me. The proper treatment of prisoners of war is most important. I am not a traitor, but my superiors would consider me one if they learned about my actions on this hilltop and the information I have given you. You hold my future in your hands. I alone know the whole story about you as a prisoner, or most of it. It is not written anywhere, nor will it be. None of your fellow prisoners have any idea I was gathering information about you. All my questions were about prisoner behavior in general.

"But like I said. One man told me much more than he should have. He made no effort to protect you. He thought he was helping me find information I would use to punish the people he was telling me about." Li place the papers on the table between them. "His name is first on the list. And he knows there is an escape plan in the works."

Swede did not reach out to take the papers. He was trying to process all that Li had just told him. From his first meeting with this Chinese officer, there had been something different about him. Especially once he arrived at Camp 3. Swede finally concluded he had more to gain at this point by trusting the man. He picked up the papers.

Page knew Swede had something on his mind other than basketball. He had missed his last two shots and kept having the ball stolen from him. When they took their next break, he pulled him aside. The other players assumed Page was doing some managing.

"What's on your mind? Something is bothering you." Page wasn't concerned about basketball. He could tell Swede was worried.

"Li told me some things yesterday that are a little strange. I was plannin' on talking with you about it later. I'm not exactly sure how to handle it. We should probably have Earl listen in, too."

When practice wrapped up the three men took a slow walk up to Hilltop while Swede explained about the list of Progressives Li had given him. While they watched the door of his hut, Swede pulled the list out of hiding and showed it to Page.

"Wow, that is a new one to me." He passed the list to Earl.

"Jesus! How the hell did we miss that?" Earl looked at the rest of the list. "Nothing else here is new."

"The guys that asked me for help with an escape are going out tomorrow night," Swede explained. "This means he set the whole thing up. Maybe I should tell them to call it off."

"First off, they will probably ignore you," Page replied. "Second, if you call it off, it tips your hand that you know something is up. We need to come up with Plan B."

"Don't make it more complicated than it has to be," offered Earl. "Pass the word to somebody we trust to tell the guys the guards know about the escape. He can say he heard some Pros talkin' about it. The guys can decide for themselves to go for it or not. That keeps us out of the picture. Especially since there is a small chance all of them are in it together to try and get Swede in trouble for assistin' escapes. I don't think that's the case, but better safe than sorry. And this bastard," he pointed at the list, "now that we know about him, we play it careful. Maybe we can use him to tell the Chinese what we want them to know."

Page grinned at Earl. "I like it. You're getting kind of diabolical. Especially the part where we use him like he is trying to use us."

Swede just sighed. "Danny Morgan, a rat. Who would have thought it?"

Spring 1952

A B-29 Can't Swim

The no escape plan worked. The men managed to get rid of everything they had stashed to take with them, which wasn't much. A canteen, some rice, a compass, and a rough map Swede had drawn for them. Ken Tarr, the man who had the map, remembered it was still in his pocket when he saw the guards headed towards his hut.

"You don't want to know," was his answer when Swede asked where he had hidden it. Ken knew the Chinese had a thing about nudity and would never have done a strip search. One of the men smarted off to the guards when they barged into his hut. Since they couldn't find any escape materials, they saved face by throwing him in the hole for a week. Page bribed a guard to bring the man extra rice and water every other day.

Two weeks later the entire camp headed out for the sports tournament at 3 North. They didn't march up to the camp, they strolled. Every prisoner and most of the guards simply walked down the road towards the camp HQ and then north up to 3 North. There was kind of a picnic attitude about the whole day. There were plenty of armed guards, but they too were simply enjoying the day.

Just before reaching the village used as camp headquarters was the river which flowed into the estuary or bay. Swede made a point of telling people around him that about 5 miles upriver was Camp 1. "If you escape and head down that road, you will need to be very careful." As they crossed the bridge over the river, they saw stacks of long beams and planks. It looked as though the bridge was going to be updated. When they went through the village, Swede and Earl smiled at each other as they remembered their work party being praised for putting out the fires they had started. Then Swede remembered Colonel Li had hinted he might have had something to do with those fires and it wasn't so funny anymore.

They arrived at 3 North in the early afternoon and were welcomed with a snack of peanuts and a fist-sized loaf of bread each. They spent the rest of the day visiting with old friends and getting caught up on the latest rumors. That night they either crowded in with friends or slept on the ground. Blankets were handed out to those who wanted one. The next day the teams competed in basketball and baseball, with the final game of each scheduled for the following morning. That evening every man was treated to a bottle of beer with their supper. Swede gave his to Earl. Page traded his for cigarettes.

Page's basketball team took first place the next morning and then watched the final game of baseball. Many of the Chinese had been around Americans in Shanghai or Peking and were familiar with both games. They seemed to enjoy watching as much as their prisoners. After more peanuts and bread, the group from 3 South said their goodbyes and headed home. They were reminded of their circumstances when a headcount was taken before they started down the road.

After passing through the headquarters village, they approached the bridge where they would turn northwest towards their camp. The bridge was much wider than before. All the heavy beams that had been stacked nearby were gone, as were most of the planks. The bridge had undergone a major remodel. As they crossed over Page nudged Swede.

"Your eyes are better than mine. What is that down there at the bend in the road?" Page tilted his head to their left. "Don't stop. Just take a gander."

"It looks like a bulldozer. A big one. And just behind it is something covered in netting. Something really big. Kind of like a plane without wings."

"A B-29 maybe? Do you know what a B-29 looks like?" Page had slowed his pace to keep whatever it was in view.

Swede dropped back with Page. "You're right. I think that is a B-29. But where are the wings? And what is a B-29 doing here?" Swede waved his arm to include their surroundings.

"Keep moving and don't stare. I don't think we are supposed to see that." Page tugged Swede back into the group as they continued over the bridge. As they headed up to their camp Bobby Hanley called their attention to something out in the bay.

"Check out those two barges headed in. I've never seen barges that big in here before. They're twice the size of the ones that bring in supplies."

Page stopped so abruptly, the man behind him walked into him. "I just added two plus two and it means big trouble. That is a B-29 back there. Those two barges are here to take it across the river to China. Two barges because the wings are probably on a trailer right behind the fuselage we saw. The bridge was too weak to support the weight, so they had to reinforce it." Page was practically whispering.

"How is that big trouble?" asked Swede.

"The B-29 is the most powerful bomber in the world. China doesn't have anything like it. I'm sure they would love to get one for themselves. The one back there must have crash landed somewhere around here and they got it before our guys could destroy it. If that one gets across the Yalu, it will mean China will have a bomber force equal to ours. That is big trouble."

"So how do we stop it?" asked Swede. "Blow up the bridge?"

"Not a bad idea," answered Page. 'But they will have it across the bridge before we can steal some explosives and get back down there. Besides, where can we get enough explosives to blow that thing up? It's pretty heavy-duty now. *We* can't do anything about the bridge. But we can arrange for somebody else to take care of it for us."

Swede looked at Page in the expectation he was about to explain what he meant. Instead, he just walked on towards their camp, glancing out at the barges in the bay. As they got close to camp, Page pulled Swede into him.

"Follow me to the main camp. Don't break off and go up to the Tiger camp or Hilltop. Just follow me."

"Do I get the chance to volunteer for whatever you are volunteering me for?" Swede asked with a grin.

"No. We have to do this. Those barges can't get to China. If we get caught, we might get shot. And I can't do it alone." Swede had never seen Page that serious before.

"The guards are just as tired as we are. My guess is they won't take a headcount until tomorrow. To be safe, find Earl and tell him if the guards make a count, he needs to mess it up. Have him get Bobby Hanley to do the same. Every time they do a re-count, it has to be off by a few. After one or two counts being off, they will give up until daylight. By then we will be back where we belong."

After dark Page explained what they were going to do. "We need to get a message out to our side so they can send some planes in here and sink those barges when they are in the Yalu. Hopefully, the Chinese will think it is just bad luck that some planes spotted the barges at the wrong time. Maybe they won't suspect anybody here had anything to do with it.

"The camp radio is just used to talk back and forth with HQ and 3 North and only during the day. At night there is a guard wandering through the area, but not just for the radio room. We get in, send a message, and get out. If we do it right, the Chinese will never know. If the Chinese are listening, all they will hear is a short message in code. They won't have time to figure out where it came from or what it means. But none of that matters. What matters is we stop that plane from getting to China." Page waited to see if Swede had any questions.

"You know where the radio is and how we can get to it? We can't just wander around over there."

"Yes. I've been in the building on a work party. They had us add on to some of the buildings. I will get us there, if you can get us through a few locks on the way. You have your picks, right?"

"You bet," nodded Swede. "When do we go?"

"Right now. We sneak over in the direction of the radio room and hide out. That way we don't have to try and sneak out of here later. With all the confusion, we should be able to get out of here easily. Then we wait until after midnight to make our way into the building. The guard who comes on duty then spends most of his time smoking and throwing stones in the river. Talk to Earl and meet me back here in ten minutes."

There wasn't much of a moon as the two crawled out from underneath the shed they had picked as their hiding spot. They were headed towards two rows of former Japanese vacation homes. Between them ran a gravel path that led down to a beach. The Japanese had long ago simply torn down that part of the original village closest to the water and put up their much larger structures. They were multi-room wood-frame houses, some two-story. Now the Chinese were in charge and they used them for offices for the camp staff. Only the guards remained in camp overnight. Everyone else spent their nights, and days off, at camp headquarters just beyond the bridge. A few of the original villagers still lived in some huts between the former vacation homes and the main housing area for the POWs. The Koreans still living there worked in the kitchen for the prisoners, which also fed the camp staff during the day. Not the same food, of course. When night came, those villagers shut themselves in their huts and ignored what went on outside. They simply didn't want to know anything that might get them in trouble.

Page knew this but still moved slowly and quietly, keeping close to storage sheds and outhouses and away from the occupied huts. There had to be no hint that they were in the area. Once they reached the office area, he crouched and waited in some bushes with Swede by his side.

"We need to see the guard," he whispered. "Once we spot him, I will be able to predict where he will be next. About once an hour he walks down this path from the shore, stops about one hundred feet from here, turns back, and goes down to smoke and throw more stones. He's gotten pretty good at skipping them into the river."

It took a while, but the guard finally made his appearance, strolling up the path towards their hiding spot. Every now and then, he tossed a pebble at a tree. As Page had predicted, the guard turned and walked back down to the beach. Once he was out of sight, Page whispered, "Let's go," and moved to his left around the houses on that side of the path. He moved slowly, staying close to the buildings, using the shadows as much as possible. Swede could see him silently counting the buildings. He stopped beneath a window that swung out to both sides. Reaching into a pocket, he took something out. As he unrolled it, Swede could see it was a piece of heavy wire. Using the now straightened wire, Page slid it between the two halves of the window, releasing the hook on the inside. He slowly opened one side and peered in.

"Give me a boost," he whispered. Swede positioned his knee so Page could step up and slide over the sill. He disappeared for a minute and returned to reach out an arm for Swede. Once they were both inside, Page closed the window and replaced the hook. There was just enough light for Swede to see they were in a small storeroom of some kind. There were boxes on shelves, buckets and mops lined up against one wall, and pants and jackets hanging from hooks above a bench. Page moved to the door and listened. Hearing nothing, he led Swede through the door and down a hall to their left. At the end of the hall was a door to the right.

Listening again before he opened the door, Page turned to Swede. "There are windows facing out to the path on the far side of this room. We need to crouch down before I open the door. We stay low and move to our right. The only door on that side leads to the radio room. Its locked. Stay low as you work on it." Then he opened the door and moved through.

It took Swede a couple of minutes to work the lock. Then he moved to the side so Page could make his next move. Page moved to the windows and looked out on the path. Moving back, he opened the door and motioned Swede in. He followed and closed the door behind them. It was pitch dark, so Swede didn't move while he listened to Page rustling through his pockets. There was a scratching noise and the bright flare of a match.

Noticing the surprise on Swede's face, Page whispered, "It's okay. The walls are tight. Just don't touch anything." Moving the match to his other hand, he lit a small candle. The room danced to life. The far wall had a bench with a large radio on it. Page carefully moved a chair in front of the radio and handed the candle to Swede. Sitting down, he reached out and flipped a switch that caused dials on the radio to light up. Once all the dials were steady and all the lights green, he pulled the base of the microphone to him. Reaching to a dial on the right, he turned it slowly until he got the reading he wanted.

"Don't drop the candle when I start talking. I'm going to be speaking Russian. I'll explain later."

Pressing down on the bar at the base of the mic, Page began.

"Prozhektor, Proshektor. Etot Bludnyy syn.

Prozhektor, Proshektor. Etot Bludnyy syn."

After a pause, a voice came back in English.
"Wait one."
Another pause.
"Go Prodigal."

"Odin sigara zheka sinyakami moye mestonakhozhdeniye.

Dva vagony prinyatiye sigara Pekin.

Zapros torgovets reshat problema.

Povtoreniye.

Zapros torgovets reshat problema.

Konets."

A short pause.
"Copy, copy, copy."

Page shut the radio down, moved the chair back where it had been, and moved to the door. Reaching for the candle, he licked his fingers and snuffed it out. Swede felt a hand pushing him low and saw the door swing open. They both moved into the main room and Page closed the door.

"Lock it back up. I'm going to check out the window."

Swede inserted his picks and locked the door. He waited for Page to move away from the window and lead the way back out. They went down the hall and slid out the window. Page took his wire and maneuvered the hook back into place. Swede guessed the whole process had taken only fifteen minutes. He couldn't help but smile. In and out with no problems. Much better than falling off the back end of a truck into the snow.

The two made their way back to the path. There Page stopped and sunk to the ground. "We are going to wait until the guard shows up and turns back to the beach. If we cross now, he might be heading up this way and spot us. So far, so good. I don't want to mess it up with a simple mistake."

As they waited, Page explained the Russian over the radio. "Somebody listens on that frequency twenty-four hours a day. When they hear my code name, Prodigal Son, they turn on a recorder. I told them a bruised cigar was at my location and two wagons were going to take it to Peking next year. Which means tomorrow. Last year would have meant yesterday. I requested a merchant fix the problem because I could not. Copy, copy, copy meant they had a good recording. Cigars are B-29s and wagons are barges. The code is designed for somebody watching military traffic.

"If the Chinese heard it, they will think a Russian was talking to the Americans in some kind of code. If the Russians heard it, they will think one of their own is talking to the Americans. Even if anybody heard the transmission, I doubt they had time to record it before I finished. In any case, nobody should think any of us are involved. If things go well tomorrow and our guys destroy the barges, some radio operator might remember hearing a strange message, but I don't think they will suspect us. If anybody gets any blame, it should be the Russians. It only makes sense they would try to keep the Chinese from getting any new weapons."

"You know," said Swede, "the Chinese were asking everybody where we had the radio stashed that we used to get all camps to quit attending their lectures? If they hear this, will they be able to tell where it came from? Will they know it came from somewhere in this area?"

"Only if they have triangulation equipment set up near here and they have it turned on tonight. Even then, I don't think we were on long enough for any equipment to work. I tell you what, even if I knew we were going to get shot for this, destroying that plane is worth it. But I just don't see them figuring it out. They can search all they want for a radio. They haven't found one yet because there isn't one. There is no way for them to know we used *their* radio. Not if we make it back before they get an accurate count. If this works, we will have done more tonight than we could on any battlefield."

Pretty soon the guard wandered up the path, still tossing pebbles. He sent one skipping up the path towards the two of them hiding in the bushes. It bounced off the path and rolled to a stop in front of Swede. For some reason he picked it up and put it in his pocket. Then the guard turned and strolled away into the darkness. Two shadows in the night waited a few minutes and moved silently across the path to the sheds on the other side. As they moved past the villager's huts and headed for their own, they began to hear some strange sounds coming from way out in front of them. Page stopped and motioned Swede to the ground. The noises grew louder.

"What is that noise? Can you tell where it's coming from?"

"You know what? I think it's coming from down near the bridge. All those creaks and groans, that powerful sounding engine noise. I bet they are trying to load the plane onto the barge. I hope your message got through."

"It got through all right." Page sounded confident. "But will they get some planes up here in time? Will the Chinese shoot our guys down if they do get here? We are right on the border. We don't see many of our planes around here, at least not very often." They listened for a few more minutes and then continued moving from shadow to shadow. Then Swede grabbed Page and pulled him down.

"Something is moving off to our left. Jesus, it's a whole line of troops, moving this way! We've got to get back." He turned and moved back to the west and up the hill. Hearing a thump, Swede looked back. Page was gone! Then he saw a shape on the ground. There was no time to ask questions. Kneeling down, he slid Page on his back, and, keeping low, continued to move away from the approaching troops. Crawling into some thick bushes, Swede felt a sense of déjà vu. He had been in bushes like these before, trying to hide from some guards. Only those guards were Korean and were moving in the other direction, not coming his way. And he hadn't been carrying someone on his back.

So now what? Can I carry Page and still stay ahead of these troops? Why are they looking for us? How do they know we are here? Should I try to stuff Page under some bushes and get away by myself? But if they find him, they might figure out he had something to do with their secret plane being destroyed. If it gets destroyed.

All those thoughts flashed through his head as he watched to see what direction the troops were moving in. Then he realized they weren't following him. They were going straight up the hill. It looked like they had stopped and turned to face the POW camp, which put their backs to Swede and Page! Just then, the clouds moved past the sliver of moon and he noticed something else. Even more troops were moving along the shore of the bay, putting themselves between the POW camp and the water. They also were facing toward the camp. There was now a long L shaped line of guards between the water and the POW camp. Given the noises he could still hear, and the troops lined up like they were, it looked like the barges would be heading out soon. Apparently, the Chinese wanted to make sure none of the prisoners swam out and attacked the barges with their bare hands.

Swede had been on this part of the hill when he, Danny Morgan, and Jim Riordan worked their way through the same area in their escape attempt the year before. He realized if he kept moving up through the trees, he could circle around and get back to the huts at Hilltop without being seen. If he moved now while it was still dark, it would be almost impossible for anyone to see him. Then if he waited near the camp until the barges were moving out into the river, all eyes would be looking in that direction. He should be able to move through the open area to the huts without being spotted. He could approach past the punishment shed, using it for cover. Maybe then Page would able to move on his own.

By the time he had carried Page up the hill, stumbling himself a few times, it was getting close to dawn. He found a spot to hide and collapsed to wait. The engine noises and the banshee cries of metal dragging on metal were louder now. Then there was a new noise, the powerful rumbling of the barges as they began to work their way through the bay towards the Yalu. Every prisoner on that end of the peninsula seemed to be up and watching. And every guard was doing the same. Swede watched as the barges made their way out towards the Yalu. Nets covered both cargoes, but they did little to hide what was underneath. The fuselage of the B-29 was very recognizable. It dwarfed the barge beneath it. The nose was crumpled and part of the huge tail missing. The second barge carried one wing and at least one engine with its propeller all bent and twisted.

Swede heard a noise from Page. He was propped up on one elbow and looking out at the scene on the water. "What the hell happened? Did I get shot?" He reached for his head as if to find a wound. And winced when his hand ran across the tender lump on his forehead. "How did I get here?"

"I carried you. You tripped on something and went down hard. If you can move, we need to get to the huts while everybody is looking the other way."

Page looked back in the direction they had been when he fell. Raising his eyebrows, he asked, "You carried me?"

"Yep, and you aren't exactly a light weight. I could have dragged you, but your big feet would have left some pretty obvious marks. I had no choice. Besides, if they found you, they might have connected you with what is about to happen to those barges. They would have been all over us looking for a radio. Who knows how many of us would get slapped around? Maybe even me. I had no choice." Swede grinned at Page.

"What do you mean 'what is about to happen to those barges'?" Page asked.

Swede pointed up. "See those contrails? Those planes have been circling around up there for a while. Any minute now, they are going to spot the barges. Then the fireworks should begin." Just then they heard a deep growling coming from the sky behind them. Three planes roared overhead, followed by three more, propellers flashing, ripping the morning apart with their noise. The barges were well out into the Yalu. The planes pulled up, their engines shaking the sky. Swede could feel the noise in his chest.

"P-51 Mustangs!" he yelled. Look at those babies go!" Page reached up and yanked him to the ground.

"Look from down here. And try not to attract any attention while you do." The planes all banked back to the east and disappeared. Seconds later they came roaring back, flying parallel with the camp and the bay. As the water around the barges erupted into a boil, a new noise ripped apart the morning air. Tracer rounds from the guns on the planes reached out and tore into the barges. All six planes thundered their way into the sky again, three banking right and three banking left.

Page nudged Swede, who was still watching the Mustangs, his mouth open in awe. "Look at the barges." The barge with the wing was dead in the water, flames starting to rise. The lead barge was trying to turn and head back to the shore.

Just then the Mustangs appeared again from the east. This time rockets leaped from their wings. Explosions seemed to lift both barges from the water. An enormous roar came from the second barge, with flames shooting almost as high as the planes. The barge simply disappeared in the smoke and noise. The lead barge, the one with the fuselage of the B-29, tilted to the side. The strong Yalu current caught it and started to carry it downstream. The tilt continued, becoming extreme. Finally, the barge rolled over and disappeared beneath the water, bow first. As the smoke and noise drifted away, more planes appeared, this time coming out of the west. Three jets flashed overhead.

"Mig-17s," Page noted. "I hope the Mustangs are well on their way home."

"It might not matter," exclaimed Swede. "Here come our guys. They must be the ones that were making the contrails a bit ago."

Three more jets screamed out of the sky and followed the Mig-17s to the east. And then it was quiet again. Smoke over the river thinned and disappeared. No planes, no barges, no B-29. The whole thing could have been a dream.

"B-29s don't swim very well, do they? C'mon, let's get into camp while everybody is still looking the other way." Swede, chuckling at his own humor, reached down, and pulled Page to his feet. With Page supporting himself with an arm over Swede's shoulder, the two moved quickly to the huts on Hilltop and disappeared among their fellow prisoners.

Page and Swede pulled it off. Their excuse for asking Earl and Bobby Hanley to mess up any prisoner count was to let people visit a little longer instead of going to their huts right away that night. Swede told Earl he had stayed and chatted with Page for most of the night. Earl seemed to accept the explanation. Either that or he knew better than to ask more questions. Everybody else talked constantly for the next few days about what they had seen in the bay that morning. Some claimed the barge had held a B-29, others just saw a huge pipe of some kind. In either case they all were thrilled to see U.S. planes come out on top of whatever it was that had gone on. The generally accepted theory was with our planes that close the war must be almost over.

The Chinese asked questions for a few days. They had their stooges asking all around to see if anybody knew anything about the raid. A stooge would approach a group and throw out a story about having heard there was a commando team in the hills, or maybe a submarine coming up the Yalu at night and sending radio signals back to the US fleet. That backfired, because when they called people in for questioning, all they heard about were their own rumors, sometimes with creative details added for good measure. First prize was the story about the black commandos who were inserted by submarine and only operated at night. Nobody could see them.

There were also rumors of an all-camp Olympics to be held at Camp 5 in the fall. Some mail from home started coming in. The men at Hilltop were finally allowed to write home. Work details continued, for the most part focusing on making camp life more sanitary and comfortable. All outhouses and latrine trenches were moved farther from camp buildings. Lime was made available. A fly killing campaign was established. For every twenty dead flies brought to the registration station, one cigarette a day could be earned. It wasn't long before the requirement was two hundred flies. All but the real nicotine addicts soon lost interest, but the fly population was greatly reduced-at least for a while.

A negative development was the removal of all NCOs, corporals and above, from the camp. An announcement was made over the new camp PA system in the morning and they were all gone by noon. Rumors spread throughout the camp. They were being sent to a separate camp. They were being sent home. They were being sent up to Camp 5. The nastiest rumor was they were being sent to China. No one had a clue.

Swede and Page spent the morning saying goodbye to Earl. The three men tried to come up with a reason for the change. Were the Chinese going to start putting pressure on the younger captives again? Would they be forced to attend lectures again? Why else remove the NCOs? Were they really being sent home?

"You two stay healthy," said Earl. "I know you are up to something every now and then, but I also have no doubt you are the good guys. Any time you need some help on a 'work detail' you just ask. Just as long as I don't have to give up too much of my rice or too many of my cigarettes." He smiled and stuck out his hand. "You take care, kid."

Then he shook Page's hand. Still smiling he said, "Try not to get him shot."

Earl gave a little wave and boarded the truck while singing a familiar tune.

The sun came up and I was told
My place in life was set.
Don't look for what you can't have
This is all you'll ever get.

I'd had enough so I set off
For places I'd never been.
Sun and sea, mountain and vale
Then I would move on again.

Radios and Reactionaries
Aug-Oct 1952

The Chinese didn't start up with lectures again, but the alternative wasn't very pleasant. The new PA system blasted out Chinese music and very slanted news broadcasts for most of the day. At least the lectures had been just a few hours at a time. The speeches read over the PA by the Progressives that had gone over to the Chinese side were the worst. They begged their fellow prisoners to see the light and join them. They could have better food and sweets on a regular basis. They could receive regular mail from home, even the packages of food and cigarettes their families sent. They could benefit from the Communist way of thinking. Capitalism was an evil that should be removed from the face of the earth. Truman and Eisenhower were war criminals. All who gave those speeches were kept in separate huts away from the rest. Even with extra guards in their area they were often pelted with stones. Earl had left behind some disciples of his own.

Swede and Page didn't do anything to attract attention to themselves after the B-29 incident. Page got more involved helping teams that were going to the Camp 5 Olympics. Swede helped with making the banners they were required to have ready before they left. There was going to be a repeat of the parade celebrating the Chinese Revolution the year before at Camp 1. Swede made as many suggestions as he thought prudent about how they might word the slogans on the banners. Just as the year before, the bootleg banners were hidden in the back of the workroom. The more correct versions were in full view of the Chinese who monitored the work.

Swede and Bobby Hanley started spending more time together. Bobby didn't bring it up in any conversation, but he knew Swede and Page occasionally got involved in what the Chinese called "incorrect behaviors." He suspected the fire down at HQ was a little fishy.

"Do you think there's a particular reason the Chinese separated us from the officers and NCOs?" Hanley asked. "The officers were sent up to their camp a year ago, so why take away all the sergeants now? What is it they are going to do to us that they don't want them to see? Or do the Chinese think we will all roll over and play dead now that we are on our own?"

"If I had to bet," offered Swede, "I would bet they will take different approaches for each group. For the officers, it will be something like – *you are more educated than the others. You can see the truth in communism. You can see how sometimes we must lead by force.* For the NCOs – *now you can think for yourselves. Your officers never let you make decisions.* For us – *they all think you are fools. Now that they can't threaten you, you can make your own decisions.* Something along those lines. All that garbage they spit out over the PA seems to be trying to convince us we are slaves to democratic capitalism. *Remove the yoke of slavery your corporate masters have placed on your necks.*"

Fewer men in camp meant more slots to fill on work details. Swede and Bobby bribed their way on to the crew that worked on barges running supplies up and down the Yalu. Guys who had been on that run before told them to be sure to take along a blanket. Riding a barge on the Yalu for a day could be chilly. Swede took his blanket and an old, ratty, overcoat he had borrowed. Once the supplies were loaded, they set out to the north, apparently headed for Camp 5. Being on the river made Swede a little nervous. All the barge crew had to do was swing left and they were in China. Once across that wide river, you might disappear forever.

On the way up to Camp 5, Swede and Bobby sprawled out on some crates and watched the fall colors roll by. "All I need is a fishing pole and I could be Huck Finn," smiled Bobby.

Swede had been thinking the same thing and grinned back. "Don't get too comfortable. Things can easily get worse. What if we have to cut all the firewood to fill these barges before we go back south? What if we don't go back south? But I guess until that happens, we might as well enjoy the ride."

"Isn't that why you volunteered? To enjoy the ride?" Bobby asked.

"Yeah, that's true. But just between you and me, I thought it would be worth our time to see what we can along the river. Do we stop at any camps we don't know about? I have this theory that these barges are the ones that would pick up the firewood Earl and I cut when we were up at Camp Sunday last winter. A little river ran near our camp. It ran north and then cut west toward the Yalu. We would haul the logs we cut to a point on that river where barges would pick it up. Up a little valley near that pickup point were some huts all fenced in. Maybe we'll get a chance to see it again. Earl and I never saw the barges. We just stacked the logs and headed back to cut more. But from what the guys say who have been on this trip, I think these are the barges that picked up that firewood.

"Even if these barges don't go there, we will get a good look at the river and any other camps that might be here. Maybe we'll spot the camp where all the NCOs went. Either way, we get to relax a little and maybe collect some good information."

As they moved up the river, Bobby began to talk about the Tiger Death March, something those guys didn't bring up very often. He said after they were captured, the Koreans hustled them north. Some days they got fed, some days they didn't. When they did, it wasn't much. The sick and wounded didn't last long. A couple of times they were loaded on trains. In Pyongyang, they were marched through the city so the North Koreans could see how weak American soldiers were. Things got worse by the week as they headed still further north. There was a column of about seventy civilians that joined them somewhere along the way. The two columns were kept apart . At night, the civilians were usually put in some kind of building for shelter, but not the soldiers.

"I slept outside a lot when I was a kid, sometimes even in the winter," said Bobby. "But we had blankets, or sleeping bags, and food, and a fire. But not on that march. Throw yourself on the ground and hope some buddies would curl up next to you. A couple of my buddies were still curled up on the ground when we left the next morning." Bobby sat without speaking for a while.

The Tiger showed up about the same time as the snow did. And he was more deadly. "You know what kept me goin'? The kids. There were about ten kids in the civilian group. A couple of them were only two or three years old. When I saw them stumble along, I figured I could make it too. Everybody watched out for the kids. We would wave and make funny faces when we got close to them. Every one of those kids was still alive when they finally put them on trucks and sent them away. But we buried a lot of our guys in snowbanks or a miserable little hill near the camps where they kept us." Swede didn't ask questions. He just let Bobby talk until he finally sat in silence.

Later in the day they pulled up to what they recognized was Camp 5. They helped unload some of the crates and were led to a nearby building for the night. They were able to talk with the POWs who helped with the crates and served them supper and then breakfast the next morning. While Bobby went down to the river to wash up, Swede talked with a couple of guys he knew, hoping they might have some recent news.

"I'm not impressed," Bobby proclaimed as the barges headed north again.

"What do you mean?" Swede looked puzzled.

"For some reason I was expecting things to be better at Camp 5. But nothing was different. Same bland food and same dirt floors. I wasn't expecting bacon and eggs, but I thought maybe some real coffee and butter for my bread."

"One of these days, Bob, one of these days. Coffee, bacon, eggs, toast. Maybe even sausage and pancakes with real maple syrup like my mother makes. Until then, we do what we can. Speaking of which, do you know what's in these crates?"

"Not a clue. Why?"

"Maybe we should take a look."

The barges pulled in at two different Chinese camps along the shore before they came to a river and headed east. A mile or so up the river they saw a pile of logs on the south bank. As they pulled up to the bank and tied off, Swede looked around and nudged Bobby. "I was only here in the winter, but this looks like where we used to stack our logs for pickup. I bet this is the same place. You go up that way maybe a quarter of a mile and the river turns south and gets narrower. And just over that hill should be some fenced in huts." He pointed into the woods beyond the logs.

It took everybody working the rest of the afternoon and into the evening to get all the wood loaded aboard the barges. The cook had supper ready when they finished. By that time, it was well into the evening, and the entire group was exhausted from the day's work. Bobby paid no attention when Swede motioned him a little further into the woods than most of the others before they tossed their blankets down. He just pulled his blanket over his head and went to sleep. Swede placed a few small stones under his blanket before he stretched out. It was a trick his father had taught him when they needed to get up early for hunting. You never fell into a deep sleep. And Swede was going hunting.

According to the moon and the Big Dipper in the night sky, Swede set out just after midnight. He headed straight up the hill, moving south as quickly as possible without making a lot of noise. The trees were thick enough that he soon could not see the river. At the crest of the hill, he crouched next to a tree and studied the little valley below. Moving from tree to tree, he moved down the hill. At the bottom, he found nothing except more trees. Reaching the top of the next hill, he could see what he was sure was the little camp he and Earl had spotted a year ago. There were some larger houses far to his left and some small sheds of some kind scattered in the small valley below him. A crude wooden stockade about four feet high surrounded three of the huts. Swede sat and watched the area for about thirty minutes. A guard wandered past the fenced-in sheds and returned to the hut. Swede then moved down the hill and approached the shed farthest from the house. He came at it from the back so he could watch towards the house and guard hut. The fence wasn't much, but he didn't try to cross it or jump over.

"Hey, in the hut," Swede called in little more than a whisper. "Is anybody in there?" He called a couple more times before he heard a reply.

"Who are you? Are you here to rescue us?" The voice was definitely American, not from the Midwest, maybe the east coast?

"No, I'm a POW on a work detail on a barge out on the river just to the north. Can you get out of there so we can talk without making a lot of noise?"

"Except for these handcuffs I could. So the answer is no. That fence isn't much. You can probably squeeze through."

Swede did just that, pushing aside some of the posts and stepping through. He kept most of the shed between himself and the guard hut but moved just enough to the right to be able to see down the valley. Once at the shed, he introduced himself to the voice inside.

"I'm Paul Larson. I came up from Camp 3 on a barge. We loaded up a bunch of logs and will probably head back in the morning. Who are you and how long have you been here?"

"I'm Dave Williams, an F-84 pilot. I was shot down about a week ago. The villagers that captured me looked like they were going to kill me until some Chinese troops showed up. They acted like they had just won a prize. I guess I was it. I've been here two days. There are two more guys in the other sheds. I hear them talking with the guards, but they never let any of us out when the others are out. Where is this Camp 3 you talked about?"

"As far as we know there are four main camps now. There were lots of smaller camps in the beginning, but now we think they have us all up near the Yalu. Camp 5 is a few hours southwest of here on the Yalu. Camp 3 is a few hours south of Five, again on the river. Camp 1 is southeast of there on a small river that flows up to the Yalu near Camp 3. Camp 2 is about west southwest of here. Two is the officers camp. They moved them all there last fall. They moved all the NCOs somewhere just a few weeks ago, but we don't know where yet."

"How long have you been a prisoner?" asked Williams.

"Since the beginning of the war, July 1950."

There was a long pause. "Damn! I thought a week was forever. I don't know if I can last a couple of years."

Just then Swede heard a noise from the guard hut. "A guard is coming! I gotta go!"

"No," said Williams. "Lay down next to the wall. He will never see you. He won't come close and he won't bother to look back around here. If you head back up the hill now, he will spot you. Trust me. Just flatten out next to the wall."

Swede did just that and listened as the guard's footsteps came his way. He figured if he had to, he could run right through the fence and keep on going. If he headed south up the hill before he turned and circled back to the barges, they might think he was from the punishment camps to the south. But Williams was right. The guard just turned and walked back to the hut. Once the guard was inside, Swede sat up.

"Why are you in these huts? What are they doing with you?" Swede asked.

"They say all American pilots are war criminals. We bomb villages and drop germs of some kind over the countryside. They want us to sign confessions. At least that's what they want me to do. I'm guessing it's the same with the other guys. When I wouldn't sign, they threw me in here. They have me cuffed to a pole. How is it that you can wander around? How are they treating you guys?"

'The first winter half of us died. Since then, things have improved a little. They still cut our food down when we don't cooperate like they want. I've been thrown in punishment cells for a couple of months at a time. But they seem to think the war might end soon and are trying to keep us more or less healthy."

A long pause again. "Half? Half of you died? For real?" Williams' voice had more than a little despair in it.

"Half," Swede repeated. "But I don't think anyone has died in any camp I've been in since last July or August. They might keep you hungry and uncomfortable, but you'll be okay. What do you know about the peace talks at Panmunjom? Is the war almost over?"

"One week it is and the next week it isn't. But they are still talking, so that's a good sign."

"I've got to get back before somebody looks around and figures out I'm not under my blanket. I'll try to get the word out that you guys are here. There is a punishment camp maybe a mile south of here. I'll try to let them know. I'm not sure what they can do, but I will try to get the word to them. That might take a couple of months. We can only get news from camp to camp when they transfer somebody."

Swede pushed a chocolate bar through a crack in the wall. "Take this. I stole it from the Chinese on the barge. I took the wrapper off so the guard doesn't spot it. And take these. They're vitamins. They were with the chocolate. Keep them hidden. If you can, get some to the other guys.

"I know what you're going through. The first winter I spent five months before I saw another American. You can do this. Maybe they'll send you to the officer's camp pretty soon. Tell them you were the copilot and just got here from the states. You don't even know the pilot's name. You were on your first flight. Lie as much as you can get away with. Just keep track of your lies. But if you have to, sign their confession. If they let you write it out, make mistakes so other Americans will know it isn't for real. If it's in Chinese, spell your name wrong or sign with your other hand. And try to contact the guys in the other huts. Hearing just a few words will make you feel better.

"I wish I could do more. Good luck, Dave Williams." With that, Swede slipped back through the fence and headed up the hill. Thirty minutes later, he was asleep under his blanket.

On the way back down the river, Swede thought about telling Bobby Hanley about Page and himself and some of the things they had done. He decided against it. He trusted Bobby completely, but what he didn't know couldn't hurt him - or anybody else. He also knew Page did some things he didn't talk about. The more the merrier did not apply to keeping secrets in a prisoner of war camp. Swede did tell Bobby about his trip over the hill the night before. He didn't mention he had talked with Dave Williams, just that there were some huts in the valley. He passed it off as another punishment camp, like 2-3, or Camp Sunday, as Earl liked to call it.

As they sprawled out over the logs soaking up the sun on the way back to Camp 3, Bobby brought up an idea. "I've been thinking. It would help if we had real news about what is happening in the world. Are we winning or losing? Are the peace talks for real? Who is going to be in the World Series? Who's hot in Hollywood? If we had that kind of real news it might be easier for some of these guys to stand up to the Chinese. It would remind them of home and who we are."

"So how do we get real news?" asked Swede. "We don't get many new guys in camp that can tell us what was happening before they were captured."

"Did you ever make a radio?" Bobby asked. A really, really, simple radio?"

"There weren't any Boy Scouts around where I lived, but I used to check out Popular Mechanics from the library. My dad and uncles would help me do some of the projects. We made a simple radio once. We used a razor blade and a pencil. We could listen to WCCO out of Minneapolis at night. We had a regular radio, so our homemade contraption was just for fun."

"That's exactly what I'm talkin' about! Can you remember how you did it?" Within a week the two had put together a simple radio receiver using a razor, a pencil, paper clips, some wire, and a tin can. What they didn't have or couldn't trade for, they stole. The antenna was the biggest problem. They had the wire but no place to string it out where it wouldn't be seen. Finally, they came up with a simple solution. Attach it to the tower behind the radio shack. They could use the route Swede and Page had taken to get back to their huts the night they sent the message about the B-29. They would only be able to make that trip at night, but figured reception would be better at night anyway.

When all the parts were in place, they picked a dark night and snuck out past the punishment hut on the edge of Hilltop. The guards had never been known to patrol out into the woods, but they took no chances and moved cautiously through the brush and trees. At the tower, they attached their wire and backed away into the trees. At first, they could find only static. Bobby bent his ear to the tin can and slowly moved the pencil tip around on the razor. Then he looked over at Swede with a grin like a kid on Christmas morning.

"English! I can hear English!" he whispered. After moving the pencil slowly for a few seconds, he let Swede listen. They had an American voice giving the latest war news.

"This is an Armed Forces Radio broadcast," whispered Swede. "We hit the jackpot!"

The two men didn't push their luck. They buried the radio in a box in the brush. They only went out once a week. Each of them knew two or three other prisoners who loved to hear rumors. They would casually mention different tidbits of information to different people each week. It was something a guard had told them, or news somebody had gotten in a letter from home. In case the Chinese were listening to the same broadcast, the two didn't spread all the news the next day. That would make it obvious there was a radio somewhere in camp. Some things they didn't mention at all. Now and then, when one of their news rumors came up in a group, Swede or Bobby would argue it made no sense. Any time the Pros started asking questions about where the new rumors were coming from, they quit talking to their gossipy friends for a while. It was important they didn't attract attention to themselves. Only Page knew the whole story.

Swede had given Page all the details about the barge trip up the Yalu. The crate he opened on the barge, the pilots and the germ warfare charge, and the radio he and Bobby Hanley built.

"If that crate was all food stolen from our mail, was it a one-time deal by somebody at Camp 5, or is it something they do all the time? Earl Stoneman and I raided a shed full of medical supplies at Camp 5. But that was probably stuff they had taken from captives or found after they overran some outfit. If they are stealing our mail, they might be keeping it somewhere in camp. Is it worth our looking for?

If we find it, do we steal it all back? How should we handle this?" Swede looked to Page for a solution.

"The first thing we can do is have some of our Progressives look around. Maybe some of the extra goodies they get are from our own packages from the states. I'd rather not go wandering around at night looking into random sheds.

"But I think you might be right. I've sent enough postcards and letters that I ought to be getting some packages back. But I've only gotten a couple of letters. How about you? Have you gotten any mail?" Page asked.

"I've only been able to send one postcard. That was in May or June. I haven't gotten anything back yet," answered Swede.

"Just one postcard? That's it? I didn't know that," Page responded.

"Same goes for all of us on the hill. We are all Reactionaries, capitalist war-mongering scum. You probably shouldn't be hanging around with us."

Page chuckled. "Give me an address and I'll ask somebody to get your folks a message next time I write. If I scatter your name and hometown in different parts of the letter, it might get through."

Cooler weather signaled the arrival of fall and a uniform exchange. Each prisoner was issued two cotton padded uniforms of the student type, two sets of underwear shorts, two shirts, a hat, and cotton gloves. Each man received a blanket and a light quilt or an old overcoat. They were allowed fires in their huts, but their wood supply was rationed. Men on work details constantly tried to sneak extra kindling of some kind back to camp. If the peace talks were going well and there had been no major problem in camp, the guards looked the other way. An escape attempt or a slowdown in Panmunjom meant unhappy guards and bruised prisoners.

The teams going to Camp 5 for the Olympics continued to practice. Bobby Hanley took over Earl's duties and filled in as a player when needed. Page asked both Bobby and Swede if they had any friends in the Progressive group who could still be trusted. True, some of the Pros actively helped the Chinese. But most were simply trying to make their life a little more comfortable while waiting for the war to end. The articles they wrote for the camp 'newspaper' or the speeches they read over the PA were often nonsense, if not downright comical. Portraying Truman as a man with a secret harem made the Chinese smile with the insult, and the POWs laugh at the absurdity.

But Page had discovered the camp commander had set up a new committee that only the 'best' of the Pros were invited to join. Their job was to bring the commander information on planned escapes and who was threatening Progressives. Information on secret radios or people giving orders was especially important. Anything about germ warfare would win first prize. Committee members were moved into a special barracks where they got better food and real beds with pillows. Page wanted to find some Progressives who were willing to change their behavior and work against the Chinese once again. He figured Swede and Bobby would know who might fit that requirement. But he was surprised at Swede's reaction, especially his language, when he heard about the newest committee.

"Son of a bitch! They're willing to turn against us for a bed? For a lousy bed? Turn against a fellow prisoner? In that case, I'll make sure those bastards have some threats comin' their way!"

"Hold up a minute. This is where we use their committee against them. We plant a map, maybe even a compass, in a Progressive hut. Then we spread rumors, just a few, about an escape plan. We let slip a few names. On the back of the map we list two or three of them. While we set up that little surprise, we can think of a few other ways to mess with them. And we need to get the word out so everybody can be extra careful around any Progressive. If we do it right, they won't be able to pin anything on any of us.

"But to really fight the committee we need some Pros who can be reasoned with. You two should be able to find some guys who are starting to feel being a Progressive is wrong. This new committee should make it easier for us to reason with them. Talk to those you think might be ready to be soldiers again. Explain they can redeem themselves if they help us out. You had some people like that at Camp 1, didn't you Swede?"

Swede looked over at him in surprise. "I didn't realize you knew that. I figured the fewer people I told, the better. But, yeah, I did."

"We will have to be careful about who we talk to," suggested Bobby. "Some might say no, but we need to make sure anybody we approach won't run back to the guards and spill the beans."

"We only need a few who are willing to continue to act as Pros but go to work for us. Bobby is right, be careful who you talk to," Page continued. "Wait until you get an answer from one guy before you try another. Then put them to work. We need to know when the Chinese might search our huts. Are any of us being watched or suspected of any kind of plot. Are there plans to send more guys to another camp? Where did the NCOs go? Are they holding back our mail? Anything and everything that will help us stay ahead of the Chinese. Anything and everything that will help keep the morale up around here, keep our guys from giving up.

"We can't just sit in our huts like sheep and wait for the war to end. They tell us the Geneva Convention doesn't apply here, that we are students, not prisoners. We need to show the Chinese, and the Progressives, we don't accept that."

To help keep attention off themselves, and the others who were helping them, Swede suggested they form a committee of their own. "We don't hide it. We make it obvious," offered Swede.

"What good will a committee do us if the Chinese know about it?" asked Bobby. Page had the same question but waited to see what Swede was thinking.

'We need to be able to talk to people without sneaking around the camp. We need to have a reason for walking down to the main camp or somebody from there coming up here. So, we form a Welcome Wagon." Swede grinned as he waited for their reaction.

"How about a PTA while we are at it," laughed Bobby.

"The Chinese love committees. We tell them every small town in America has a Welcome Wagon, a committee of people who help the poor peasants when they move into town because the bank took their farm. The committee helps them get a place to stay and helps them fix it up. They see that the peasants get enough to eat, have a job to make them feel like they are part of the community. They talk to people who might be troublemakers, so things in the community run smooth. The war will end soon, we just want to make sure there is no trouble in camp until then. The Chinese will eat that kind of talk up. We get to move around from camp to camp without much hassle. And it won't just be the three of us. We can get lots of guys willing to help. We can even get our sources with the Pros to join. They can tell the Chinese they need to be part of the Welcome Wagon to keep tabs on what they are doing. We can have all the meetings we want. I believe they call that a slam dunk."

"Swede, you are a devious man." Page chuckled. "A devious man."

3 South

Nov-Dec 1952

November came, and it was time for the teams to head out on the trip to Camp 5 for the Olympic games. They boarded trucks early in the morning and headed towards camp HQ. Once in the village the trucks pulled over and waited. More trucks appeared from the south. As they slowed and pulled past the 3 South trucks, men began to recognize each other. The new trucks were from Camp 1. The men called greetings out to each other and then headed up to 3 North where the scene was repeated. After an uncomfortable four-hour ride, they turned west and headed out on the peninsula to Camp 5.

It was a little chilly to be playing games outside, but the men soon began enjoying themselves. They all understood it was a Communist propaganda ploy, but they didn't care. More importantly, it was an escape for them. They got to be treated well for a week, and they got to meet old friends and exchange information. The exchange of information was probably the biggest morale booster for the POWs. They caught up on the latest news from home. Marilyn Monroe had a new movie out called *Monkey Business*. The Yanks had won the World Series. Nobody knew for sure, but it looked like Eisenhower was going to be the next president. The Chinese never announced good news over the PA in the camps. They were afraid Eisenhower would use nuclear weapons if he got elected. Since the election was over, Ike must have won. If he had lost, the Chinese would be more than happy to let the POWs know. The POWs knew the news you did not hear was often as important as the news you did hear.

One of the first faces Swede saw was Earl. "Guess what?" yelled

Earl as he swatted Swede on the back. "I found out where Camp 4 is. It's where they sent all of us important sergeants. It's about as far north of Camp 5 as Camp 3 is to the south. They put us to work building a rock wall between two sections and put barbed wire all around. The roughest part is we have to walk quite a way out of camp to get firewood. The good news is they are building real barracks with lights and stoves. It's colder up there, so the stoves will help this winter. I've been in worse places.

"Hey, I met some guys you know. Mike Randall and Jack Usury. Randall is top notch but that Usury sure is a grouch. Lucky for me, he's not in my company."

"Jack Usury, a grouch? That's not the way I remember him." Swede wondered what had happened to change Jack.

Just then they heard a yell. "Swede! Page!" They looked up to see Trigger waving at them.

The week went by fast. Swede's basketball team was knocked out of the games mid-week, so the friends had time to visit – and ask lots of questions. Nobody knew of any deaths in any of the camps for the past year. Nobody knew of any successful escapes, but lots of people had tried. Most spent a month or more in whatever nasty "hole" was used in that camp for their attempt. The information about the deaths and escape attempts was important to know – and to share. A couple of the senior officers were held in separate huts outside of Camp 2. At the most, they were able to wave at a POW who managed to get near on a work detail. People were still sent to the punishment camp beyond Camp 2 where Swede and Earl had spent most of the last winter. And there was a rumor of an even more remote camp where pilots were interrogated about germ warfare. Swede didn't come right out and say he had talked to someone there, but he did drop a few rumors about the existence of the camp itself.

The parade at the end of the week was again supposed to be a major Communist propaganda coup. There were even movie cameras to record it. Some of the men took off their hats and looked directly into the cameras so the folks back home might spot them. Others scowled and displayed a discreet middle finger. Swede was pleased to see he wasn't the only one to come up with banners that didn't quite meet the Chinese spirit of the day. "Chairman Mao for President" had probably given its creators lots of laughs. Swede saw some puzzled faces in the reviewing stand as it was translated for the generals and political officers. "Send the War Mongers Home" caused a few frowns on the reviewing stand. But it could be taken a couple of ways so they must have figured it was best not to attract attention by having the guards pull it down. There were plenty of "Proletariat" this and "Capitalist" that to make the generals happy. The guys in Camp 5 had created a "Yanks Win Again" sign they claimed was in tribute to the New York Yankees winning the World Series, but their explanation failed to win over the monitors.

After the final celebratory meal, everybody was loaded in their trucks and sent 'home'. Both the Chinese and the POWs looked at the week as a win for their side. They were correct.

The ride back to Camp 3 was different than on the way up. The excitement was gone. They were headed back to the boredom of the daily routine. The cold reminded them winter was near. Most of them in the truck had survived the first year and would never feel the same about winter again.

"Why did the Chinese wait until this time of the year to have their little Olympics? September would have been a better choice. Not too hot, not too cold." Bobby Hanley wasn't asking anybody in particular. He was just thinking out loud.

Walt Fairmont had been the catcher on the baseball team. Walt couldn't run very well. He had lost some toes to the cold that first winter at Bean Camp, and considered himself lucky it was just his toes, and only a few at that. But he could still catch! And he had an answer for Bobby's rhetorical question.

"A friend of mine from Camp 5, Gabe Goessling, has a theory. He says it was planned this way because of the elections at home. He says the Chinese don't understand our elections, so they figured Stevenson was handpicked by Truman. Truman used the bomb in Japan, so if Stevenson won, he might use it again, here in Korea. Eisenhower was our top general in World War II, so they figure he is still a general and will either use the bomb or push north and invade China. By showing how great they are treating all of us, they figure to get world opinion on their side. By holding the games just after the election back home, they figure to have the front pages full of happy POWs playing games. And our winter jackets make us all look well fed. Happy, well fed American boys playing baseball and basketball. You can't drop atomic bombs on that picture. At least, that's what Gabe says."

"This Gabe sounds pretty smart," offered Bobby. "What did he do before the Army?"

"He was going to be a lawyer, but he took a year off before his last year of school. When they opened the draft back up in '48, guess who got a letter from Uncle Sam?" Walt sang the answer. "He's in the Army now," as he pretended to blow a bugle. Then he started laughing. "I just realized. Gabe is from Chicago! Famous trumpet man from out Chicago way? Get it?"

A few days after they got back, Colonel Li brought Swede in for "questioning." He placed a canteen and a small package wrapped in paper on the table. "Hot tea," he said. "Sweetened. And some rice balls with fish. Drink all the tea now but save some of the rice for later."

"Later?" asked Swede.

"When we are finished here, I am going to have to place you in the punishment shed for the night. I have a blanket here for you to take with you. In the morning, leave it on the ground at the back. The next man can use it and do the same."

"The punishment shed? Why is that?"

"My superiors are starting to ask me questions about you. Their new committee has told them you were responsible for some of the banners at the Olympic games that demonstrated incorrect thinking. They think you escaped before you came here to Camp 3. You are hiding the truth. Maybe you are the leader of the refusal to attend the camp lectures."

"And why is the committee saying these things about me."

"It is not the committee. It is the man I told you about before. Your friend Morgan."

So, Swede spent the night in the punishment shed. He didn't tell Li they had already snuck a blanket into the shed to keep any occupant warm at night. Now there would be two blankets. From personal experience, he knew even two blankets wouldn't keep anyone very warm when the real cold hit.

The next day Swede and Page talked about how to handle Danny Morgan. Swede told Page he had talked with a friend in Camp 5 when he and Bobby went north on the barge before the Olympics. The friend had told him that when he, Earl, Dick Shea, Fred Moeder, and Danny Morgan had all been sent to Camp 5 last December for

325

their sentencing, Danny Morgan stayed in Camp 5. The other four had gone to penal camps at 2-3. They assumed Danny had been sent to a penal camp also. It wasn't until his friend brought it up that Swede realized Danny had never really said where he had been for those three months.

"My friend told me Danny stayed at Camp 5, but not in any kind of punishment cell. The word was he spent those three months living with the Progressives, but never came into the main camp. For some reason, instead of being sentenced to a penal camp like the rest of us, he was given special treatment. And now Li tells us Danny is giving information to this new committee. It looks like he has switched sides."

Danny Morgan was the only child of parents who never really wanted children. They were good parents, but seldom willing to get involved in activities that required much of their time. Danny played with the local kids after school and in the summer but was never part of any regular teams or clubs. He tried hard to fit in, but the older he got, the more difficult that became. He began to resent the popular kids for their ability to be part of a group. He never had the size to take out his frustrations on anybody, but he was quick to point a finger at any behavior of others that might get them in trouble. That made it even more difficult to make friends. He saw the Army as an opportunity to finally be part of a team. That would have happened if he had been able to set aside his constant resentment at the success of others. His fellow soldiers often found themselves in trouble for things they knew were not their fault. They began to suspect Private Morgan. The less he was accepted, the more resentment he felt.

Private Danny Morgan was exactly what the Chinese were looking for. Someone unhappy with the world around him, someone looking for approval, someone eager to be part of a group. Someone who was so eager they did not care what the group did, as long as it welcomed them into it. A few words of approval, a few rewards for the desired behavior, and the Danny Morgans in the camps were hooked.

For Danny, it was that desire to be recognized with little effort on his part. For others, it was fear. Fear of physical discomfort, fear of hunger, fear of death. For a few, it was plain ignorance. They were easy to convince their current predicament was the fault of the US

Army, or the US government, or even the American people back home. Whatever their reasons, there were too many Danny Morgans.

Because Danny Morgan was telling tales and Swede was getting attention from the Chinese, Page suggested he stay away from the radio for a while. The snow was making it hard to get over there without leaving obvious tracks. Swede decided to make one last trip over and bring the radio back to hide in camp. It was small enough to keep hidden, and he wouldn't have to make another later on.

The next moonless night, he slipped into the trees behind the punishment shed and made his way over to the radio shack on the Yalu side of the camp. He took his time, pausing to look and listen before moving on. He saw no sign of guards on the way over, so he didn't bother to watch for a while before moving to where the radio was hidden. Putting the tiny receiver in his pocket, he moved towards the radio tower, winding the antenna wire as he went along. At that point, he had to move into the open as he pulled the wire from the ground and detached it from the metal poles. Just as he finished, he heard a metallic sound. Turning to see what might have caused the noise, Swede saw a guard just ten yards away, his rifle pointed right at Swede's chest.

The guard was between Swede and the camp. He could turn and run but the Yalu was only yards away. He could rush the guard, but the man looked about ready to pull the trigger as it was. Any movement from Swede and the guard would fire. Swede slowly raised his arms, hoping he would get a chance to toss the radio and the wire. Still looking directly at Swede, the guard called out. Swede heard a response from farther back in the buildings and then the sound of running. A second guard appeared, unslinging his rifle as he saw what was going on. The first guard said something, and his partner approached Swede to search his pockets. So much for ditching the evidence. Swede was about to spend some cold nights in a cell.

A few days later, Colonel Li was called up to Camp 5 to meet with General Chen, the senior commander of all the POW camps. His predecessor, General Peng, had been returned to China due to illness. Peng was a survivor of the Long March and close to Mao. Chen was determined to make a name for himself, to claim the recognition he felt he deserved. It was General Chen who had selected Li to head up the search for any prisoners trying to assume leadership roles in any of the camps. The officers were isolated at Camp 2 and the sergeants all gathered in Camp 4. But General Chen was a paranoid man. He knew Peking was watching. When all the prisoners in all the camps had refused to attend their educational classes in the spring, he became convinced there was a group sending orders throughout the camps. Maybe these orders were generated by some of the POWs themselves, or maybe they were being sent in somehow from the outside. In either case, now that he was in charge, Chen was determined to find the source of those orders and stop them. He was sure his next promotion, or demotion, depended on it.

Chen had selected Colonel Li based on his rank, his knowledge of the English language and these Americans who spoke it, and because he knew Li was vulnerable. He knew Li would be worried his wife's death would reflect poorly on himself. That meant he would want to succeed. Chen could read some English, but had no personal experience working with Americans. Colonel Li was just the tool he needed to impress Peking.

"General, I have heard only a few vague rumors of a Finnegan who may be giving orders to the prisoners. I believe these stories to be nothing more than our prisoners amusing themselves at our expense. 'Chasing a wild goose' they call it. Or Finnegan could be nothing more than someone trying to earn a reward for telling us what they think we want to hear.

"I have found no evidence of a leader, a commander, who is issuing orders. I am sure some of the officers make attempts to send simple orders. Stand fast, remain strong, we are Americans, that type of thing. But that is all they can do, if even that. We have them all in Camp 2."

"But do we Colonel? Are we sure some officers weren't told to disguise themselves as common soldiers so they can issue orders secretly? I believe you are wrong, Colonel. There is truth to your rumors. We have recently found a carving in Camp 1. It is meant to look like a simple drawing of a tropical island, but I have found hidden messages in it. And it is signed by this Finnegan you don't believe in." Chen pointed to the back wall of the room.

Hanging on the wall was another much smaller wall. On the smaller wall someone had carved an island scene, complete with palm trees and an outrigger canoe. Far offshore, a whale was breaching.

"It was on the wall of a punishment cell, a place the guards would usually not see. I believe it was how they passed orders to each other. Only a hard-core reactionary would be placed in that cell. Someone who would try to give orders to other prisoners. And two of those people signed their names."

The general pointed to the bottom right. There Li could see "Finnegan was here." Then the general pointed to the far left. Li had to move closer before he could see a log cabin surrounded by pine trees, smoke rising from the chimney. It was smaller than the rest of the carving. Peeking over the tops of the pine trees was a face and the inscription "Kilroy was here."

The general was getting excited, his little round face changing from pale to pink, his hands dancing in the air as he went on. "You see, your Finnegan carved this scene to give coded messages to others. When they understood the message, they were to sign their name. Like this Kilroy has done. Had the commander at Camp 1 not been so eager to show me his discovery, we could have simply watched to see who else signed. But he had the wall removed and sent to me.

"The log cabin represents their president Lincoln, who led a war to free slaves. Finnegan is saying he is the commander who will lead a revolt. When the prisoners revolt, there will be a rescue force arriving by sea-or water. Battleships will send in their landing boats." The general pointed to the canoes and the whale. "Our camps are all on or near the Yalu. I have informed Peking of my findings so they can prepare for such a rescue force."

Li was shocked. This man was in charge of all the prisoners? His interpretation of the carving showed his complete lack of knowledge of Americans and their culture. He had no doubt the island scene and the log cabin had been carved by different people. 'Finnegan' had probably carved the much larger island scene first. 'Kilroy' didn't want to ruin the bigger picture, so he added his smaller touch in the corner. It was obvious the general had never heard of the American tradition of drawing 'Kilroy was here' wherever they went in the world. This Kilroy was simply following the tradition, big nose and all. The general's interpretation of the canoe and whale as battleships and landing craft? Li had no explanation for that at all.

Finnegan was probably dreaming of a much warmer place he hoped to be one day. Kilroy probably dreaming of home. The island was most likely put there in the winter, the cabin in warmer months.

Finnegan might be an actual prisoner's name, but Kilroy was not. But Li knew that to explain any of this to the general was not in his own best interest. So, he waited for Chen to speak.

"I want you to find these two men. Go through the records of all the camps. Start with Camp 1, but they may have been transferred to another camp. Check Camp 2, the officers camp, next. Find this Finnegan, and we will find their command structure.

"I have been told you recently discovered a radio in your camp. Find more about it. Was it used to send orders, to receive orders? Are there other radios? See to it the other camps look for similar radios. We may be close. When this Finnegan is found, Peking will reward us both."

Upon his return to Camp 3 South, Li had Swede brought from his cell for questioning. Given what General Chen said, Li thought it likely Swede would be sent to Peking as an example of how hard the general was working to discover the leaders giving orders to the prisoners. He pushed Swede to make a confession before the general decided to make him a scapegoat.

"You are going to be punished. You can limit that punishment by showing your willingness to confess to your crimes. Say the right words. You will no doubt be sent to a penal camp. For how long and under what conditions will depend on your level of cooperation. Refuse to confess, and you will just disappear in the middle of the night. They will then read your "confession" over the camp PA. If you make your own confession, the whole camp will hear your words from your mouth, not a speech written by a political commissar."

A week later, on a cold, snowy day, Swede stood on a small platform in front of the entire camp. His fellow POWs sat on the ground in front of him, huddled together to stay warm. The senior Chinese officers sat in comfortable chairs in a large tent. The wall of the tent facing the prisoners was open, but they were all dressed warmly and supplied with tea by their staff.

Swede knew what the Chinese wanted. He had learned from some of the older soldiers that the Chinese used self-confession and public shaming with their own troops. He had played word games with them in Camp 1. If he used the right words and phrases, the Chinese would hear a message of self-criticism. His fellow soldiers would hear something quite different.

"You know why we are all here. Most of you have been through this before. I am here to 'correct my mistakes,' 'to confess my crimes.' *That brought smiles to their faces.* They say I have escaped five times. They say I used a radio to send and receive orders. That I gave orders to stop attending daily lectures. They say I spread rumors.

"I do not deny the basic charges of our captors. I have tried to escape. No, that is wrong. *Oops, frowns.* I did not *try* to escape. I escaped. But then I was captured again. *Their smiles are back.* I have not escaped five times, like the Chinese say. Not quite that many times." Swede grinned. "But I do confess to escaping. And I confess I was never successful. I was never able to outwit our captors, or nature. From those experiences I no longer feel it is possible to escape." *That should make them happy.*

"People sitting in Panmunjom have drawn a line that is hundreds of miles south of here. Escaping this camp is not your biggest problem. Walking those hundreds of miles, through these mountains, through enemy controlled territory, that is your problem. How do you plan to do that? *Satisfied smiles.*

"But it is our duty to escape. If you think you should try, go ahead. If you have a plan and feel duty-bound to try, then you should. *Careful, those smiles just disappeared.*

"But there is more for me to confess. I cannot stand by and see others punished for something they did not do. I have learned from our Chinese teachers that we must accept responsibility for our behaviors. *Yep, they liked that.* I am the one who built the radio that was discovered."

That remark brought complete silence to the assembly. The POWs knew what was happening. Whether or not Swede had built the radio, he was now taking the blame off any others. He was offering himself up to the Chinese. With him standing there, using the phrases they were all supposed to learn, the Chinese would have no choice but to accept his confession. That meant the camp would get regular meals and would be allowed fires in the evening again. To not do so would make the Chinese lose face. Everyone became focused on what Swede would say next. The Chinese more than the Americans. They were happy. Here was a known reactionary, standing in front of the entire camp, and confessing to his crimes! This is what they worked for.

Colonel Li sat with the other camp staff. He knew what his fellow officers were thinking, what they thought they were hearing and seeing. But he was seeing something else. He was seeing a brave man send a message to his fellow Americans.

Swede went on. "I did build a radio. Just like the ones I built when I was younger. Just like the ones you probably built. Right out of Popular Mechanics. So, yes, I confess to building a radio. *Lots of smiles now.* Remember how it worked? A razor, a pencil, some wire. And you know all it can do is receive a signal, and not very well at that. *The Chinese aren't really paying attention now. They are only hearing the words confess and radio. They don't hear me telling every prisoner in the camp how to build a radio of their own.* You can't send messages. But I confess I did build it.

"I can't confess to spreading rumors. I told people what I heard. News about home, news about the war, news about the peace talks. Just news that makes us feel good, that gives us hope. For some reason, our captors don't want us to know these kinds of things, don't want us to have hope. That is a crime they must confess.

"I can't confess to giving orders. I am a private in the US Army. Privates in the US Army don't give orders. I do confess to being glad when we all stopped attending those lectures. No, not glad, proud! *Uh oh, they are listening again. I gotta make this quick.* Proud like the brave soldiers of the Chinese People's Volunteer Army who treat us so fairly in this camp. *That will make them happy again.* Proud because when we stopped attending the lectures, we became soldiers again. Any soldier in any army would feel proud about that. When we stopped attending those lectures we didn't riot, we didn't harm anyone. We accepted the fact we are soldiers, but also that we are prisoners. We didn't attempt to take over the camp. We just stopped doing what we should not have been forced to do in the first place.

"So, I confess to some of what the Chinese call my crimes. *Don't yell for this next part, just keep your tone regular.* Now I call on you to confess your crimes. Start acting like soldiers again. You are prisoners, yes. But you can still be soldiers. Stand up for yourselves. Quit cooperating at the expense of your fellow soldiers. At the expense of your pride.

"Yes, we are prisoners. But even prisoners have rights. Our captors have chosen not to allow us these rights. *I think somebody just signaled the guards to get me out of here.* So now I call on our captors to confess their crimes. They say I have broken the rules. But they break the rules every day. Where is the food, clothing, and shelter prisoners of war are supposed to be given? Where is the medicine we need? Where is our mail? Why are we still sleeping under rags and on the ground?

"But those are questions you will have to ask. I can see the guards are here to take me to my trial." At that point, the guards grabbed Swede's arms, not too roughly in front of the entire camp, and led him away. One by one, the prisoners stood. Soon the entire group was standing. They stood in silence, their respect obvious.

Swede expected some severe consequences because of his confession. After the guards took him away, he was shoved into the back of a truck and sent down the road to camp headquarters. Three days later, he was still waiting for those consequences. His cell wasn't comfortable, but it was just a cell. He was fed twice a day and allowed to empty his bucket every morning. There were other prisoners in other cells. They were all being treated the same. But every time a door opened, or a guard came in the room, Swede expected the bellowing and punching and beatings to begin. What he didn't know was Colonel Li was working hard on his behalf just a few buildings away.

"This prisoner is just a boy. He cannot possibly be a commander of any sort. Yes, he built a radio, and yes, he has escaped. But he publicly confessed to those crimes, just as we constantly ask these prisoners to do. You saw his fellow countrymen stand when he was led away. They respect him for his confession. If we go too far in punishing him, we will lose face. It will be more difficult than ever to get information from any of the prisoners. Why not send him to the penal camp, but not with other Americans. If he is a leader of any kind, he can't do much leading if he has no contact with other Americans. Place him with the British prisoners. They will treat him as a former colonist, as a commoner. He will not have his fellow Americans to keep him company."

A few days later, Swede was called out of his cell. Once again, he found himself in front of a panel of Chinese officers. Once again, he learned he had been found guilty without even having a trial.

"Pole Lawson, you have been tried and found guilty of crimes against the Chinese People's Volunteer Army. You are sentenced to one year in a penal camp."

On the ride north towards Camp 5, Swede thought about his sentence. One year? Even the Chinese thought the war would be over soon, within a few months at the most. Would he be held beyond the end of the war? Would it be in solitary somewhere, maybe in Camp 2-4? Could he last a year doing the kind of labor he and Earl Stoneman had done a year ago? Could he last a year all by himself? Would he be shot 'trying to escape'? All kinds of nasty thoughts ran through his head. He realized he was doing the same thing as when he was first captured. He was letting fear take control. It was time to slow down and think about what needed to be done to improve his situation.

The cold was Swede's first problem. He was going to need more than just the blanket they had tossed at him after he climbed into the back of the truck. The only other thing in the truck was the crate he was sitting on. Looking inside, he found a raggedy coat. It was oil-stained and had a few rips and tears, but most of its cotton padding was still there. Next, he was going to have to keep an eye out for a chance to "borrow" another blanket. To help with that task, Swede wrapped the blanket he did have around himself and donned his new coat over that. His hands were now free to quickly grab anything worth grabbing, and he presented the appearance of someone who needed a blanket. For the second Christmas in a row he was all alone, on his way to a new camp. He could only hope this time he got a better room at the inn.

As the truck bounced and rattled its way north, Swede thought about his last two and a half years. He was fairly sure his parents knew he was a prisoner. No mail had arrived from home, but he knew they would have written. The Chinese decided who got mail and who didn't. Page was confident his message had gotten through to Swede's folks. Worrying about home wasn't going to do him any good. But when he got home, would he be able to hold his head up when his uncles asked about the POW camps? Would they understand about the confessions he had given? Had he done the right things so far? The answer he finally gave himself was yes.

Prince and Rasputin

Winter 1952-53

Improvements had been made to the roads. Still, the truck bounced all the way to Camp 2. After a few hours walk from Two, Swede began to recognize the terrain and then the cottages in the valley of what Earl Stoneman had christened Camp Sunday. One of his guards spent just a few minutes in the main house and returned with two new guards. They escorted Swede further east to the rough road bordering the river and turned north. As they walked along the river, Swede recognized the small valleys where he and Earl had worked. Just beyond was another small valley with the usual assortment of cottages and huts. Here Swede was given plain rice and hot water, his first meal since his meager supper of the night before at Camp 3. He sat on a log in the snow and took his time eating. From the noises and the smells, the guards were having a much better supper of their own. He could also hear American voices coming from the smaller huts.

When they were ready, the guards took Swede up the little valley, away from the river. They followed a path through the snow, the trees closing in around them in the dimming light. The buildings behind them faded from sight. A few minutes later the outline of a single hut appeared. As they approached, Swede could see it resembled a typical Korean hut, except there was a crude fence of saplings and wire surrounding it. A small shack stood at the entrance to the fence. As they approached, Swede realized it was a guardhouse, complete with guard. Following some conversation among the guards, the gate was opened, and Swede motioned inside. His two escorts bid their goodbyes to the guard and headed back down the valley to the warmth of their cottages.

The gate guard unhooked a simple latch and motioned Swede inside the hut with a big grin. "Ding hao. Ding hao." He gave the impression he knew something Swede did not. The hut was dark, just a flicker of light coming from a bucket being used as a stove. Swede could see figures moving around inside but could not make out any features.

"Hi. I'm Paul Larson, just up from Camp 3."

At first, there was no response. Then, surprisingly, a voice with a strong British accent said, "So you're the American bloke who likes to rat on his pals. Your Chinese friends told us you were coming. They won't be of much help to you in here, Yank."

Swede was sure he could hear growling from parts of the room. It looked like the Chinese had arranged for his fellow prisoners do their bellowing and punching and beating. His eyes still hadn't adjusted to the dim light. He knew he couldn't spot even one man coming at him, let alone take on a whole room. He was going to have to talk fast if he wanted to avoid some broken bones, at the very least.

Then a deep voice from the back asked a question. "Did I ever tell you blokes about the time I shared a cell with Rasputin? He was like a ghost. He could walk through the bars from his cell into mine. But when he did, he ate my food and drank my tea. Then he pissed on my leg. Boys, meet Rasputin, in the flesh."

Those remarks brought forth even louder growling. Swede could sense men circling around him in the dark. A large man stuck his face into Swede's. "Ya won't be walkin' through any bloody walls when we get through with ya, Yank. I doubt you'll be able to walk at all!"

Swede hadn't had time to process the voice from the back of the room. Then the voice got louder. "Step back there, boys. I've got something to say to our Commie lovin' Rasputin first." The shadows in front of him parted and a large figure approached, stopping an arm's length away. For a few seconds, the entire hut was silent. Then the large man reached out, grabbed Swede, and gathered him in for an embrace that felt like it would crush his spine.

"Swede! How are you lad? I see you haven't improved your ways. Still refusing to learn the truth, are you? It's good to see you again, son. Come on in and meet the boys. Boys, meet Swede, the American Rasputin. This man saved my life! He's no more a friend of the Commies than you or I."

Then it all began to make sense. "Prince! I don't believe it!" Swede hugged the big man back. His vision had adjusted, and he could see the other men in the hut backing away and staring at him like he was molesting the queen.

"Boys, I told you a Yank had helped me out after I was first captured, but I never told you the whole story. Put a little more kindling on that sad excuse for a stove and let me tell you a tale."

"Except for the few of you who are not Glosters, more's the pity to you, you'll remember Hill 327 in February two years ago. After that battle, the regiment was pulled back to the Imjin. But I went out with my Yank counterpart, their S-2, to see what we could see that might help even the odds. As you might recall, we were a bit out-numbered." That brought some wry chuckles from the group, as just over five hundred of them were captured at the Imjin. Four thousand UN troops had faced twenty-seven thousand Chinese along the Imjin River that April.

"We were able to get a fair picture of what the Chinese had in store for us and were headed back to our lines when the jeep hit a mine. The others were killed, and I was a bit out of sorts when I came to. The Chinese dragged me into a cave until night-time. They must have thought I was worth handing over to their officers. They didn't knock me around, but they didn't do anything for my wounds either. My leg looked nasty. The officers though, that was a different story. One unfriendly fellow spoke English and was convinced I held the clue to the Chinese army sweeping you lot into the sea. When he finally gave up, my fingers were swollen from his boots mashing them and my face had gotten too familiar with his fists. They threw me in the back of a jeep, and I woke up on the cold floor of a jail cell somewhere.

"I could hear a voice but couldn't make out where it was coming from. I finally looked across from the cell and spotted a shadowy figure in a little box. I couldn't hear very well, and my eyes were about swollen shut. Then that figure just crawled right through the bars on his box and came over to my cell. He put his face down to look into my cell and whispered to me. The blanket around his shoulders hid his body. He was just a face with wild eyes and blood and hair. When he walked through the bars of my cell, I was convinced I was in a loony bin with Rasputin!"

The men in the hut were oblivious to the cold and discomfort as they listened to the story. They knew nobody could walk through the bars of a cell, yet there was something about this story that had the ring of truth, something about this story that told them it had special meaning to their sergeant.

Colour Sergeant Anthony Tomkins was a fifteen-year veteran of the British Army. He had been with the Gloucestershire Regiment, the Glosters, since Dunkirk and had fought in Burma. The mission was first in Colour Sergeant Tomkins' world, and his men were next. And they loved him for it. They had been at Camp 1 when he was finally released into the main camp. The fact he was assumed to be dead only added to his reputation. And now this 'Rasputin' was part of that reputation.

"Rasputin tried to feed me the rice the guards had left when they tossed me into the cell. My jaw was too swollen for me to chew. When he realized the problem, he picked the half-frozen rice from the bowl, popped it into his mouth, and started chewing. I thought he was stealing my food! Once he had it all mushed about, he dribbled it into my mouth a little at a time so I could swallow it down. Then he did the same with the frozen tea.

"Next, he took the blanket from his shoulders and tucked it around me like a mother with her babe. Then he checked my wounds. He told me he was going to have to clean up my leg or it was going to get infected. He didn't explain just how he was going to clean it! Tell the boys how you cleaned my leg, Rasputin."

"Why Prince, I pissed on it, of course," replied Swede, grinning the whole time. "It wasn't like I had any water to boil, or anything to boil it in, or any fire to boil it with. And that wound was full of dirt."

The men in the hut weren't quite sure how they should react to that statement. Laughter came to mind for some, but this was their colour sergeant, their "Tom." Laughter might not be appropriate at the moment. And who was Prince in this story?

The problem was solved when their colour sergeant burst into a loud guffaw. "That's right. He bloody well pulled out his trouser snake and pissed on me. And you should thank the good Lord he did. I tell you, boys, without this man's help that night and many days and nights after, I wouldn't be sharing these glorious accommodations with you today."

Over the next week, some of the troopers got the story from Swede as to why he called their Tom by the name of Prince. He had never seen a British uniform before, let alone a British soldier. Above the stripes on the arm was a little crown. Swede told them he just assumed their Tom was some kind of royalty, like a prince or something. So, Prince it was. Given what he had done, the men were more than willing to ignore military protocol and allow the familiarity. A few days later the myth of Rasputin was set in stone when Scout Sergeant Tomkins told of another event.

"It was late one night, not long before they released us to the main camp. The fat guard, Harry, came in drunker than I had seen him before. He staggered around and yelled at me for a bit, then went to jabbing at me with a pole. I couldn't move very well, so, as drunk as he was, his jabs were still hitting home. Then he opened my cell door and started aiming for my head. I saw a shadow come out of Rasputin's little box and come up behind the guard. Rasputin grabbed that unkempt man by the seat of his pants and the back of his jacket and slammed his head into the bars of my cell. Twice. I thought the noise alone would wake the entire camp. That guard dropped like a stone. Rasputin dragged him out of my cell and into the outer office. Then he came back, locked my cell, and disappeared back into his box. He told me later he made it look like the guard had tripped when he came in the building and knocked himself out before he even got to our cell block. There was no ruckus when they found him in the morning, snoring away. I don't know that I would have survived that encounter had Rasputin not stepped in."

Conditions in the hut were a bit grim. They weren't packed in wall to wall, but it was crowded. They were only being fed once a day and poorly at that. The Brits told him their stove had been replaced by a small bucket. They were given a small amount of charcoal each day and no more, no matter the temperature. They weren't in a Korean home with its in-floor heating system, but just a storage shed of some kind. One room and a dirt floor. Each man had one blanket. As cold as it was, the circumstances reminded Swede a little too much of the first winter.

Prince said the camp commander, Colonel Zhao, was not a happy man. His prisoners paid a price for that unhappiness. He was easily upset and quick to replace their two daily meals of rice with sorghum, sometimes making it only one meal a day. When he was in a nasty mood, he reduced their charcoal rations, forcing the men to shave kindling from boards on the walls. Everyone in the hut was a hard-core reactionary. Even the recent request they sign a birthday greeting for General Peng, commander of the Chinese People's Volunteer Army, was met with silence. But now two men in the hut were starting to show signs of malnutrition. Corporal Blake, a medic, said he was beginning to worry about his two patients.

"If conditions don't improve, or if we can't get them some vitamins, these two are in big trouble. And others could follow. But every time I ask to have a doctor see them, the guard says, 'Him no sick, him lazy.' It seems to be their automatic response to the word 'doctor'. I'm pretty sure they have medicine and maybe even food in that shed down near the guard quarters. In the hut I was in before they put me up here, we had a sick trooper. I saw the camp doctor take a guard to that shed. When the guard came back, he gave us some pills he said were APCs. Our guy got better."

"Can we get in that shed," asked Prince.

"It's locked and close to the guard huts," answered Blake. "I don't see how."

"Are you sure these men need those vitamins?" asked Prince.

"Either better food or a heavy dose of vitamins," responded Blake.

Prince looked over at Swede. "So, Rasputin, can you still walk through walls?"

"If we can get to the building, I can get in. But we have to get there, get in, get the vitamins, and back again, without the Chinese knowing. Other than that, no problem." Swede wasn't grinning when he answered.

Over the next few days, a few suggestions were made, tossed around, and discarded. The main obstacles were the guard outside their hut and the snow that would show tracks. Swede thought back to his first adventures outside his cell at Camp 1. He had waited for a snowstorm only to realize there were tracks all over. Nobody would ever be able to see the ones he made. But this was different. To hide his tracks among all the others meant he would have to walk out the door and past the guard. The chances of a sleeping guard were slim. A sleeping guard on the way out *and* on the return to the hut was too much to expect. The solution came to him when he heard Blake complain that sleeping on the dirt floor wasn't helping the situation. Swede took a good look at both the floor and the walls of the hut.

"We can make a door in the back wall. We just need to find

something hard with a pointy end."

There was some rustling around in the corner. The large man who had threatened Swede when the Chinese first brought him into the hut spoke up. "Are these hard and pointy enough?" Corporal Owen Thorpe had been with the SAS during World War II. A leg injury at the end got him sent to the regulars. Once he realized the Glosters were higher up on the ladder than most regulars, he settled in and adapted to a lesser level of excitement than he was used to. But he continued to look at problems differently than most soldiers. When he found some old nails buried in the dirt floor that were making sleep difficult, he didn't just chuck them away, he put them in his pockets. You never knew when something like a sharp nail might come in handy.

"Perfect," answered Swede. "Now let me ask a question. What do the walls look like on the outside of this building?"

Thorpe gave Swede a strange look but decided to humor the lad. "The boards run vertical, not horizontal. From the inside, it looks like each board runs from roof to ground, but each board is actually two. They meet halfway down, right here on this small beam." Thorpe pointed to a beam that ran from corner post to corner post on each wall.

"But how do we cut a door with these nails," he asked.

"We don't cut a door. We don't have any saws, and it would be too noisy if we did. We dig our way out."

"We dig a hole, not cut a door? With these nails?" Thorpe was beginning to think maybe this Yank wasn't so bright after all.

"Let me show you." Swede moved to the back wall. He pointed to the tips of nails showing on the inside of the beam. "We dig around these nails to loosen them so we can push the boards out. We should only need to work on two boards. We leave the nails in the boards and widen the nail holes in the beam just a little. When we are ready to leave, we just push the boards away, crawl out, replace the boards, and be on our way. I just need to come up with a way to pull the boards back on when we get back inside. We go out during a snowstorm at night. The storm will cover our tracks."

Thorpe slapped Swede on the back. "For a youngster, you have a devious mind. I like that."

It only took a couple of days to loosen the nails to where they could push the boards away from the wall and crawl out. Only one man could work on the boards at a time. The effort required to constantly scratch away with a nail kept the man working warm, so there was no shortage of volunteers. The wood on the bottom was so rotted they didn't need to work on the nails there at all. They waited until dark to see if their secret door was going to work. Swede carefully pushed the boards away from the wall, not enough to crawl out, but just to be sure they could remove the boards and then replace them again. A good kick, even less, would dislodge them, but the guards seldom came into the hut. The fence outside connected to the hut at each back corner instead of circling it completely. Their door opened directly to the forest. The next step was to wait for a heavy enough snowfall at night. There had to be enough snow to cover their tracks near the storage shed, and on the way back to their hut. A snowstorm hit four days later.

After their evening meal of sorghum and tea, both delivered cold, Prince sat with Swede and Owen. "This looks like it will last well into the night. Do you two want to try your little scheme tonight?" Swede and Owen looked at each other and nodded. They had already decided to go.

Using the little spy hole, they waited until they figured the guard was asleep in his shack. Two blankets had been slit in the middle to create a poncho for each man. The boards were removed and the two crawled out. With whispered 'good lucks' from their friends, they headed into the trees and moved east down their little valley.

Owen Thorpe had decided he should take the lead. He doubted a young American could make his way through the woods better than someone with an SAS background. He didn't want to take so long the storm might end before they could make it back and have their tracks visible, but he wasn't about to go running through the woods either. The forest was thick with bare-limbed deciduous trees and large pines scattered about. It was very dark, so they would only be spotted if the Chinese had a guard posted in the middle of the trees. And they were sure that was not the case.

It was one of those snowfalls with large flakes gently floating down. There was almost no breeze. It was a cold night, but they had prepared with extra wraps around their legs, wool ponchos, and rags wrapped around their hands. The two men kept ten feet between them and moved slowly, pausing to look and listen. The tree trunks came at them as blurry shadows as they worked their way through the woods. All they had to do was keep the upslope of the hill to their left and the downslope to the right. That kept them moving east towards the path that followed the river. The guard huts and the storage shed were on the west, or near, side of that path. Once they could see the outlines of some buildings, they crawled under the overhanging branches of a large evergreen and took the time to watch for a while. There was no movement around the cottages and huts that made up the camp, just the smell of wood smoke. A few of the huts held fellow POWs, but this was not the time to visit. It would be a couple of hours before an unlucky replacement would trudge up the hill to relieve their gate guard. They had to be back before then.

When they were ready, they moved back into the woods and then towards the river and the storage shed. Dark as it was, they could see vague outlines of the huts. When they neared the path, Swede tugged Owen down behind a tree.

"We should go out to the path along the river and then follow it back to the huts. Any tracks we make will blend in with those already there. If we go at the shed from the woods, we might leave noticeable lines in the snow, even if they fill in."

Owen nodded in agreement, again impressed that this kid would think of that. They walked in a slow crouch as they approached the shed. The door faced the guard huts and, even in the dark, they still might be spotted by anyone looking that way. Swede tugged Owen down again and continued to the shed door on his hands and knees. When they reached the door Swede simply sat back against it and watched the camp for a few minutes. He reached into his pocket for something and turned to the door. Owen wasn't sure, but thought the kid might have lock picks. It didn't take long before the door swung in. Owen followed the kid in and pushed the door closed.

"Damn. I forgot it was gonna' be so hard to see what we are lookin' for," whispered Swede. Just then a match flared. Swede had to close his eyes against the sudden brightness.

"Aren't ya glad I came along?" asked Owen, holding up a book of matches. "Let's see what kind of treats we can find." Using one match at a time, remembering to put the used matches back in a pocket, the two men found stacks of C-rations, first aid kits, blankets, and a pile of boxes of different sizes. Using a fresh match, Swede looked carefully at the boxes.

"This is mail from home! These are all addressed to different guys. Probably guys right in this camp somewhere. Those bastards! I'll bet there are all kinds of things in these boxes we need, and they keep it all piled up in here." He was getting a little loud at the end.

"Shhh. Let's not wake up our friends out there." Owen could hear the anger in Swede's voice. "Now is not the time to get off track. We need to decide what to bring back and get out of here."

Each man took a blanket and wrapped it around a carton of c-rations and a handful of vitamin and APC packets they removed from first aid kits they found. They could only carry so much and didn't want to make it obvious they had been there. At the last minute, Swede threw a small box from the mail pile onto his blanket. Using cloth bandages from the first aid kits, they tied the ends of their bundles and threw them over their shoulders. When both were ready, Owen cracked the door a bit to peek out. Crawling again, they moved outside. Swede reached back and swept out any snow they had tracked in. Then he clicked the lock back in place.

They returned to their hut by following the furrows they had left in the snow on the way down. This created four tracks in the snow. They figured one track in the snow would attract attention, but four tracks spaced ten feet apart would be taken for drifting or maybe animals of some kind. The tracks they had left on the way down were almost gone, so it didn't look like any signs of their movement in the area would be left. When they reached their hut, they quietly brushed the snow off each other and crawled through.

"Corporal Blake, you take charge of all the goodies. See to it our two patients get as much good stuff as they can handle, but go slow for a few days. We don't want to send them into shock. Most of this goes to them and any others you think are borderline. We'll take one can of meat for the rest of us and mix it in with whatever gourmet delight they bring up this morning. But only one.

"We can wrap the vitamins and APCs in a rag and bury them in the corner. For now, cover everything else with a blanket. Until we use all the foodstuffs up, we will bury it in the snow during the day and bring it in at night. We can't chance a surprise inspection by the guards. But they won't bother us at night. The cardboard we burn for heat. We can use lids from the containers for cutting and the cans themselves we can melt snow in for drinking or catch rain later in the spring. Everybody be smart. If our keepers catch on, we'll all be down the loo." Prince looked around at the group. "And now Rasputin has a present for us to unwrap."

Swede and Corporal Thorpe had given the group a detailed report on their mission down to the main camp. Prince thought it best for everybody to know as much as possible about the layout of the camp. Swede showed them the package he had grabbed in the shack before coming back. He explained about the crate he had spotted on the barge headed north from Camp 5 in the fall.

"Given what I saw in that crate on the barge and what they have down in that shed, I'm pretty well convinced the Chinese are getting a lot more mail for us than they are handing out. This box is from a Mrs. Thomas Webster in Biloxi, Mississippi, to a Private George Webster, POW Camp 5, The Democratic People's Republic of Korea, care of Chinese People's Committee for Peace, Peking, China. Wow, that's quite an address.

"I had a pal who refused to write home," offered Stanley Wilson. "We had to include 'Against Yankee Aggression' on the return address. He said he didn't have any great love for the Yanks, but he wasn't going to play Chink games."

"How often you are allowed to write home and how many letters they deliver to you depend on how well your attitude is adjusted," explained Prince. "How many letters have you been able to send home, Rasputin?"

"Three," grumbled Swede. "And I haven't gotten any back yet."

"That is because you are too impurdinint," laughed Prince. "You must learn the truth!" In a more somber tone he added, "Don't you worry. The folks back home are writing. Our warden friends here just aren't delivering. Maybe we will just have to deliver our own mail.

"Now open up Private Webster's package and see what he has to share with us!"

Mrs. Webster had sent what any mother would send to a son who was a prisoner of war; woolen socks, mittens, and scarf, some Hershey bars, Juicy Fruit gum, Geritol vitamins, a packet of cocoa mix, and a can of Spam. For years, the men in that hut would fondly remember Mrs. Thomas Webster from Biloxi, Mississippi.

Charlie

Some days his head was clear, but usually there was a fog over his brain. Lately that fog was not as thick, but still there. When he felt a dark buzzing cloud begin to settle into his head, he knew it was going to be a bad day. The darker the cloud, the louder the buzzing, and the lower into his head it fell, the more painful the experience. Then it hurt to interact with the world outside his head. Sometimes it was painful simply to open his eyes.

He didn't know why this happened. His oldest real memory was of stumbling alongside a bunch of soldiers. His head hurt, his neck hurt, and he couldn't talk. It was only by listening to those around him he came to understand he was in the Army, there was a war somewhere, and they were all prisoners. He remembered nothing before that, not even his own name. He could hear through the buzzing in his head and knew the people around him called him Charlie. Eventually, he realized the uniform he had on said Charlie. For some reason, he knew that was not right, but could not come up with whatever it might be. So, Charlie he was.

He did have flashes of memories. Often they were violent. Confusion, explosions, screams, blood everywhere. He was dressed in white and covered in blood. Sometimes he was running, sometimes he was holding someone else. A person he knew but didn't. With these memories came an overwhelming sense of guilt that remained after the fog lifted. The only way he found to deal with the violent memories was to worry about people around him. When he focused on someone else's needs, the violent flashes stayed away.

His memories became a little clearer. He still didn't know his name. There had been a battle of some kind. Men had been in his care. Explosions came and they were dead. A person or persons hurt him. Next, he was in a line of men. They tried to talk with him, but he couldn't understand what they were saying and couldn't tell them that. He simply couldn't talk. His head and throat hurt, especially when he tried to talk. There were more lines of men. Some kept stumbling, so he helped them. Sometimes they died. More lines of men. One of them seemed to understand him. It became important to help that man. They stopped walking, but it was very cold, and he was constantly hungry. More men died. When people around him died, the pain in his head got worse. They walked some more and lots more died. Then a place where fewer and fewer died. It got warm and soon no more died. The violence in his head faded. Certain things brought it back, but he couldn't figure out why. The fog and noise would start and his world hurt for a while.

One day Charlie realized things were beginning to make sense. He was an American soldier in a prison camp run by the Chinese. He understood what it meant to be an American but had no specific memories from before that battle. He could read on the few opportunities he had something to read. He could write. He could understand everything his fellow prisoners said. But if it referred to anything before the battle, it simply had no meaning. He understood they were talking about food or family or a movie, but they weren't real concepts to him. He knew he probably had this thing called family but didn't know what that meant. He knew he had been to a thing called movie but didn't understand what that meant. He came to accept his strange reality rather than fight it.

Mike Randall became his anchor. Mike seemed to understand what he was going through and helped him calm down when the violence got into his head. Another much younger man had shown him a respect he didn't fully understand but welcomed. He helped that man fool the guards and escape. His voice gradually came back, but only at a bare whisper. Even that hurt if he tried to say too much. Life developed a certain normalcy for him, if normal meant existing only in a prisoner of war camp with nothing from the past to compare it to.

Once there were only a few men who needed constant attention, Charlie's focus turned to the Chinese. He assumed they were responsible for the pain in his head and the deaths of so many fellow prisoners in the first months. He also clearly saw what they were trying to do to those still alive. They wanted to turn the prisoners against everything they had been taught. Tell lies about your friends. Accuse them of stealing food or saying bad things about the Chinese. Write letters full of lies. Renounce your values as a soldier and an

American. Working against the Chinese became his new crutch. When he focused on battling with them, his head stayed clear.

It wasn't long before that focus got Charlie in trouble. He couldn't personally speak out against the Chinese in group meetings, but he could whisper to individuals. And he did a lot of whispering. He even started whispering to those he knew to be Progressives. That eventually lead to an invitation to join some others who were not living up to the spirit of cooperation the Chinese desired. They had all earned a truck ride from Camp 1 to Camp 3.

Charlie arrived in Camp 3 South in late September 1952 to find a few men who had been on the march with him in the beginning. He remembered the day Swede and Ray Parker had joined their column. They weren't so much captured as swallowed up. Charlie was with Ray when he died at Camp 1 after surviving Bean Camp and the march to Camp 1. Henry Page was also at Camp 3. Charlie learned from Page there were two places called Camp 3. They were at South and there was another called North. Page also filled him in on what had happened to Swede since he left Camp 1 in August. His arrival meant he was in time to help with the creation of posters for the October parade. Charlie took great pride in his creation of a smiling Mao Tse-tung with the slogan "Up Mao." He especially liked the olive branches he drew on Mao's tunic pocket.

It was while working on the posters that Swede told him about Red Sedlinski. Red had agreed to keep posing as a Progressive while gathering information on what the Progressives and the Chinese were up to. Charlie had seen more than a few prisoners, mostly younger guys, get caught up in the Chinese system of indoctrination. One man in each hut became responsible for walking up to the interrogator's huts in the morning and bringing back the article or question of the day. The men in the hut usually made that same man write out responses which got them their food quota for the day. The interrogators would often have some candy or cigarettes for the go-betweens when they dropped off the day's responses. They would pretend to be friends and ask seemingly innocent questions about other prisoners. Pretty soon the men forced by their hut to take up the job of go-between were seen as Progressives by the same men who had so readily forced them into the position in the first place. Red was a perfect example. But he realized what had happened and wanted out. Charlie understood he was to cover for Red if Swede could not.

When Charlie heard about the plan to spread the word to all camps to quit attending lectures in the spring, he found a new cause. Nobody paid a lot of attention to him. The Chinese were a little afraid of him. They thought he was crazy and stayed away until he did something that brought attention to his Reactionary ways. He could only talk to his fellow POWs one at a time, and then for only short conversations in a harsh whisper. With this latest cause, he focused his attention on two groups. He spread the word about the spring plan to as many POWs as he felt could be trusted. *Here's the plan. Get on board. Spread the word.* When Red told him about a Progressive who was having doubts about his behavior, Charlie would approach him with a different message. *Why are you so willing to cooperate with the enemy? Have you taken a good look at what you are doing? Are you really willing to give up the values you grew up with? Would your family approve?* The shock of hearing logic from the camp crazy was often enough to bring them back into the fold.

When Swede was sent to a penal camp at the beginning of the new year, Charlie grew closer to Page. He kept Page current on whatever news he was able to pick up. Once Page realized how the Chinese ignored him, he began asking Charlie to look and listen for specific information. Were there Russians around, were there hidden camps anywhere, what was happening at Panmunjom, were they keeping an eye on any particular prisoners? Charlie enjoyed playing the game. There was a certain sense of professional accomplishment. The more he concentrated on fooling the Chinese, the less his head hurt. The less his head hurt, the better he was at fooling the Chinese. Whenever it seemed like someone was getting suspicious, he became Crazy Charlie and wandered away. Since Crazy Charlie couldn't talk, many people assumed he couldn't hear either. Many Progressives, and even a few Chinese interrogators, gave Charlie plenty of information he then passed on to Page. And then there was the Charlie only a select few people saw. They were the prisoners put in the hole for more than a day or two. There was never anything crazy about him as he slipped them a blanket or some needed food.

Charlie had fully understood what was happening as he watched Swede's confession about the radio. The whole production was masterful. Swede tossed the Chinese a couple of bones. He used all the correct phrases to announce his guilt in front of the entire camp. He told his fellow POWs he didn't think they could escape. But then he went on to say if you think you can escape, give it a shot. He confessed to building a radio. Then, while the Chinese were basking in that little victory, he told everyone how they could build their own. He talked about his faults, then mentioned the obvious faults of the Chinese. Knowing he was about to be hustled out of sight, maybe to be shot, he challenged everyone to take pride in being an American soldier once again. Masterful! Charlie fully intended to use parts of that speech in his little whispers with Progressives. *You heard Swede say he was proud of what he has done. What about you? Are you proud of what you have done? Would your family be proud?* Oh yes, between himself and Red Sedlinski, people would be hearing about that speech for quite some time.

Camp 2-3

Winter-Spring 1953

"You know you have to go back to that storage shed, right?" Prince and Swede were sharing blankets trying to stay warm. Their hut was still low on Colonel Zhao's list. Food and heat were equally minimal. "What you and Owen brought back gave us all a boost. But McAndrews and Moore aren't out of the woods yet." With a chuckle, he added, "So the two of you need to go back into the woods."

"I won't argue with you, Prince. We've been hoping for another snowstorm. This time we plan to bring back some firewood as well. Now that we know the lay of the land, maybe we can find a way to get down to that shed without needing a storm to cover our tracks. I've seen deer in the woods when we were out on firewood detail. Maybe we can find some of their trails to use. But I think we need to wait for one more storm before we go again."

While they waited, Corporal Thorpe decided they could stay warm and drive away the boredom by practicing self-defense techniques he knew from his days in the SAS. He explained it to Swede as "a bit like your Rangers in the last war, but better." There was no room in their hut to throw people around, so the training was limited to simple hand to hand techniques. A few participated, most were content to watch.

At one point, Private William Sharkey, a tough Liverpool lad, made it obvious he considered a good right hand to the jaw to be better than what Thorpe was offering. "There are many that agree with you, Billy. But I am not one of them. Come up here and demonstrate what you mean."

William Sharkey didn't like to be called Billy, and Owen Thorpe knew it. He also knew Sharkey would be mad and throw a real punch, exactly what he wanted to happen. Before he was fully upright from his seat on the ground, Sharkey launched his right, a perfect uppercut headed directly for Thorpe's chin. Owen slipped to his left and misdirected the blow, which positioned him behind Sharkey. Without hesitation, he slammed the edge of his hand to the base of Sharkey's neck, who simply dropped to the floor, out for the count.

After gently slapping Sharkey's face to bring him around, Owen helped the man up and dusted him off. "Well done, William. In most cases you would lay a man out with that punch. But what I am trying to demonstrate is that, with some training, you can win most any encounter with another, whether he is armed or not. All right then, who's next?" He spent the next hour teaching simple pokes and jabs that help disarm a man at the least; and render him completely unconscious at the best. Twice-a-day lessons soon had a few of his students showing real promise. "Not quite ready for selection into the SAS mind you, but I might put in a good word or two if you want to have a go."

The snowstorm came soon enough. Swede and Owen donned their cold weather wraps and slid out their back door. They followed the same route down to the storage shed until they got near the road. Swede crouched near a large pine and motioned Owen down. "Let's look for a deer trail of some kind. We can brush snow on our tracks when we go back, and the deer will walk over the whole thing again. Less chance somebody might notice. A simple pine branch will cover our tracks on the path as we head down to the shed."

It wasn't long before they found what they needed and headed to the main camp and the storage shed. When they got within fifty feet of their target, both men stopped to look and listen. When they moved again, Swede was in front and took only a few steps at a time. There was no moon and the snowfall was heavy, but caution was necessary here. They still didn't have a good idea of how the area was guarded at night. As Swede rounded the corner to get to the door, he was surprised by a grunt and a shadowy figure rising in front of him. A guard had been sitting in front of the door! Without even thinking, Swede smashed his hand into the side of the man's neck, just as they had been practicing. The man dropped before Owen could reach him with a follow up blow.

"Get the door!" he whispered, as he grabbed the man under the arms. Swede was quick to get the lock open and they dragged the man inside, closing the door over behind them. "Take his rifle. If he starts to come to, bash him on the head." While Swede covered the guard, Owen grabbed what he thought they needed. Then he began grabbing random packages, shaking them before he opened a few.

"What are you looking for?" Swede asked in a whisper. Owen seemed to have a reason for only opening some of the packages.

"Booze," came the reply. "Mothers might not send alcohol, but wives or girlfriends will. Killing this guard is the last thing we want to do." Finally, Owen held up a small bottle of liquor in triumph. "Eureka! Now here is what we do. This man must have broken in here and gotten at some of the special goodies. They find him in here in the morning, smelling like a brewery, with an empty bottle of America's finest, and some chocolates thrown around for good measure, and our friend is in trouble. Sure, he'll tell about being jumped by somebody in the dark, but if we cover our tracks, they won't believe him. If we are lucky, he didn't have time to figure out what was happening before you put him down. Young Mr. Sharkey might be a believer yet after we tell him this story. Now pour some of that down his throat. Don't worry about spilling it. We want it all over him.

"Even if he wakes up before they find him, there's a chance he will decide to cover everything up rather than admit he was goofing off on duty. Either way, we might get away with it."

When they were ready, the two slipped out the door, leaving it ajar, and headed back up the path with their supplies. Swede motioned Owen on while he grabbed a large pine branch and moved back to the shed. Then he walked backward while sweeping out their tracks. The heavy snowfall quickly covered the marks left by the branch. When they reached the large pine close to the path where their deer trail came out of the woods, Swede continued sweeping. He kept that up into the woods for fifty feet before tossing the branch aside.

"I don't think any tracks will show up even ten minutes from now, let alone in the morning. Lead on, Macduff."

"It's 'lay on,' but at least you're familiar with the Bard. Now follow me, Yank."

In case there was a surprise inspection over the next few days, they buried the supplies in the snow in the woods. Swede or Owen went out at night to get what they would eat up before morning. They also brought in some wood for their miserable little stove. It was obvious they couldn't go back down to the shed for a while.

"I think we should send two people down every night for a week. They stay hidden and watch to see if the Chinese are trying to catch any mysterious thieves. They can get a better idea of guards around the camp. But I don't think getting too close is a good idea for a while. Meanwhile, I would like to go over to 2-4 to see what's happening. There might be some guys there that could use some vitamins. Even a friendly voice would be good for them. What do you think?"

Swede was asking Prince. Getting back over to 2-4 had been on his mind since he arrived at 2-3. Was Dave Williams the pilot still there? He had explained about seeing the camp with Earl and again with Bobby Hanley. But he wasn't going without permission. For the first time since he had left Mike Randall at Camp 1, Swede felt he needed a superior's OK before he went on any adventure.

"If Corporal Thorpe here will volunteer to go with you, I think a look-see would be a good idea. Will you need a snowstorm before you go?"

"What do you think, Corporal Thorpe, do we need a storm to cover our tracks?" Swede looked at Owen. Swede had no doubt Owen would go with him.

"We should wait for a dark night, but I don't think we need to wait for snow. If we get some, that would be sugar in our tea. We can just sit back and watch without getting too near the camp. Let's wait a day or two and see what happens."

There was some light snow off and on over the next few days, but nothing big enough to cover their movements. On the fourth night they set out. A few other men had asked about going out with them, but the consensus was to keep the number down until they got a better idea of the terrain and the layout of 2-4. Volunteers could get out of the hut and feel like they were contributing again by going down to watch the guards in the main camp.

Swede took the lead on this trip. He had an idea of the area from his previous visits. They covered their tracks as best they could twenty feet back from the hut. From there on, it didn't matter. There had never been any sign of guards patrolling through the woods. They moved as quickly as they could without getting all sweated up, pausing just before the crest of each little hill. Hiding their movements, they took the time to see what was on the other side before moving on. Swede was sure all buildings at 2-4 were in just one small valley. He was also sure it was less than a mile north of 2-3.

They smelled the camp before they saw it. Wood smoke rose from simple chimneys on three of the larger structures to their right as they looked down into the valley. There was more to the camp than Swede had noticed before. He could see the three small huts enclosed by the crude brush fence where he had talked with Dave Williams. Closer to where he and Owen crouched, on their side of the hill, were two more huts. Each had its own fence. Swede knew there were more huts farther down the valley, as he and Earl had seen them when they hauled firewood past the valley a year ago.

They sat and watched the little valley until Swede was shivering from the cold. Then they moved down the hill toward the nearest of the two solitary huts. Each of them had a handful of vitamin pills and a chocolate bar wrapped in a rag. The thinking as they prepared for their little reconnaissance was that any prisoner isolated from the others would be easier to approach and most in need of some food.

As with their own hut, the forest came right up to the back of the first hut. They approached from tree trunk to tree trunk until they were behind the hut. The fence and the hut itself shielded them from anyone looking up the hill. It had been decided Swede would try to make the actual contact with anyone inside since they would most likely be American. A British accent might confuse them. Swede tossed a few small sticks against the wall of the hut. After his third toss he got a reaction.

"Who's there?"

"We only talked to one man, Norman Brunnel. He says there might be fifty POWs held there altogether. Mostly aircrew, most of them pilots. He was shot down three weeks ago and spent a few days at what sounds like Camp 5, then a couple more days at Camp 2. He's been up here for two weeks. Norm says he's been in the little hut we found him in the whole time but gets messages snuck in from the other huts. The Chinese want to know how the new F-86 turns so much better than the earlier models. So far, he has them convinced he was flying a C model, he was shot down on his first flight, and he wasn't carrying any bombs. There are two more new guys in the other two huts near him. They haven't been feeding him much, so he was really happy to get our little CARE packages. He said he would try to get some of the stuff to the other two huts. We told him we would be back within a week if we could. He also said there is more talk at home about the war being over in a few months."

Owen snorted. "Don't get your hopes up yet. We've been hearin' that same rumor for at least a year now."

"What's the terrain like between here and there?" asked Prince. "Is it safe to go back?"

"There are two hills after we cross over our ridge here. The camp is on the far side of the second ridge." Owen Thorpe waved his hand in the direction of the camp. "The ridges are heavily wooded but the valley less so. We didn't see any human tracks between here and there. We'll have to check, but unless they have a manned post to watch over the valley, there's no problem going back and forth. We can't stroll along like we're on a picnic outing, but we mind our manners and Bob's your uncle."

Swede looked at Owen with a bit of a grin on his face. "I think I agree with my uncle Bob."

Prince smiled as he watched the other two men. Owen Thorpe wasn't the most open of people, so it was interesting to watch the two interact. Even with their obvious differences, they got along well. The other men in the hut were no wallflowers, but Owen and Swede seemed able to ignore altogether the fact they were prisoners of war in a cold, uncomfortable hut somewhere in North Korea.

"I sent two of the boys down to watch our camp here. They say it doesn't look like the Chinese are guarding the storage hut. Instead, they are keeping an eye on the prisoner huts. Two guards patrol each hut. They change off every hour. So, my question is this. Do you think you can get in and out of the storage hut without getting spotted? Or should we not chance it anymore?"

Swede and Owen looked at each other. "We can't let all that food and medicine just sit there," answered Owen. "We should be able to get in, gather up a good haul, and leave the place looking like we were never there. Then we lay off for a while. We only give the goodies to our sick and anybody in an isolation hut either here or up in the camp north of us. Camp 2-4 you call it, Swede?"

"That's the designation we gave it at 3 North when we realized there seemed to be four small camps out here in the direction of

Camp 2. And Corporal Thorpe is right. We can't just ignore all those supplies. Boxes are just kind of thrown in there, so if we are careful, nobody will be able to tell anything is missing. Winter shouldn't last much longer. We just need to get a few guys through some rough spots until then. Maybe we'll get lucky and the war will be over tomorrow. But right now, I need to wrap up in a blanket. I'm cold."

Once Swede was curled up on the ground in a blanket Prince looked over at Owen Thorpe. "Is he OK?"

"He wasn't his normal self out there last night. Maybe we are pushing a little too hard. We can wait a day before we head down to the storage hut."

But waiting a day wasn't going to help. Swede was sicker than any of them knew.

He was just floating, floating along, looking up at a dull gray sky through a twisted web of bare tree branches. *Am I dead? Is this what it's like? I can't feel my body. I don't hear a sound. Is this my soul? Is that all that's left? If I'm dead, why didn't my life flash before my eyes. I don't like that sky. Where am I going? On my way to Purgatory or Valhalla I guess, depending on whether Mom or Grandpa is right. I don't even feel sad. Is this how it...*

My Lime Green Harley
Spring 1953

Reality came back slowly. He felt hot and then he was out again. He felt cold and was out again. Eventually, he felt hungry and became aware of voices around him. It felt like he was in a bed, but that didn't make any sense. He hadn't been in a bed since Japan. Corporal Blake's face hovered over his as he asked how Swede felt. There was real concern in his eyes.

"Welcome back, Yank. Are you ready to start pulling your weight around here now? You made me work there for a while. But I think you'll be okay. Take another sip of my special soup." It wasn't exactly soup, but it was hot and had some definite flavor to it. Then Swede was out again.

When he woke, Swede realized he wasn't in their hut anymore. He was in a room with real walls and a wooden floor. Owen Thorpe was there watching Swede looking around in confusion. "We've been upgraded. The camp commander decided to move us into this house, probably because peace talks seem to be on again. We're about fifty yards up the valley from our old accommodations. A definite improvement. You even got a bed."

Still not fully coherent, all Swede could do was whisper, "I floated. I was dead."

Owen looked at him with concern, then he understood and laughed. "So you did. It was rather a grand procession. The boys hoisted you up like royalty when we moved up here. They were enjoying the day so much you're lucky they didn't drop you. But you weren't dead. Blake says you had a nasty fever. He did wonders mashing up some of the vitamins we borrowed from the shed and feeding it to you in tea. He did the same with some of the food. I wanted to feed you some APCs, but Blake said you were probably having a malaria relapse. Looks like he won that argument. We are in a real house now, with a real stove. Some of the boys think you might be a lucky charm. Do you think you can get sick again to see if things improve even more?" With a grin, he winked at Swede.

Prince filled in the details. The camp commander, Colonel Zhao, had decided the group had been punished enough, although nobody was sure what they had been punished for. He had them moved into a nearby abandoned house. It had real doors and windows, an actual porch front and back, but was otherwise completely bare. Best of all, it had a real stove located in what the boys called the parlour. They were allowed to collect firewood every day. Meals were back to twice a day with a snack for lunch, either a handful of peanuts or a fist-sized loaf of bread for each man. Food was delivered from the main camp. That meant they had communication again with the POWs down there. Messages hidden in the bottom of the food buckets said the peace talks were going well. There was even supposed to be an exchange of sick and injured prisoners soon.

Swede chuckled when he heard that. Prince looked at him with a puzzled look on his face. "What?"

"Do you see any injured around here? When was the last time you saw an injured man? They all died two winters ago." There was a hardness to Swede's voice.

"You have a point. But we did have some men at Camp 1 that had toes or even feet amputated and survived that winter. Hopefully, they have made it this far and will be sent out soon. I'm quite sure that is the reason for all this." Prince waved his hand around the room. "They are fattening up the sacrificial lamb. They want us to look good when our turn comes."

He went on to explain what they had been up to since Swede got sick. He had sent people out to continue scouting both locations, Camp 2-4 and the storage shed down at the main camp. They had solid knowledge of the guard routine down at the main camp and around the storage shed. They knew the layout of camp 2-4. It was more complicated than they thought. There were a hundred and fifty POWs in larger huts close to the path and the stream.

The huts where Norman Brunnel was held were the most concerning. Men held there were completely isolated from the other POWs. They were given one small, mangy, blanket and fed once every two or three days. There was a latrine bucket in each hut, but they were not allowed out to empty it. They were taken from their hut only for interrogation. Questions focused on germ warfare, aircraft capabilities, and who was giving orders to all the camps. At times they weren't even taken out of the hut but questioned right there in the smell and the mess.

They had learned all this from Norman. He was able to get Care packages to others in nearby isolation huts by hiding them in the one outhouse he was allowed to use during the long interrogations. The guards seldom entered his hut or that one outhouse, most likely because of the atrocious smell. Each package the British shoved through the back wall of Norman's hut was already wrapped in a rag. He was never sure who got what package, but they were gone on his next visit to the outhouse.

Owen and the others who made the trips up to 2-4 were reluctant to approach any of the other isolation huts. For one, Norman had told them there was a machine gun set up down near the interrogator's huts. It was never manned when he was taken out for questioning, but it was there. Also, the chances of being spotted or someone talking increased with any new hut they approached, especially with their tracks in the snow. On the other hand, someone in one of those isolation huts not getting the extra food and medicine might not survive. Winter was on its way out, but there were still cold days and even colder nights.

"With the move up to this house, we have two new problems," explained Prince. "This place is bigger, more comfortable, and we have a stove. But the fence goes completely around the house. It's not much of a fence. We could push through it easy enough, but it would create a real ruckus. I'm guessing that's the only reason it's there. So, we can't just sneak out the back. Second, it turns out the guards down at the main camp are carefully watching the storage shed after all, especially at night. There are two guards on watch every night. They are in another small hut about fifty feet away and look right at the door to the shed. We haven't been able to get anything new out of there for over a week now. What is left is hidden in our old hut, but it's almost gone. We need to solve both of those problems soon."

Swede solved the first problem that night. He spent lots of time sitting in the sun on the back porch of his new home. The area immediately around the house was clear for twenty or thirty feet out to the five-foot high fence. There was no way to get over the fence without making a lot of noise and probably breaking the fence in the process. Then Swede noticed one large branch sticking over the fence from the trees on the other side. Someone could throw a rope over the branch and pull himself up. Then he could crawl to the tree and slither down. To get back he had only to reverse the procedure. But there was no rope. Until he went to bed that night.

The bed, the only one Swede had seen in almost three years, had been just a rectangular frame. The Chinese had given Prince some rope to weave back and forth to make a support for pine boughs they allowed to be cut for a mattress. That was how they carried Swede from the old hut to the house. The plan was to use the bed for anyone considered too sick to sleep on the wooden floor. Swede had never given any thought to what supported his comfortable pine boughs. Until that night. Once he discovered the rope, he explained to Owen how they could get out to visit Norman or the food storage shed. Owen went over the wall twenty minutes later. He worked his way back to their old hut, went in through the back, and got some packages for Norman. After delivering them and explaining why they hadn't visited in a while, he returned, climbed up the tree, and dropped back into their new yard. Swede slept on his pine boughs that night, but they were on the floor.

Once Swede was up and about again, Owen suggested they continue his self-defense training in their back yard. They also talked about getting back into the storage shed. What they had hidden away in their old hut was almost gone. As they talked about guards and schedules, they realized their own guard schedule was much more relaxed than it had been. There was only one guard at the little shack in front of their house. The guards rotated about six in the morning, noon, six in the evening, and around midnight. For the guard rotation in the morning, two guards came up the hill. They carried the buckets of morning rice and tea. That was now the only time of the day the guards did a headcount. Since people were moving about getting their breakfast, it would be easy to fool the count. Two or three men could easily get themselves counted twice. Which meant they no longer had to hustle back after delivering food up to Norman's boys, as they had begun to call them, or watching the main camp.

Prince didn't think Swede was healthy enough to go for long walks through the woods at night and Swede agreed. He spent time trying to solve the problem of getting back into the storage shed now that guards seemed to be watching it more closely. He also spent time exercising to get his strength back. Corporal Blake kept an eye on Swede to see he didn't push too hard. Which he did.

"I thought you Americans weren't too keen on exercise," remarked Blake as Swede went through a series of pushups and squats.

"What gives you that idea?"

"When we first got to Camp 1, you Americans were already there. You were a bad lookin' lot. Every day, burial details were busy on that hill to the north of the camp. Boot Hill I think you called it. Every day. Twenty or thirty a day.

"On the second or third day after we got there, our PT instructor sergeant had us all out in the morning for some exercise. We did that every morning for quite a while. At first, no one in the American compound seemed to pay any attention. About the only activity I recall were the burial details. Gradually you started to join in. I guess that made me think you weren't much for exercise."

"I was there at that time," Swede explained. "But in a cell up near headquarters. I got there about the first of January. They dragged your colour sergeant in sometime in April, before the rest of you got there, I think. I had been with the column headed north in October when I escaped. From what they told me, they got to a place called Bean Camp in January. They were on the march from when we left Seoul in September until January. Then half of them died on the march from Bean Camp to Camp 1 in April. I guess they were about exercised out when they got there. But I also heard your people did a lot to encourage our guys to get off their butts and start living again. We should thank you for that.

"By the way, I think I have an idea how we can get into the storage shed to replace all the medicine you used on me. If I haven't already, I sure want to thank you for getting me through that. Now we have to get in there and get more CARE packages up to the guys north of us."

"I think our best bet is what we did at 3 South. There was a punishment shed that was a miserable place to spend a few days until we remodeled it. That's what we need to do to the storage shed down at the main camp." Swede was explaining his idea to Prince and Owen Thorpe.

"I get the impression the shed is guarded pretty close at night. But what about during the day? Do they have extra guards then too, or just at night?"

Owen turned to his left. "Robertson here is our expert on the guards down there at the main camp." Robertson was a slim lad with a permanent grin on his young face. He had enjoyed his assignment of sneaking around to put together a detailed understanding of guard routines. Between prowling around at night keeping track of the guards and whispered conversations with prisoners down there, he knew exactly who was guarding what and when.

"They only have a special watch on that shed at night. During the day there is no special detail just for the shed. But there is a chain on the door now that rattles even when the wind blows."

"Good. That means they are only payin' attention to the door, the front door. But we are going in the back door." Swede grinned at the group.

"What back door?" asked Owen. "There's no back door on that little shed."

"There will be as soon as we remodel it," explained Swede. "Just like we did to that punishment shed. As I recall, the backside of that shed is right up against a bunch of brush and trees. We sneak in there and put a little door in the back of that shed. It just needs to be big enough for somebody like Robertson to crawl through, get what we need, and wiggle back out."

"How do we put in a door of any size without making enough noise to get caught? The guards in the hut across the way will hear us." Blake just shook his head. "There won't be any other noises at night."

"We won't do anything at night. We'll rob the bank in broad daylight, pardner." Swede's idea was to sneak down during the night and hide in the brush behind the shed. During the day, they could inspect the back wall and determine exactly how they would get in. If they were lucky, the boards would be as rotten as the ones in their old hut. Then they would get the men in the camp to create a disturbance far away from the shed during the day. That was when they would break in. The guards would be on the other side of the camp and the noise from the ruckus would cover any noise required to get in. Once they had their little back door, they could continue their night raids to get what they needed.

Four days later a ruckus broke out far away from the storage shed. One man accused another of stealing his motorcycle and riding it around camp. The accused then took off on the motorcycle again, even racing past the camp commander's office. He was caught when he ran it into a tree on the edge of camp. Far away from the storage shed. The guards were completely confused as they couldn't see a motorcycle. They had never seen a Keystone Cops movie either, or they would have recognized the antics that followed the wreck of the alleged motorcycle - a lime-green 1938 Harley-Davidson Knucklehead, so the owner claimed.

"My Harley, my lime green Harley," the man moaned, "How am I gonna fix that fender? I don't have the tools to fix that! And who around here sells that color of paint?"

Everyone finally calmed down. The camp commander 'confiscated' the motorcycle, forbidding the riding of any motorcycles in or around camp-just in case. Just then someone yelled "Fire!" It was some time before that was put out. Later, the consensus of the prisoners was that there must have been a faulty muffler on the motorcycle. How else would the back of the outhouse have caught fire? During all that noise and confusion, no one heard the protest of a few nails as boards were loosened on the back of a storage shed.

Cecil B. DeMille would have appreciated the whole production.

Clean Again

Spring 1953

Spring brought more than warmer temperatures and green growth. The week before Easter most of the men down at the main camp at 2-3 were escorted the few miles back to the officer's camp at 2-1. For three days they enjoyed a picnic-like outing, playing baseball and basketball, eating good food, and visiting fellow prisoners. They came back in time for another good meal on Easter Sunday. The Chinese had heard ham was commonly served for Easter dinner and slaughtered a pig. One pig didn't go far, as Prince and his men in the house on the hill were invited down to join the hundred or so men below for their Easter feast. But there were treats, even a bottle of beer for each man. Especially enjoyable was being able to freely mix with men they had only been able to whisper a few words to in the past. Again and again, they heard the story of the motorcycle and the fire. Almost the entire camp had simply gone along with the plan, accepting the less they knew the better, content with feeling like they had helped pull the wool over the *wolf's* eyes.

Best of all was the news from Camp 2-1. The talks at Panmunjom were going very well. In a few weeks a prisoner exchange was supposed to take place. This was to be for the sick and wounded. In a few months all POWs would be returned home. Rumors of an end to the war had been around for over a year. Some saw this as just something else to get disappointed by. Then the guards started to talk about going home. Maybe this was the real thing! When the men on the hill were told they would be allowed to bathe in the river twice a week, and use the new bathhouse recently built in the main camp once a week, most of them became believers. Photos of clean and healthy-looking prisoners would make the Chinese look better when the exchange took place.

To counter the good news were the stories that had been told at 2-1 about a nasty camp nearby where aircrew were being pushed hard to confess to germ warfare. Most of the men from 2-3 were not aware of the camp just to their north. Only two knew the reason for the motorcycle caper. Prince hoped to keep it that way. Too many cooks stirring the pot would cause problems. If the guards at 2-4 became more alert, the CARE packages wouldn't get through. As far as they could tell, news of the coming prisoner release hadn't changed anything up there. Those men still needed help.

The House on the Hill, as Prince and his crew began calling it, received some guests. Three guards escorted a prisoner up the hill one afternoon shortly after Easter. As they came closer, it became obvious one of the guards was an officer. Swede didn't pay much attention to the Chinese, but he thought the prisoner looked familiar. When the four stepped past the guardhouse and approached the house, Swede realized who it was. Charlie!

Why was Charlie there? Should he say something, or should he not let on he knew him? If the Chinese sent him there to be punished, would it be better for Charlie if they weren't aware they knew each other? Then the officer spoke, and Swede got another surprise. The officer was the one who had questioned him after Colonel Li had found him in that snowstorm more than two years before.

"I am Lieutenant Bo. I have been sent here to conduct interviews to see if you have learned the truth. Only then can you be exchanged for the courageous Chinese soldiers being held by the United Nation aggressors. This man is not well. I leave him in your care." At that point, the lieutenant's eyes searched the group as if he was looking for something. Then he turned and motioned the guards to head back down the hill. Charlie simply walked past the others and entered the house without talking.

Once they were inside, Charlie broke out into a big grin and shook Swede's hand with both of his own. Then Swede pulled the man into a hug. "Charlie! It is good to see you! What did you do to get sent out here in the middle of nowhere?"

"Colonel Li arranged to send me here," Charlie could only manage a scratchy whisper, but at least he could talk now. *"He said the Chinese wanted to hide me so I wouldn't get sent out with the release of the sick and wounded. They don't want to send a crazy man home. And they think I'm crazy. Which I suppose*

is at least partly correct. Colonel Li said they will send me home after most everybody else.
People won't be paying much attention then." And then in even more of a
whisper, *"I have some other news from Colonel Li. When we are alone."*

Swede introduced Charlie to the group and explained his difficulty
speaking. He also explained what Charlie meant when he said the
Chinese considered him to be crazy. Turning to Charlie, he asked,
"Do you still have bad spells?"

"Not as often, but they still grab me sometimes. Now that I'm with you again, maybe
they will stay away. You could always help me work through them. But I'll miss working
on the Pros to get them back on the straight and narrow. I don't suppose you have many
of those around here."

"No, but we do have a few projects you can help with. Don't worry,
we'll put you to work." Swede chuckled and threw his arm over
Charlie's shoulders. "It is really good to see you again."

Lt. Bo started in on his interviews the next day. Guards brought up
a small table and two chairs, which they set up just out of earshot
near the house. He first asked the reason for the individual being sent
there and if he was aware of any crimes committed by fellow
prisoners. The answer to that question was never yes and he never
asked again. Then he asked questions about where they had grown up
and what life was like back in England. Sometimes he even asked if
he was pronouncing a word correctly. The lack of concern about
whether they had "learned the truth," and his seemingly genuine
interest in their life back home, puzzled the prisoners.

"What is this guy up to?" asked Owen. "Is there some reason we
shouldn't answer his questions? Are we giving him too much
information? I can't see any point to what he is asking."

"I feel the same way," responded Prince. "And I can't decide what
we should do. Do you know this man, Swede? Is this some kind of a
setup?"

"I don't really know him. He questioned me when he and his
colonel found me delirious on a road the second time I escaped. The
lieutenant questioned me before the colonel talked with me.

"I know the colonel, Colonel Li. And I trust him. He took lots of
chances to help us. When he questioned me that first October, I told
him about prisoners being shot on the march. Then he showed up at
Camp 3 when Earl Stoneman and I finished our sentences at the
camp just south of here, and I brought it up again. A few weeks later
he said he had asked a lot of questions, unofficially, and found I had

been telling the truth about the executions, and more. He showed me his report and said he wanted me to take it. I refused. He told me what was in it, including that the major in charge of the Tiger Death March was probably in charge of 2-4, questioning aircrew about germ warfare.

"Then he gave me some papers with the names of all the Progressives that were being stooges for the Chinese. He told me if the Chinese found out it would be the end for him. He let us know when the guards were going to raid our huts or try to set us up to catch us escaping. He said he wouldn't betray his country but was completely against the way we were treated. He has backed up everything he said. So, yeah, I trust him.

"He arranged for Charlie to be sent here, just like he did with me, I think there is a good chance both of us would have just disappeared if he hadn't pulled some strings. Charlie says Li told him to tell me that Lt Bo speaks for him. Meaning I should trust Bo."

"What if this is all just a setup?" growled Owen.

"I've spent lots of time asking that question myself," answered Swede. "But set us up for what? He would have had to start planning at least a year ago. If the rumors are true, the war is about over. Even the commander here is being a nice guy. And I still have the papers Li gave me. They are probably a death sentence for him. I think we should just be cautious and see what Bo does."

Bo continued his interviews over the next few days. Finally, it was Swede's turn. When he sat down in front of the Chinese lieutenant, Swede didn't say a thing; he just waited for Bo to begin with his questions. The lieutenant looked at him for a bit and then leaned across the table. Reaching out slowly, he brushed the hair back from Swede's forehead. Understanding what Bo was doing, Swede sat back and gestured to the scars on his forehead and neck.

"These weren't there when we first met. Some of your countrymen got a little enthusiastic with their re-education efforts. But you look pretty much the same.

"I noticed you seemed to be looking for someone the other day when you brought our newest member of the club up here. Would that be me?"

Bo smiled. "Ahh, Colonel Li told me you might not be too friendly in your welcome. He will be happy to know you are well. He knew you would be sent to join your English friends instead of fellow Americans. And he knew efforts would be made to make you unwelcome when you arrived. But that was all he could do. Others wanted you to be shot while trying to escape again. He also arranged for your friend Charlie to be sent here. Our superiors consider those of you in these camps to be in a place where you can do no harm. You were both 'on their radar.' I think that is the expression you use. Am I correct? I hope to improve my English while I am here.

"I also know another friend of yours. He asked me to say hello. And to give you this message, that today is just another page in the history books."

Swede sat stunned for a few seconds. That was the code phrase Henry Page had said they should use to identify someone they wanted the other to trust completely. The phrase he sends his greetings and salutations meant the person could not be trusted. Either Page was telling him to trust Bo, or Bo had tortured Page to get the phrase from him so he could fool Swede. That didn't seem to make much sense. Bo would first have to know he and Page had code phrases. He didn't have time to think about it much before Bo went on to talk about Page.

"Henry Page is different than most prisoners I talk to. He doesn't seem to be bothered too much by the fact he is a prisoner. Much like you and these Englishmen here. You don't seem worried or afraid."

"*Should* I be worried or afraid?" asked Swede.

"Let me try to explain. Colonel Li told me all about his conversations with you. About the list he gave you with the names of those Americans you should not trust. About the document he put together describing the killing of prisoners and their treatment that first winter. He told me you were not willing to take that document and why. I have it with me now. I am supposed to convince you to take it with you when the next prisoner exchange takes place. Until then, I have it hidden away.

"He told me how he helped you and the others 'modify' a hut so it was less of a hardship when he had to keep his superiors satisfied he was punishing you for not cooperating. He also told me he thinks you and Page were involved in a fire that burned the records of many prisoners. And he thinks the two of you might have been involved in the sinking of an American B-29 in the Yalu as it was crossing to China on barges."

Swede tried hard to show no reaction to that news, but apparently wasn't successful. Bo held up his hands as if in surrender. "So I have no need to try and trick you into doing something I can punish you for. I could have you shot by giving that information to my superiors, even if it isn't true. But that is not why I am here. I need your help."

Bo waited to see how Swede was reacting. When he seemed to relax, Bo continued.

"The Colonel explained to me how he feels about what is happening. He says there was a change in China after the defeat of the Nationalists. He especially saw it when he went home for his wife's funeral. The government is now treating the people much like they are the new enemy. He met with a close friend who told him he saw the same changes. He thinks he will come under suspicion when this war is over because he worked with the Americans before and he associates with you again as an interrogator. I will also be under suspicion because I worked with him.

"He told me I must leave with you when you are exchanged. He says I will have a better life in America as a defector than in China as one who has been poisoned by working with Americans. Henry Page says he will do what he can to help me when we get to the United Sates.

"I am telling you all of this now because I need you to trust me. I think maybe the message from Page was telling you he trusts me. I hope so, because I need your help. I will carry the documents from the Colonel when we leave so you cannot be caught with them. Hopefully, they will help me earn some trust with your superiors. But I won't be able to escape without your help." With that, Bo sat back and waited for Swede's reaction.

Swede could easily read the worry in Bo's face. There was also sincerity there.

"Wow, that is a lot to take in," responded Swede. "Now I'll tell you something. Colonel Li also sent me a message." He paused there. He wanted to see if there was any hint of being caught in a scheme on Bo's face. There was none. Just curiosity.

"The Colonel says I should trust you. Page's message says the same. And Charlie agrees with them both. So now we need to talk, because I could use *your* help with a few things."

Swede, Prince, Owen Thorpe, and Master Sergeant Ed Suermondt sat naked on the bank of the stream. They had two buckets of water, one for washing and the other for rinsing. They were washing up as well as they could while they waited their turn in the tub of hot water in the bath house. Suermondt was the senior man in the main camp at 2-3. The motorcycle caper had been his idea. He and Prince had been in contact for some time now, but this was their first conversation in the open daylight. Ed was explaining what they had learned from their visit to Camp 2-1.

"We already knew 2-1 was the officer's camp. Last fall they moved about half of them a mile down the road. That is what you have been calling 2-2. There are two hundred and fifty men in the two camps. Mostly officers, but a handful of enlisted, for some reason or another. They think the Chinese divided them up because the schoolhouse they were in was too small. Right now, their living conditions are a little better than ours, but their first year was rough. Lots of time spent in isolation for poor attitudes. Their senior man has been kept alone in a hut about a hundred yards from the camp since they got there.

"A lot of their time in isolation was for escape attempts. There were over forty attempts last year. Not one successful, of course. But the best news we heard was about the peace talks. They told us about the first prisoner exchange and that turned out to be true. Given the way Commander Zhao is treating us lately, it seems maybe the war really is over. He told me the first truckload of my guys would go out in a week or so. But some of the guards are saying they will only go back to one of the regular camps, and then be released from there. In either case, it's a start, the beginning of the end, maybe."

"At least we will be able to go home smelling a little better," added Thorpe.

"About time, too," agreed Swede. "Smelling better, I mean. I don't know how much longer I can stand the smell of your armpits."

"I'm pretty sure it's not my armpits you've been smellin'," replied Thorpe. The group all chuckled and nodded in agreement with that remark.

"Yeah, I know," agreed Swede. "I was just bein' polite." That brought outright laughter from them all.

Swede watched the others as they continued their banter. Smiles. Laughter. That had meant bad news for almost three years now. But maybe Suermondt was right. The beginning of the end. Maybe this time would prove his uncles wrong. Maybe these smiles would not mean things were about to get worse. In the meantime, it was good to feel – and smell – clean again. It was good to hear birds in the trees and feel the sun's warmth on his back. If he just looked at the trees and grass across the stream and ignored the Chinese guards chatting away at the bath house, he could almost be home.

Then he tuned back in to the conversation.

"I think we need to confront Zhao about the mail and packages in the storage shed." Ed Suermondt was talking. "Some of that stuff might start spoiling."

"Why don't you and Prince play ambassador," suggested Swede. No one else in the camp referred to Sergeant Tomkins as 'Prince," but neither did they challenge Swede's doing so. They didn't know the whole story, but knew enough to realize there was a special bond between the two.

"Play ambassador? Why not just tell the bastard we want our mail?" challenged Suermondt.

"Because we aren't out of here yet and I would like to continue to get a hot bath once a week. We all know how Zhao can turn nasty on us." Swede looked directly at Ed Suermondt. "Throwin' it in his face might get our bathwater thrown in ours. But the two of you can hint that you have heard of mail being held back in other camps. You respect him for his fair treatment in this camp. With the war about over, you would hate to see him get in trouble like some other camp commanders. Maybe he could check to see if any of those commanders are holding our mail also. He can blame one of the other camps and paint himself as the good guy.

"Like that. Play ambassador,' smiled Swede.

Ed Suermondt looked at Prince and Owen with a puzzled expression on his face.

"Every now and then the kid comes up with a good idea," chuckled Owen.

The day before Prince and Suermondt talked with Zhao, Swede and Owen snuck down to the storage shed to get a rough idea of how much was in there. If Zhao did turn it over, they wanted to know if he kept much for himself.

"Why don't we just take it all right now?" asked Owen.

"Because then he would have to search for it. And he would find it sooner or later. Then he would have to punish somebody, or everybody. And we would lose it all. If we lose it, all we can't help the guys over at 2-4. This way we just might get most of it right out in the open.

"If Zhao keeps too much for himself, we find out where it is and then steal it. He won't be able to complain because he supposedly just turned it all over to us. If he decides to go back to his old ways, we let him know we will be very loud in our complaints. This close to the end he doesn't want to mess up his chances for his next promotion. That's my theory and I'm stickin' to it." Swede grinned at Owen.

That afternoon Swede got out a watercolor set they had found in the mail packages. Using some wrapping paper from the packages, he made two maps. They were duplicates, showing where the camps were and rough guesses on distances between them. He gave one to Prince and kept the other. Maybe one of them would be successful in sneaking the map out when they were finally sent to Panmunjom. They both felt it was worth the risk to get the information out.

At 2-3 and 2-4

Summer 1953

"I need your help. But I am not sure how to ask." Bo was looking worried. "I want to understand what Americans mean when they speak, but I don't want to upset you."

Swede grinned. "Go ahead and ask. If it upsets me, I will say so, and we can start over. What's on your mind?"

Bo was very hesitant. "Why is it that so many American soldiers are…are uneducated, and..uh..and have no fathers?" He rattled the last part off quickly and sat back as if to avoid an expected blow.

"Uneducated and have no fathers? I don't know what you mean."

"Every day, in every camp I go, I hear Americans call each other 'dumb bastard.' That is how you say it, 'dumb bastard,' yes? Bastard means having no father, yes?" Bo held up an American dictionary, the cover just barely recognizable, the spine broken and tattered.

Swede looked from the book back to Bo a couple of times, not quite sure if he understood what was going on. Then he started laughing. He couldn't stop. This was maybe the funniest thing he had heard or seen in years. Finally, he noticed Bo's expression was jumping back and forth between embarrassment and anger. Swede brought his laughter under control and waved his hand.

"No, no, I am not laughing at you. But you have just shown me my countrymen through different eyes. And I see how you are confused." Swede brushed away the tears.

"Let me try to explain. Americans swear a lot. You have an expression 'ben dan', am I right? It means a stupid person, or something like that?"

"Yes, yes, ben dan, stupid egg. It is often used." Bo's anger was gone.

"But you don't really mean a person is an egg, do you?"

"Americans use the word bastard all the time. We don't think of what it means in the dictionary anymore." Swede gestured towards the tattered pages Bo clutched in his hand. "It is just something we say. One time it is calling a person a bad name in anger, another time it almost means a friend. If you are my friend and I introduce you to others I might say, and this bastard here is my friend Lieutenant Bo."

"So how do I know if I am your friend or enemy when you call me a bastard?" Swede could see Bo was more confused now than he had been before.

"It all depends on context, as my English teacher used to say. Context means the situation in which I use the word. If I look angry and I say this bastard here, it means you are not my friend. If I am smiling and say this bastard here just beat me at poker, it means you are my friend. Probably.

"If I am not smiling, maybe it means you cheated me. Context. What just happened when I used the word? Think of the word rain. It can be a little rain that will be good for the crops or too much rain that will wash them away. Context. But that doesn't mean you should go around calling people 'bastard' just because you like them. You still have to be careful."

Bo looked puzzled for a moment, a bit of a frown on his round, friendly face. "So then poor bastard does not mean a man has no professions *and* no father?"

"No professions?"

"No...no...no things! Poor bastard does not mean a man has no things and no father?"

"No professions, no things?" Swede was a little lost on this one.

"Wait. You mean no *possessions*...no things...no money! OK, you mean does poor bastard mean a man has no money?"

"Yes...I think. So a poor bastard is not poor and is not a bastard?"

Swede chuckled. "Exactly. It almost means you feel sorry for the man. You kind of like him, but life is not good to him. But a sorry bastard is not a man you like. It usually means he is not honest. A sorry bastard is someone who cheated me when we played poker. Unless he is my friend and we always cheat each other when we play poker. Then maybe he is a silly bastard. This silly bastard tried to tell me he had four aces when I already had one in my hand!

"And a stupid bastard is not a good man. A dumb bastard is just someone who is not too smart, but a stupid bastard is a man you do not like. You might call a friend a dumb bastard if he just did something wrong, but you still like him. But if you call your friend a stupid bastard, he will be angry."

"Then what is a goofy bastard? Goofy is a dog in your comic books, yes? Does a goofy bastard act like a dog? Wait! ... He acts like a funny dog!"

That really got Swede laughing. Then Bo joined in the laughter. One would look at the other and laugh even louder. They would settle down and then it would start all over.

Finally, Swede calmed down enough to say, "I just realized how confusing all this must be to you. You must think all Americans are goofy bastards." Then he started laughing again. Bo looked over at him and barked. That almost brought both to the ground.

"if you think this is confusing," snorted Swede, "wait until I try to explain motherfucker!" By that time, tears were rolling down his face again.

That conversation was just one factor in the two bonding. Each also had a high level of respect for Colonel Li. There was something about Page which made Bo admire him, but he wasn't sure exactly what it was. Swede knew exactly why he admired Page but knew better than to give too many details to Bo. For one, he knew there was a very slim chance Li or Bo, or both, could turn out to be conning him. He didn't think it was very likely, but knew the fewer people who were aware of Page's background, the better. It was the message Charlie had brought from Page that was the biggest factor in his trust of Bo. Page asked Swede to help Bo. He said to use Bo to get messages back to Colonel Li or Page himself. Whoever got the message would relay it to the other. And there was no way Page would have sent the code with Bo unless he meant it. The Chinese would never be able to get him to give up that code. Swede was positive about that.

So, Bo and Swede became friends and partners in crime. Swede and Charlie helped Bo understand the quirks in the English language-as spoken by Americans anyway. They told him it would only confuse him if he tried to understand British slang as well. Bo set out to get Swede as much accurate information about the set-up of 2-4 and how the POW exchange was going.

And the POW exchange was happening. Bo said from what he knew all prisoners would be returned to a UN exchange point over the next couple of months. Why they were not all released at once, he did not know. A few truckloads had already been sent out from Suermondt's group. Bo said the guards were right. Those men were only being sent to one of the regular camps and then later sent out from there. He had not heard the reason for that move either.

There were other signs the war was over. Colonel Zhao had told Prince and Suermondt their men could freely move back and forth between Prince's upper camp and Suermondt's lower huts. A headcount would still be taken every morning at each location. Men at the upper camp would take all meals with the larger group down below. And meals were the best they had ever been. There was no difference now between what the guards ate and what the prisoners ate. Zhao said he hoped the prisoners would refrain from any escape attempts. No one successfully escaped from his camp so far. Why bother trying now when they would be going home in a few weeks?

Zhao mentioned something about a neutral nations commission and Bo confirmed the news. A commission to supervise the prisoner exchange had been agreed to at Panmunjom. Neutral nations inspection teams were visiting POW camps on both sides to help coordinate the exchange. So, when a truck with strange markings pulled in to 2-3, it wasn't a complete mystery. No one understood the **CFI** painted in large black letters on the door of the truck, but Prince recognized the Dharma Chakra of the Indian flag. The men on the hill sat back and waited to see what unfolded.

The driver was a dark-skinned man who could easily be considered Indian, but the man who stepped down from the passenger seat looked American. Certainly European. Both were wearing military clothing with a CFI patch on the sleeve. The darker man had a smaller version of the flag on the door of the vehicle. The other man had a different flag on his sleeve. The whole scene became much more interesting. Maybe another batch of prisoners was going home. The group watched as the two men entered Zhao's office. Within minutes Bo also arrived and went in.

Word got around the camp that something unusual was happening and more men gathered around, keeping a polite distance. Anything that interrupted the boredom of their day was most welcome. Swede worked his way over to where Owen and Prince sat with Ed

Suermondt.

"Do you have any idea what sifee means?" asked Prince, pointing to the truck.

"C F I," read Swede. "Communist Forces International?" he guessed.

"Could be, none of us have a bloody clue," answered Owen.

"That is the Indian flag on the door," offered Prince. "Not your Indian," he smiled at Swede. "India Indian, as in the country of. I'm guessing they have something to do with the neutral commission Bo told us about."

"Did you fellows get a good look at the white guy?" asked Ed. "He could be your brother, Swede. An older brother, maybe, but a brother."

Fifteen minutes later, the four men came out of the hut and approached the area where the bulk of the prisoners sat on the ground. As they got near, it was obvious they were all speaking Chinese. Then Zhao yelled out something to the nearby guards and they hustled away.

"I think he wants us all gathered here together," said Prince.

"Is that good or bad?" asked Swede.

While they waited for people to be brought down from the House on the Hill, Zhao and the others looked at some nearby prisoner huts. Next, they visited the kitchen and the bath house.

"Looks like some kind of a bloody inspection," offered Owen. "Now they inspect. Would have been nice to have an inspection or two a couple of years ago."

"If you didn't like the accommodations, Corporal Thorpe, you should have complained to the management," suggested Prince in a mock growl of authority.

"I did try to check out early, but that didn't go over too well with the bloody management," replied Thorpe with a chuckle. "As I recall, that's one of the reasons we were given that spacious hut we spent most of this last winter in."

"Don't be such an ingrate, Thorpe," growled Suermondt in his own mock growl. "It is obvious you have not seen the truth. You must reconsider your attitude."

"You shurd not be impurdinint!" laughed Swede. That earned him a few pebbles tossed his way.

The inspection team returned. Colonel Zhao nodded to Lieutenant Bo to address the group. Zhao showed a certain deference to Bo. Not only did the young lieutenant speak excellent English, but he was known to have been sent there by Colonel Li. It could only help to have Bo make favorable comments about Zhao in his reports back to Li.

"This is Simon Bishop of the Polish detachment to Custodian Force India. With him is Captain Kunal Patel of the Indian Army, commander of the CFI forces for all of Camp 2. They are here by agreement of deliberations at Panmunjom. Mr. Simon Bishop will explain in more detail." Bo stepped aside and Mr. Simon Bishop stepped forward. Swede agreed with Ed Suermondt that the man could be a relative. He also noticed Bishop had no rank insignia on his uniform while the Indian captain had three gold circles on his collar.

Bishop spoke in perfect English. "I am with the diplomatic corps of the Polish People's Republic. Captain Patel, as Lieutenant Bo stated, is with the Indian Army. We are an inspection team of the Neutral Nations Supervision Commission. The captain and I have been tasked to observe your part in the ongoing prisoner exchange. We understand that your treatment has been improved at Colonel Zhao's direction and there are no serious health problems in your company. We shall be in and out of this camp as the exchange process reaches completion.

"As you know, some of your comrades have already been sent on for exchange. They went from here to Camp 5, and from there on to Panmunjom. You will eventually do the same. You will travel by truck, and sometimes train, as you complete your journey. The process is slow and will take some weeks, maybe longer. Colonel Zhao has told me another group of twenty-five will leave here tomorrow. The captain and I will leave here and visit the other companies, continuing to travel back and forth until the last of you return to your forces."

With that, the announcements were over, and the four men returned to Zhao's office. Some of the prisoners wandered over to look more closely at the CFI truck. Others gathered in groups to talk about this newest development in their lives. Since this was the first official word an exchange was really happening, there were lots of smiles in the camp.

When Bishop and Patel finally left the Colonel's office, Bo walked with them to the truck. The prisoners around the vehicle all backed away and at least pretended to be paying no attention to the new men. Bo and Bishop wandered out to the road and talked for a few minutes. Finally, they shook hands, Bishop hopped into the cab, and the commander of the CFI forces for all of Camp 2 drove them away.

The day returned to normal, which meant everyone offered his opinion on when they would finally leave camp to anyone who would listen. The Polish diplomat who looked and talked like an American was also the topic of many a conversation. The fact many had heard him talking with Zhao in Chinese just added to the mystery.

Later in the day Swede managed to get Bo off to the side to ask questions about the CFI. He was concerned their presence might interfere with Bo getting information from Li or Page. He had some specific questions for Page that needed to be answered soon if they were going to come up with a workable plan to get Bo safely to the American lines.

"Simon Bishop will be no problem for us. He and Colonel Li are friends. They went to school together in California. He brought some news. Colonel Li is being sent back to Shanghai. He thinks it is a routine assignment now that the war is ending. But he is also worried it might not be. I am not to return to Camp 3 to see him or Page. The colonel says it might be dangerous for me. Someone might decide I should be sent back also.

"The colonel says I should trust Simon Bishop as I would trust him. Bishop gave me a message that only the colonel could have told him. No one else knows the frequency we used to monitor Russian radio communications. Because no one else knew we were doing so. That was not part of our assignment."

"You can trust him but keep me out of the picture." Swede was firm in that statement. "There are people here who think I am a fool for trusting you. That doing so is dangerous. You have more than proven to me that they are wrong. But it is hard to see your enemy as a friend. If people here think I am also trusting a Polish diplomat, they might quit trusting *me*. So don't tell this Bishop about me."

"You don't think Colonel Li has not already done that?" Bo asked.

"I don't know. But my world is already crazy enough. I don't have room for a Polish diplomat just yet. Speaking of crazy, you have to make at least one more trip back to Camp 3. We need to get some information from Page. And you can ask him to check on this Bishop character."

Charlie had been there when the CFI team came into camp. Swede told him about the message from Li that Bishop had relayed to Bo. He wanted to get Charlie's input on the whole situation.

"You trust Li, right? He has given you all kinds of reasons to trust him, right? And you trust Bo, right? Right?"

"Right, absolutely, both of them. I have no doubt about either of them," answered Swede. "And Page trusts them and you trust them. But now a Polish diplomat is going to help us? It almost seems too much. I know one thing for sure. I am not gonna mention this to Prince or Owen."

"That makes sense. If they have to know at some point, we can explain it then."

Charlie went on. *"Did you get a message to Page yet? We need a frequency to contact the Army once we are headed their way with Bo."*

"Yeah. Bo is going to get to him in the next few days. Colonel Zhao thinks Bo needs to interrogate some Reactionaries back at Camp 3. When you say 'we' that means you have decided to help me get Bo out of here?"

"Yes. The trick is going to be knowing when we should leave. If they tell us it will be our turn to go out on the exchange trucks the next day-we leave that night. But if they tell us we have thirty minutes before our trucks get here, that makes everything a little more difficult. We need a plan worked out now. That's why we need the radio frequency from Page. Because he will probably get sent out sooner than us."

Even with all the new developments, Swede and the others still had to keep an eye on 2-4 and keep delivering the CARE packages. Part of the process they had developed was simpler now. They no longer had to break into the storage shed. It was much easier to leave their House on the Hill at night, even sometimes before dark, and get over to 2-4. But approaching the isolation huts over there without being spotted still required caution.

The relaxed rules at their camp meant they now included some quality rice and even hot tea in their deliveries. The rice was cold by the time they got to the huts, but they kept the tea warm. Suermondt had come up with two canteens and a length of rubber tubing. Once they contacted the prisoner, they poked the tubing through the wall and filled his cup with warm, sweetened tea. As they delivered their tea and poked the rice and any other goodies through the wall, they exchanged information with the man inside. News of the ongoing prisoner exchange was a better morale booster than the food and tea.

Three days after Bishop left, Swede and Owen got a surprise from the first prisoner they visited that night. He said most of the prisoners at 2-4 had been sent out that day. As far as he could tell, only the men in the isolation huts were left. He also said the crazy Korean officer who came into the camp to interrogate the men in the isolation huts had brought a Russian with him the day before.

"He said the man spoke English," Swede reported to Prince, "with what he thought was a Russian accent. He was wearing what seemed to be a Russian uniform. They had gotten angrier than usual when he couldn't answer their questions about the fire-control system on the B-29 gun turrets. They were punching now instead of slapping. He thought he had finally convinced them he was an F-84 pilot, so they left to punch somebody else around. He had heard that interrogation and they were just as nasty in that hut. Both the Russian and the level of violence in their visits are new."

Owen looked worried. "We can get them better food, but what do we do about the beatings? We can't just bust in there and stop them. He said both the Korean and the Russian wear pistols. The Russian threatened to shoot him a couple of times."

"He described the Korean," added Swede. "He's this Major Chong something, the one Johnnie Johnson calls the Tiger. The one Colonel Li told me was up to something at 2-4. This guy is bad news. When I was first captured, I saw him walk up to a captain and blow his brains out with that pistol of his. He was in charge of the death march Johnnie Johnson was on. They executed nuns on that march!"

"So, what are you saying? We should do something about him? Like what?" Owen asked.

"We can't let him kill those men up there," Swede answered. "This is almost over. We can't let those men be killed this close to going home."

"Do we kill him instead?"

"There would be some nasty repercussions in that case," offered Prince. "We need to think this through very carefully. First, let's find out as much as we can. How many men are getting this treatment? Is it just smacking them around, or more serious? With most of the men gone it will be easier to keep close to the few that are left."

"Would Colonel Zhao help?" Can we talk to him?" It was clear

Swede was upset about the whole issue.

"Maybe those CFI guys are the ones to talk to. It sounded like their job was to see we were being treated OK." Owen was thinking out loud. "I don't think Zhao is our friend. If we say anything to him about what is going on up there, we will have to explain how we know. And then about stealing the mail, even though it was ours. He just might use the whole thing to make himself look good. You know, catching the nasty Reactionaries in a plot. But maybe you can talk to Bo and see if he can help. You say he is on our side, right?" Owen looked at Swede.

"He said he had to go to Camp 3, but when he gets back, I'll see what he thinks."

Dammit, thought Swede, *I knew we were smiling too much. This doesn't look good.*

The whole group from the House on the Hill was on the march again. Headed north, not south. Not south towards Panmunjom, but north towards China - or Russia.

Early that morning trucks had pulled up at the main camp and Ed Suermondt and the last of his people were loaded on board. After quick goodbyes and wishes of good luck, the trucks roared away. Before the dust settled all the men from the House on the Hill were ordered to gather their possessions and meet back at the lower camp.

"Looks like we're next," offered Corporal Blake, smiling like he had just won the Irish Sweepstakes. Swede didn't feel much like smiling. Bo wasn't back yet and there were still the prisoners at 2-4 that needed help. He wasn't sure what he would do if they were loaded on to some trucks. He couldn't just leave Bo. Then they were formed into a column and marched north from Suermondt's empty camp. There were no smiles now.

"What do you think, Yank?" asked Owen Thorpe as they trudged along.

"I doubt they are going to shoot us, at least not now," replied Swede. "They wouldn't have bothered to let us get our blankets if they were going to shoot us."

"Unless they want the blankets to bury us in," offered Prince from in front of them. "Keep a sharp eye out. If we round a corner and spot a machine gun set up on the road, we'll need to act fast. We can either rush it or scatter and run for the woods. I'm not saying that's what they have planned, but it sure is a possibility."

"*Look at the guards,*" Charlie whispered. "*Too casual, walking too close to us. They aren't worried about anything. There might be plans to shoot us, but the guards don't know anything about it. No machine guns yet.*"

"If we keep heading north all day, we will have to make some decisions tonight." Prince was deadly serious in his tone. "Try to get some info from the guards. They might be able to tell us what is going on."

Then things got better, or worse, depending on how you looked at life. The column rounded a corner and turned left off the road into what some of them knew to be Camp 2-4. Which meant they weren't headed towards China. But it also meant they were now in the lion's den, so to speak. This is where men were kept in isolation and harshly interrogated.

Prince looked over at Swede and gave a shrug. Is our glass half full or half empty?

Just off the road was a house, almost identical to their House on the Hill, even to the flimsy fence surrounding it. The big difference was the entry through the fence and guardhouse twenty feet from the front door of the house. There was a guardhouse but no gate. A well-worn path ran from the porch, straight out the gate, and on towards the road. Colonel Zhao's deputy, Lieutenant Kuang was there, standing on the porch. His English was not on par with Zhao's, but he could get his point across.

Kuang waved his arm at the house. "New home. Colonel Zhao and many men go now. No problem. I stay to care for you. But you must do you part. You must cook all food." He pointed to a smaller hut nearby. "House for food. You cook, you gather wood, you clean pots. Too many men go, you must do you part. Cook for all camp." At that point Kuang waved his arms to encompass the whole area.

Fifty yards away, just up the slope of the hill forming the northern edge of the valley, were two larger huts. Swede and Owen knew them to house the Tiger in charge of the camp and his guards for the isolated POWs. Similar buildings just behind their new house had housed the recently departed POWs. Further back up the little valley were the isolation huts. The valley floor was about sixty yards wide and gently sloped up to the west for a hundred yards, almost identical to the valleys that held the three parts of 2-3. Scattered trees dotted the valley floor and thickened on the slopes to either side.

"Bathe in river OK," Kuang continued. "Firewood, you go only this way." He pointed back south towards Suermondt's camp. "No go this way," pointing north, "and no go this way," pointing up the valley.

"No escaping." Kuang was serious. He was in command now, his first such command. It would look good on his record when he returned to China. Any mistakes and he would be a lieutenant forever. "No escaping," he repeated. "You go home soon. Week. Month. Soon. Enter new home now." At that point he barked orders to the guards. Most moved around the house and carried their gear into the two houses just beyond. One moved out onto the road and began walking up and down. Swede watched another move up the southern slope, remove a tarp from a machine gun, and set himself on the stool behind it. The weapon pointed directly at the front door of their new home.

.

Camp 2-4

August 1953

Jiao barely remembered a time when Americans were not a significant part of his life. As far as he knew, he was twenty-eight years old. His earliest memories were of a small, bare room, buried deep in the heart of Shanghai. He had shared that room with his grandparents. Other families, distant relatives of one kind or another, squeezed into various other rooms in the little house on their crowded longtang-or lane. As soon as he could walk, Jiao wandered as far as he could, exploring his surroundings. His grandparents were simply too old and feeble to do anything other than scold him for being away so often. The others in the house pretty much ignored him.

Jiao had no memories of his parents. He just knew the two old people in his room felt a certain affection for him and everybody else considered him a nuisance. By the time he was five, he was bringing home a coin or two a week that he managed to beg or steal. He turned those 'earnings' over to his grandparents, who were immediately relieved of them by the family that owned the house. Luckily, he consumed on the spot the occasional pastry or cup of rice he managed to acquire on his wanderings.

For some reason, Jiao found he preferred to earn rather than beg for those few coins or cups of rice. Even as a six-year old, he could carry messages or perform little errands. As he grew older, and wandered farther from their longtang, he discovered the foreign communities of Shanghai. The foreigners were more willing to reward a cute little guy for simple tasks than his fellow Chinese were. When he discovered the Bund, it felt like a different world altogether.

The farther he got in his wanderings the bigger the buildings grew. Streets were paved. There were even smaller streets that you could walk on next to the big street. Huge windows of glass displayed goods he had never imagined and often didn't understand. When he finally worked up enough courage to venture all the way out to the Bund itself, there were even more surprises. People of all sizes and colors in strange clothes, speaking in languages that made no sense. Giant carts that carried people up and down a wide street, sizzling and snapping as they moved on iron tracks. A river crowded with small wooden boats and huge iron monsters that moved without poles or sails. Giant policeman everywhere, Sikhs with their turbans and beards.

He soon found that a little boy in simple peasant clothes was not welcome on the Bund itself. But just a few steps away was the working city: the warehouses, simple restaurants, gambling houses, bars, tailor shops, butcher shops. Men could get a haircut and have their shoes shined at the same time. If needed, they could go down the street and buy a brand-new pair of shoes, even a suit. These streets were made for Jiao. He could easily earn enough money each day to buy a meal and bring a few coins back to the tiny home he was growing to dislike. When he could, he snuck in some extra food or maybe a warm cap for his grandparents. Too often these items were taken by others in the house. His grandfather began to suggest to Jiao he might find somewhere else where he could live. Just in case.

It was about that time Jiao discovered American Marines. They often wandered the streets just off the Bund. They were generous with their candy bars and cigarettes. Both were valuable items in the barter economy. It became easier for Jiao to stay away from the crowded longtang of his grandparents for a few days at a time. The Americans became used to his constant presence and willingness to do odd jobs. He never stole from them, a problem they frequently encountered with street urchins. So, on the day he returned to visit his grandparents and was told they had both died, he knew what to do. Before anyone could search his pockets for whatever he had brought for his grandparents, he turned and left. The next day he approached the Marine he often ran errands for and explained, with his limited English and pantomime, what his situation was. He was seven years old.

That Marine, a man with four stripes on his shirt who called himself

Schneider, arranged for Jiao to sleep in a storeroom of a bar he owned with Mr. and Mrs. T'ang. There was a bar with a small restaurant attached, and rooms above where men visited with the girls that waited on tables. Jiao earned his keep doing odd jobs for the T'angs. He also washed and guarded the Jeep his American sometimes drove. Over the next few years Jiao lived a good life, often wishing his grandparents were still alive so he could help them. He became comfortable in English and learned essential phrases in Japanese and French. Staff Sergeant Schneider relied on him more and more in his everyday dealings with the locals.

The good life changed in 1937 when the Chinese and Japanese went to war in Shanghai. Jiao had seen death often enough, but only the aftermath, bodies seemingly asleep in the street. This was different. This was violent, rampant destruction. This was seeing friends bleed to death in the street. This was watching tanks crush mothers and their babies running to escape street battles. It shook him to his core, not hard to do for a twelve-year-old.

Life after the battles were over never returned to normal. The Japanese controlled the city and normal now included dodging patrols and regulations. However, there were positives. Mrs. T'ang became his mother and her six girls his sisters. They would have spoiled him rotten had Mr. T'ang not kept him busy.

By the time he was sixteen a few of his sisters had become more than that. Jiao was young, good looking, clean, and honest - traits they didn't often encounter in their line of work. Then his world changed. In late November 1941, the 4th Marines were pulled out of Shanghai, marching out of their compound with their band playing and thousands of Chinese waving goodbye. Jiao was not among them. Staff Sergeant Schneider sat down with him at the bar two days earlier and talked about his future. He knew the T'angs would treat Jiao like a son, but the Chinese and Japanese armies would both view him as just another body to be used for their purposes. He gave Jiao a letter of introduction in case the Americans ever returned to Shanghai, not that he had much hope that was going to happen any time soon, if ever. Schneider was fairly certain he would not be returning. He was correct. Staff Sergeant William R. Schneider was killed on Corregidor five months later.

The next four years were hard for Jiao. He found the violence he had experienced during the Japanese takeover of Shanghai was mild.

Now he witnessed entire neighborhoods being destroyed, thousands of deaths by every means imaginable, including that of the T'angs. At first, he was forced into a work gang for the army, then conscripted into the army itself. He fought against the Chinese Nationalists as often as the Japanese. By the time the war against the Japanese ended, he had been wounded twice. Along the way, it was discovered he spoke English well and understood it even better. Since he had extensive combat experience, he was placed in a frontline unit responsible for listening to the radio chatter of the Americans advising the Nationalists in the new war. When the Nationalists left the mainland for Taiwan at the end of 1949, Jiao thought he would finally be discharged. Before that could happen, he found himself involved in his third war, assigned to guard American prisoners in Korea. He was sick of violence and found associating with Americans once again to be enjoyable, even though he was appalled at how they were treated that first winter. He did what he could, whenever he could, but was limited by the circumstances.

Had Jiao not known English, he would have most likely been discharged. He had no education and a leg wound limited his ability to move quickly. But he was a veteran. He knew how the army worked. He was respected by his fellow soldiers. And he spoke English. He could serve as a link between the American prisoners and their guards. And maybe, just maybe, he would hear useful information for his commanders. Once the penal camps at 2-3 were opened, he was sent there. Prisoners sent to 2-3 were the troublemakers, the hard-core reactionaries. If anybody was going to be plotting escapes or some kind of revolt, it would be them. General Chen was still hoping to find his "Finnegan," the man he was sure was somehow giving orders to all the prisoners. Having guards that understood English watching over these prisoners might give him some leads. Jiao didn't try to hide the fact he spoke English. He enjoyed talking with Americans again. Somehow those wily Yanks managed to hide all their escape plans from him, so he seldom had anything to report to his superiors. Every now and then he mentioned that someone had made a disrespectful remark about Chairman Mao. He never was able to identify who made those remarks. However, never reporting anything would have created problems for him.

By the time Swede joined Prince and Owen at Camp 2-3 he had adopted Henry Page's practice of being friendly to the guards. When cigarettes became available from their raids on the storehouse, he used them as a way to approach guards when no one else was around. When he had first offered Jiao a cigarette, he was surprised by the perfect thank you in response. The two never had the friendly relationship he had with Bo, but sometimes exchanged stories of their lives and experiences at war. They didn't try to hide those conversations, but didn't go around slapping each other on the back in front of their respective peers either. Jiao especially liked Swede because he didn't immediately change Jiao to Joe, like the Marines he met in Shanghai usually did.

When Swede looked up and saw the machine gun pointed right at their new home, he recognized Jiao as the man behind it. Once everyone had settled into the new routine, he wandered up the slope and offered Jiao a cigarette.

"You are not an American Marine, are you?" Jiao smiled. "It was American Marines who first introduced me to the corrupt Yankee way of life, and it all started with their cigarettes."

"I would never try to corrupt you, Jiao." Swede grinned back. "I might hope to get some information from you by offering another cigarette, but never try to corrupt you."

"You will never get any information from me, a soldier in the Communist People's Volunteer Army," answered Jiao, as he took the second cigarette. "But I am willing to pass the time of day with an American such as you because you might give up some secret plan to win the war. My superiors would probably reward me with a whole pack of cigarettes for such information."

From Jiao, Swede learned the machine gun was inoperable, set up for show only. First Colonel Zhao, and now Lieutenant Kuang, hoped the machine gun would keep the prisoners from getting any ideas about escape. Jiao also knew the British troops were scheduled to leave by truck in a day or two.

"Just you and the other American, the crazy one, will stay. You will go later when some other Americans come through on their way from a camp farther north of here." Swede didn't like the sound of that but tried to hide his reaction until he knew more.

"I have heard stories about some other prisoners in the huts farther back in the trees, some American officers. Will Charlie and I be put with them?" Swede wasn't sure how much Jiao was willing to talk about but figured it was worth a shot.

"No. Those are men we call the Major's pets. He visits them a lot. You do not want to be with them. That Korean major is a sick man." Jiao circled a finger near his ear to mean the Major was sick in his head. "He has a Russian with him this past week. When they ask questions of the men in those huts, there is a lot of noise. Some of the noise comes from pain." Jiao had recognized the noises. They were the same he had experienced at the hands of the Japanese in the dark cells of Shanghai. "And there is only one of them left. The others have all been returned to the camps they came from. The Major asked them questions about germs and secret orders. Now he and the Russian ask this one man about radars and special weapons in airplanes. When the Russian is here, they only ask questions at night."

"Are you sure the man is a Russian?" asked Swede. He and Owen had talked with a prisoner in one of those huts a few weeks past. He hadn't mentioned a Russian.

"I grew up in Shanghai. There are lots of Russians in Shanghai. This man is Russian. And they have another man with them. I think he might be American, but that doesn't make sense."

"Another prisoner?"

"No, he came in the truck with the Russian. He slept in their house with them. At night he went to the prisoner huts with them but did not go in. He listened from outside."

"You saw this? An American who is not a prisoner helping the Major and the Russian?"

"I did not see them the night they first arrived. But everything else, yes. Can you tell me why an American would be helping this mad man and his Russian friend?"

"Your Lieutenant Bo told me some Americans are refusing to be exchanged. But I can't think of any good reason an American would go so far as to help interrogate fellow Americans." Swede looked at Jiao for a bit. "Would you be willing to help me watch this man to see what he is up to? Let me leave our house and follow when they question the prisoner tonight?"

Jiao smiled just a bit. "Don't you have plans to talk with that man and deliver one of your packages to him?"

Swede's heart almost stopped. Could he act like he had no idea what

Jiao was talking about? Was it already too late for even that? Before he could come up with a response, Jiao continued.

"A few months ago, some of the prisoners who left yesterday were doing some strange things in their camp. They were arguing about a motorcycle that was not there. I could see they were up to some sort of trick, so I looked around the camp. When I saw some men sneaking away from a storage shed, I checked to see what they had been up to. For the next few nights I watched as you and your English friend took things from that shed and delivered them to men in these huts here. When I looked in the shed, I realized what you were doing, and that the commander had been stealing your mail.

"When they sent me to guard Americans, they said I should watch to see if any of you were trying to escape or plotting some Reactionary activities. They didn't mention what I should do if I found you helping prisoners that were being mistreated. Then I remembered you, that scar above your eye. You shared your food with me more than a year ago when they sent you here to work in the forest. One day the cooks gave us an empty box and you understood how much trouble it would be to go back and get more food. You shared yours with us. Your friend that day was not so willing. And now you were risking punishment, maybe even getting shot, to share your food with other prisoners.

"So, I will not notice if you leave the hut tonight." Jiao just grinned as Swede stood in shock. "You should go now. We can talk more tomorrow. Maybe then you will be able to explain to me what the crazy major and his Russian friend are up to."

Owen Thorpe insisted on going with Swede that night. The fence hadn't been repaired in a long while and they were able to slip through it behind the house. They moved slowly, searching for any twigs that would snap under their feet. The moon was only in its first quarter and mostly hidden by clouds at that. When it tried to shine through, they waited. They did not have far to go. Once they were close to the shed holding the new prisoner, they hid behind some bushes. They needed to see where the mystery man positioned himself by the shed to listen to the night's interrogation. Once they had him in sight, they could move closer.

Sounds of conversation came from the Major's house for about an hour before they heard the door open and the voices approached the hut through the trees. All three of the men were speaking English, but too quietly to be understood. One of them remained outside the door as the other two entered. He simply sat on the ground and put his ear close to the wall. Almost immediately there was a scuffle inside the hut.

"Get up, pilot! Yes, we know you are a pilot. Don't lie any more about that. Get up, we have more questions for you!" Swede was sure that voice was the Tiger. But the questions came with a Russian voice.

"What is TARZON? How does it work?" Swede and Owen both looked at each other and mouthed 'Tarzan?' at the same time. What kind of question was that?

"Edgar Rice Burroughs? Tarzan? I don't understand."

"Burroughs? Is he the general in charge? Where is his base? How many B-29s are there? Do they all use TARZON?" The Russian sounded excited!

"General? Burroughs is the author. Tarzan is his story. What does Tarzan have to do with B-29s?"

"Burroughs is the author? He designed TARZON? But how does it work?" The Russian was getting worked up. He wasn't getting the information he wanted.

"Yes, Burroughs is the author. Tarzan of the Apes. Burroughs wrote it. They even made movies. Tarzan the Ape Man."

"Movies? Tarzan of the Apes? More lies? TARZON, TARZON! Tell me how TARZON works," bellowed the Russian. The distinct sounds of someone being punched came through the walls.

"Tell me!" More punching.

Both Swede and Owen jumped as a loud rattling came from the front of the hut. The man outside was shaking the door. The Tiger and the Russian pushed their way out. The voices were excited, but low. All three were talking at once. Finally, one cut through the night. "Listen to me!" Swede jumped again. The voice was familiar.

"He thinks you are asking about a book! A book! Tarzan of the Apes. Edgar Rice Burroughs wrote it. Tarzan! Not TARZON. Not radio guided bombs!" Swede was sure he knew that voice. But he couldn't come up with a face or a name to go with it.

The Korean and the Russian went back inside. There was a rattling noise from within the hut, almost like chains being dragged across something.

"Sit up, pilot! No more about your books. Tell us what you know about radio-controlled bombs on the B-29. Your generals call it the T A R Z O N program."

"I don't know a damn thing about B-29s. I'm an infantryman. We might as well go back to talking about Tarzan movies. Those I can tell you about. But I don't know a single thing about B-29s!" The voice was strained, tired, even weak.

What followed was a bellow of rage, a loud crack, and the thud of a body hitting the ground.

"Don't kill him!" It was the Korean again. "I have questions for him! Go! We can come back later." With that, the door to the hut crashed open and both men stepped out again, stumbling over the man crouched outside.

"You told us he was a B-29 pilot! He hasn't answered any of our questions about B-29s." The Russian was apparently aiming his accusations at the third man. They continued towards their house in the distance.

"No, I told you I thought he was a crew member on a B-29. I knew him in Africa and Italy. By the time the war was over he was an officer. The next time I saw him was in 1948. It was at Carswell Air Force Base in Fort Worth, Texas. We provided security for bomb sights delivered to SAC bases. I told you about the security unit I was with and the nuclear storage sites. We had delivered the sights right out to the flight line. We stood around in the heat while the stuff was unloaded. I watched a B-29 land and taxi over to the hangar where we were. As the crew walked by, I recognized him. He was in flight gear and yukkin' it up with the others like they knew each other. I told you he was an officer at the end of the war, and I told you I saw him get out of that B-29. I never said anything about being a pilot."

Owen and Swede moved through the brush, following the three men as they approached the house, listening to their conversation. Swede was sure he knew the voice of the third man. Then they passed through a sliver of moonlight and Swede stopped in shock. Usury! Jack Usury! The third man was Jack Usury and he was giving the Tiger and the Russian all kinds of information on a fellow American so they could interrogate him! Owen finally nudged him, motioning with his head they needed to keep following. The trio was just about to go inside.

Owen led a dazed Swede to the side of the house so they could hear anything else that was said. The Russian was disgusted, both with the fact he had gotten no information from the prisoner and with Usury for misleading him.

"Forget your B-29s! The information I already gave you on nuclear storage sites is worth its weight in gold. When I get back, I will be an ex-prisoner of war. They will give me my choice of assignments. I'll ask to be transferred to my old unit. The information I can get will make you an important man back in Russia. And you will make me a rich man. Don't screw it up because of that clown over there!"

"He's right." The Tiger joined in. "The two of you go back to your camp. I have more questions for our 'pilot' out there. Tomorrow, the British prisoners here are being sent to Panmunjom for exchange. Neither of you can be seen here. I will join you tomorrow or the next day."

"What about the prisoner out there? What do we do with him?" asked the Russian.

"I will either have him with me when I join you or I won't. Either way I think we make him disappear. I will handle it. I have done it before. Now you need to leave." The Tiger sounded as if he already knew what his plan was for their prisoner.

They waited until the Russian and Usury had left and then moved back towards their hut. Swede convinced Owen to go back and fill Prince in on what they had heard. He wanted to check on the prisoner and give him the vitamins he had in his pocket. He didn't tell Owen, but Swede wanted to make sure the Tiger didn't go back and hurt whoever was in that hut. It was his intention to kill the Korean if he harmed the prisoner anymore.

Swede waited before going into the hut. If the Tiger came in while he was trying to help the prisoner, they both might get shot. He still carried a pistol strapped around his waist. Sure enough, not long after the Russian and Usury drove away, the Tiger headed back to the isolated hut. Swede moved in to hear what was happening.

"We have met before, haven't we, American? You were there when I executed your captain for giving orders to his men. You have just become a problem. Unless you can give me some information I can use, you will join your captain in the same manner."

"What can I give you? I am an infantryman, a regular soldier. I don't know anything you don't already know."

"What about this Finnegan I am told is sending orders to all the camps? Is he a prisoner? How does he get his orders from camp to camp? Where are the hidden radios? My superiors would reward me for this information. I would reward you. We should help each other. Then you can go home like the rest of the American vermin." With that, the Tiger left the hut and returned to his house. Swede waited another half hour and then simply walked into the hut.

After hearing Usury's explanation of how he knew the prisoner, Swede was sure he knew what he would find. He stood inside the door, waiting for his eyes to adjust to the dark. Moonlight helped to see shapes, but nothing more.

"Mike? Mike Randall? Is that you?" Swede waited. Then he heard the chains again.

"Who's there? I already told you I don't have any information to give you."

"Mike, it's me. Swede. Are you OK?" There was a long pause. The chains rattled again.

"Swede? Swede? We thought you had escaped. Or had been shot. Are you really here? Cuz if that's you, I could use a little help. I think that crazy Korean is going to shoot me."

Swede could see a lantern on a small table. There were matches next to it. He got on his knees and held the lantern close. When he got it lit, he turned the wick down as low as he could and put the lantern under the table and back against the wall. It cast out just enough light for him to make out Mike Randall sitting up against the far wall. A chain ran from his ankle to a post in the wall. A bucket in the corner couldn't disguise its purpose. Mike's face was badly bruised, but otherwise he looked healthy. Swede walked over to him, knelt on the ground, and gave him a big hug.

"You look good, Swede. Clean. A little older than I remember you, but good."

"Yeah, well you don't. And you don't smell all that great either." Swede smiled. "What's with the chains and the bucket? You couldn't get a better room? Hey, I've got some things for you!" Swede reached inside his pocket and unwrapped the vitamin pills and chocolate bar he had brought along. "Take two of the pills and eat the chocolate. Then try to take two pills a day until they run out. That's based on the advice of a pretty good medic I know. He's in a hut just out by the road.

"I can't get you out of here right now. I mean, I could, but then what."

"The bastard that has me in here says I'm a dead man if I don't tell him about somebody named Finnegan who is supposed to be giving orders to American prisoners through some kind of radio network. I don't have a clue to what he is talking about. This guy is nuts. He's the same Korean who shot Captain Winslow the day you joined our column. He recognized me. I think he figures to shoot me no matter what I tell him."

"I heard him mention Finnegan. That's almost funny. No, that is funny!" Swede chuckled. "Okay, maybe that's what we use to keep him happy for a few days. The British guys are supposed to leave tomorrow. Hey, Charlie is here with me, did you know that? He and I are supposed to stay here for a few days until the guys from Camp 4 come through on their way out. When that happens, we can either sneak you onto one of the trucks or I will steal a jeep and get you out that way."

"Camp 4? I was at Camp 4. I got called up to the commander's office and was told I had to go with this Korean major. We drove to a couple of houses not far from here and his Russian friend joined us. Then we came down here." Randall paused. "Charlie is here? Why is Charlie here. He was in Camp 3 last I knew. Why are you here. And where is here?"

"This is 2-3. It's a penal camp. This is my second visit up here. Charlie is here because the Chinese think he's crazy and don't want to release him until the very end. They don't want any bad publicity until they get all their own prisoners back.

"And it wasn't just a Russian that joined you and the Korean major. Jack Usury is with them."

"What? That doesn't make any sense. Why would Jack Usury be with a Korean and a Russian?" Randall sounded like he thought Swede's brain was a little too baked.

Swede spent the next hour filling in all the details. He also explained how Randall could use the whole Finnegan story to buy some time. As he listened, Mike Randall realized Swede did indeed look a little older. More than anything else, it was his eyes. They weren't the smiling blue eyes he remembered from their time in Seoul. There was a certain edge that hadn't been there before, a look that said tread carefully.

When he returned to the house, Swede woke up Prince and Owen to explain what he knew and get their advice on what to do. They all agreed breaking Mike Randall out right then would get them nowhere. Owen said he would stand guard near Randall's hut. If the Korean Major came back and it looked like he was going to shoot Randall, Owen would create a racket and hope that would stop him.

"If we are going out tomorrow, I will have plenty of time to sleep on the ride to Panmunjom. But you get some sleep." Owen patted Swede on the back. "You are going to need your wits about you in the next few days."

By morning nothing had changed. The major's jeep was still outside his house, but he remained out of sight. Bo returned mid-morning, driving his jeep. Simon Bishop followed in the CFI truck. They brought news that the trucks for the British would arrive by mid-day. They would stop for a noon meal and then continue, taking Prince and his group with them. Bo also managed to let Swede know he had contacted Page, and just in time. He was in a group that had been sent out of Camp 3 the day before. He also told Swede he had more information for him but would wait until the British were gone before explaining.

While the British were getting ready to leave, Swede talked with Jiao. He explained about a lone American being held by the Korean Major and the Russian. He asked if Jiao could arrange for some food and sweetened tea to be given to the American in the hut. It might be easy to do when the British were being served their meal. He offered a pack of cigarettes as a bribe for whoever might be willing to do so.

Jiao refused the cigarettes. "That will not be necessary. Someone from the kitchen will see to it he is taken care of. They do not like the way those prisoners of the Korean have been treated. With the special guards of the Korean gone, it will be easier for them to get the American some food."

He looked at Swede carefully. "Will you help that man escape? Are you worried the Korean major will hurt him?'

"I'm worried he might shoot him. He is asking questions that have no answer. Some generals think there is a prisoner in charge of all the prisoners, someone who gives orders through secret radios. There isn't. I told my friend a story he could use, a story he could stretch out over a couple of days. I think we have that much time."

"Trucks to take you and your sick friend to Panmunjom are supposed to be here tomorrow," offered Jiao. "If the Korean will not release your friend in that hut to go with you, what will you do?"

"I don't know," replied Swede. "But I won't leave him here. I will have to try and get him on the trucks." Jiao saw how serious Swede was.

"This is not just another American. This is a friend of yours?" asked Jiao.

"Yes. A good friend." Swede explained to Jiao about the Korean major, the Tiger, and how he shot prisoners early in the war. And then shot many more on the Tiger Death March. That he had recognized Mike Randall and had him chained in the hut.

Jiao thought for a bit after listening to the story. "We have heard rumors about that Korean. I believe you. There are some others here who will help. We will watch the hut during the day and help you watch at night. Tell me when you have a plan and how we can help. I will see that your friend gets a good meal today."

Swede spent the rest of the morning saying good-bye to Prince and Owen and the others. This was harder for him than leaving home four years before. Then he was looking forward to an adventure and assumed he would only be gone for a few years. Now he knew it was unlikely he would ever see any of these men again. Owen argued for Swede to sneak Charlie and himself on one of the British trucks.

"If it was just Charlie and me, I would do it. But I can't leave Mike Randall behind. I'm hoping when the trucks with some Americans come through for the two of us, we can make a fuss with Lieutenant Kuang. The Tiger outranks him, but I plan to convince Kuang he will be rewarded for preventing an incident that might cause problems at Panmunjom."

The trucks full of British prisoners finally showed up, dust billowing everywhere as they screeched to a halt on the road in front of the camp. For Prince and Owen and the others, it was a family reunion. Prince and his group had been sent to 2-3 nine months before. Swede was not aware of any prisoners dying since the early fall of 1951, two years prior. But when someone was forced into a truck and sent away, you just never knew what might happen to them. The meal prepared for them made it seem they were having a picnic, with tea instead of beer and rice instead of burgers. But it was a happy day for all. Even Swede found himself smiling at times at the pure joy shown by the British.

As they were about to board the trucks, Prince gathered his men. Owen reached into his pocket and pulled out a small brass badge to hand to Swede. It had a Sphinx on top with the word Egypt underneath. Owen waved his hand towards the men.

"I want to give this to you on behalf of all of us. This is the badge from the back of my cap. Only the Glosters wear two cap badges. The Regiment earned that distinction in Egypt when they fought off Napoleon's forces attacking from the front and the rear at the same time. You have had our backs in this camp. We want you to have this as our way of saying thank you."

Each of the British soldiers shook Swede's hand and boarded the trucks. Owen, and then Prince, said their final goodbyes and were hauled over the tailgate by their men. As the convoy began to pull away, every man in the last two trucks, the trucks holding Prince and his men, stood up, waved their caps, and began to sing.

"For he's a jolly good fellow, for he's a jolly good fellow, for he's a jolly good fellow
And so say all of us, and so say all of us, and so say all of us."

The trucks disappeared into the dust, but Swede could still hear the voices of his friends.

For he's a jolly good fellow, for he's a jolly good fellow, for he's a jolly good fellow
And so say all of us, and so say all of us, and so say all of us.
AND SO SAY ALL OF US!"

Headed Home

August 1953

The last of the singing faded away and the dust settled. All that could be heard was the distant growling of engines. Swede stood looking down the road, turning the cap badge over and over in his hand. Simon Bishop walked over and patted him on the back.

"They thought well of you." His voice expressed admiration.

"They were…they *are* good friends." Swede found it difficult to speak.

Bo waited for a bit. Then he approached the men and said, "Let's talk. We have some things to tell you."

Bo helped Swede get Charlie back into their hut. The short march up from 2-3 had been too much for Charlie. Not physically, but mentally. He had become mute again and was frightened by noises and quick movement. Once Charlie was wrapped in a blanket, the others moved out to the small porch and squatted down.

Bo explained about his visit back to see Page at Camp 3. "We got the frequency you asked for. And we have a plan that we think is just what we need." He looked over at Simon Bishop.

"As an official representative of the Neutral Nations Supervision Commission, I have with me documents ordering me to escort two American prisoners-of-war to Panmunjom. Lt Bo of the Chinese People's Volunteer Army is to accompany me. We are authorized use of an official Custodian Force India vehicle. All Korean and Chinese units we encounter on the way are to provide food and shelter, even armed escort, if that becomes necessary. The two American prisoners-of-war are believed to have typhus. That should keep people from being too nosy." Simon pulled an envelope from his pocket and removed a very official looking document, grinning at

Swede like he had just played a royal flush.

"Is that real? How did you get something like that?"

"I really am an official representative of the Neutral Nations Supervision Commission. Just in that capacity, it would be perfectly within my role to escort some prisoners to Panmunjom. I also happen to be a good friend of Colonel Li Chen Hong. He asked that I help both yourself and Lt. Bo here to get safely out of the country. That means get you to Panmunjom. I typed up the document myself. Once it is destroyed, there will be no record of my involvement. We just need to work out the details on how to get you out of camp." Simon sat back and grinned again.

Swede spent the rest of the day taking care of Charlie and watching the Tiger's house. Charlie was almost catatonic. The march up from 2-3, as short as it was, had set off the demons in his head. When he wasn't sleeping, he sat and stared. The Tiger wasn't active either. Swede was sitting on the porch of the house as it got dark, positioned so he could see both Charlie inside and Randall's hut. If the Tiger approached it, Swede planned to listen outside to make sure Mike was safe. Bo and Simon walked through the gate and joined Swede. All three sat in silence for a while.

"Strange," Simon offered. "It is peaceful here this evening. You could almost forget there has been a war going on."

"I could," answered Swede, "if a friend of mine wasn't chained up in that hut and being threatened by a crazy Korean who has committed war crimes. This is almost over. I can't let it end with the senseless death of another friend."

"I could also almost forget this war," offered Bo, "if I wasn't about to betray my country and never see my family again. But I will do everything I can to help your friend, Swede. I agree, any more death now is senseless."

"I would argue that any death in war is senseless," said Simon. "What has been accomplished here? Has anything changed since the beginning of this war? Have the small changes in the border between north and south been worth the tens of thousands, hundreds of thousands, of deaths? The last war made no sense either. But there was no choice when the Germans and the Japanese made it clear they would not stop until most of the world was under their thumbs.

"But in every war, who pays the biggest price, who dies the most deaths, who loses their homes and their livelihood? It is the people, the people who are caught between two armies, the people who suffer the most. Then again, it is those same people who sit back and let the Hitlers and the Tojos form those armies. Any death in war is senseless because war itself is senseless. That's why when I had a choice between China, America, or Poland, I chose Poland. They are the least aggressive. They have suffered at the hands of many invaders. When Germany invaded, Poles charged German tanks while riding on horses, armed with swords. Poland understands the futility of war better than most countries.

"So I chose to use diplomacy as my weapon against war itself. My father wanted me to choose the church. My history studies showed me the church, religion, has far too often been the worst of armies. So here I am. Trying to see this war ends as quickly and as peacefully as it can. Getting prisoners safely home is a big part of that.

"It is important for me also, Swede, to help get your friend out of here. And maybe after this is over, I can do something to bring the Korean major to justice. But I disagree with you, Lieutenant Bo. I don't see you as betraying your country. China was once my country also. China was my soul. But when your Colonel Li and I met, we both were concerned with what was happening in China. Both sides, the Nationalists and the Communists, cared more for taking power than for helping the people. But you care for the people. You have made a choice: the best way to help the people is to leave the Army, to leave China. Hopefully to work to bring China and America closer together. Helping the Chinese people is not betraying your country. The Chinese people *are* your country.

"Sun Yat-sen and Chiang Kai-shek both left China because they knew they couldn't help the Chinese people if they stayed. Why should you feel doing the same is betrayal?

"That ends my lecture for the day." Simon smiled at the two younger men. "Let's talk about what we do tonight and tomorrow."

The Tiger questioned Mike Randal again that night. Swede sat outside the hut, listening, prepared to rush in if he thought the Tiger was going to shoot his friend. But Randall used the information Swede had given him to buy some time. He used the Tiger's desire to find the mythical prisoner giving orders over a radio to send him down a path to nowhere. He sprinkled interesting tidbits into a long narrative of his time at different camps. He was also careful not to mention the first months of the war and the execution of prisoners. Then he got to the important part.

"When we first got to Camp 1 there were rumors about someone getting information to the UN about bad conditions in the temporary camps. And those camps were shut down. When we got baths and haircuts and were issued our new clothing, new rumors surfaced about a group in contact with the UN. But those rumors came from the British troops in camp, so it was hard to tell if it was British or Americans who were in contact with the UN. I heard a name once that sounded like Milligan or Finnegan.

"Nobody mentioned any radios until we got to Camp 4. Then we had prisoners from all the camps. There were more stories, more rumors. But every time radios were mentioned, it was somebody talking with the Russians. There was a rumor that somebody in Camp 3 had sent a radio message to the Russians when the Chinese were trying to get a wrecked B-29 across the Yalu on a barge. Russian planes with American markings sank the barges. The Russians don't want the Chinese to get their hands on a B-29. The Russians think when this war is over, the Chinese will be their enemy. I never did hear if a B-29 was destroyed at Camp 3, so I don't know if that story is true or not." Without explaining his involvement in the destruction of that B-29, Swede had told Randall the basics. He figured the Tiger either already knew about the incident or could easily find out. The bit about Russian planes with US markings was believable enough. He was sure somebody like the Tiger would buy a story like that.

Mike Randall could almost see the wheels turning in the Korean major's head. If he could prove the Chinese and Russians were working together and ignoring the Koreans, his superiors would reward him with a promotion. He would be important again, not sitting in a smelly hut talking with this dirty American chained to the wall. He would be brought back to Pyongyang, maybe even to give a report to the Leader himself, Kim Il-sung!

At that point, Randall began talking about any random thought that came into his head, giving the Korean a reason to leave and think about how to get his new information to his superiors, and which superiors would be most likely to listen to him. After he was gone, Swede brought Randall some food and tea, courtesy of Jiao. As much as he wanted to, he knew taking the chain off wasn't a good idea just yet. Jiao had suggested to Swede he sleep behind Randall's hut. That way he would hear any disturbance if the Korean came back. Randall was chained so the door was not locked in any way. But if Swede was inside when the Tiger decided to come back, there would be no escape for either of them. Swede grabbed a blanket and worked his way back up to the hut. Once there, he knocked gently on the wall and told Mike Randall what he was up to.

"What's the story behind this Finnegan guy?" Mike asked Swede. "The Korean's eyes lit up when I mentioned him in connection with somebody sending orders to the camps."

"It's probably best you don't know right now. Once we are out of here, I can tell you the rest." Swede paused for a bit. "I thought you and Jack Usury were friends. He told me once about the two of you serving together in Italy. Why would he turn against you?"

"I have no idea. If he was drinking again, I might blame it on that. But he can't get more than a little home-made booze here. For a while he resented my getting promoted while he didn't, and even lost some stripes. I thought he had gotten over that. We got assigned to different huts once we got to Camp 4. I didn't see him much after that."

"When he and the Tiger and the Russian talked after they left your hut the other night, he mentioned something about getting re-assigned to his old unit when he got back. Somehow that would get him information on nuclear storage sites and it would make him rich. Do you know what he was talking about?" asked Swede.

"That sounds like he intends to spy for the Koreans or the Russians. If he thinks I know, I'm a dead man." Randall paused. "If all three of them come in here to question me, I'm a dead man!"

Swede had been poking at the wall and came to a realization. "If they all come in, I'm coming through this wall. It feels flimsy. The trucks from Camp 4 are supposed to be here tomorrow. When they do, we'll break through this wall and get you on those trucks."

"Maybe you can get through the wall, but what about this chain?" Mike asked.

"I have a few tricks that will take care of that chain." Swede answered as he fingered his lock picks hidden in his jacket. Get some sleep and be ready tomorrow when you hear the trucks get here."

Except for a few mosquitoes, the rest of the night went peacefully.

In the morning Jiao talked with Swede for a bit and then suggested he and Charlie eat with the guards. Swede decided it would be better if he just took some food to Charlie and kept him inside. When Charlie went back to sleep, Swede met with Bo and Simon Bishop out on the road. It would appear as if they were discussing the arrival of the American prisoners from Camp 4.

Bo had talked with Jiao. "He's sure the Korean and the Russian are using some old houses just north of here as their base when they aren't here. There is a small road, just wheel tracks, five minutes north of here on the right. An old wooden bridge crosses the river. Just beyond are two houses hidden in a small clearing. The Korean had a couple of the guards help him take a prisoner there a few weeks ago. The Korean often spends time there and then comes back to interrogate a prisoner here. We just have to hope that is what he does today. Then we can grab your friend and sneak him on the trucks from Camp 4 when they get here."

"And if the Korean doesn't go up there before the trucks get here?" Swede asked. "I won't leave without Mike. We'll just have to break him out just before the trucks are ready to leave. Maybe we can get the men to create some kind of noisy disturbance that will attract attention. But if we can't get Mike out, I am staying. I can hide out for the day and get him out at night. You two can wait down the road and we will work our way to you."

"Is he going to be in any shape to walk?" Simon asked. "You said he has been chained."

"I'll carry him if I have to."

Lt. Kuang showed up just then with news the trucks from Camp 4 were due that afternoon. They would eat and be on their way. He smiled at Swede, "You will be on your way home. Soon we all can go home." He walked back towards the cookhouse to supervise the preparations for the trucks. Six trucks, he had been told. Six trucks with twelve POWs and one driver and mechanic each. There was no need for guards. The prisoners were going home, no one would bother trying to escape.

Swede and the others spent the rest of the morning watching for the Tiger. The brush and the trees hid the Tiger's house, but they could see the door to the hut where he had Mike chained. If he headed that way, they would know. Again, they talked about how they would get Randall onto the trucks. With eighty men milling around, it should be easy enough to get him on a truck.

406

"But how do we get him out of the hut?" asked Bo. "And how do we get the chain off. It won't be easy to sneak him on a truck with a chain dragging behind him."

"Jiao and I are going to break in through the back of the hut. We talked about it this morning. He and I will be less conspicuous than either of you helping. We'll wait until there is enough racket down here to hide any noise we make breaking through the wall."

"What about the chain?" asked Bo.

"I'll take care of the chain," answered Swede. "That should be the easiest part of the whole plan."

Both men looked at him as if waiting for more of an explanation.

"If it works, I will explain later. If not, it's best you don't know."

The trucks rolled in on time. There had been no sign of the Tiger, so the four men got ready to put their plan into action. The prisoners came out the back slowly and stood stretching as they eyed up their new surroundings. Some of them noticed Swede standing inside the fence around his house. When they noticed Bo and Simon Bishop in the background, they became curious. What they thought they were seeing was one Chinese guarding two Americans. The buzzing started as they nudged each other and pointed toward the two Americans. The buzzing grew louder as some noticed the markings on Simon's jacket.

Then there was a shout that made everybody jump. "Kid!" Swede looked up to see a tall American with shaggy hair waving his arm and running towards him. "Kid! You're still standin' on two feet! I'll be damned, Swede, it sure is good to see you." Earl Stoneman grabbed Swede in a big hug and lifted him off his feet. "What are you doin' out here in the middle of nowhere?"

Swede stood there, a big grin on his face. "I'm waitin' for all you big shots from Camp 4 to show up and give me a ride home. What took you so long?" Swede realized he was grinning but knew this time it was OK. Together, he and Earl could solve most any problem.

"C'mon, let's get a handful of lunch. There's something we need help with and we don't have much time."

"Mike Randall is in this camp? In that hut? Over there?" Swede had explained about Mike Randall, the Korean major, his Russian friend, and the need to get Mike out and into one of the trucks in the short time they had left.

"Exactly. We need a diversion down here so we can break in through the back wall and get him out. We get him in the truck when everybody loads up. If the guards do a headcount, we hide him or screw up their count. We need to get Charlie in the trucks too. His head is really messed up again. Do you have somebody we can depend on to take care of him? A medic maybe?"

"Yeah, I know just the guy," replied Earl. "Let me find him and get him over here. You get Charlie ready to go. When do we start the diversion?"

"You have your guys ready. When we are ready to head up to Mike's hut, give them the signal. I'll meet you back here and we can get Charlie set. Then we go."

Earl headed off to get his medic and give instruction to the men he had in mind for creating a diversion. Swede found Bo and Simon and quickly explained what he had in mind. "You two follow a little after our convoy leaves. Mike and I will drop off the trucks and you can pick us up. We will be the two prisoners you are escorting. Bo here can be our Chinese driver. Then we stick to the original plan and head for Panmunjom." After talking with them, Swede went to find Jiao.

"There is going to be some more invisible motorcycle type mischief. Any help you can give that will add to the confusion will be appreciated. We are going to break our guy out of the hut and on to the trucks. And I want to thank you for friendship. Good luck to you." The two men shook hands.

As Swede looked for Earl, Bo hurried up to him. "Look, the Russian just put your friend in his jeep and is driving away!" Swede looked through the trees to see the Tiger headed for the road. He turned left and headed north.

"Let's go! We'll take your jeep. If he's headed where I think he is, it won't be a problem. If he keeps going north, we'll just have to run him off the road." Earl showed up just then with his buddy the medic, wondering why Swede looked so comfortable talking to a Chinese officer. "C'mon, Lieutenant Bo is going to take us for a ride in his jeep. Stay low until we get away from camp. Give the signal to start the ruckus. You," he grabbed the medic and pointed at Charlie, "get that man on the trucks. He's got some kind of shell shock. You need to stay with him until you turn him over to the medics at

Panmunjom. Let's move, people!" Swede paused to have a quick word with Simon Bishop and then headed to Bo's jeep.

Bo swung his jeep onto the road and headed after the Korean. When they got far enough down the road, Swede and Earl sat up. "Well hell," growled Earl. "One minute I'm headed south to Panmunjom and all the American food I could eat, and the next I'm headed back north to a rice diet again." He smiled at Swede. "Damn, kid, it sure is good to see you again! What's your plan here? You do have a plan, don't ya?"

Swede looked over at Bo. "I hope he's headed for his secret little camp. We need to stay back far enough so he doesn't see us. You know the cut to his camp, right? Go as far down that road as you think we can without them hearing or seeing us. We leave the jeep in the road so nobody can get around it and get away from us. Then we sneak in and get Randall. If we can, we take the Korean with us too. We turn him over to the UN so they can put him on trial. Pretty good plan if I do say so myself." He grinned at the other two. "Hey, it's all I got. We fill in the details when we get there.

"By the way, Earl, this is Lieutenant Bo. He's a friend of mine and Colonel Li's. He's coming out with us. After we get Mike Randall."

"Out? Meaning Panmunjom? Coming over to our side? What about the guy that looks like your brother? Is he in on this too?"

"That's Simon Bishop. He's a Polish diplomat. He's got the paperwork to get us out of here. You and I and Mike Randall are going to have typhus. Simon and Bo here are our escorts."

"And I thought that fire at headquarters back in Camp 3 was complicated. Sounds like you've gone pro. Or nuts." Earl chuckled at his own humor. "Okay, one last little adventure before we go home. But this is the last one. We *are* headed home after this, right? Jesus! I sure hope I have grandkids so I can tell them about our little adventures."

Bo slowed the jeep as he came up to the road leading to the bridge and the Tiger's hidden camp. Sure enough, fresh vehicle tracks were visible. He headed down through the trees until they came to a wooden bridge. It looked like it would fall into the stream if you took one step out on it.

"If we go over that, it will make way too much noise," said Bo. "And I'm not sure we would make it anyway. We can leave the jeep right here. Let me turn it around and back it up to the bridge. There is no way anybody can get past. Those lousy bastards are screwed, right?" He looked over at Swede, smiling. "See, lousy bastards. Not poor bastards. I've been practicing."

The three men hurried across the bridge. Once on the other side, they moved into the trees and continued following the road. After a few simple turns it ended in a small clearing. On the near side was a hut with the Tiger's jeep parked in front. On the far side, about forty yards away, was a more solid-looking home. The Russian's truck was parked there. The woods surrounding the clearing were thick enough to allow them to move closer without being seen.

Earl motioned the others down and continued towards the back of the hut. He crawled slowly, pushing leaves and sticks aside. There was no window for a quick peek, so he sat next to the wall and listened. It wasn't long before he moved back to the other two.

"Two voices," he whispered to them. "One with an Asian accent and one American. The American is answering questions but not making any sense. I don't think the Asian understands. Nobody is yelling or getting punched yet."

"We need to get Randall out of there. The Tiger isn't going to let him go after this. Any ideas how we get in without being seen by the Russian? Or Jack Usury."

"What's Usury got to do with any of this?" asked Earl.

"For some reason, he's giving the Russian information about Randall."

"Jesus!" Earl thought for a bit. "But Usury isn't in there with the Russian. I saw him get on a truck when we left Camp 4. We turned off to get here. The other trucks continued on the main road."

"That's good. One less pair of eyes to spot us over here. So, any ideas how we get inside?"

Bo spoke up. "The door opens to the road, not the house. We hug the wall until we get to the door, listen to see if we can tell where the Korean is standing, and rush in. I will go first. Seeing a Chinese face won't upset him as much as seeing one of you. Then we jump him."

Earl looked over at Swede. "Better than anything I got. How about you?"

"Sounds good to me. Let's get back up to the wall and listen to them." Nodding to Bo, he said, "When you are ready, move around to the door. We'll follow your lead. Everybody be careful. We don't want to make any noise before we go in the door."

The three moved across to the wall and listened. Bo looked around the corner and waved his hand forward. Looking to see if the others were ready, he reached for the door. Then he stood up, tugged it open, and ran in, Swede and Earl right behind. Neither of those two could see what was happening, so they simply ran blindly behind him. And ended up in a pile of bodies on the floor.

Bo had heard Mike Randall ask if he could have another drink of water. Assuming that meant there was some water close by in the hut, Bo waited until he figured the Tiger would have something in his hand other than a weapon. Then he opened the door and rushed in. The Tiger was on the other side of the room, handing a cup to Randall. As he turned to see what the noise was all about, three bodies collided with him. Everybody went down in a pile.

Earl was the first to recover. He jumped up and pulled the door closed, then turned to see what the others were doing. The Tiger was almost upright, reaching for his pistol. Swede could see what was happening and trying to push Mike Randall off him so he could get at the Tiger. Bo was still stretched out on the floor. Earl grabbed the first thing he saw and swung for the Korean's head.

The Tiger dropped like a rock. Swede grabbed for the pistol and pointed it at the Korean, waiting to see if he made any further moves. Mike Randall made it to his knees and reached over to grab the Tiger by the hair. Just as he was about to launch his fist into the Tiger's face he stopped. Looking up at the others, he said, "He's dead." Swede relaxed and let his arm drop. Realizing Bo hadn't gotten off the floor yet, he bent down and touched the man's shoulder. "Bo, are you okay?" Then he noticed the blood.

The Korean had been turning in reaction to the noise when Bo collided with him. Swede and Earl hit the Korean next and they all went down on top of Bo. The stool he landed on shattered. One leg broke into three pieces, one of which punctured Bo's chest. The young Chinese lieutenant was dead.

Mike Randall was free. A good friend was dead. Swede's brain locked for a few seconds. Then he looked at Earl. "Get the clothes off the Korean!" Earl stood looking down at the Korean and then the object he held in his hand. "C'mon Earl, get his clothes off. Just do it!" By that time, Swede was working his lock picks on the shackle around Mike Randall's ankle. "Now get yours off," he said to Mike.

"You need to switch clothes. I'm going out to the jeep. I'll be right back."

By the time Swede came back in carrying a can of gasoline, the other two were getting the clothes switched. Swede grabbed the chain and locked the shackle around the Korean's ankle. Then he stood and looked at the others. "We're gonna make it look like the Korean killed you, torched this place, and left. Then he lost control on the bridge and went over the side. We'll have to take Bo with us and deal with his body later. Then we'll stick with the original plan and have Bishop get us out with the orders he wrote up."

They emptied the gas can over the body and around the hut. Swede kicked a small hole in the wall where the shackled body lay. The men checked to see if anyone was outside the Russian's house and carried Bo's body out to the Korean's jeep. With Earl driving, they pulled away as if leaving, but stopped behind the hut. Swede got out and tossed a match in through the hole. Then they drove away.

As they approached the bridge Swede told Earl to drive across to Bo's jeep. They carried his body to that vehicle and then backed the Tiger's jeep to the middle of the bridge. While Mike Randall cranked the steering wheel hard to the right, all three men pushed the vehicle over the side.

"I hate to bring this up," said Randall. "We need a body for them to find." All three men knew what he wasn't saying.

"I don't think we do," offered Swede. It isn't long before this enters into the Yalu. The damage to the bridge should be enough to make them look for a vehicle. If they find it, they'll look for a body. By the time they start looking, a body could be long gone in the current. If they don't notice that something has gone off the bridge, they will just assume he took off. After bashing a prisoner over the head and burning his body, it would make sense for him to disappear. What did you hit him with anyway, Earl?"

"Hey, I just grabbed the nearest thing I could see. I didn't realize it was metal until after I had already swung at him," explained Earl.

"That was the metal bar he was going to heat up and use to start burning holes in my leg if I didn't give him the information he wanted," explained Randall. "Since I didn't have a clue what he was asking about, I was going to be in big trouble. He said nobody would hear me scream."

"He was going to kill me. Thank you, thank you both." Mike Randall was quiet as he spoke. "I was going to try and get his pistol, but he was careful. I would have been another missing in action report if it wasn't for the two of you. And your friend here, Swede. I'm sorry."

"What do we do next?" asked Earl. "Wasn't your friend Bo part of the plan to get us out of here?"

"Yeah, he was. But now we pull over between here and the camp and hide until dark. Then I sneak into camp and explain things to Bishop. You two will go with me but sneak past the camp and wait for me to pick you up. Bishop will follow and we head out in both vehicles, just like the plan. While we wait, we bury Bo in the woods. I don't want to dump his body in the river. And I'm going to need the Korean's jacket and pistol.

"After I talk with Bishop, I'll take this jeep and make a stop in the camp, pretending I'm the Korean. I need to get in his hut. Chances are nobody will see me. They aren't guarding anything anymore. If things went well, they think we are on the trucks and long gone. He came in and out of that camp at all kinds of hours. If they do see me, they will see a guy with a pistol strapped on him. They will see the crazy major they are all afraid of."

"You can't drive in there with this jeep," said Randall. "It sounds too different. His had a knock to it that this one doesn't."

"He's right," agreed Earl. "That other jeep had some engine problems. But that's an easy fix. Pull off here. After we bury your friend, I'll adjust some spark plug wires."

Two days later the CFI truck that had been following a convoy of POWs on their way to the exchange point near Panmunjom continued south instead of turning off for the holding camp. Nobody paid much attention to the CFI vehicles, or any Neutral Nations vehicles, for that matter. They didn't bother anyone, and if their presence helped the prisoner exchange, the Chinese were happy to tolerate them. The truck continued to Panmunjom.

Before they ran Lieutenant Bo's jeep over a cliff, the four men had used the radio to contact the people Page had said would be listening. So a lone, unscheduled, vehicle coming into the UN receiving point was quickly waved over to the side and disappeared amid many similar trucks. A day later, the truck headed back north, the driver all alone in the cab.

The three ex-prisoners-of-war were treated pretty much the way they had been dreaming about for a couple of years. Lots of good food, beds with sheets and no bugs, clean uniforms-even mail from home. They weren't separated from the other POWs, but weren't exactly allowed to wander around Freedom Village. Mike Randall pointed out to the other two the little differences in how people reacted to them. Then he pulled them to a table in the corner of a mess tent.

"Listen carefully. We have to have our story straight. This is how it goes. Swede was about to break me out of my hut when the trucks from Camp 4 showed up. He asked Earl to help. As you were sneaking off to the far side of the camp to get me out, the trucks took off. When you got me out, we hid in the woods. We figured the Chinese would think we were on the trucks and not bother to look for us. We headed down the road in the middle of the night and found a truck stalled along the way. Earl here got it running and we were off. We would pull off into the woods and wait for a convoy of POWs to go by and follow them. When they looked like they were stopping for the night, we pulled off. The next day we did the same thing.

"We don't mention Bo or Bishop. We don't mention the Korean major. I will say he had me there to interrogate me, but often left for a day or so. There must be some guys through here already who were held there earlier. They'll mention him too. Any questions about what happened to you before you got me out, just tell the truth. But we can't get involved in the death of a Korean officer, a Chinese officer, or any talk about being helped by anybody from the Neutral Nations Commission. Everybody good with that?"

"That's the most logical train of thought I've heard since I got off that truck a few days ago and found the kid there," said Earl, grinning at Swede.

"I don't want to get in the habit of agreeing with Earl's logic, but that sounds about right. Let's just say Earl did the drivin' and there were spare gas cans in the truck. We got some food one time in a village. We didn't want to risk that a second time, so we just went hungry. Speaking of which, who wants more pie? I'm buyin'." Mike Randall noticed there was humor in Swede's voice, but not his eyes.

Two days later they were on board the USNS Marine Adder, headed for San Francisco. Besides returning POWs, the ship carried soldiers returning home from the war. The first thing Swede noticed was the POWs and soldiers were kept separate. Even when on deck, they were not supposed to cross rope barriers. The first full day at sea, another difference became obvious. The men who had been labeled as Reactionaries by the Chinese were often treated as lepers by other ex-prisoners. Then came the interrogations.

Everybody expected to be questioned about their experiences. Describe the camps. When were you there? Who was in charge of each camp? What did he look like? What did you call your camp? Swede was surprised when he was told there were over one hundred and fifty POW camps, most of them temporary, like Bean Camp. But the map they had drawn up of the permanent camps turned out to be quite accurate.

Those were reasonable questions. Even when asked if he knew any POWs who had cooperated with the Chinese, Swede was not surprised. Some men had done so at great cost to their fellow prisoners. But he did not expect to be accused of cooperating. Was it not true he spent time talking with a certain Chinese colonel? Was he not friends with some of the guards, even giving them cigarettes that belonged to the prisoners? Wasn't he responsible for the death of a fellow prisoner during an escape attempt? Where had he been from October 1950 to April 1951? Why did he prefer living with British prisoners rather than fellow Americans in the same camp? Why had he allowed himself to be brainwashed? Hadn't he stood up in front of his fellow soldiers and confessed to crimes against Communism? That was the first time he heard the term 'brainwash'.

At first Swede tried to give reasonable answers to the questions. In the evening he would talk with Earl and Mike Randall to compare notes. It became obvious there were plenty of men who had cooperated to some degree with the Chinese that now were trying to deflect attention from themselves. They were now casting doubt on the behavior of many Reactionaries. When he tried to explain that to his interrogators, he got nowhere. He became louder in reacting to what he considered insulting questions. Then he simply refused to answer any more questions.

"I have given you detailed answers to these questions day after day. I know others are telling you the same things. We are giving you a detailed picture of what American troops will have to go through if we go to war over Communism again. We can be prepared the next time. Because we sure weren't this time. But you aren't listening. So, I'm done here." Others did the same. Then the comments started to come from some of the ship's crew or soldiers who had not been prisoners.

"How do you like the chow? Probably not as good as you got while bein' a good little Commie in the camps."

"While I was gettin' my ass shot at you jokers were playin' basketball with your Commie friends up north."

"I hear you guys got all the smokes you wanted and had three square meals a day. All I got was lousy C rations. Must have been tough sittin' out the war in those camps."

Most of the men making those remarks hadn't even been in the army when Swede was captured. Earl was one of the first to throw a punch out of frustration. Others followed. Then some of the prisoners were called to a special session in the mess hall. There were no sandwiches or coffee to be seen when they filed in. Both had, until then, been available around the clock for the returning POWs. Swede looked around the room and realized the whole group had been classified as Reactionaries by the Chinese. Most of them had gotten into arguments with their interrogators about the tone of their questions. And more than a few had gotten into bigger arguments with non-POWs on board.

A major Swede had seen a few times during his interrogations walked in and the group came to attention. He called at ease and told them to go ahead and sit. Swede noticed there was no Combat Infantryman's Badge on his tunic. Yet he had the 'I was there ribbons' from two wars.

"I'm sure you men had some bad days in the camps. But you have to understand, the other men on this ship fought for three hard years. Every day they were out there. Every inch of ground they bled over, every Christmas they sat in the cold, they had you in mind. Everything they did was to get you home."

The major may have meant well in some strange sort of way, but he lost his crowd with the first sentence. They gave him a little more time to start making sense, but it only got worse.

"These men have seen harsh combat, they've had buddies die, but they have also seen the pictures and even movies of you in your camps. Playing baseball and basketball, marching in parades all smiles while you held banners that read 'Down with War.' They've seen the pictures of you sitting at tables full of food while the Red Cross handed out mail from home. They've seen the letters you sent home with 'Against American Aggression" written on the envelope. They've heard about the statements you signed calling the folks back home capitalist pigs." His voice was getting louder. "They know what life was like in those camps." And now almost angry. "And they damn sure know what *they* went through! Now you people need to settle down and quit causing problems!"

Apparently realizing he may have overdone it a little, the major tried a friendlier tone. "Sure, maybe these guys make some remarks every now and then. But you can take it. Just ignore them. Some of them were still getting shot at just a few weeks ago. Let them blow off some steam. But the fighting has got to stop."

The ex POWs sat there, looking at each other in disbelief. Then a man in the back of the room spoke up. Swede turned to see who it was. He was a short little guy, but there was nothing little about his voice.

"Let me tell you how *my* buddies died. On the third day of our march north, three days after we tried to stop tanks with pistols and rifles, cuz that was all we had. Billy Simmons couldn't walk no more. He'd been shot in the guts and the Koreans wouldn't let nobody touch him. He couldn't walk no more so they shot him. Shot him in the back of the head and shoved his body in the ditch. They didn't shoot Sam Belmont. They didn't have to. First, they starved us. Then they marched us day after day. They didn't give us no blankets when it got cold. I woke up one morning after sleepin' on the frozen ground and there was Sam. Eyes lookin' right at me. That's how Sam died. He frozed to death!

"And, yeah, I seen the Red Cross. It was three days before they put us on the trucks to go home. The Chinese marched twenty of us down to the river and told us to clean up. Then they gave each of us clean shirts. They sat us down at some tables in front of a building that had been spruced up. They told us to wait. Some people would be coming to visit but we wasn't to talk to 'em. When we heard some trucks in the distance they hustled out and piled all kinds of pots and kettles on those tables and put real plates in front of each of us. When the trucks stopped the Chinese took the tops off the pots and kettles. The food was steamin' hot! Some Red Cross people got out of the trucks and stood around while the Chinese took pictures. Our guards made sure to stay off to the side so they wouldn't be in any of those pictures. The Red Cross people were all friendly like and smiles, but they never tried to talk with us. Then they got back in their trucks and drove away. As soon as they were out of sight, the Chinese took all that food away. There was rice, biscuits, bottles of beer, even somethin' that looked like chicken. My buddy tried to grab a biscuit before they took it away and got smashed in the head with a rifle.

"There was your Red Cross! And they didn't hand out no mail neither. In three years I got two letters! Two! The first was to tell me my Momma had died! The second was to tell me Pa was sellin' the farm. Those bastards only let us have our mail when it was bad news! So, don't go tellin' me I got to settle down and quit causin' problems. You got your truth all twisted up. Maybe we ain't no heroes, but we sure as hell warn't on no picnic for three years either!" As he sat back down the room erupted in applause.

"All right, people, settle down. At ease! I don't want to hear any more back talk. We know what went on in those camps. The men who were released in Operation Little Switch told us all about it. They told us a bunch of you had cooperated with the Chinese and got put in special camps where you got better treatment. They told us you would be troublemakers. Now listen up! The next man that starts a fight with any of the other soldiers on board will spend the rest of this little voyage in the brig! Try earning a little respect!"

The man might just as well have said "You shurd not be impurdinint!" For a second Swede was back in Camp 1 being interrogated. He jumped to his feet.

"We don't want your respect! We know who we are and what we've done. The respect of someone like you has no meaning for us. If you ever speak to us like that again, you'll have to swim home. I've had my fill of clowns like you who can't think beyond the margins of the manual. You're still using the old rules. I've got news for you. The rules have changed. There is no manual for what we went through. If you could get your head out of your ass you would be asking us to help you update the manual to get ready for the next war. We were beaten, starved, our buddies were shot or froze to death, some of us spent weeks or months in solitary. We learned what choices we had.

Sign or be beaten. Sign or starve. Sign or be shot. Sooner or later we signed. The Geneva Conventions didn't exist!

"But you dumb bastards can't figure that out! You don't even try to figure it out. You just think we are all traitors who confessed to crimes because we aren't patriotic enough. And that means they win."

By that time, some of the men in the room were almost growling. Then they started applauding again. A deer in the headlights look came over the major's face. He practically ran from the room.

Not all the interrogators were on the same page as the major. Some of them saw exactly what was going on. Swede pulled one aside a day later and asked if they could talk. He explained about Red Sedlinski, how Red had come to Swede asking what he should do to correct his behavior. Red had agreed to spy on the Chinese as he still pretended to be a Progressive. He wanted to make sure that went in Red's record.

"Funny you should bring that up," said Lieutenant Patterson, the interrogator, "Another returnee brought up that name a couple of weeks ago. A Henry Page, as I recall. He said pretty much what you just told me. I noted it in Sedlinski's file. I'll add your info and see that it gets sent up the chain. Page had a lot of things to say about you too. All good, I might add."

"I'm glad to hear he made it out OK," said Swede. "Not that I had much doubt, but you never know. Page was quite the character."

"Let me ask you something," said Patterson. "There have been articles in the newspapers lately about how all of you were brainwashed by the Communists. How do we understand what a prisoner went through? How do we judge whether an individual cooperated with the enemy? Is a little cooperation okay? Where do we draw the line for too much? Because I gotta tell you, it looks like everybody cooperated at one time or another."

"I can tell you this," offered Swede. "The biggest battle for each of us was not with the North Koreans or the Chinese. Our biggest battle was with ourselves. Every single day we battled with our conscience and with our heart. Have I done enough? Have I done too little? Should I give some of my food to my sick buddy? If I do, will I get weak and die? Should I escape or should I stay here and help my buddies? If I refuse the demands of the Chinese will they cut food and water for the whole hut or just me? Should I lie when they ask questions? Will they find out? Will they hurt my buddies if I lie?

"Cooperate? Maybe you can call it that. But in the hours, or days, or even weeks, before you broke and signed, you argued with yourself and the men in your hut. If I sign this will I be a traitor? Will they feed us if I don't sign this? Will they shoot me if I don't sign this?

"Every day we had to live with those kinds of decisions. And the next day it started all over again. We will have to live with those decisions for the rest of our lives. Unless you were there, you can't judge those who were. I think most of us have long forgiven the ones who went too far, except for the very few cases where somebody caused the death of a fellow POW. They can never be forgiven.

"It's strange. We signed up to fight the enemy. But we never expected to have to fight the way we did in those camps. We weren't trained for that. The scars from that fight are on our souls, not our bodies."

Patterson had noticed the scar on Swede's forehead and the marks on his neck. His medical record listed a wound on his arm. He waited until Swede relaxed and then reached to shake his hand.

"Thanks. That will help me when it comes time to write up my final report. And maybe it will help people up the chain understand better. Not that I'd hold my breath on that."

"I'll give you another helpful hint," added Swede. "At Camp 1 the Chinese had tiny little punishment cells we called dog kennels. They were wooden cages. Some people spent months in them. The little rooms you built to conduct your interrogations? They remind a lot of us of those dog kennels. I'm surprised nobody has gone off the deep end and destroyed one."

Patterson just looked at him, almost in shock. "You're right. We don't understand enough to judge."

The men who had been in the room for the major's lecture played a game after that. Whenever they spotted the major on deck, one of them would walk past and make a friendly remark.

"Nice day for a swim, huh Major?"

"Man, it must be a three-thousand-mile swim home from here, don't you think, Major?"

"Don't get too close to the side there, Major. You sure wouldn't want to fall in. We'd probably never find you."

It wasn't long before the Major disappeared. Word from the crew was he never strayed far from his cabin for the rest of the trip.

Finnegan Found

Fall 1953

By the time the Golden Gate Bridge came into view, new uniforms had been issued, complete with stripes, ribbons, and patches. Swede discovered he was a Sergeant who was authorized to wear a series of medals and badges. He had no idea what most of the medals were for. When he asked, the overworked clerk handed him some papers. "Oh yeah, you're supposed to carry these documents with you. Apparently, the MPs are stopping soldiers coming back from Korea with lots of ribbons on their uniforms. I hear some guys like to pin on extra ribbons to impress the girls back home. And with all the fruit salad you have there, I guarantee they will stop you. The papers say you are authorized the medals and badges listed. Just show them to the MPs. And don't let them keep the papers, I'm pretty sure you will be stopped more than once.

"And somethin' else. This authorization came right out of Washington. Somebody went out of their way to make a point all those medals are legit. You must be some kind of war hero."

Earl helped Swede make sense of the medals and documents. "The three blue ones mean you served in Korea during the war. You have a Good Conduct medal here, only because the desks back in Washington don't know how you misbehaved over there." He grinned at Swede. "But these others, with them and a dime you can get a cup of coffee anywhere. The papers say the Silver Star is for participating in a classified operation behind lines and saving a superior officer from capture. Care to explain that?" Earl looked at Swede expectantly.

"That must mean when I helped Page sink those barges and he tripped and knocked himself out. He was an officer on a special assignment when he was captured. I suppose he knows somebody in Washington."

"I kind of thought the two of you might have been connected with the show that morning. It sure was a sight to see the markings on the '51s when they flew over! OK, the Bronze Star is for your actions on some hill. Must have been just before you were captured. The combat V device is from that time too. The second Bronze Star is for action involving saving a UN officer from serious injury or death from the guards. The Commendation Medal is for actions as a prisoner-of-war involving another classified operation behind enemy lines. What's that all about?"

"To be honest, I'm not sure. Page did manage to talk me into doing some things that probably weren't very good for my health. I know the Purple Heart is for when I got hit in the arm on the hill before I got captured. But that little oak leaf means a second award, right? I'm not sure what that's all about."

Earl looked at him with one eyebrow raised. He pointed to the scar on Swede's forehead, obvious now with their new GI haircuts. And then he pointed to his neck.

"But not many people know how these happened," argued Swede.

Again, Earl gave him the raised eyebrow.

"Oh yeah, Page again. I suppose you're right."

"You know, I like the guy, but there was is something about him that isn't quite kosher. I'll tell you one thing; he must have some pull to get these authorized. If you re-enlist, a record like this should get you most any assignment you want. Just try to make it somewhere Page isn't."

"Yeah, well, re-enlistment isn't very high on my list of things to do."

"On the other hand, you do have a couple of marks against you. You are an ex-pow. In case you haven't noticed, we seem to be kind of 'persona non grata,' as you educated types like to say. Being that we all went and got ourselves brainwashed." Earl twirled his hand around his head. "And then there are promotion boards. At some promotion board, somebody is going to know you sounded off to that major the other day, and you won't get the promotion. But enough happy talk. Let's go get a cup of coffee." Earl laughed and patted Swede on the back. "Don't worry, I've got the dimes."

Both Mike Randall and Charlie had been flown back to the states from Japan, so it was just Swede and Earl standing at the gangplank saying goodbye. Earl had some friends he wanted to look up in Oakland. Swede had decided he would spend some of his back pay and go home by train. Not sure what he would do with his life, he thought he might as well see a little of the country before making up his mind. Earl thought it was a good idea.

"You've been halfway around the world, but you saw every new place through the eyes of a kid. You're a different person now. But don't ride the rails like I did. Get yourself a real ticket and enjoy the sights on the way home. Look at the trip as an experiment. If you see lots of signs that say 'Dogs and soldiers stay off the grass' you'll know the Army might not be a good career move. But if you can't buy a drink in any bar from here to home you might consider re-enlistment. Now that I'm a real NCO, I need to give career guidance to youngsters like yourself." Earl had been promoted to Staff Sergeant and already had a year time in grade. He had decided not to turn it down, to see if the pay increase was worth it.

"Take care, kid. I'd be proud to serve with you again, anytime, anywhere. If you ever need a reference for a new job, you tell 'em to talk to me." With that he was off, singing his favorite tune.

> *The sun came up so I set off*
> *For places that would welcome me.*
> *Blue skies and warm smiles are easily found*
> *If a traveler you're willing to be.*

> *The sun came up and I set off*
> *My place in life was set.*
> *I would only be what was best for me*
> *And never look back in regret.*

It took Swede five days to get home, including a side trip to the Grand Canyon. He was glad he made the stop. Looking out over something so majestic and timeless seemed to ease whatever it was he carried inside. He knew it was there, but just wasn't sure what it was or what to do about it. He also didn't know he was tracing the steps of Colonel Li, Simon Bishop, and Henry Page as they had traveled across the country years before. The trip had helped each of them make some life-changing decisions.

A Greyhound bus and a salesman's Studebaker finally got him home. He had sent a telegram from San Francisco to say he would be arriving in a few days. He figured if his folks didn't know exactly when he would get home, they couldn't plan a party. The last thing he wanted was a bunch of people asking questions they wouldn't understand the answers to. His own bed and his mother's pancakes and sausage were all he wanted for a while.

After a week of pancakes and rebuilding some fences, the subject of his future came up. It wasn't his parents that brought the topic up, but his uncles. Swede had noticed they treated him differently than before. He seemed to be their equal now. They had asked a few questions about his experiences without pushing for details. He realized they understood what he wasn't saying, so felt comfortable giving some of those details. They enjoyed the story of how he had cleaned both the wound on his forehead and a British NCO's leg.

"So, other than going into a career in medicine, with your skills at treating wounds, what other plans do you have? You'll get fat pretty soon on your mother's cooking and won't be able to catch any of the pretty girls in town who are talking about you." The question came after supper one night, the whole family on the veranda enjoying the fall evening. Mike Finnegan had been invited out for supper and a visit. He was older and slower than when Swede had last seen him, but perked up when he heard the question. So did his mother.

"What's this about treating wounds?' she asked.

With a dirty look towards his Uncle Kurt, Swede ignored his mother's question. "When I enlisted, I thought it would be a way to save some money for college. I didn't really have a plan beyond that, and I still don't." Swede noticed the oldest of his younger brothers was paying close attention to the conversation. "I don't really want to farm," almost a sigh of relief from his brother, "so I suppose I better enroll in college somewhere for the fall semester."

"Oh my goodness," his mother blurted out, "I forgot to give you your letter. It came just before you got home."

As she went inside to get the letter, Mike Finnegan spoke up. "College is a good idea. You might want to try a major university, maybe even somewhere in Europe. The more you can expose yourself to different people and ideas, the better person you become. Don't spend too much time thinking of plans for the future. Let the ideas come to you."

The screen door squeaked open again. "Here it is," said his mother, extending a letter to Swede. "I didn't open it, but it looks like it's from some business in Minneapolis."

The letter was from Meyer Merchandising in Minneapolis. A Mr. David Jorgenson, Director of Recruitment, extended his greetings and suggested Mr. Paul Larson come in for an interview.

"It has been suggested by an associate of ours, Mr. Henry Page, you might be a good fit for our company. At Meyer Merchandising we deal with products from all over the world. Your recent experiences would seem to give you an edge at understanding cultural differences. We offer excellent wages and subsidize higher learning opportunities. We would welcome an opportunity to discuss details with you.

"Enclosed are vouchers for round trip bus travel to Minneapolis and lodging at the Andrews Hotel. Upon arrival at the hotel, please call our office to arrange your interview time.

Meyer Merchandising
310 S 9ᵗʰ St
Minneapolis
phone Lincoln 8931

Andrews Hotel
Corner of Hennepin Ave and 4ᵗʰ St South"

The use of Henry Page's name was certainly interesting. Maybe Page would be there. It would be good to go over events since they had last spoken. And he had questions about Jack Usury. Borrowing some clothes from his father, he left for Minneapolis two days later.

Walking the few blocks from the hotel to Meyer Merchandising, Swede gave some thought as to what he expected at his 'interview.' He wasn't sure there was a job involved, probably something more like questions about the past three years. He undoubtedly had some information that people like Page would be interested in, but he also had questions of his own.

When he entered the building and told the receptionist he had an appointment to meet with Mr. Jorgenson, she led him down the hall to a door marked Records. There he was led past the desks and filing cabinets of busy clerks to a door marked Break Room. Another door in that small room led to a short corridor and an elevator. They joined a man with a cart full of cardboard boxes with various labels on them and all rode up to the third floor. Another receptionist led him to a door marked Personnel. She knocked, opened the door, and stepped aside for Swede to enter.

The room wasn't the fancy office Swede had been expecting for a large company. There was a desk and some shelves along one wall, but the other three were brick. There were no windows. The wall on the right was mostly lined with file cabinets. The room was large enough to include a large table and four comfortable looking chairs. Hanging on the wall behind the desk were pictures of small boats and sailing ships of various sizes, some with closeups of two or three men gathered on the deck. The man behind the desk fit the pictures. His hair was gray, cut much like Swede's. His eyes were brown, his face tan from years of sun and wind. He wore a white shirt with no tie. He waited until Swede was finished taking in his surroundings and then stepped from behind the desk to greet him with a smile and a handshake.

"Mr. Larson, I'm Lawrence Houston. I've been looking forward to this meeting since a mutual acquaintance suggested it. Come on over and sit. They should be bringing in some iced tea and snacks. I know you must have a few questions but let me give you some background first."

Pulling a chair back from the table, he offered it to Swede and then took the one opposite.

"This is not the kind of business you probably think it is. We invited you here because of a mutual acquaintance you know as Henry Page. His name is Alex Haynes. We work for an organization you may not have heard of, the CIA. Central Intelligence Agency. The CIA grew from the Office of Strategic Services that was put together in the beginning of World War II. The OSS was basically a spy unit, a behind-the-lines unit, that fought the Germans and the Japanese during the war. Six years ago, the CIA was formed because of the need to continue doing that kind of work against the Soviets and the Chinese, and a few other people.

"Nothing I've told you is classified in any way, so I'm not giving away any secrets here. But there are secrets you might give away. That's the primary reason Alex asked me to speak with you. He says he sent you a message to be careful of what you say and who you say it to. You haven't spoken to him in a while?" Then he paused. "You don't mind answering some questions about it all, do you?"

"No, not at all. It was about nine months ago that I last saw Page. We were at Camp 3 at the time. We've sent some messages back and forth since then, but I haven't seen him. There are two other people who have been involved in some things since then that might connect to Page, but I trust them."

"That would be Master Sergeant Randall and Staff Sergeant Stoneman, right?" Houston asked. He saw no reaction from Swede. "You don't know how much you should trust me, do you?" He went over to his desk and picked up a sheet of paper. "Alex sent this along with his suggestion I speak with you. He said I would probably need to show it to you before you would say much." He handed the paper to Swede.

Swede   Hope to see you soon. Today is just another page in the history books.

One more time, Swede had no choice but to accept the message as being authentic. Again, it was just too much to think otherwise. "This is the second time he has sent me this message. I almost wish we hadn't set it up. But I am going to accept it as valid. We set it up because we trust each other. There are only three others I trust as much."

"Who are the other three?" asked Houston. "I'm only asking because I'm interested. Would Randall and Stoneman be a good guess for two of them?"

"Absolutely. Without them I might not have survived. It wasn't in the room keeping me alive. It was in my head keeping me alive." Houston nodded at that answer as if he understood perfectly. And Swede was sure he did.

"What is it about this Sergeant Randall that makes him one of the three?"

"Mike Randall kept quite a few men alive in the early months of the war. He was standing right next to his captain when the Tiger shot him. Some of the captain's blood was on his fatigue shirt. He could have quit right there, like so many others did. But he took charge, even though that was why the captain was shot in the first place. I wasn't with him on the worst of the march north or at Bean Camp.

But others told me he never gave up. For guys like me with no idea what was happening, he was exactly the kind of person we needed in charge. He is one of the few real leaders I saw in my four years in the army.

"Jack Usury told me Mike Randall was commissioned out of the enlisted ranks during World War II. After the war he was busted back to Staff Sergeant. He stayed because he believes in the army, not because it was a safe job. I could see that the first day I met him.

"Speaking of that, Page sent me another message just before the war ended. He said I wasn't to talk with anybody about Jack Usury. I wasn't to report him as being involved with the Tiger and a Russian. Do you understand why? He was an American, helping them torture Mike Randall!"

"Alex got word back to us about Usury. We didn't want him taken into custody. Chances are this Tiger was careful and nobody else knows that Usury was involved."

"Why wouldn't you want him taken into custody? That doesn't make sense. He's a traitor. To his country and to his friend." Swede stared at Houston, waiting to hear a response so he could point out how wrong it was.

"Oh, he's a traitor alright. He intends to sell the Russians nuclear secrets when he gets his next assignment. Alex clued us in. And he will be court-martialed as a traitor. But not until we let him feed the Russians a lot of information that we want them to have. We will either convince him to cooperate or simply see he only gets his hands on the kind of information we want him to get. We haven't decided which approach to take yet. But he won't be giving the Russian any real secrets."

Houston looked directly at Swede. "Now is the time for me to tell you that you can't tell anyone what we talk about here. You will either be one of us when we are finished, or you won't. But because you are so involved in what Alex was up to over there, you have information we can use. Even if you decide not to stay with us, we still need to talk about information that is classified.

"So yes, we know about Jack Usury. And we intend to use him as much as we can before we get around to any court-martial." Swede could see he was serious.

"Did Alex get you that message about Usury through this Lieutenant Bo?"

"Yes, he got back to camp a day or two before we got Mike Randall away from the Tiger and headed down to Panmunjom."

"From what little Alex was able to tell us, I thought Bo was coming out with you."

Swede explained the rescue from the Tiger's hut, how Bo was killed, and how they pushed his jeep into a river to fake an accident. Simon Bishop was going to ask questions when he got back to make it look like he was looking for Bo. If it looked like he was under any suspicion, he was simply going to return to Poland on a Neutral Nations aircraft.

Houston asked detailed questions about Colonel Li, the sinking of the barges and the B-29, and the other incidents Page and Swede had been involved in. "I'm not trying to get you to spill any beans on Alex. That's not the point. This is what we call a debrief. I need to get your view of each operation. When Alex gets back, I will get his. That will allow me to better understand each operation and determine what works and what doesn't."

"Page isn't here? When will he get back?" Swede had hoped to see Page again.

"Hopefully, he's on his way back now, but it will be a long trip. You know, from what Alex has been able to tell us, and from a cable Washington received from the British military, you seem to have a lot of the leadership qualities that you admire in Alex and Master Sergeant Randall. You don't have a lot of experience yet, but your natural talents seem to be far ahead of people the military spends thousands of dollars training to be leaders. Have you considered staying in and making a career of it?"

Swede just shook his head. "I know my thinking is a little twisted from my experiences over there. But there was little that made me admire the military. We weren't ready for what we had to do and didn't have the weapons to do it. Too much of our leadership fell apart on day one. I don't ever want to put myself in a position like that again. A position where the people making decisions shouldn't be, and I can't do anything about it.

"Mike Randall and Jack Usury helped me understand our survival was almost completely dependent on how we dealt with our situation. We weren't going to get much help from the military or the government. We weren't important enough. The idea of sacrificing yourself for your country loses much of its appeal when you realize your country doesn't care. At that point, you focus on helping yourself and your friends survive because that's all you can do."

"But you did more than help yourself and your friends survive," offered Houston. "You took risks for people you didn't know. That cable from the British was detailed. You saved a man's life by breaking out of your cell and fighting with a guard. You saved a man without even knowing his name or nationality. You risked your own death to do that. You outwitted the Chinese to steal food and medicine for men you didn't even know. Not just once or twice, but on a regular basis. Page thinks you did the same thing in other camps.

"And based on the cable from the British I'm guessing the third person that earned your trust was a British prisoner?"

Swede simply nodded his head in acknowledgement. Houston waited to see if Swede was going to elaborate any on that point. When Swede stayed silent, Houston continued speaking.

"You deserve much more recognition than the medals the military has awarded you. But that won't happen, since the recognition you deserve would bring attention to the failures you mentioned.

"So, if you aren't thinking of staying in the military, what are your plans? College? The family farm?" Houston waited for a bit to see if Swede had a reply. "What about coming to work for us? You already seem to have a knack for what we do."

"What makes you say that?" asked Swede. He had enjoyed working with Page. There was a part of his brain telling him that maybe he could do what Page did.

"Let me answer your question with two questions of my own. How did you get the Chinese looking for somebody called Finnegan who was responsible for sending orders to all the camps? What part did you play in the camps refusing to attend the Chinese group re-education efforts?"

Swede looked at Houston in surprise. How could he possibly know anything about that?

"Hey, this is what we do. We collect information. Your buddy Earl Stoneman told us quite a bit." Houston paused again, watching Swede's reaction. "So, tell me about this Finnegan and convincing a couple thousand GI's to all quit attending lectures on the same day."

They spent the rest of the afternoon talking about how, in early winter of 1952, a handful of Reactionaries at Camp 3 were frustrated with the way so many people were cooperating with the Chinese. Not cooperating in a big way, but not standing up to the Chinese in the way the group thought American soldiers should. The group knew everyone was worried the coming winter would lead to as many deaths the first had. They knew it would be hard to convince people to quit cooperating then. They had all experienced the Chinese willingness to cut off food for huts that didn't cooperate. But in the spring, with warmer weather, maybe then people would listen. They picked a day near Easter because everybody would know when Easter came around. Since Reactionaries were constantly being sent to other camps to break up their groups, it was easy to spread the word.

"I was surprised when it worked," explained Swede. "The Chinese started asking who was responsible for the order. I suggested to a Progressive who was spying for me to drop the name 'Finnegan' in the hope the Chinese would go off on a wild goose chase. There is a Mike Finnegan at home who is kind of an adopted grandfather to us. His name just popped into my head."

"You had people spying on the Chinese for you?" Houston was smiling. "They were spying on you and you were spying on them?" He couldn't help but laugh.

"We had to know who they were watching. I had a few guys who were willing to keep acting like a Progressive to get information back to us. I made sure the interrogators on the way home took their names."

"So your source was able to convince the Chinese they needed to find a prisoner by the name of Finnegan who was the ringleader of all this?"

"I've thought about that. I doubt that Red Sedlinski was able to do all that by himself. Maybe others picked up on the name and rumors took off from there. Then I heard the Tiger questioning Mike Randall. He was asking about a Finnegan and radios. That was just a few weeks ago."

"Why did you take the risk to stop at this Tiger's hut back at Camp 2-4 after you rescued Randall?" asked Houston. "Wasn't that pushing your luck, driving right into the camp like that?"

With another look of surprise Swede asked, "Earl again?"

"Yep. Like I said, we collect information from all the sources we can."

Swede shook his head. "It was dark. The jeep looked and sounded like the Tiger's. I wore his jacket and the belt and pistol. Anybody who saw me thought they were looking at the Tiger. The guards stayed away from him. They thought he was nuts. And they knew he was mean."

"So why the visit to his hut?" asked Houston.

"If they had caught on to the fact Mike was missing, they would have started looking. And the obvious thing to do would be find the vehicles that passed by the camp going south. I wanted them to think Mike Randall was the body in the fire and the Tiger was the one missing, that he had either drowned or headed for the hills after killing a prisoner. My initial plan had been to capture him and get him to Panmunjom.

"Earlier I had Bo ask Page for a frequency the Russians would use. I was going to plant it as the incriminating evidence when we captured him. When Earl hit him and we decided to do the body switch, I realized the frequency would still work. I scribbled the frequency down on some paper next to his radio. On the same paper I wrote 'Finnegan.' A little clue to help them find what they were looking for. My hope was sooner or later the Chinese would notice it and start thinking they had finally found their Finnegan."

"Actually, not a bad plan," offered Houston.

"Well, I hoped it would at least give us enough time to get out. And maybe it would cause some problems between the Chinese, the Koreans, and the Russians."

"Now I have some questions for you," Swede said, "since you have all this information you collected. Can you tell me what happened to a Danny Morgan? Last I knew was cooperating with the Chinese and was one of the worst Progressives."

Houston looked at him. "You don't know?"

"Know what?"

"His name is on the list of those Americans who decided to stay, to go to China rather than return to the states. Twenty-one Americans and one Brit."

Swede sat, stunned. Decided to stay in China? That made no sense.

"Crazy, right? The papers are using them as an example of how all of you were brainwashed. Not strong enough to stand up to a few questions." Houston waited again to see how Swede reacted.

"Yeah, I caught that attitude on the ship on the way home. Quite a few of our own interrogators seemed to feel that way." Swede just shook his head.

"What about Charlie? Did Earl tell you about Charlie? Do you know what happened to him?"

"Albert Grasneer," said Houston. "Master Sergeant Albert Grasneer. He was in charge of the Division Mess in Japan and better than most at his job. He went over in the first few days to see that 'his boys' got fed right. Grasneer was helping deliver a hot meal to a company when the Chinese hit them. The experience must have been too much. He's probably in a psych ward back in San Francisco. He's not the first to break, and he won't be the last."

Swede sighed. "He seemed to be getting better. Then we had to march from Camp 2-3 up to 2-4. It wasn't more than a few miles, but it must have reminded him too much of the march earlier in the war. I liked him, but I was never sure how to help him."

"There are people with multiple degrees who can't help guys like that." Houston waited again. "What about you? Does all this talk bother you? Make you feel like you're back in Korea in some camp?"

"Maybe it's eating at me and will all come out someday. But I know what I did and what I didn't do. I feel okay about all that." Now Swede waited for Houston to react.

"One last question, at least for now. Why was Page in Korea in the first place?"

"He was investigating what we thought was an attempt by an American soldier to contact the Russians in Japan. The Russians don't have an embassy in Japan, but there are a couple of businesses we use if we want to send an unofficial message. This soldier's wife was spotted in one of those businesses. Alex was in Tokyo on another assignment, so we gave him the job of looking into it. We 'assigned' him to the soldier's unit. A week later they were shipped over to Korea. It turned out the wife was trying to get help finding their house girl's parents. They had sent their daughter south with relatives after the last war but couldn't get out themselves. She figured the Russians might be able to help. Not too smart, but not exactly espionage.

"His original assignment was collecting information on Russians in North Korea, so he stayed. Dedication or foolishness? But he did get important information for us. You even helped." Houston grinned at Swede.

"So, back to my question. What's next for Paul Larson? I'm sure we can use you. You're a little raw. You'll need some training. Some of that would be on a college campus. That would give you an idea of what it means to be a civilian in the regular world. You haven't had that experience yet. Before you would get into specific training, you could decide not to stay with us. You could go on your way and owe us nothing."

"I tell you what," offered Houston. "It's late. Go back to the hotel and have a good meal on us. In the morning, if you think you want to work with us, give me a call and come back over. If not, thanks for the good job you did over there, and thanks for filling in some details for us. Stay another day at the hotel. Your bus ticket is round trip, so you can get home with no problem." He showed Swede out of the building and shook his hand. "No matter what, know that I agree you should feel comfortable with your conduct over the last three years. You earned those medals on your uniform. Even if you just hang it up in a closet and only take it out on the 4th of July. Don't ever doubt that."

Swede took a long walk before returning to the hotel for the evening. He had hoped to talk with Page, to ask if working for these people was a good idea. There was still a lot he didn't know about the organization. Were most of the people like Page and Randall, or were there still a lot of them like the major on the boat home? What kind of training was involved? The idea of going to college and being able to back out if he didn't like the CIA appealed to him. He would still have a lot of options left.

On his way over from the hotel the next morning, Swede felt good about his decision. He was about to embark on a career. If it turned out to be a bad fit, he could easily change direction. He found himself smiling as he entered the building. Again, he was guided through the building and up to the third floor. On entering, he found Lawrence Houston at the table with two other men, both about his age. Lawrence rose to greet him.

"Mr. Larson. I'm glad to see you back. You saved us the embarrassment of a public scene at the hotel." He motioned to someone behind Swede. The door had never been closed behind him and now two military policemen stood there. Swede looked back at Houston, completely puzzled.

"You are under arrest for treason. The information you freely gave us yesterday backs up what Alex Haynes had reported." Speaking to the two behind him, Houston said, "Put the cuffs on him and take him over to our people at Fort Snelling. Go out the side entrance. Now get him out of here."

Swede could hardly believe what was happening. How could he have judged this man so badly? How could he have misjudged Page so badly? Treason?

With a man at each elbow, he was marched out of the room and to the elevator. Neither of the two men said a word. Swede looked at them, wondering what they were thinking. Did they think he was a traitor? Then he just leaned back against the wall of the elevator and hung his head.

Leaving the elevator, they headed down the hall to a door that led to a small room. One of the men said to the other, "Watch him. I'll go get the car." He pulled the door open and went out into the street. Swede sat down on one of the two chairs in the room, put his head down, and stared at the floor. Waiting until his guard looked away, Swede rose and swung his arms over the man's head. In a few seconds, his chokehold had the man slumping to the ground. Easing the man to the floor, Swede took one of the chairs and blocked it under the handle of the door leading ouside.

Slamming the door open, Swede walked in and tossed the handcuffs on the table where the three men sat in surprise. "Are there any other tests you have for me this morning?"

After the few seconds it took for them to close their jaws, all three burst out laughing. Finally, Houston settled down enough to ask, "How did you know? Wait, you didn't hurt those guys, did you?"

"No. One of them is waking up on the floor downstairs right about now. The other is probably running around to the front of the building to get back in."

Houston rose and offered his hand to Swede. "I apologize for the trick. But we wanted to see how you would handle it. So how did you know it was a setup?"

"Their shoes, for one." All three looked at Swede, waiting for more of an explanation. "Their shoes were a mess. No MP would be caught dead in shoes that looked that bad. They didn't call me any names or take any jabs at me with their clubs. Real MPs would have been very unhappy with somebody arrested for treason. Not to mention one of your "MPs" looks just like a civilian who was pushing a cart around here yesterday."

Shaking their heads and laughing, the other two men rose to shake his hand and introduce themselves. Houston shook his hand one more time. "I'm glad you came back this morning. I know Alex would have been disappointed if you hadn't."

Swede reached inside his shirt. "I had to come back this morning, no matter what. I need to hand these over to you. I didn't bring them yesterday because I wasn't sure if you were going to be the right people to get them." He pulled out the documents that Colonel Li had offered him back at Camp 3. Bo had hoped to use them as a bargaining chip in his plan to defect. Swede kept them when they buried Bo.

"These have detailed information about the mistreatment of POWs in the first year of the war. There is also a list of Americans who cooperated with the Chinese, including their level of cooperation. I had the idea if I turned them over to the interrogators on the ship on the way home, they would simply disappear. I'm hoping you will put them to good use. I have plenty of reasons to believe Colonel Li was accurate and honest in putting this together."

Taking the documents from Swede, Houston paged through them for a bit. Then he set them gently on the table and looked at the other two men.

"Gentlemen, I think any doubts about our decision yesterday can now be set aside. Mr. Larson here helped one of our best people conduct valuable operations behind enemy lines. Probably saved his life during one of those operations. Now he delivers material to us that will help put to rest the lies coming out of China about how our POWs were treated. He has worked with a Polish diplomat that we need to keep track of. He obviously knows an influential Brit. To top it off, he seems to have a connection to a Chinese colonel Haynes suggested we try to establish a relationship with. And he accomplished all that just with instinct and raw skill. Imagine the possibilities with professional training."

Lawrence Houston offered Swede a chair at the table. "I think we may have found a Finnegan of our own. Let's talk about how you might fit in with us."

The Recognition They Deserve

The actions of the main character of this historical fiction novel represent those of hundreds of American POWs in miserable camps along the Yalu. Most of his actions are based on real events. Even the incident with the motorcycle.

The details concerning the Tiger Death March are accurate. Conditions and death rates for marches prior to reaching permanent camps are accurate. The petition at Camp 5, which made clear the number of deaths that first winter, is real. Camp locations and conditions are accurate, as are the movement of groups of prisoners from Bean Camp to Camp 1, Camps 1 and 5 to Camp 3, NCOs to Camp 4, and officers to Camp 2. The Kennel Club in Camp 1 was real. POWs considered Reactionaries by the Chinese were often put through sham trials and sent to Camp 2-3 for punishment. An all-camp Olympics was held at Camp 5 in November of 1952. In the earlier athletic competition at Camp 3, the men from 3 North marched down to 3 South. The sequence was reversed for this story. There was a Progressive committee formed to turn in POWs for planning escapes at Camp 1, not Camp 3. Colonel Li is modeled after a Chinese instructor at Camp 3 who passed news to some prisoners about the war and hinted at who the Progressives were in the camp.

The Chinese labeled the main camps as 1 through 5. In my earlier book, I added the additional identifiers 1, 2, 3, and 4 to avoid confusion in discussing the smaller sub-camps around Camp 2. Camps 2-1 and 2-2 held officers. Camp 2-3 was a penal camp consisting of scattered huts to keep problem Reactionaries separate from the other camps. Camp 2-4 was even more secluded and believed to primarily hold aircrew. Camp 3 consisted of northern and southern segments as described in the chapter titled 3 North. The southern segment, 3 South, is described in the chapter titled Camp Sunday.

In books and debriefs about the Korean War POW experience,

many Reactionaries mention they were segregated from other soldiers on the voyage back to the states and questioned more harshly than in the camps.

Cordus H. Thornton had earned the Bronze Star in World War II. Serving as a 1st Lieutenant in Korea, he was captured in July 1950, part of the same column of prisoners as Johnnie Johnson. Thornton was executed in November at the beginning of the Tiger Death March as an example of what happened when prisoners could not keep up with the pace of the march. He was buried at the site of his execution.

Mother Beatrix was a seventy-five-year old French nun who first came to Korea as a missionary in 1906. She had asked for permission to remain in Seoul if the Communists invaded. When she collapsed on the Tiger Death March she was shot.

The Tiger, Korean Major Chong Mhyong Sil, took command of a column of about seven hundred and fifty prisoners, fifty-nine of them civilians. Over nine days of marching through snowstorms and over mountain passes, about ninety died from exhaustion or were executed for failure to keep up. The survivors refer to that time as the Tiger Death March. The Tiger himself executed the first prisoner on the march, Cordus Thornton. The Tiger was in command of the group from 1 November 1950 until sometime in January. It was rumored at the end of the war the Tiger had been sentenced to two years in prison for selling POW rations on the black market. The death rate on the Tiger Death March was greater than the death rate of Americans on the Bataan Death March.

Major Thomas A. Hume was arrested at Camp 5 and charged with "publicly insulting the workers of the Chinese paper-making industry." He suggested a question they were forced to discuss was not worth the paper it was written on. He was held in isolation and repeatedly beaten over a three-week period. When he was released from isolation, he told his fellow officers he was supposed to inform on them to the Chinese and they should not trust him. Hume did not recover from those beatings and died two weeks later.

Father Emil J. Kapuan was captured in November 1950. He died in May 1951 when the Chinese refused him any medical treatment. They did not like the respect he earned from his fellow prisoners by constantly helping them, even giving his food to the sick. In 2013 he was finally awarded the Medal of Honor for his actions just prior to capture and while a prisoner.

Wayne "Johnnie' Johnson was eighteen years old when he was captured in July of 1950. Between then and October 1951 he recorded the names of almost five hundred soldiers from his column who died or were executed. His list included name, rank, unit, date of death, and hometown. He was beaten when the list was discovered but had a copy hidden away. At the end of the war he informed the Army, but his information was ignored until 1995. Johnson was awarded the Silver Star in 1996.

Just prior to completing this book, I came across information on another individual. Tibor Rubin was awarded the Medal of Honor in 2005, both for actions just before capture and while a prisoner. Rubin constantly broke out of his hut and stole food from enemy warehouses and gardens to give to his fellow prisoners. As was the case with Wayne Johnson and Emil Kapuan, his fellow prisoners worked hard for years to get him recognition for his actions. They credited him with saving the lives of at least 40 men. The three examples of Johnson, Kapuan, and Rubin illustrate how actions above and beyond the norm were ignored for years. Had it not been for the persistence of a few, the American public would have never learned what these men did. How many others received no recognition at all?

The general public is almost completely unaware there were ever Americans held as prisoners-of-war in Korea. That knowledge is not forgotten—we never bothered to learn it in the first place. This book is my attempt to shine a light on their experience and bring to those men the recognition they deserve.

John N. Powers
Wittenberg, Wi

About the Author

John N. Powers enlisted at age seventeen and served as an intelligence operations specialist in the Strategic Air Command, Vietnam, and then Europe. He earned bachelor's and master's degrees in history and education at the University of Wisconsin-Stevens Point. After teaching for thirty-one years he worked as an emergency room coordinator for ten more.

Powers created the web site *northchinamarines.com* for family members of 203 US Marines captured in China on the first day of WW II. Research on that topic led to the American Ex-POW organization asking that he write some articles about the POW experience in Korea and Vietnam. That work resulted in the book, *Bean Camp to Briar Patch-Life in the POW Camps of Korea and Vietnam.*

Finnegan Found is his first attempt at historical fiction. If you enjoyed reading the novel, please consider leaving a review on Amazon and Goodreads. Those reviews will help others discover this long overdue story. Hopefully, you do not consider that request to be "impurdinint."

The Cover

Why is there an upside-down mailing address on the cover? Why does the map look like it was hand-painted?

Think back to when Swede was sentenced to one year in a penal camp and placed in the hut with the British prisoners. He and Corporal Owen Thorpe broke into a shed in the hope of finding some medicine for two sick troopers. They discovered the shed was full of packages that had been sent by families of the prisoners, but never delivered by the Chinese. When they left that shed after finding the medicine they were looking for, Swede grabbed a package at random. The package was wrapped in brown paper and addressed to Private George Webster. His mother had sent George candy bars, vitamins, gum, cocoa mix, and a can of Spam. All worth more than gold to POWs on a starvation diet in the middle of winter.
When news of the beginning of a prisoner exchange reached the camp, Swede used a paint set he had found in other packages to draw two copies of a map showing where the POW camps were located along the Yalu River. He and Prince planned to sneak the maps out and turn them over to military intelligence. What did Swede use to draw those maps on? The wrapping paper from George Webster's package.

Made in the USA
Middletown, DE
11 October 2020